Praise ...nson

"A strangely be[...] ...[n]ew love and of connections and separations with a gothic turn, this is a book that will have you thinking long after it's done."
—Parkersburg *News and Sentinel*

"This is a stunning debut: a haunting, extraordinary tale told by a born storyteller who combines humor, heartbreak, and real suspense."
—BERNARD CORNWELL,
New York Times bestselling author of *Agincourt*

"A haunting tale of timeless love. The vibrant voice of Hannah's heroine brings the lonely coast of Scotland very much to life, complete with the taste of oatcakes and the tang of smuggled claret. A surprising, rich, and rewarding novel."
—LAUREN WILLIG, author of *The Orchid Affair*

"A charming and heartbreaking account of love and loss."
—*South Florida Sun-Sentinel*

"An extremely original piece of storytelling with a thoroughly unique heroine."
—DEANNA RAYBOURN,
bestselling author of *Dark Road to Darjeeling*

"Darci Hannah's debut novel has something for everyone: romance, mystery, humor, historical detail, a feisty protagonist in Sara, and a stunning Scottish setting."
—ANNE EASTER SMITH, author of *Queen by Right*

"*The Exile of Sara Stevenson* is an intriguing read, telling a tale of a great romance that survives death—and time." —BookLoons

"Like the gales that sweep over the desolate north coast of Scotland, *The Exile of Sara Stevenson* gathers force and delivers an atmospheric tale of love, passion, and loyalty. Like the lighthouse lamp at the symbolic center of the novel, details of the story that at first seem inconsequential or mysterious gather into one great beam of light, illuminating a conclusion that shows the power of love to transcend death and even time itself."
—LAUREL CORONA,
author of *The Four Seasons: A Novel of Vivaldi's Venice*

By Darci Hannah

The Angel of Blythe Hall

The Exile of Sara Stevenson

The
ANGEL
of
BLYTHE HALL

The
ANGEL
of
BLYTHE HALL

A Historical Novel

Darci Hannah

Ballantine Books Trade Paperbacks
New York

A Ballantine Books Trade Paperback Original
Copyright © 2011 by Darci Hannah

Published in the United States by Ballantine Books, an imprint of The Random House Publishing Group, a division of Random House, Inc., New York.

BALLANTINE and colophon are registered trademarks of Random House, Inc.

LIBRARY OF CONGRESS CATALOGING-IN-PUBLICATION DATA
Hannah, Darci
The angel of Blythe Hall : a historical novel / Darci Hannah.
  p. cm.
ISBN 978-0-345-52056-2
eBook ISBN 978-0-345-52057-9
1. Heiresses—Fiction.   2. Brothers and sisters—Fiction.
3. Kings and rulers, Medieval—Succession—Fiction.
4. Intrigue—Fiction.   5. Supernatural—Fiction.
6. Scotland—History—15th century—Fiction.   I. Title.
PS3608.A7156A54 2011
813'.6—dc22 2011002945

Printed in the United States of America

www.ballantinebooks.com

9 8 7 6 5 4 3 2 1

Book design by Virginia Norey

For David and Janet Hilgers,
my parents, my angels

And for my nieces Dana and Jenna,
whose mother really is an angel

Acknowledgments

My heartfelt thanks to:

Linda Marrow, Junessa Viloria, and the rest of the fabulous team at Ballantine for wholeheartedly embracing the Blythes; Meg Ruley, literary agent and guardian angel; my husband, John Hannah, for being the most enthusiastic supporter of the tales I write (especially during football season), and for rolling up his sleeves, gathering the troops, and tackling the groceries, laundry, and all manner of petty chores so that I could keep the pages coming; my father, Dave Hilgers, for his unshakable optimism, encouragement, feedback, and lively discussions on the nature of good and evil; my mother, Jan Hilgers, who taught me that the greatest blessing in life is family; my son Jim, for providing stimulating conversation, for dreaming big and being fearless, for taking care of all our technical needs, and who just might recognize in a young king of the same name and age some striking similarities; my son Dan, whose easygoing demeanor, enthusiasm, and complete dedication to everything he does is inspiring, and for providing music, laughter, wit, and plenty of material for this story; my son Matt, for his comedic diversions and for challenging me with "Hey, Mom, if you really want to write a great book you need some quality kills. Nothing says awesome like a dagger between the eyes!," which I found disturbing yet intriguing; my brothers Randy and Ron Hilgers, whose adolescent antics prepared me for sons; Sandy Cobb, for being more like a sister than an aunt; Tyler Schnute, for sharing his musical talent, and all the young men of Calamity for the beautiful rendition of *Loch Lomond;* Scott Specht, for unknowingly providing Julius Blythe with one of the best off-the-cuff remarks I've ever heard; longtime friends Jane Boundy and Stacy Enxing Seng, for the laughter, encouragement, support, and memories; dear friends Cyndi Lieske and Rachael Perry, for their gift of words, and all the South Lyon Writers; Brenda Hilgers, Kay Rauch, Carol Rauch, Bob and Teresa Hilgers, Larry and Irene Newquist, and the incredible network of family and friends, near and far, who are too numerous to mention but cherished all the same, and whose enthusiasm and support keeps me writing; and to my late sister-in-law, Diane Johnson Hilgers, who believed in angels, collected them, taught me about them, and who gave to us before she left two of her own.

With gratitude and love,
Darci

The
ANGEL
of
BLYTHE HALL

PROLOGUE

Blythe Hall, Roxburghshire,
Scottish Borders

LIKE A TENACIOUS WEED, THE MEMORY OF THAT SUNNY
spring morning eleven years ago, in the year of our Lord 1481,
still haunts the recesses of my mind. I was only seven at the
time, and had wandered far beyond the castle walls to play
with my new puppy, a little black-and-white collie I called
Rondo. I knew I would be summoned home eventually, but I
never heard him until he was at the meadow's edge. It struck
me at once that his horse had been urged to a reckless speed, a
speed that was familiar yet far too fast for his young years, or
so our father had constantly chided. Julius was twelve and utterly incorrigible; so, perhaps, was I, because I secretly
thought he and his little steed moved with the most mesmerizing elegance I had ever seen. The moment I heard the
pounding hooves, I stood and grabbed the wiggling Rondo
lest he run us both over in his great haste. But as soon as I did,
I realized he knew all along that we were there.

"Quick, Isabeau!" my brother cried, jumping from the little horse before it came to a complete stop. I could see he was

distressed, yet there was gleam of wild excitement in his eye. I knew this look, I had known it all my life, for it revealed that something terribly important was about to happen. Yet before I could form a single question, or utter a protest, I found myself plopped on his saddle with Rondo squirming in my arms and Julius's lithe, agile boy's body behind us urging the horse to the same reckless speed.

"Julius!" I found my lungs at last. "Please slow down. What are you about?" I shouted, for we were going too fast and I was afraid of dropping my puppy. Julius, intent on something far greater than my excited questioning, never answered me. But he didn't need to because I saw them myself the moment we crested the hill.

Gathering on the banks of the river Tweed, still dripping, with steel helmets and long pikes glinting in the late-morning sun, was a great body of mounted men. I knew even back then that they were Englishmen and not a band of local reivers; and I knew by the way Julius rode that they could only be heading for one place: our home, Blythe Hall.

The moment they saw our little horse heavy with two riders—two child riders—racing across the grassy slope heading for their target, a cry rang out and a pack of armed horsemen broke from the main group to give chase. I saw that they had a slight advantage on us and meant to cut us off before we reached the castle gates. My brother saw it too and somehow managed to drive the horse even faster up the slope that led to the bridge. I looked at the looming fortress that was Blythe Hall and saw that men were already on the parapets with bows pulled taut and eyes glued to our pursuers. Our archers were excellent shots, and the steel-helmeted men who came to take our castle began to fall back as dark arrows took to the sky. But not all of them were deterred—not the man who made a grab for the halter of our racing horse.

"Leave off!" Julius cried, kicking the man's huge arm away as he reached for the frothing mouth of our steed. I had been holding Rondo tightly, frightened to let go, frightened to move, and knew I was being no help at all. The man made a grab again, this time running his horse into ours and bringing it so close that I could smell his stale breath. The two horses jostled, Julius reacted quickly, and the man missed his target again but found Rondo instead. The meaty hand, wrapping around the dog's head, yanked hard. I was holding my puppy so tightly, so protectively, that I was nearly pulled from the saddle.

"Let go!" Julius ordered. "For God's sake, Isa, let him go, or you'll be pulled from the saddle too."

I should have let go. I knew even then my value as a hostage. It was said that Blythe Hall had never fallen. However, the gates of that impenetrable fortress might be weakened a great measure with the laird's children as bargaining chips. But I didn't think of that; I only thought of Rondo and held his squealing, wriggling body even tighter until I felt my legs come away from the horse's side. And still, like the stubborn child I was, I held on, becoming a human bridge between the Englishman and my brother.

I don't presume to know what thoughts possessed Julius at that moment, just as I never saw the dagger in his hand, but I did see the shock and horror in the Englishman's eyes seconds before the blade slammed into his throat, a mere inch above the top of his cuirass. A terrible spurt of blood burst forth, and the man flopped backward, his helmet crashing onto the lathering flanks of his horse and launching Rondo into the air. Time seemed to stand still as I twisted my body to follow the arc of the black-and-white puppy as he flew across the blue morning sky. I felt Julius pulling me back, yet I stretched for Rondo, fighting my brother with my fingers splayed, aching to grab the scruff of the dog's neck. I was no match for Julius's strength. My body was heaved upward just as Rondo's parabolic flight was coming to an end. I still reached, and by some miracle I caught him by the leg as the horse hit the bridge, hooves clamoring frantically for the open gate.

My father, having watched the whole desperate chase from the parapet with his archers, was there the moment the gates crashed behind us. Relief and anger fought for control over his impassioned face as he pulled us one by one off the blowing horse and into his arms. "Julius," he said, "God as my witness, I never know what possesses ye, or if ye are sent me by God or the devil. Ye nearly got yourself killed, lad, and I'm sorry to think I love ye all the more for it. Now go and get some food, for we've got our work cut out for us this day." Then he turned to me. His face was still livid with anger, yet his eyes had gone soft with a sudden hint of moisture. "Isabeau, ye know better than to run off without telling a soul, child. That mangy cur nearly cost ye your life, and your brother's as well. Nothing is worth that. Ye must learn when to let go, my dear lass. For love of that pup alone ye should have let go." He looked at the now motionless, limp ball of fur in my arms. His hand reached out, as if he meant to take Rondo from me, but he thought better of it. "Take ye off to the tower, Isabeau," he added softly. "Madame Seraphina is there waiting for ye."

I had been greatly shaken by the events of the morning. A man had died by my brother's hand; more were dying as the battle raged on, and Rondo, the puppy I had loved and nearly sacrificed my life and my brother's for, had gone stiff and cold. Mme. Seraphina, my nurse, had tried several times to take him from me, but I would not let him go. I think I believed that if I held on to him long enough—until my brother and father returned unharmed, and Blythe Hall and all her people were safe—then Rondo would be safe too. But I don't really remember what I believed, only that I was not ready to believe that he had died.

The day wore on in tiresome battle. The air was filled with the cry of fighting and dying men. Fires had been started on various rooftops and put out, and the women were slowly called away to bring food and water to the exhausted warriors, or to attend those who were injured, or to see to the animals, and soon I found myself alone in the tower, momentarily forgotten. That was when I took Rondo to the special room at the very top of the old keep—up the six flights of spiraling stairs that led to the only room in the entire castle that my father had forbidden anyone to enter.

I knew why he had shut it off from the world the way he did, covering all the furniture in white cloth and never sweeping the floor of the many layers of dust that had settled. He wanted it to remain the same as it looked the day he left it, the day my mother had died giving birth to me. That it was special to him, I respected, but it was special to me as well. To a curious child the discovery of the forbidden tower room was like uncovering a treasure, not only because of its vaulted ceilings and the arched windows that were filled with colored glass and had a magical way of transforming light, but because of the woman who lived there. I once told Julius about her, but he didn't believe me. He was a knight-in-training and very busy. He didn't have time for childish stories, and he never ventured near this room. I knew better than to tell my father.

It was nearing twilight, and the light that filtered through the colored glass was tempered by a golden hue. I crossed the floor, my little slippers leaving their mark in the dust, and found the spot I was looking for. I set Rondo down where the yellow light from the saint's halo fell, and sat back, watching as the dust I had disturbed fluttered in the shafts of dazzling light. "Please," I said to the saint and all his trumpet-bearing angels. "I need your help." And then I stared into the beams of soft light, tears clouding my vision, until I heard her voice.

"Isabeau," the voice said very quietly. "Are you crying, child?"

I turned and saw her, the white lady. I always felt happy when she came, for she was beautiful, like an angel, only she didn't have wings. But the little boys who accompanied her did, and I watched as they stepped from the shafts of light, where they sometimes hid, to gaze upon Rondo with their lovely, quizzical faces. I could not speak.

"What have you there?" asked the lady, walking around me. She knelt beside the little boys and looked at Rondo, her eyes wide with gentle inquiry.

"His name is Rondo," I told her. "And . . . and he died today."

"He died?" she repeated, and then: "No, Isabeau. Rondo is not dead, only sleeping. Come here and touch him for yourself."

I did as she told me, and when I knelt beside them, she wiped a tear from my cheek and dripped it onto the puppy's fur. She then took my hand and placed it over the tear that had stained Rondo's still, small body. "Do you feel him breathing?" she asked. I shook my head. "Well then, you must try harder. Close your eyes and feel how he breathes, how his tiny chest rises and falls."

I don't remember how long I spent trying to feel Rondo breathe before I heard my father's voice. The sound startled me, for he bellowed a name that wasn't my own in a gasp and a cry of such anguish that I didn't at first realize it was him until I turned to the door. The sun had nearly set and the room had lost its luster, but I could still see his face as he stood there, framed in the doorway. He was covered in soot and streaked with blood, and his eyes, burning with an intensity that frightened me, held to a spot just beyond where I was kneeling. It was then that I realized that he was looking at the white lady, and to my astonishment, I saw that she was looking at him as well.

He cried the name again, *Angelica,* and stumbled into the room on weary legs. The white lady stood slowly, and said in a voice that was the very essence of serenity wrapped in all the sorrows of the world: "William . . . oh, William . . ." And then she smiled at him with a longing I could not comprehend. It was the last thing I saw before my father, crashing into the furniture as he made his way toward her, scared her and the little boys away.

She was gone, yet he continued calling her name as he ran around like a madman, searching every corner and recess of the old tower room. But I knew, and was trying to tell him, that once she was gone you could never find her until she chose to come back again. Frantic, and wrought with a grief so palpable that it tore at my own heart, he dropped onto his knees beside me, grabbed me by the shoulders, and shook me as he cried: "Where is she? Where has she gone, Isabeau? Oh, God! Oh, God, child, where has she gone?" Then, unable to utter another word, he began to sob. I was sobbing too, because I had never seen my father cry.

That was how Mme. Seraphina and Julius found us, my father on his knees speechless and in tears, and me standing beside him, dumbstruck, in the middle of a darkened, shut-off room. My father told Seraphina what happened—how he saw the woman he called Angelica, the woman who was my mother. He then ordered servants to remove the sheets, to sweep the floor, to light all the sconces, and to bring him food, for he was not going to leave. And I shall never forget the look in Julius's eyes, the harsh, accusatory look as he grabbed my hand and dragged me away while Rondo, tail wagging, followed us out of the room.

I never saw the white lady or the little boys again. To this day I refuse to believe that I ever saw them at all.

Chapter 1
THE CALLING

Republic of Venice,
October 1491

A LIGHT, VEILING FOG HAD SETTLED ON THE CITY AS he traveled the silent, snaking waterway through the *sestieri* Cannaregio. The black water, lapping gently at the shallow boat, seemed to swallow the scant light offered every now and then by torch or the odd hanging lantern. It was unsettling, but he was glad of it, this hungry darkness, this cloaking mist. He had taken pains to conceal his own identity as well, as this meeting required, lest he be seen traveling this desperate path by any of his men. Around another corner and through the black tunnel of yet one more bridge, and there it was, the old palazzo eerily illuminated by four hissing torches on the pillars of the lower arcade. While the gondolier, obviously no stranger to this address, expertly piloted the little craft toward the landing place, the traveler turned his hawkish gaze to the façade, or what he could see of it through the mist and flickering firelight. The once beautiful imported stone, adorned with rows of expertly crafted ogee windows, their fine arches topped with quatrefoil embellishments and exotic marble tracery, arose four stories out of the canal. In its day it had likely been the jewel of the old waterway, but now, tucked away in what had become the rougher quarter of the *sestieri,* it looked as shabby as old lace. He imagined it smelled like old lace too—old lace, stale sweat, and fading flowers—once one passed under the crumbling arcade and was let inside the piano nobile. And he wondered again what fool notion had driven him to come here.

As soon as the gondola was tied onto the pole, he stood, his golden head and piercing blue eyes concealed by the hood of the black cape he wore, and tossed the gondolier a coin. "Stay here," he said in perfect Italian. "I shall be back in a moment." The gondolier, a wiry old man, smiled a nearly toothless smile by way of response and settled down in the bottom of his craft. He fished out a ripe plum and took a sideways bite that employed all his remaining back teeth.

"Nobody," he said, chewing, the fleshy fruit shaken lazily in his direction, "who visits this *casa,* signor, stays only a moment." He took another bite.

The traveler's eyes, dark and liquid in the shadow of the hood, widened in response. "In general, I imagine that's so. But I didn't come here to linger."

The gondolier's face split into a wide, gap-toothed grin. "Ah, you are nervous. It is your first time, no?" The very notion seemed to tickle him. "Pleasure should not be rushed, signor. You, my young friend, will linger."

There was really no polite response to this, and so, leaving the old man to relish his own conclusions, he jumped out of the boat and headed for the crumbling arcade knowing that he wouldn't be inside those walls any longer than he had to, because tonight pleasure wasn't in it.

After gaining entrance with a password and a heavy amount of coin, he was whisked up the stairs to the piano nobile, the grand parlor of the old palazzo. Climbing, he could hear the faint music of plucked strings and melodious flute interspersed with high, lilting giggles. That was not uncommon in such a place as this. Yet nothing, not even his own vast experience, could have prepared him for what was on the other side of the door. The guard paused a moment to unlock this newest obstacle, uttering, "Enjoy your visit, signor." And then, without another word, he found himself thrust inside the grand parlor, his power of speech abandoning him as his eyes registered the writhing scene before him.

It was a dazzling vision of ancient Greece—a hedonist's vision—brought to life by a very savvy Venetian. The first thing that struck him was the number of people in the vast room partaking of its delights. Usually the parlors of these places were moderately empty, most business being conducted in the private rooms upstairs. But here that rule did not, apparently, apply. He stood for a moment as his eyes took in the erotic ambiance, every sense heightened by the wanton display of sex and lust. At the far end of the room a group of customers, dressed in short togas and carnival masks, gathered near a marble colonnade to watch a man dressed as a satyr, or perhaps even Pan himself, entertain his throng of nymphs. The man-goat, a remarkable creature with little horns sprouting from his raven curls, oiled chest, and legs covered in goat hair that, unfortunately, did nothing to detract from his spectacularly erect organ, stood under the arch playing the panpipes. The traveler didn't much care for the panpipes, and truthfully, although they were played with a lot of heart, they were utterly discordant. However, it was not the music or the satyr that had the men so enthralled. It was the seven willowy nymphs dancing barefoot in sheer, flowing, gossamer gowns. Correction: they weren't really dancing so much as frolicking. Yes, they most definitely were frolicking, moving between potted trees and crumbling columns, teasing both horny satyr and paying guests alike with erotic gestures and suggestive movements that left little to the imagination. The masked men, he noted with grim satisfaction, were about to get exactly what they paid for.

In the center of the room was another eye-grabbing attraction in the form of a marble reflection pool. It was a wonder of a thing, complete with a magnificently sculpted bubbling fountain, only it wasn't water that spewed from the erect phallus of this huge marble satyr but wine. More nimble women frolicked here beneath the rose-colored liquid as it drenched their voluptuous bodies, turning their thin Grecian gowns into wine-stained skin. The women, playful as kittens, were seasoned sirens of seduction, driving their male guests to frenzy by touching, teasing, and feeding them from their own dripping lips.

"Dionysus, god of wine, inspirer of madness and wondrous ecstasy, I am your slave," he uttered softly to himself as his eyes held the scenes before him—from the mood-setting art on the walls and the lush greenery of the potted gardens to the trays overflowing with fruits, sugared nuts, and cheese set near the low couches where couples lay entwined, heavy with lust. "But please, have mercy on me this night." He closed his eyes and fought to expunge the raging fire in his blood—the glorious madness that so easily took him. But he would not be a slave tonight—not here, and certainly not now. Four deep, cleansing breaths, and he opened his eyes again; the prophetic statement of his smirking gondolier rang through his over-taxed brain: *You, my young friend, will linger.*

Damn him, he was lingering.

It was then that he silently cursed Dante for being the misbegotten whoreson he was. The wily little Venetian never warned him of this and was no doubt having a good laugh over it too. And he had been very wrong: this place smelled nothing like old lace. It smelled like paradise, and he cursed himself again for pursuing the task that brought him here tonight. Unbeknownst to him, he had paid heavily to partake in a good old-fashioned Greek orgy, and he felt it a real shame to have to forgo the pleasure. He would likely kill Dante for this.

"Signor?" came a sultry voice behind him. He turned and looked into the eyes of a dark-haired, dark-eyed Venetian beauty dressed like a goddess. In her hands she held a white toga and plain black carnival mask. "Will you take off your cloak and join them . . . or do you prefer a private room?"

He smiled at her and pulled back the hood concealing his face. The girl, he saw with returning satisfaction, froze where she stood and stared at him in speechless wonder. One might have thought such a reaction to his golden, northern looks would have gotten old after a while, but today, in this palace of pleasure, it was welcomed; a small consolation for his troubles. "Thank you, my dear, but no," he replied coolly, with just a hint of the urbane. "I'm after something quite different."

"Really?" The goddess's large black eyes looked both naughty and delighted at once. "But, signor, I can provide *different* if you wish?" The way she pronounced *different* elicited the rise of one golden eyebrow.

He let his cerulean gaze rake her from head to toe before offering his sweetest, most disarming smile. "Very well," he said, and handed her a slip of paper. He watched with satisfaction as her open and inviting features darkened.

"*This* is what you came for?"

"Shocking, isn't it?"

"What . . . what kind of man comes here . . . at this hour, for . . . *this*?"

"Only the kind of man who has total mastery over all his urges."

Her dark eyes sparkled with devilish mirth as she let out a trill of laughter. "Really? I've never known such a man to exist. A real saint among us sinners, are you? Or is it that you prefer—"

"No, and no," he replied before she finished. "And I believe it would hurt your pretty little head to puzzle out exactly what I am. So, shall we just get on with it?"

It was several moments later—after the full, mesmerizing hips had stopped swinging as she led him upstairs—that he found himself standing before a door on the very top floor of the old palazzo. The sultry music and engaging voices of the piano nobile below were but a soft echo. He wondered again why he had listened to the daft Venetian. The goddess, holding him with suspicion and just a touch of disappointment, prepared to knock on the door. A sardonic smile crossed his lips, and he nodded.

"Signora Evangelista?" she called. "You are expecting a visitor?" There was a faint reply to this, and the goddess, hearing it, turned to him and cautioned that he should wait. Without another word she slipped inside the room.

He waited a good ten minutes before the goddess reappeared, noting that her beautiful dark eyes were not coy or teasing any longer but suffused with pity and something close to fear. "The signora . . . will see you now."

She was about to slip away when he grabbed her by the wrist and, pressing her to the wall with his hard body, kissed her roughly and very thoroughly on the mouth. "I'm sorry," he whispered, noting that she had gone breathless. His fingers were entwined in her thick tresses, and he bent back her head to kiss the column of her olive neck. Her breath came in short, bursting gasps. "I'm a liar," he said near her ear. "I have no mastery over any of my urges at the moment."

"Then I shall wait for you," she uttered, her voice suddenly thick. God, she was a beauty.

Delivering one more kiss, he released her. "No," he said with finality. And then, without looking back, he walked inside the darkened room perfectly ignoring his exploding senses and that voice of reason inside his head that warned against such foolish desperation.

⁊⊚

He had never been a patron of necromancy and regarded the whole notion of dabbling in the spirit world not only distasteful but a cartload of, well, the slipperiest kind of excrement. The practitioners of the art were little better, mere actors supreme in the art of deception. He knew all this; the parlor below was proof enough. Yet still, he was here.

"Well, don't just stand there gawking like a mute fool, boy! Come forward." The voice, crackling with impatience, had come from the direction of a huge chair.

The old woman, the legendary owner of this crumbling palazzo whom he had gone to such great pains to see, was in reality a wizened, wrinkled wraith of a being who looked more like some naughty, misshapen child who had plundered her mother's jewels and makeup to engage in a game of pretend. Still, he had to admit that this petite old woman, dressed in garish finery and peering at him from the depths of the vast chair, was mightily unsettling. So too was the room, for that matter. For here was a shrine designed to create a legend. It was filled with Grecian antiques. Marble busts, short columns supporting heavy vases and chipped pottery, wondrous wall hangings of the finest cloth, were all cast in an ominous red hue. This, he saw, was achieved by four hanging lanterns encased in red Venetian glass. A little brazier sat on the floor next to the old woman's chair with a silver pot simmering over it. The heat provided warmth on the chilly, damp night, while the burning coals served to illuminate her weathered face from below, casting the Roman nose, the thin, painted lips, the sunken eye sockets ringed in black kohl, in wavering shadows. Although old, her painted skin no longer plump and vibrant with youth, he could tell she had once been a beauty. A fine veil covered her white hair and was kept in place by a circlet of gold studded with jewels. Of course they were real, likely the spoils from her many conquered lovers. He guessed the reason the lovely goddess had taken so long in this room was to complete the illusion of Signora Evangelista Continari, the High Priestess of Cyprus, as she was more commonly known—a self-proclaimed descendant of Aphrodite, goddess of love, teller of fortunes, finder of lost souls. Doubt clouded his mind again, yet he had to admit, as far as seers and necromancers went, she was quite the consummate professional. No silly hocus-pocus here, but a real actress. God knew he loved a good performance, but not in matters as dire as this.

Her old red-rimmed eyes, black and sharp as a raven's, held his. A wave of sickening regret washed through him. "So," she spoke plainly, "you have finally decided to seek my counsel."

"When being fleeced I prefer to be a willing party," he replied amiably. This caused the painted eyebrows to rise. "And while we're on the subject of parties, may I add that you're one of the few women I've ever met who really knows how to entertain her guests."

Her old lips pulled into a wry grin as she indicated that he should take the seat across from her. "I find, Signor Blythe, that if one wants to make lots of money, one has to first understand the hungers that govern before one can exploit them. Take, for example, your cloth merchant, your spice merchant, and even our glassmakers of Murano. All have learned to exploit a growing hunger. I am no different."

"An old, insatiable hunger you've tapped into, I see." It was said with genuine appreciation as he took the offered seat. "And I commend you. You're quite exceptional at it."

"I take it Dante did not tell you the nature of our business?"

"He's a very modest young man, is Dante. All he said was, 'She runs an old brothel.' Not a complete lie. Don't tell me he worked here?"

"He was one of the best satyrs I've ever had," she said ru-minatively, her liquid black eyes softened now, still holding his. "Seldom sober, never sated . . . passionate about his work."

This caused him to laugh, and he offered, "You'll be happy to know he's not changed."

"Dear Dante." Focusing on him again, she added with bit-ter challenge, "I had to kick him out—for the sake of the girls and my business. Did he tell you that? He had too much promise to fall victim to such useless emotions. Amore, Signor Blythe, is a weakness that, like a sickness, devours the soul. Lust, however, is another matter. You do not love, do you?"

"No," he replied levelly. "But we are not here to discuss my virtues, or your misguided grandson. I am here, Signora Evangelista, because I was told you could help me locate a man."

He remained calm and unmoving as her black eyes scoured him quite naked. "And you do not believe that I can."

"I am here. That is all you need concern yourself with."

"Very well," she said. "And who is this man you seek?"

He found it odd—that the quest that had brought him across Europe and throughout the Mediterranean should end here, in this unchancy place. But he would not stop now. "I am looking for the man who once wore this ring," he said. As he spoke he took from his pouch a magnificent ring of gold and handed it to her.

He watched as the old woman hungrily examined it under the rose light, twisting and turning it over in her age-gnarled hands until they began to shake. She looked up. "He is a seeker, this man, one who is on a personal quest."

"Aren't we all?" His voice was edged with sarcasm as he watched her through hooded eyes.

Her serene countenance darkened as her sharp gaze pierced his skeptical heart; he saw that her hands were still shaking. "You are a wanderer, a frivolous wastrel, not a seeker! There is a difference. You have been thrust on an aimless path by your own foolish machinations. This man," she proclaimed, her raspy voice growing stronger, "is a true seeker—a man guided by divine beings."

"And you can see all this? Or did you merely read the inscription on the ring?"

"You mock me?" The words were firm and harsh, and her old black eyes narrowed in warning. "What is it you want, Signor Blythe? Surely you have not come here... you haven't paid my price to play the fool."

"What I want," he said slowly, lacing his elegant hands together while pressing forefingers meditatively to his lips, "is for you to tell me where that man is." Forefingers still together, he pointed to the ring. "Not what he's after, not that he is driven by divine beings, but where I can find him."

"You assume that he is still alive."

"I assume nothing," he replied, and for a moment he believed she had caught the slight edge of desperation in his voice. "Be he living or be he dead, I wish to find him," he concluded and gave a humorless smile.

She sat back, nearly swallowed by the huge chair, and studied him at leisure from the shadows. Then, finally breaking the silence with a grin of pure malice, she said: "Very well, Signor Blythe, then let us dangle our toes in the spirit world."

❦

He supposed this is what he had come for, the promise of answers that went beyond cold trails and dead ends. But still, nothing in his experience, nothing in all his travels—in all the lands he had fought and bled in—prepared him for what came next.

He watched in silence as Signora Evangelista pulled a pot from the brazier and carefully prepared a tea of pungent herbs and powdered substances, most of which he could not name.

The smell of her potion, that of rotting vegetation swirling around wet wool with an underlying stink very similar to camel shit, suffused the air, and he felt he might be sick. But he fought it off, transfixed by a perverse desire to see this old witch fulfill her obligation; after all, her price had not been cheap. The wrinkled lips pressed to a little cup, quavering as the first drops of the vile mix went down. If it tasted at all like it smelled, then she indeed was not only a good actress but incredibly devoted to her craft. She sat very still, and then, closing her black eyes, she tossed the rest back like a thirsty sailor, wiping the dribbles from her chin with the sleeve of her gown. After a theatrical pause, her papery, wrinkled eyelids flew up with a startling suddenness. She looked at him with black orbs distant, and then she picked up the ring and placed it on her finger.

His eyes, unmoving, silently admired her pluck as she waited to summon her spirit guides. As if on cue, her body convulsed with a sudden jerk and her head lolled back dramatically, hitting the wood of the high-backed chair. He raised a brow at the sound. It had to have hurt. Nonetheless, he was perversely transfixed by the performance, knowing in the rational part of his brain that he was the biggest kind of fool. He should have just stayed in the grand parlor and enjoyed the orgy.

The old woman was very still now. A cold wind blew in from the canal, ruffling the light curtains. He felt it on the back of his neck, felt it travel like frozen fingers under his hair and send a wave of icy chills down his spine. It was a warning, an instinctive response, and he knew he should leave at once. But he ignored the impulse—because he was riveted to Signora Evangelista's bold performance. The old woman remained deathly still as her gown fluttered in the intrusive breeze.

And then the wind came again.

This time there was more force to it, enough to throw the

shutters back on their hinges, causing a loud, resounding crack. Turning, he saw that the curtains were protesting violently and jumped from his chair to close the shutters, toppling an expensive vase in the process. But the wind, oddly contained inside the room, did not stop. He watched, awestruck, as a current began circling, building in force, growing until it howled in his ears. Other vases toppled. The fine wall hangings were ripped off their hooks. And he knew, without doubt, that he was in the middle of something unholy. He also saw that the old woman understood it too. Her eyes were wide with horror; her red-painted lips had parted as a guttural scream formed in her throat. His eyes held hers, but no sound came from her lips. He took a step toward her. Her face contorted in a look of unbearable pain. He was about to run to her when the lanterns, all four of them, exploded in a burst of rose-colored glass. Shards shot through the air on the demonic wind, and he found himself pressed to the floor in the swirling darkness, his breath coming heavy, his mind and body awakening to the instinct that had kept him alive when he had walked in hell, or whenever entering the heart of a battle. This was a little of both, but unlike anything he had ever before experienced.

He fought his way back to the chair as the wind kept howling around him, driving razor-sharp glass and broken pottery at his body. He pulled up his hood and, shielding his eyes as best he could with his arm, caught sight of Signora Evangelista. Now cast in monochromatic tones from the scattered embers of the brazier, her entire body was convulsing; her black eyes, wide under the sheer fabric of her veil, were disturbingly blank, and he watched as they rolled back in her head until only the whites could be seen.

This was not an act.

Something had gone frightfully wrong. Perhaps the tea had been poisoned. Perhaps a storm like none this city had ever known had blown in, causing the strange wind; for he would cling to any possibility rather than yield to the suspicion that an unseen force had taken hold of the old woman, causing her frail bones to rattle the chair that was at least twice her size. And then, suddenly, from deep within the High Priestess of Cyprus came a voice that only the likes of the devil could own.

He could hear someone pounding on the door. It was the young woman, the goddess he had told not to wait. Damn her, but she had waited, and her frantic cry touched him as she pleaded to be let in. But he would not bring her into this.

The demon voice pulled him back.

The old woman was now speaking in a language he did not know, had never heard, and he had heard many. It was harsh and guttural, as if the earth had ripped open and was vomiting brimstone. Yet there was a cadence to it, an allure to its dark madness that encircled him, and visions of the naked bodies below, writhing, coupling in unending rapture, held him to the spot as the gnarled hands of the old woman came for him. He saw that her eyes were still white; her painted mouth was uttering words, but her legs weren't moving. By God, she was floating on the wind! He then saw the blue pall of death on her face and knew she was gone. His blood froze in his veins; he couldn't move if he wanted to.

The hands of the dead body were coming closer. His eye caught the glint of the ring he had given her—the ring of his father. He reached for it, his fingers nearly touching those of the possessed priestess, and he cared not what happened. He wanted his ring back. Yet before he could grab it—before he could touch her—a flash of light tore through the room, stilling the raging wind, silencing the demonic babble, and blinding him completely. The shock of it thrust him backward, sending him tripping over the Kurdistan rug and cracking his head on the leg of a chair. He hit the floor, landing on the wreckage of broken glass and pottery, but he felt nothing. Shielding his eyes from the bright light, he heard the unmistakable voice of his mother. "Julius, my poor, dear child, it is time to stop running."

He sat up, straining to see her face, but the light was too strong. Somewhere, he knew, the goddess was still pounding on the door. But his heart was beating too loudly, and his face, inexplicably, felt damp. "Mother?" he uttered, seized with fear, hope, disbelief. His arm came over his eyes.

"Julius, go home."

"I can't go home!" he cried, and caught the unnerving thread of fear that lined his every word. "I can't," he reiterated with persuasive finality. "Not until I find him."

"My dear, misguided soul," replied the voice of serenity. "You have courted demons enough; it is time, my son, to face your own. Leave your father be. What you seek from him will be delivered by the messenger you have already chosen."

"What?" he gasped. He felt emotionally eviscerated and feared he was mad, the madness touching him as it had touched his father. His eyes burned at the thought, and his cheeks stung. He brought his fingers to his face and saw blood mingled with tears. By God, was he actually crying?

And then he smelled her.

The horrible stink of the room, the rotting vegetation and camel shit, had gone, and in its place came the pure and heavenly scent of roses and warm sunlight. It had been years ago, he had been only five, but he would never forget her scent. Thoughts of home came flooding back, entangled with memories both good and painful, and a vision of a marble angel above an old archway. An angel. A messenger. A warrior of God. The one who would hold the key to his absolution. "Gabriel!" he gasped, finally understanding.

She did not speak again, but he could feel her answer. A burst of love, pure and blinding, radiated through him. He wanted to bathe in it; he wanted it to last forever. But it did not last. It was ebbing away, leaving with one clear message:

"Go home to Blythe Hall." And then she was gone, and the light with her. The room turned dark once again.

He awoke next to the body of a dead woman and felt he must vomit. The stink was back in the room, now accompanied by the smell of death. He heard the frantic pounding of fists. He sat up, saw the ring on the gnarled old hand, and took it. He put it on his own finger and walked to the door, bleeding, bruised, and utterly shaken. The goddess was there, waiting as he knew she would be, only her face was now pinched with fear.

"Signora Evangelista...," he began, but could say no more. Her large, imploring eyes, pooling with tears, failed to move him, and he left her standing there, with a hand over her quivering mouth. He continued quickly down the dim corridor, descended the many flights of stairs, walked past the private rooms, past the piano nobile where the bodies now lay naked and spent, and down yet more stairs until he passed through the crumbling arcade where a guard bade him good night.

"Get up," he told the gondolier, who was sleeping peacefully in the bottom of the boat. The old man sprang awake, confused at first, until he took a good look at his passenger's face.

"Sweet merciful Christ," he uttered and broke into a wide, toothless grin. "What the hell happened to you?"

"I lingered," Julius Blythe replied, and sat down on the cushioned seat. It was then that he noticed he was shaking. The gondolier noticed it too and, through a look of rapt admiration, handed him a handkerchief to daub the blood streaming down his face.

"You lingered!" he laughed as he cast off, the bow of the sleek boat heading for the dark waters of the canal. "Indeed you lingered, my young friend, but I would say you got your money's worth."

"I got more than my money's worth," he answered softly, unable to return the smile. The old man laughed heartily at this, but Julius could not join him. Instead he pulled up his hood and wrapped himself tightly in the folds of his cloak, hoping that would stop the shaking.

He did not stop shaking.

Gabriel. The name came to him as they traveled the lonely waterway in the small hours before dawn. Gabriel, he had uttered, remembering the white light that had pulled the name from the jaded recesses of his mind. Unfortunately, he knew exactly what it meant. "Well then," he said to himself while looking heavenward, where one lonely star had broken through the mist. "If that's how it's going to be played, then by all means, let the game begin."

Chapter 2

BLYTHE HALL

WITH MY OWN THOUGHTS HELD CLOSE AND MY ermine-lined cape pulled closer still, I rode in silence, absorbing every detail of the undulating land of Roxburghshire. I let my eyes wander over windswept, heather-covered hills and down the sides of wooded valleys where the intrepid Tweed, appearing a mere whimsical stroke of an artist's brush, moved like a peaty-brown viper weaving its way east and to the sea. It was wild, desolate country inhabited by a hearty, often lawless breed of people, yet no one could deny its beauty or its allure, least of all me.

But one doesn't return home, especially to a place like Blythe Hall, without feeling some form of unease. I had been thirteen the last time I laid eyes on the brooding Borders fortress that was my ancestral home, and five years had filled the space in between, most of which was spent in the convent at Haddington and then serving King James, the fourth of that name, and his remarkable aunt, the spinster Princess Margaret Stewart. Because James came to his throne a minor, being only fifteen at the time, and was yet a young man near my own age, he was still a bachelor. The nobles, of course, were scouring the royalty of Europe to remedy this, yet try as they might, there appeared to be a real shortage of suitable princesses available for their young king. Lucky James. I, unfortunately, was not so lucky. In fact, Scotland, I learned, was bursting at the seams with men, young and old, noble or otherwise, all very willing to marry a young woman of noble birth, especially one who was the sole heir to a large and propitiously placed Border estate. It was a daunting situation for any young woman, and for me it was especially so because the king was not only my dear friend but my legal guardian. And it was his duty to make it my duty to marry, and marry wisely.

I'll be the first to admit that I was not overly wise where men were concerned. I blame this on my father and brother, both frightfully damaged specimens of their sex, who engendered my love and my heart and then abandoned me. On the opposite end of this scale was the king, a rare fine example of all that a man should be—brave, wise, kind, and chivalrous, and utterly untouchable. Aside from kindly servants, dear friends, and exhausting relatives, I found the whole swirl of savvy courtiers befuddling. And so, to preserve my own sanity, I decided it was time I heed the sagely advice of Princess Margaret and take control of my own destiny. And my destiny was to be the Lady of Blythe Hall. In this I had no regrets.

What I did regret, if I were to be totally honest with myself, was my decision to wear silk hose and not good old stout wool ones better suited to long hours on horseback and the blustery winds of the Borders. I might also have regretted leaving court as hastily as I had, jumping at the king's offer to accept his escort and not waiting for my own to arrive. And certainly, if I had been one to dwell on past foolishness, I would have regretted eating the cheerfully offered *marag dubh*, as Tam, my groom called it. The dear lad said his granny had made the blood pudding especially for me, and took the liberty of fortifying the black sausage with a special mix of herbs and whatnot to ward off evil. Tam's use of the word *whatnot* was suspect, but since I had no wish to encounter evil on my journey home, I took a polite nibble; Tam's granny, although well meaning, was not known for her cooking. True to her reputation, the blood pudding was cold and slimy, tasteless but for the strange effervescence of river moss, and uniquely granular. Tam, however, being a superstitious lad, insisted I eat the whole thing, and now the kind yet unpalatable offering sat in my stomach, churning away like sour milk on ill-smelted lead. Although I had eaten the blood pudding yesterday morning and hadn't suffered much at the time, I was certain my queasiness was a latent reaction to this and in no way a result of any regrets on my part for acting so rashly.

"God's knuckles!" The expletive hit my ears with the same startling unease as the memory of the blood pudding. "Pray don't tell me that's where we're going?"

I looked at the source of the outcry, my dear friend Marion Boyd, niece of the late Earl of Arran, youngest child of Arran's brother, Sir Archibald Boyd of Nariston, and favorite niece of the once powerful Sir Archibald Douglas, fifth Earl of Angus, or Bell-the-Cat as he was affectionately known. Having spent a good deal of time at court, and having been around powerful men her whole life, Marion was lively, beautiful, and wildly self-indulgent, and although her behavior was scandalous at times, she was my dearest friend. At first I had no idea what she was complaining about, only that she was complaining about something again. Yesterday it had been the overwhelming amount of mud we slogged through, then the hardness of her saddle, and this morning the good brothers of the Cross Kirk Friary in Peebles were awarded for their hospitality an earful about their weak ale and burnt oatcakes. Noting that her bejeweled glove was still quivering aloft, and that her finger was waggling accusingly at some indiscernible point in the distance, I followed it.

My heart stilled.

In the distance, in a wooded glen not far from where the Tweed parted ways with the Teviot, the top of a great stone tower could be seen poking above budding trees and a tangle of tenacious shrubbery. Although the very top of the noble gray tower was all that was visible from here, it didn't take a practiced eye to see that we were no longer in the fertile heart of our country, nor was this the center of courtly civility. We were in the grip of a land battered and scarred for centuries by hostile, warring forces, and the great castle before us was but another vigilant sentinel guarding the gate to Scotland. Only it wasn't just another castle, it was Blythe Hall.

"Umm," I began cautiously, noting the puzzled look on Marion's face and not wishing to cause her further regret, for she had been rather eager to accompany me on my journey home. "Yes, I . . . believe that it is."

She raised a perfectly plucked eyebrow. "You believe that it is, or it is?"

"What if I said it is? Would you hate me very much?"

"Dear heavens above, Isabeau, nobody could ever hate you, although I'd have perfectly good reason if I did. You've dragged me through mud, bog, and frightful hills, and fed me nothing but rubbish for the last two days, and it's now threatening rain." I was awarded her most dazzling and sarcastic smile. "Forgive me if I assumed your home would have been a little more civilized and imaginative than that bleak pile of stones over there. It does have a roof, doesn't it?"

"Of course it does," I replied, hoping I was correct, for it had been a long while since I'd been home. "And it's not bleak and unimaginative. You do understand where we are, don't you?" This last question I asked a bit loudly, so I'd be heard above the building wind and the jangling of horse harnesses. Yet I could see that Sir Matthew Beaton, Master of the King's Guard, who just happened to be riding on Marion's other side, heard me as well, for his lips, surrounded by a neatly trimmed beard, pulled into a smile. It was this small gesture that urged me to continue. "They don't call these the Borders, Marion, because they're bordering on the same luxuries as Stirling Castle, or Linlithgow, or even Edinburgh. This is not a stroll down the High Street where one straps on her pattens and goes a-calling, and where everyone you meet invites you in for mulled wine, almond cakes, and the latest gossip. But it does have its own particular kind of charm."

"Charm?" replied my lovely companion, her perky brows raised high beneath the gabled velvet headdress of emerald green. "Really, there are so many other words that spring to mind, but *charm*, Isabeau dear, is not one of them. However, I must admit I was getting a wee tired of almond cakes." I watched as her large brown eyes, heavy with doubt, scanned the windblown pine and scrub, the rogue tufts of grass, the chickweed, bilberry, and bedstraw interspersed amongst the blanket of purple-dusted heather. Marion, although a lively soul, did not enjoy being separated from luxury.

"As you'll recall, you were tired of a great many things, Marion, including the vigilant eye of Princess Margaret," I gently reminded her.

She cast a quick glance at the long line of armored men riding behind us, both of us quite aware that the closer ones were trying very hard to appear as if they hadn't been hanging on our every word. She looked back at me and grinned. It was a look that usually preceded mischief. "I was, wasn't I?"

"Did you know it was Princess Margaret who suggested I take you with me in the first place?"

"Really?" she replied, looking mildly amused. "And why do you think she thought of me for this enlightening little journey?"

"I believe she admires your spirit and thought you could use a little excitement," I suggested, then added with a remonstrative grin, "and not because of your bold and rather public declaration of love for her nephew, although that certainly didn't help."

At this Marion tossed back her emerald-covered auburn tresses and laughed. It was a well-crafted, silvery, tinkling laughter that drew admiration from our guard as it would have from any man within hearing. "The reason serving at court was at all bearable, if I may be so bold, was because of her charming nephew, Jamie." Her smile was languid and indulgent as she rolled his name off her tongue. Sir Matthew, I saw, had the decency to blush and look away.

"Really, Marion, James is your king and not some young buck to be toyed with. He has more important things on his mind these days than to dally and idle his time away with silly maidens."

"What could possibly be more important than dallying?" she mused aloud while staring boldly at Sir Matthew. That poor, dear man. Had he known the details of his assignment— that he was to escort two young, unmarried noblewomen and their retinues from Edinburgh to a remote border castle, and that the temperament of one of those noblewomen, Mistress Marion Boyd of Nariston herself, was anything but proper and chaste—he might have been wiser to decline the mission. But he was a loyal man, and one who dearly loved his young king. And he would suffer the boldness of my pretty friend like the honorable knight he was. "Well, I suppose you would know, wouldn't you?" she added, capping off the wistful smile she had been holding on our escort with a pointed look. "Because we certainly know that His Highness thinks very highly of you. After all, the man has lent us the gallant Sir Matthew and the cream of his brave young men." She cast a glance behind her and smiled coyly at the armor-plated, close-riding men-at-arms. Turning back, she said, "You never did tell me, did James send you away, or did you leave of your own volition?"

The tone of her voice implied that I was more to the king than his cherished friend. I might have been annoyed if the accusation came from anyone besides Marion. "As I told you before, I left," I began, smiling sweetly, "because it was time I start looking after my own affairs."

This time the coy playfulness left her face entirely, and she nodded. "How very fortunate you are to be your own master. But you won't hold that title for long, I'll wager, for I hear there's a list in the possession of the king that's filled with the names of eligible men lining up to be the next Lord Blythe. Isn't it exciting?" she offered conspiratorially, drawing her palfrey close to mine. Although Marion clearly thought this was exciting, the truth was, just the mention of such a list in the king's possession sent shivers down my spine. Ignoring my look of fear, Marion whispered, "And speaking of Lord Blythe, do you know what would make that daunting pile of rubble you call home infinitely more charming?" Her eyes flicked to the looming fortress, with not only the tower but a jumble of steeply pitched rooftops, soaring chimneys, and plenty of crenellation along the high walls visible. "Julius. Julius would make it charming. Did I tell you I heard he was back?"

"What?" I pulled to a halt. The man directly behind me hadn't expected the sudden stop and was forced to cut left to avoid collision. This caused a chain reaction ending with one unlucky knight riding straight into Mme. Seraphina. My governess was not overly fond of horses, or obtrusive young men save for dear Tam, but she was quick, and her meaty hand whacked the young man's face before he knew what hit him. His companions, wisely dropping back and navigating with a little more care, chuckled. I turned back to Marion. "That's impossible," I hissed.

Marion's liquid dark eyes held mine as she reined in her own mount and spun around. "Is it? He's Julius Blythe, remember?" And her lavish smile made me believe it could be true.

Julius was my older brother. He was not only charming and brilliant, bred on luxury and heir to a fortune, but also a traitor and an outlaw whose life was forfeit the moment he stepped on Scottish soil. And that was the reason I was now heir. It was rumored that he had escaped to France four years ago, after the disastrous battle outside of Stirling, on the very ground where two hundred years before, Robert the Bruce had defeated the English. It was now referred to as Sauchieburn, and it was where King James III, battling a rebel force of his own nobles, met his end. Battling one's own people was bad enough, yet adding further insult to injury was the fact that the king's own son, my dear friend James Stewart, only fifteen years of age and titled the Duke of Rothesay at the time, had been employed as the rebellious force's nominal leader. Some claimed it was in self-defense, and I believe that it was, for James III was a superstitious man and had grown more wary of his firstborn son with every passing year. Young James had been raised in Stirling by his mother, and after her passing the king cautiously kept him there, or far from his circle and the men who moved about him, because of his fear that one day the young prince would overthrow him. It was rumored that this notion came from a court astrologer who read it in the stars shortly after the young prince had been born. *A Scottish lion was to be devoured by his whelps,* the prophecy had declared.

I didn't believe in prophecies. They made one behave foolishly, and in my opinion the king had behaved very foolishly. His fear became a powerful weapon that turned against him and paved the way for the prophecy to come to fruition. The whole affair was a disastrous mess that had split the country in two and ended in regicide. James III was murdered far from the battlefield, and his son, my dear friend, was crowned King of Scotland by the men who had brought it all about. James had never forgiven himself for what had happened at Sauchieburn; to this day, although he had received absolution from Pope Innocent VIII, it was the sin that still lingered in his heart, and he had vowed to me, in private, that he would repent for it until his last breath. James was a man of his word, and I believed him.

My father had always been loyal to the kings of Scotland, regardless of policy, and James respected that. My brother, however, was not so honorable and was found to be working not only with the rebel lords but with England as well. And the plot he was said to have been concocting would have been enough to topple the entire nation. Knowing that any claims to his inheritance had been forfeited, he somehow managed to escape, presumably to France, where he disappeared. For all I knew Julius was dead. The only blessing to this blight on the family Blythe was that my father never knew of it. He had left Scotland the year before Sauchieburn.

I kicked my horse. "Even if he is, by some miracle, still alive, he'd be a fool to come here," I remarked, heading toward the castle. "And he could never penetrate those walls, even though by every right they should be his. Julius should have thought of that before rubbing elbows with that devil King Henry."

"You would turn him away? Your own brother?" Marion had come abreast of me, urging her little mare to keep up. She was not normally a fearless rider, but she had met Julius once, and she had heard plenty of stories. And as everybody knew, once you met Julius—shameless, immoral, crooked, beautiful Julius—you fell under his spell.

At length I finally replied with forced bravado, "It would be my duty to king and country."

I heard Marion laugh as she dropped behind, unable to keep pace as I raced over the uneven moorland, trampling heather and new-sprung moor grass, my eyes burning with the threat of unshed tears. I'd like to think it was the wind, but I knew better. And in her laughter that trailed me like a hound on the scent was all the mockery I had endured these many years on behalf of my mad father and my spoiled, self-serving, insatiable brother. Blythe Hall, that impossible fortress, that tarnished jewel mired in the Thieves' Waste between England and Scotland, was a monument to madness. And now it was mine.

☙

The rain started the moment my horse's hooves touched the bridge. A loud crack of thunder shook the earth as lightning danced through the rolling, black clouds. And then the deluge came, the kind of drenching rain that penetrates thick wool and plasters expertly coiffed hair to the skin. The stream below in the wooded ravine, acting as a would-be deterrent to any who thought to attack the castle, swelled with the runoff, and the drone, even louder than the pounding rain, unsettled my horse. The beast capered sideways, threw its head, and reared. Sir Matthew pulled up beside me and grabbed the halter.

"Easy now," he soothed. His words were directed at my horse, but somehow I knew they were for me. And then: "I dinnae ken about thon young lady, but right now, Mistress Isabeau, Blythe Hall looks more inviting to me than any place in the entire kingdom."

"Thank you, Sir Matthew," I replied, and turned my eyes to the imposing gatehouse at the other end of the bridge. On either side of the gate were two round towers, thirty feet high, with the pointed archway between them. The great gate was closed and no guard could be seen, which was odd, especially on a day when the mistress of the castle was to return home. It was then that my eyes traveled to a space just above the arched gate. There, sitting in a protective niche above the grand entrance and fashioned out of imported marble by a rather gifted Florentine sculptor, was the image of an angel, wings unfurled in descent as if newly sprung from the heavens. The ethereal being, adorned in flowing robes with unbound hair, held a sword aloft in one hand and a shield at the ready in the other; he was an archangel, a warrior of heaven. On his shield was a thistle, the emblem of Scotland. The angel's head was slightly bent, while the eyes, large and blankly lustrous, gazed down with heavenly detachment on all who stood before the gate. The sight, after so long away, caused my skin to prickle and flush with contradicting heat as my heart, impervious to the wind and rain, began to beat with a fierceness I seldom felt. It was the Blythe Angel, our family crest, with the motto beneath it in French: JE SUIS PROTÉGÉ. I am protected. It was the madness my father believed in and proclaimed before any who happened across our gate. It was the madness my brother perversely embraced and shamelessly flaunted. And it was a madness I vowed would never touch me.

"Indeed," I uttered, pulling my eyes from the compelling winged warrior and turning my full attention to my escort. "It certainly does, and once we dry off, we shall make the Great Hall echo with our laughter before the night is out. I have not come here to cower, Sir Matthew, but to celebrate and make this castle, and her people, great once again. But first, I believe," I said, the bravado trailing from my voice, "we must get through those gates. They did receive word we were coming?"

"A messenger was sent, my lady. Whether he was received or no' we're about to find out." Sir Matthew gave a perfunctory grin, then cupped his hands around his mouth. "In the name of King James IV, open the gates!" Sir Matthew had the lungs of a sailor. Although his voice carried above the wind, driving rain, and raging stream, he was required to call out four times before a soggy head finally appeared in the gatehouse. The moment it did, the gates were opened.

A flurry of activity followed our entry, and the courtyard came alive with grooms and servants; horses were relieved of their riders and whisked to the stables. Above the clamor of armored men, exhausted animals, and servants struggling to unload heavy baggage, there was heard a cry of "My lady! My lady!"

I turned to see a man heavily cloaked, his dark hood pulled low over his face as he hastily ran toward us. But when he got to within five feet, he stopped. The hood came back, allowing the rain to soak the bemused and puzzled features, for I could see that he was staring at me just as intently as I stared at him. He was a man at one time as familiar to me as my own father, and though I hadn't seen him in more than four years, he was a welcome sight. Time had touched him as it had touched us all, only perhaps he suffered from it a bit more than most, for his position was not an enviable one. The jovial face had grown thinner and was now etched with deep lines that formed rivulets for the assaulting rainwater, and where once his hair had been a glossy brown, it was now heavily streaked with gray. The bright blue eyes were the same.

"Isabeau," he uttered, his face alight with pleasure. And then he blinked, ran his eyes over the chaos in the courtyard, and cried, "By God, lass, what the devil are ye thinking coming here?"

"It's good to see you too, Hendrick," I replied with a faintly admonishing smile, and put my arms around his lean frame for a long-overdue hug. "Have you not heard?" I said at last, looking up at him. "The king has graciously released me from his court, and now I have come home. Is that not wonderful news? I've finally been given leave to assume the duties of mistress of this old hall. And how good it does my heart to see you! But may we not continue this conversation inside? Although I think the rain's just grand, I'm afraid Marion's soaked to the bone, and if her hair comes undone again, we all will suffer for it."

Marion poked her head around Sir Matthew to glower at me.

"Marion Boyd, Sir Archibald's daughter?" Hendrick questioned, peering at the pretty face now buried in the folds of her thick crimson cloak. "God's teeth!" he chided, turning on Sir Matthew. "Ye daft loon, ye bring me the two bonny lasses here . . . now?"

"Make that three, Hendrick," said Mme. Seraphina, coming up behind me. At the sound of her voice the old steward stopped his ranting and looked in the direction of the speaker. His face, still handsome with age, turned as red as a rose in bloom.

"Hendrick, the rain," I reminded him. "May we come inside now?"

"Of course . . . of course ye may, lass," he said, and began ushering us under the timber-covered gallery that led to the Great Hall. "But God as my witness, lass, I wished ye had warned me of it."

⊷⊷

Sir Arthur Hendrick, or Hendrick as he preferred to be called, was my father's steward and the keeper of Blythe Hall and all her holdings for these many years and more. He was the man who collected the rents that had kept me in comfort at Stirling, Linlithgow, Haddington Priory, and Edinburgh; the man who employed the staff and saw to the tenant farmers and shepherds, to the fishings and the warrens and the peats and the crops; and the brewers, and the carpenters and the others who made Blythemuir profitable. He was the one who kept meticulous records of all income and expenditures and saw to the shipments of the wool and hides. He was the man who garrisoned the castle when the English were on the rampage. It was the heavy burden my father had yoked him with before his disappearance, and I had now come home to help him.

"Isabeau . . . Saints in heaven, it really is you!" he marveled aloud for the second time as we sat before a roaring fire in the Great Hall, our sodden cloaks drying on brass hooks, a mug of hot spiced wine in our hands. Upon our arrival he had ordered the kitchen fires lit, sent servants to the dormers where the folding beds were kept, and set in motion the machinations of a hasty homecoming celebration. It was apparent that Hendrick, a capable and orderly man, was overjoyed by our arrival. Yet it could not be denied that he found my sudden appearance quite troubling. "I'm sorry," he apologized, knowing that his intense scrutiny was making me a little uncomfortable. "'Tis just that it's been so very long. When ye first arrived I thought I was seeing a ghost. Ye must know ye are the spitting image of your dear mother. I would ha' sworn you were her if I dinnae know better."

I smiled softly and touched his hand. "You forget. I never saw my mother."

He sat back in his chair, nostalgia and warm wine animating the deep lines of his face, and then looked across at Sir Matthew. The large, handsome knight, now void of chain mail and surcoat, was relaxing in one of my father's vast chairs in a very well cut doublet of blue over hose of cream. He looked content as he mindlessly swirled the wine in his goblet, yet one could see some polite tension still on his face. This was undoubtedly caused by Marion, who, out of a perverse desire to torment, was sitting closer to the king's man than proper etiquette dictated.

"A rare beauty, she was," Hendrick's maudlin voice continued. Sir Matthew looked at him and nodded in mild agreement. "A kind word for everyone, she had. Blessed with a heart of gold and the face of an angel. Isabeau here is no different. She has the same eyes, clear and pure as aquamarines they are, but her hair, instead of the fine spun gold of Angelica's, is more the color of the delicate apricot—thon golden egg of the sun, as the ancient Romans called it. Ha' ye ever eaten an apricot, Master Beaton?"

The knight, transfixed, shook his head.

"Why, 'tis as delicate as a rose and as fragrant and sweet as manna. It is a fruit early to ripen yet lasts only a moment before it must be picked and eaten. I have never tasted the apricot, but my lord Blythe was very fond of them." A distant, wistful smile crossed his face. "And your hair, Isabeau, is the very essence of the apricot your father so loved, of that I'm certain." Then, as if he remembered something important, his smile slowly faded and he blurted: "But whatever possessed ye to come here, and with your friend Marion Boyd forbye? Ye were both safely kept and happily living at the palace in Edinburgh."

"That is very true, Hendrick, but the king sent a message," I reminded him politely, if not a bit sternly.

"A message? But I never received any blasted message! Had I known what ye were about, I would ha' sent the messenger right back with another message tellin' ye tae stay put."

"But why? This is my home, Hendrick. I've been away far too long already, and I'm nearly nineteen now and old enough to manage the estate."

His eyes widened as he leaned forward in his chair. "Aye, I'm certain ye think it so. But things are rough here just now. Why, if the English haven't gotten a wild hair up their arses . . ." He stopped short, cleared his throat, and began again. "What I meant tae say was that there are certain families across the border that ha' got it into their wee pickled brains tae cause trouble."

"What kind of trouble?" Sir Matthew asked, coming alive in his chair.

"Why, the usual kind, man. The kind the bloody English delight in!" He leaned forward. "There was never a skirmish or even a warning, but four nights ago all our sheep went missing. One thousand head forbye! Vanished in the middle of the night, they did, and neither hide nor hair of the beasties has been seen since."

"All the sheep have been stolen?" I exclaimed a bit too loudly. This was indeed bad news. Our sheep, some of the best in the land, were prized for their wool and had always been carefully guarded. Alexander Blythe, my father's cousin and a prosperous Edinburgh merchant, relied on our wool for his burgeoning cloth trade, and in turn, the king relied on

Cousin Alex to help finance his military endeavors. This loss of sheep—one of the main sources of income for the people of Blythemuir—was like a battle wound that if not staunched quickly and properly would turn mortal.

"What about the shepherds?" Sir Matthew asked pointedly. "Certainly they must have seen something?"

At this mention of shepherds, Hendrick's face reddened alarmingly. "The shepherds are gone too."

"What? Are they dead?"

"No. I mean, I dinnae think so. 'Tis just that we've not been able tae find them. 'Tis as if they've fair vanished."

"They've vanished?" Sir Matthew replied incredulously. And then his intelligent, gold-flecked eyes narrowed at the steward. "Have you tried tracking them?"

"Of course we've tried tracking them, man! What the devil do ye think we are, idiots? We've even brought out the hounds too, but the damn beasts just run in circles." He paused to toss back the rest of his wine. "'Tis unholy, I tell ye, the way they bay at the sky all befuddled like. They've run in every direction, too. Ach! 'Tis maddening to watch. And with all this rain what's left of the trail has been washed away. Jonny Kerr . . . ye'll mind Jonny Kerr the bailiff? He and thirty of his best men have gone on the Hot Trodd looking for them, only they havenae come back either."

Sir Matthew raised a brow and offered gently, "And do you think they've vanished as well?"

"Oh, for bloody Christ, I dinnae know!" chided Hendrick, looking annoyed. "Knowing Jonny, they're likely outside of Carlisle by now, at yon roadside inn drowning their losses in ale and taking out their frustration on the bonny English lasses. Forgive me," he added, addressing Marion and me and turning slightly red with embarrassment.

"There's nothing to forgive," I replied. "But you say they've been missing for four days?" I looked to Marion. I could see she found the whole situation rather amusing.

"Aye," Hendrick replied with rancor. "And if they're not found in two, then they're lost to us by law. Bloody fools! Our lads will be left with no choice but tae lift what's due them from the other side of the border."

"And you're certain it was the English?"

"Aye, I'm certain! Nobody saw anything, and the more volatile families hereabouts swear they weren't involved. I've no bone tae pick with anyone, and no one has seen our sheep. It has tae be the work of the English."

"Or the devil," Sir Matthew Beaton offered in an undertone. "Has anybody else been robbed or attacked?"

"Not that I know of. But I've sent word tae Lord Hume in any case, warning him that our lads are on the Trodd." Lord Hume, as everyone knew, was now Warden of the East March. He was personally responsible for administering justice and keeping peace in the thief-ridden Borders. It was an impossible duty given the amount of raiding and bloodshed that went on here.

"Hot Trodd! Thieving Englishmen! Vanishing shepherds! My, how terribly exciting!" It was Marion who broke the spell, her large brown eyes glistening in the firelight as her fair cheeks, rosy with warmth, appeared incandescent beneath her thick auburn hair. She had abandoned her soaking headdress upon our arrival, leaving her glossy tresses to tumble down the back of her splendid emerald gown—a gown made from the finest double-cut velvet. She was, as always, a sight to behold. "We sit here in this brooding border fortress while the English are on the rampage. And as everyone knows, the English not only ransack, burn, and steal all they can, they rape and kidnap as well. Mostly, I hear, they just rape." Her dark eyes gleamed with unchaste excitement as they flicked to Sir Matthew and lingered. "Perhaps Sir Matthew should sleep in my room tonight . . . on the floor, of course. Why, with so many hot-blooded Englishmen about, a lady is wont to have extra protection. After all, I believe the king would want it so." Her hand, delicate as a lotus flower, touched his sleeve.

Sir Matthew Beaton, a tall, strapping, well-built man in his early thirties, battle-hardened and unafraid of the most horrible danger, flinched as if her slender white fingers were the glowing prongs of a fire iron. His face, although partially hidden by a light-brown beard, turned red as a beet.

"My dear young lady," said Hendrick, coming to the knight's aid. "Although ye have a valid point, I'm happy tae say that willnae be necessary. Aside from the fact that Mrs. Beaton might not approve of the sleeping arrangement suggested of her husband, these walls are impenetrable. Upon my honor, no Englishman or enemy has ever seen the inside of Blythe Hall but for those who were invited. Besides, dear Sir Matthew and his men deserve a good night's rest—in a proper bed forbye, after what they've been put through, I'm sure." These last words, added in haste, were punctuated with a wry smile.

"But look," he said, turning from Marion and her feigned look of scandalized shock to motion to the arched doorway under the musicians' gallery. Great silver platters were being whisked into the room by a small army of servants. The capacious hall, filled with quiet chatter, fell silent as the first hint of roasted meat infused the air. "Why, bless me! Hot food," he declared as trenchers and pitchers of ale appeared on the table before us. "If you're anything like me, I'm sure all this excitement . . . all this talk of thievery on top of your weary travels, has made ye fair starved."

ॐ

The arrival of food was indeed a welcome diversion from the wilder thoughts of roving Englishmen, and the magnificent hall, with its spacious hammer-beam vaulting, colorful tapestries, intricate carvings, plush chairs, arched windows, chandeliers, candelabras, sconces, and great stone fireplace, came alive as hungry men, smelling of horse and leather, attacked the food with a driving purpose. They were a merry lot, the King's Guard, and most were familiar to me, since I'd served at court on and off for four years. The fare might have lacked the culinary splendor of the palace in Edinburgh, or even the Guard's Hall where the men dined, but the spit-roasted venison, stuffed game birds, and dishes of roasted leeks, parsnips, and carrots—seasoned with salt, pepper, and a dusting of cinnamon—followed by various cheeses, nuts, berries, and fresh churned butter, could hardly have been better served. It was devoured, in appreciative silence, and washed down with plenty of fine heather ale.

"M'lady," inquired Hendrick, sitting back in his chair, smiling and sated. "Shall I break out something a bit more fitting the celebration of the mistress's return?"

"Oh? Indeed!" I replied happily, setting down my cup. "Please do that." He motioned to his servant, and a moment later a cask had been carried into the room and opened.

"A rather nice malmsey," he informed me with an impish grin and a conspiratorial look. "A wee New Year's gift from your cousin Alex that I've been saving for a special occasion."

Still the storm raged around us; thunder, punctuated by lightning, echoed through the Great Hall, and the men, not to be outdone by nature, began to sing.

"Oh my," whispered Marion, hitting a note somewhere between delight and disdain. And then, quite suddenly, she giggled. The thunder of lusty voices, some in tune, some dreadfully out of tune, rose high into the rafters and hung for the space of a breath, before flittering down to caress us, their lady hosts, in a refrain that ran:

"But I would give all my halls and towers
Had I that bright birdy in my bowers
But I would give my very life
Had I that lady to my wife!"

"See?" I said, feeling a sliver of pride for having reached the place of my ancestors whole, unscathed, and surprisingly happy, even if all our sheep had been stolen. "Did I not tell you that Blythe Hall had charm?"

"Charm?" A fine, mocking brow lifted. "I've never thought bawdy ballads charming before, but yes, I believe I shall like it here very well." She turned her attention from the throng of bellowing men to Sir Matthew. With dainty precision she touched his sleeve again.

"God's teeth, but 'tis good to hear music in this hall!" Hendrick bellowed, startling all who were close to him, including Marion, who jumped. Sir Matthew quickly removed his arm from her grasp and nodded in restless agreement. "Perhaps Isabeau would honor us with a wee tune on the lute . . . or harp? Why, did ye know she had the voice of an angel when she was a wee girl? There was nothing in all the land tae compare to it, except maybe for . . ."

"Julius," I finished, looking squarely at him. "Hard as we might try, no one could ever quite compare with the seraphic Julius."

His eyes, wide and blankly amiable, flickered. "Ah . . . no. Why, that's not what I was about to say at all. What I meant to say was the choir at the abbey . . . of Haddington. They've a mighty fine choir there."

It was my turn to look mildly surprised. "Really? The choir? You do know that I sang in the choir?"

"Aye." He forced a smile. "All those voices blending together in organized harmony . . ."

"You were never at Haddington, Hendrick. How could you possibly have heard the choir?" I signaled for one of the servants to bring both instruments.

"I . . . I dinnae actually hear it," he clarified, his blue eyes round and guileless as an owl's. "But I heard about it . . . from your cousin."

It was then that I smiled, catching the old man at an even

older game because we both knew, for a certainty, that the choir at Haddington was not the first unutterable thought that came upon his lips. The men, in visibly high spirits brought about, no doubt, by the end of an arduous journey and sweetened with hearty food and fine malmsey, quieted down to a gentle hush when they saw that I held the instrument in my hand. It was a cursory politeness, for I believed they'd rather keep singing, but I had been asked, and I would honor my father's steward with a song. The truth was, Julius wouldn't have even waited to be asked were he here. He would have picked up the lute and led the men in bawdy song before the meal was even done, bringing them to tears of laughter with his wit. Men loved Julius. You could feel it whenever he was near. But this was my hall now. And I chose the harp.

Pushing all thoughts of my estranged brother from my mind, I began to play. The last time I had played the harp was for the king, for his pleasure, for his often tormented soul. I thought of him now as I plucked the strings, singing one of the songs I always sang to him. It was the song that calmed his anxiousness, a song with a melody so pure it was easy to get lost in, and he would often close his eyes as he listened, relaxing his strong, expressive face while he hummed along. The men in the hall had fallen under its spell too, and not a sound could be heard—no clinking of goblets, no scraping of benches across the flagstones, no voices hushed in whispers— just the soft patter of rain, my voice, and my harp.

As I sang my song thinking of the king, I was quite taken by surprise as another face pushed all thoughts of him from my mind. It appeared before me, clear as day, with a presence so alive it filled every recess of my mind. For the love of God, I had no idea whose face I saw, but he was magnificent, and perfect, and he literally took my breath away.

I stopped singing.

Music continued to emanate from the strings—as if by

some magician's trick—my fingers moving of their own volition. I saw the music, as I always did, only now it was born of
the smooth fair planes of this stranger's face: golden, radiant,
alive, and hauntingly perfect. I was unaware of what exactly I
played. I could hear the strings vibrate, each note filling the air
with heavenly serenity, but it was faint and surreal, as if coming from somewhere other than where I was. But it didn't
matter. Nothing mattered, because I knew that somehow my
destiny was entwined with the stranger who filled me. This
knowledge coursed through every fiber of my being, growing
in strength, pulsating with every heartbeat as it flowed toward
my soul with startling truth.

This was not, however, a prudent discovery to make in a
hall filled with inebriated men—inebriated men with curious,
liquid-eyed gazes. And I was just barely conscious of this. Yet
more important, I wanted this moment—this vision of such
sublime rapture—to last forever. I closed my eyes and turned
inward, fighting to memorize every haunting detail of his
face, the very essence of what or who he was. I wanted to
smell him, to touch him, to taste him, to bring him to life
in my memory. But this conscious act caused my vision—
a vision of a man so perfect that he could only be fashioned by
the hand of God—to fade. My fingers stumbled as he disappeared, and a broken note rang out. I opened my eyes. My
fingers scrambled to continue their unconscious flow of me-
lodic purity, but I only managed to make the instrument
squeal in discordant protest.

Marion, watching me with eyes wide and aggrieved, inhaled sharply. The men shifted uncomfortably as I fought to
regain my composure and recapture my vision. But it was too
late. It faded entirely. The handsome face with the compelling
blue gaze, straight, aquiline nose with slightly flared nostrils
and thoughtful, sensuous lips, began swirling in a confusion
of light and darkness until it was swallowed completely. And
from the roiling blackness emerged the face of a man I knew

only too well. Startled, and with heart pounding furiously in my chest, I dropped the harp at the same time that a great clanging erupted outside in the hallway. The men of the King's Guard, highly alert to danger, sprang at the sound, entirely forgetting their mugs, the recent musical disaster, and the fact that they were unarmed. Their full attention was pulled to the entrance. The great oaken slab flung backward on its hinges with a resounding bang, revealing Sir Matthew's anxious squire standing beneath the magnificently carved doorway heralding the coming of the huge, dark-haired, dark-cloaked man behind him: the other haunting man of my vision.

Chapter 3
UNINVITED
GUESTS

IT WAS AN ODD, UNSETTLING FEELING THAT WASHED over me as I stared at the dark visitor, a man so deeply imbedded in my subconscious that even the most sublime vision I had ever experienced was overcome by the power of his presence. It was more than uncanny, the ability he had to appear where he was least expected. And that he was here, materializing from the night with the soft rain and damp earth still clinging to his cape—on the very eve of my homecoming—was so unbelievable that it had to be more than mere coincidence.

"My lord, forgive me," cried Sir Matthew's man, his face pinched with excitement as he addressed his lord at the high table. "Sir George Douglas, Lord Kilwylie, has arrived with his men. They've come fresh from a skirmish with the English and seek lodging for the night." Like a piece of juicy gossip at court, the words *skirmish* and *English* buzzed through the great room on the besotted tongues of the men-at-arms, electrifying the air with the promise of action and the spilling of English blood. Sir Matthew, no different from his men, sprang to his feet with high color and eyes aglow and in four great strides was on the other side of the head table addressing the newcomer.

"By God, Douglas, where were ye set upon? How long ago?"

Sir George, a rogue and rising member of the very powerful Douglas family, of the Black Douglas line, and nephew of old Bell-the-Cat (the Earl of Angus), was a familiar at the court of King James and one of the most revered and decorated knights in all of Scotland. He was also well acquainted with the Master of the King's Guard. Yet given all that, one would still think a chance meeting here, in Blythe Hall, could only be surprising; yet Sir George didn't look entirely surprised. "Why, Sir Matthew," he declared from the doorway, languidly removing his fine leather gloves while a wry smile played about his lips. His eyes, a spectacular shade of pale green, settled on me then, and I was disquieted to find that there was no surprise in them, just unconcealed pleasure. His gaze lingered over me for a moment or two longer before he brought his attention back to the man he was addressing, the twinkle of mischief quite gone. "How provident it is to find you here, and with a detachment of the King's Guard at your heels. But I doubt you've come all this way to administer swift justice to the thieving throng that just set upon us . . . not ten miles from here."

"Ten miles?" replied Sir Matthew thoughtfully. The way he said it, the sweeping glance at his eager men, gave one the impression that he was actually calculating the distance and the chance of his men running down the bandits in the dark of night, over unfamiliar ground and with a driving rain at their backs. Sadly, I understood this was a tempting proposition for a fighting man.

"Brazen lads indeed," Sir George replied mildly, seeming

to know what the other knight was thinking and looking fabulously unconcerned. "But let me assure you, there's no need for alarm. 'Tis true we were set upon this night by a group of masked ruffians while we were pleasantly about our business in Jedburgh, but by all means they're well into England by now, or should be if they know what's good for them."

"Masked ruffians?" Hendrick asked, looking askance at Sir Matthew. "Forgive me for doubting ye, Kilwylie, but if they were masked, how did ye ken they were English?"

"Because a Scot would never be so cowardly as to hide his face," our dashing visitor proclaimed, complimenting every man in the room. "Cattle lifting is a matter of pride, Hendrick, as any of the reiving families of these parts will tell you. The English, however, have very little pride in anything, and can only hope to further their cause by igniting the blood feuds already rampant in these parts. I've no idea who else was attacked, but I believe there'll be merry hell to pay tomorrow. A clever, cowardly plan it is, to be sure," Sir George concluded gravely.

At this mention of English reivers Hendrick's eyes lit up. "Tell me, Kilwylie, did ye happen to see any sheep with them? I only ask because one thousand head of ours were lifted four nights ago."

A thoughtful expression appeared on Kilwylie's handsome face as he regarded the steward. "I'm sorry to hear it, Hendrick," he said, and there was little doubt that he was. "We didn't see any livestock with them, but they could have very easily been hidden in a nearby vale. It was dark, and these lads knew very well what they were about—a prettily planned attack by a roving band of thieves out for a swift profit. However, once they realized who it was they set upon, they were most anxious to get away. Perhaps tomorrow, after we've rested a bit, we'll hunt them down for you and return your sheep. Leave to a Douglas what others fail to do," he said with a brazen smile as his eyes, piercing and spectacular under the disheveled dark brown curls, settled once again on me. This time he did not look away.

It was then, looking into those familiar eyes, that I understood the real reason he had come. Somehow, as always, Sir George knew where to find me.

"Truthfully," he continued slowly, his smile turning softly reflective as he walked toward the dais of the head table, "championing the house of Blythe on such a cause would be a great honor. However, should I do so, I'd like to ask a wee favor in return."

The word *favor*, combined with the intense look in his eyes, confirmed my suspicion: Sir George, the renowned Lord Kilwylie, was once again on the hunt, and his prey of choice, as it had been for some time now, was me. I was sorry to admit that it caused me to doubt if there had been a skirmish at all. The thought was mildly flattering, but recalling my resolve and my duty to Blythe Hall, I pushed it aside. "That list, Marion . . . ," I whispered surreptitiously to the amused face next to me, all the while staring at Sir George, "the one in the king's possession listing applicants to be the next Lord Blythe? Sir George's name wouldn't happen to be on that list, would it?"

"At the very top, my dear," she whispered, her lips poised in a grin of irony.

"Oh, dear Lord," I uttered, and slowly stood to face my newly arrived guest. Behind a placid smile I took a deep breath in an attempt to muster my strength and sharpen my wits, for I would have need of both if I was to survive under the compelling gaze of Sir George Douglas. This I had learned from experience, for not long ago, in a dimly lit corridor of Linlithgow Palace, I had let myself be pinned against a wall and kissed most unchastely by this very man. He had been, I believed, rather drunk at the time. I had been very tired, or at least I had told myself that I was. It was the first time I had ever been kissed and, to my horror, I grew hot at the memory.

Sir George, seeing me blush and no doubt guessing the cause, smiled broadly.

The man had a beautiful smile, and I faltered in spite of my resolve. I had to remind myself that this was my hall, my tilt-yard, and not some darkened corridor in a lavish and rowdy royal palace. I cleared my throat, steadied my nerves, and addressed my visitor, aiming to wipe the grin from his shapely lips. "My dear Sir George, what a surprise it is to see you here. And, to honor the wee favor you're no doubt about to ask: of course. I wholeheartedly agree. Feel free to help yourself to as many of our sheep as you like, for it is a truth that we here at Blythe Hall take a real pleasure in rewarding those who serve us well. And unless I'm mistaken, I believe you have offered to serve us."

The darkly alluring knight, taking obvious pleasure in my taunt, stopped ten feet short of the dais and laughed heartily along with the other men. Damn him, but he had a rich, resounding laugh, and it echoed through the hall like a peal from an enchanted horn. Try as I might to resist, the sound elicited a slight, hesitant smile from me. "My dear Isabeau, as I've told you numerous times, I am your humble servant, yours and yours alone. Indeed, I have come to serve you," he said, his laughter subsiding as the unsettling green eyes held my own. "But as for sheep . . . I believe you know very well that I have not come here for sheep. Unlike your uncouth neighbors, I have no need of sheep." This he proclaimed while raising an eyebrow to the room in what might have been a lewd gesture. Given how the king's men laughed, it likely was, but Sir George Douglas did not dwell on being lewd. He was driven by another purpose altogether. "What I do have need of," he said, his singular attention focused on me, "is to speak with the king's own angel, far away from the doting eye of her very protective royal guardian. Because you see, I heard a rumor that this angel was finally given leave to return home."

"How . . . how did you hear this rumor?" I asked, shaken

further by the fact that he had even cared to know about my movements. Although the hall was warm, a slight shiver ran through me.

"Rumor?" he said with a hint of disapproval in his voice. "A part of me hoped it was rumor. And to answer your question, I'm a gentleman after all." His eyes, touched with mischief, settled upon my companion. "I shall not reveal my source."

"Marion!" I uttered, and noted that my companion was grinning at the man. At the sound of her name her smile drooped to a frown of displeasure as her eyes shot to mine.

"Well, it's not true," she defended in a testy whisper. "And it's not polite to assume things of your friends."

"Why were you grinning?"

"I'm grinning, Isa dear, because you have the incorrigible Sir George on a leash." Her voice was soft, belying the excitement in her flashing eyes. "'Tis as I've said before, the man's daft with the want of you. How can ye not see it? Why, you're the envy of every red-blooded woman in the kingdom. Go on, give him a tug. He's primed to topple like a felled oak before ye, and a man on his knees is a splendid sight to behold." Marion, a self-proclaimed temptress, and one who was always offering such suggestions for my benefit, waved encouragingly at Sir George. This caused an irritatingly broad grin to appear on his face, just before he made a courtly bow in her direction. Sir George Douglas, after all, was another of Marion's well-connected cousins.

Ignoring them both, I continued. "Very well, you found out through *mysterious means* that I was returning home. Tell me, Sir George, have you come all this way just to speak with me? Or were you indeed set upon by masked men and now in need of a place to rest?"

"Truthfully, my dear, it is both these things. My men and I were attacked as I was on my way, ironically, to offer you my protection on the off chance that this rumor I heard was true.

And I see that it is true. Isabeau Blythe," he said, and his beautiful voice this time was intended solely for me, for his strong, pleasing face had softened and his mesmerizing eyes were glued to mine. "I have come here on this night driven by an overwhelming desire to protect you. I barely understand it myself—how overwhelmed I become at the thought of you. I could hardly tell you at court, but I would be remiss indeed if I didn't tell you now—here in your own home, surrounded by your own friends—just how much I—"

I cut him off before he embarrassed us both. "I'm honored!" I blurted, entirely given over to nerves and some sort of primal fear. "Truly, I'm honored. But I assure you, we are very well provided for here already."

With a widened stance and hands firmly planted on his compact hips, he uttered a rather dramatic "Oh my." The magnificent head then tilted, and he beheld me as if I were some bewildering and pitifully misguided creature.

In truth, I had always found Sir George a disarming man—albeit a man seldom without a witty barb on his tongue or a fawning woman on his arm. He had a presence that drew the eye whenever he entered a room or appeared on a field of contest. Certainly his great height and dark, Celtic features were hard to overlook, but it was more the heady mixture of conceit, bravado, and palpable sexuality that made him so compelling. Sir George Douglas was a knight of great renown, and his reputation was one of a brash and loose-living man. I had always considered him dangerous company for one such as me. And I certainly didn't need Marion Boyd telling me what it was that drove him here on this night. It was plain as day in his expressive eyes.

I swallowed and forced what I hoped to be a placating smile onto my lips, because I knew that for my own good, as well as the good of my people, it was not wise to have a man such as Sir George within the walls of my ancestral home any longer than proper hospitality dictated. For I had not come all this way—had not endured all that I had—to step back into the shadows of a powerful man and relinquish my dreams of making Blythe Hall great once again. Sir George was a capable man, but I feared, as well I might, that he would devour me whole. "Of course," I began, "you and your men are welcome to spend the night. And if you truly wish to join our men on the Trodd, I won't stop you. In fact, I welcome the offer. But after the animals are returned, I'm afraid you must go."

"Go? And leave you out here all alone? Never!" he averred with eyes glinting like polished emeralds. "The notion's ridiculous. I know your ilk seem to believe they are protected by angels, but can an angel as pure and kindhearted as yourself possibly be prepared for this wild and violent existence— even if you are protected?"

Damn him again, but Sir George had a gift for unnerving me. In the space of a breath he had exploited my one true weakness by playing on the daft notion that the Blythes were divinely protected. He knew the story, as most of Scotland did, but his choice to remind me of it now when I wished to forget it was no coincidence. I fought to control my rising anger, for I now realized that Lord Kilwylie was not accustomed to losing. But neither was I.

"Dear Sir George," I began, mustering my composure. "I truly appreciate your concern, but you forget. Are you not yourself a paradigm of this wild and violent existence? And I'm not referring to your behavior here in the Borders, which is notorious at best, but to your actions at court."

My barb was not lost on our captive spectators, and the hall erupted with laughter. Marion, sitting beside me, offered a sincere "Well played." And dear Sir Matthew beamed with appreciation from across the table. Sir George Douglas, however, was not put off in the least and grinned salaciously.

"Indeed!" he declared, much to the delight of the fighting men. Clearly, Sir George had no humility.

"And I'm not playing!" I said at Marion in response to her comment, my eyes still glued to the incorrigible knight.

"Oh, but my dear," she replied delicately, excitedly, "I think that you finally are."

I should have been rankled by Sir George's cool demeanor, his sardonic grin, but I was more disquieted to find that I could hardly pull my eyes from him, and so I just stared in helpless wonder, absorbing every handsome, windblown, rain-soaked, unnerving inch of him as he moved closer. Try as I might, I could not deny his allure.

"It is a truth," he began, standing before the head table, his face utterly serious, "that in the past I have been careless in my conquests. Like a ship without a rudder I have tossed about, wandering aimlessly through the wild seas of my youth with a willing sword and willing body. But I am done with all that now. I need a rudder, Isabeau," he said earnestly, his mesmerizing eyes holding mine with frightening intensity, "and a pure and heavenly light to help guide me the rest of the way."

I heard a sigh, high and breathy, just before a hard, pinching pressure seized my leg. The dumbfounding spell that had come over me whilst listening to Sir George was broken. My face, under his intimate gaze, felt flushed, and I feared my heart would escape my very body. I glanced at Marion, the source of the sigh, and she squeezed my leg again. Damn her! She held me with her narrowed eyes as her full lips pursed into a little O. Unfortunately it was a common expression for her. She was demanding that I encourage him, demanding that I play his game. I slapped her hand away and replied in as sweet and polite a voice as I could muster, "You honor me with your sentiments, sir, however, this is hardly the time or place to discuss such personal matters."

"Oh, but you are wrong, my dear. This is exactly the time and place. King James has finally let you return to the home of your father, and you have arrived here not as a child but as a beautiful young woman. Dear James knows as well as I do that you need a suitable husband beside you if you are ever to manage out here. It is unthinkable, Isabeau, you in this border fortress all alone ... without companionship ... without a husband and master. You need protection—something a little more substantial than a whimsical motto, just as I need a virtuous woman beside me ... to keep me on my new and worthy course. And, forgive me, but the good Lord could hardly have created a more enchanting or virtuous creature. But I hardly need to tell you my feelings. I believe I've expressed them once before, in Linlithgow. Unless I'm terribly mistaken, your desires are the same as my own."

The men in the hall, glossy-eyed and beaming, were clearly entertained by this public declaration of what appeared to be a marriage proposal; but I was not. That kiss in Linlithgow, searing, intimate, and utterly unexpected, still haunted me. Sir George knew it too, but I had not come home after four long years away to be humiliated before my own hearth.

"Your sentiments are poetic if not a little misguided." I smiled purely for the sake of our audience. "But, again, I must reiterate that this is not a matter to be discussed here, nor," I continued, looking boldly into his forthright gaze, "do I believe I'm in need of a master."

Like a sudden shift of the wind, all caprice left his face, and he said, "While that may be true, Isabeau, have a care for me, won't you? I've never been in doubt of your ability to master your own affairs. But I've had masters aplenty. Did you ever consider that perhaps what I need is a mistress?"

"You've had plenty of mistresses."

He grimaced, as if wounded. "You know what I mean! Do you think it easy for me to come here and lay my heart bare before you? Toy with me if you must. Deny me if your pride absolutely demands it, but let us look at the facts here. All your sheep have been lifted. And your band of merry followers, unless they find them soon, will undoubtedly retaliate.

You say you have no need of a husband as your lord and master, then what will you do when you have a blood feud on your hands? Are you prepared to lead your men into battle? Are you prepared to bury the husbands, fathers, and sons of Blythemuir who will die defending your land and livelihood? I ask you again, why would the king allow you to come here alone and so unprepared? You have scores of retainers yet no actual kinsmen left but for your merchant cousin, his sniveling son, and your cowardly, outlawed brother. How will you manage without a proper husband, a man who can bring the support of his clan to answer for all your affronts—to even, perhaps as in your case now, go on the Trodd?

"By the way," he added, staring across the table that separated us and, with irksome sangfroid, plucking a hunk of cheese from a platter, "speaking of the devil, how is Julius?" He took a bite and while still chewing, continued, "'Tis been an age since we last met. I believe the last time I saw him he was fresh from England, dressed in finery and spangles after sitting with King Henry's counselors bargaining for more lands in exchange for the young heir to the throne of Scotland." He swallowed. "My, what a brazen lad he was. He could have done great things. What a pity such brilliance was squandered in drink, deceit, and debauchery."

And there it was; he had struck my final weakness and with such force and artfulness I could barely think, let alone breathe. He had come here this night catching me fresh from the splendor of King James's orbit and expertly begun his campaign for my affections. He professed his desires, and once he realized that I would not admit publicly my desire for him, he began illustrating to me, and every guest in my hall, how unsuited I was for the role I had so stubbornly chosen to play. But I had remained unmoved. And then, because he was a man and quite unaccustomed to losing, he had cleverly struck at the heart of the matter—the very source of my stubborn pride. He had reduced me to teary-eyed vulnerability by bringing to light the maligned character of the man who should have been lord of this castle. Speechless, heartbroken, and filling with unutterable shame, I stared at the great knight before me as he chewed thoughtfully on his cheese. His eyes were tender and apologetic, but the set of his jaw was firm. I wanted to speak, to refute his wild claims, but I couldn't. Because we both knew they were all true.

The entire hall fell silent awaiting my reply, but for once I had none. It seemed an age waiting in this oppressive stalemate where the sound of the soft rain hitting the roof was nearly deafening, and the crackle of the low fire seemed hungry enough to devour me. The young Lord Kilwylie stood prosaically before me, his penetrating gaze softening, as if willing me to accept the generous offer so publicly placed at my feet. It was tempting: anything to avert the disaster that must follow. And then, thankfully, another voice rang out, shattering the stifling silence.

"Actually, drink, deceit, and debauchery only serve to enhance brilliance, I find. Don't you, Georgie lad? And let me tell you, at the moment I'm feeling *exceptionally* brilliant!"

Sniffing, wiping my eyes covertly with the sleeve of my gown, I turned to the speaker, as everyone else had. It was one of the King's Guards, a man whose form and face were hidden in the shadows of his crimson-and-gold-trimmed cloak. Then the speaker, in a rather theatrical gesture, jumped up onto the trestle table and threw off the king's livery. Silence gripped the room in tribute to the golden hair, the deep-set blue eyes, the fine features, the well-made slender body clothed entirely in black. It was unfathomable. It was Julius.

It had been over four years since I last laid eyes on him. His clothes, well fitting and made of finely worked black leather, lacked the flair he had once worshipped in his youth, but they somehow did him justice. He was still lethally handsome, perhaps more so than ever if Marion's silent, jaw-agape adoration was any measure, but his body was leaner, his face thinner, no longer full with the flush of willful youth. Julius was a man now, approaching his mid-twenties, and he carried himself with an unfamiliar worldliness that was as compelling as it was mysterious, forged no doubt by years of hardship and unspeakable trials; yet in his eyes there still burned a glorious madness.

Julius was not alone, I saw. His two henchmen (and I believed that's exactly what they were) stood at his signal, also discarding the royal livery they had used as a disguise. They were quite a sight to behold, I mused—these two souvenirs of his travels—and how they had passed for loyal Scots guards I could not guess. The one, a large, wild-eyed heathen of a man with bushy red hair and the broad, high-cheeked, blunt-nosed features of the Scandinavian, looked utterly unhousebroken. The other, by contrast, was a beautiful, olive-skinned young man near Julius's own age and build, with raven-black hair and lovely eyes of onyx. Aside from the piratical gold earring glinting from the depths of his locks, he perfectly oozed urbanity, indicating that this little pet of Julius's was most definitely housebroken. I gazed at the men in wonder, suddenly realizing that Julius had been here, in Blythe Hall, since the feast began. It was an unsettling thought. Just how long he had been with us was a mystery, as was the fact that he had slipped in unnoticed. Damn him.

"Julius Blythe!" Sir George exclaimed, his rich voice shaking the rafters. In my shock I had walked around the table to better see my brother and his new friends and found myself standing beside the young Lord Kilwylie. I looked at him and saw that he was just as shocked by the intrusion as I was, but then, having better control over his emotions than I did, his features hardened into an expression of guarded wariness. I placed a hand on his arm, looking at him with both inquiry and trepidation. His hand came over mine in warm reassurance as he whispered, "Stay close, my dear. Your brother and his wee friends, as I'm sure he's well aware, are the only men in the room who are armed."

Julius, with singular focus on Sir George, replied from his perch. "It is I, my dear, a limb of hell and the root of all evil!" An insolent grin split his face. "Don't look so surprised, Douglas. I told you I'd be back one day, if not for a friendly hello, then at least to thank you for the lovely cruise you arranged for me." Although he spoke with measured precision, it was obvious he was touched by liquor. "And a Blythe, amongst other things, always keeps his promise. Hello, sunshine," he said darkly, mockingly. "I am come home too. Marvelous, isn't it? Let us break out more of the good stuff, shall we, Hendrick? For not only has the angel graced us with her presence this night, but the prodigal son has returned as well. Although I make no pretense of being welcomed warmly, nor do I expect a fatted calf, you'll be happy to hear, all of you, that I'm most definitely protected." At this signal his companions, like two mismatched but well-trained hounds, walked forward and flung open the doors under the gallery.

Like the gates of hell opening to release an evil into the world through the beautifully painted archway came a press of the roughest sort of men, well armed and meanly dressed in leather jacks—the quilted armored coat of the region—baggy breeches, and muddy riding boots. Julius waited on his lofty perch like the cunning raptor he was until all his rugged followers appeared under the arches. There must have been at least forty men who took command of the room, and once everyone was in place and the men-at-arms surrounded, Julius continued. "And, I'm sorry to inform you, in case you were hoping for a miracle, Georgie lad, but all your men are tightly bound and sleeping snugly in the stables. Consider it a gesture of benevolence, for by all rights I should have slit their miserable throats, and I believe you know why. But let us not discuss our sordid business here"—he threw his arms wide as he slowly looked around the magnificent hall, his glittering smile bent on all the unarmed guards—"on this most joyous of occasions: our little homecoming!

"Hendrick," he said, addressing the dumbfounded steward. "I must thank you for the meal. Delightful. But may I suggest more guards in the gatehouse next time? Other than that one small oversight, you've kept the place in respectable order, I see. My dear *faither*"—he rolled the word off his tongue using the language of his youth, his smiling face a vast contradiction to the disdain in his voice—"I'm sure would approve." And then the intense azure gaze settled on Sir Matthew.

"And do my eyes deceive me, or is that Sir Matthew Beaton? I must commend you, sir. Really, you've top-notch men. Very professional. Utterly disciplined. But, I'm sorry to say, not as desperate as mine are. There's a real advantage to working with desperate men, I find. Because, whereas my men have nothing to lose, yours have everything. But I shall let you keep your comfy billet, good pay, and dull lives in exchange for your purses. And that reminds me, I must thank you for the generous donation of fine swords. You may rest assured that they will not hang in some palatial armory gathering rust." At that moment Julius gave a signal, and one of his men threw him a sword. From the look on Sir Matthew's face it must have been his own. And while Julius's attention was thus turned, the outraged knight made a brave but desperate lunge.

Sir Matthew was one of the king's finest fighting men. Yet even as quick and well trained as he was, he lacked that quality that had made Julius remarkable. With deceptive agility, and movements as fluid and deft as if orchestrated by the royal dance master himself, the altercation was over before it started. Sir Matthew's arm had been grabbed and yanked around high on his back, landing the knight facedown on the table. Julius, booted foot pressing on Sir Matthew's back, stood over him with sword held an inch from the knight's neck.

"It would be foolish, really, to try anything at this point. My men are armed; yours are not. Your men have purses;

mine do not. And that is how the balance of wealth shifts. So, if you're quite finished playing games here, I suggest you sit back and enjoy the unfolding drama. It promises to be quite entertaining."

Sir Matthew, humiliation marring his strong features, acquiesced to the younger man. Julius, smiling serenely, sheathed his new sword and lifted his boots two of his men grabbed the knight and yanked him roughly from the table.

And then, inevitably, he turned his attention to me.

His eyes, so like our father's, held mine with a twinkling and slightly mocking gaze. He was compelling when he wanted to be, and I found myself, for the second time in the same day, unable to pull my eyes away. "Sister dear," he said smoothly, in a voice that was low yet pitched to reach every straining ear, "my, how you've grown. Tell me, are you still conversing with angels, or only coarse wee devils like my lord Kilwylie here?" He turned to the man beside me and made an exaggerated, courtly bow. Standing once again, he settled his gaze back on me. It was then that I saw that the blue eyes had turned hard and cold as glacier ice.

"Gentlemen," he continued, his voice now sharply mocking. "Before you stands the very fruit of heaven. Is she not enchanting? From an ugly duckling has sprung a rare beauty," he quoted. "Yet I must confess, my little sister was never ugly, only willful and flagrantly misguided." He tilted his head gently to the side, sneered, and leapt off the table as lithely as a great cat. "You may also note," he continued as he walked toward the high table, "what a heavenly touch on the harp she has, and a voice more alluring than any siren's song. But her performance, if you'll allow me to be frank, lacks discipline, confidence, and heart. You never did have much confidence in your abilities, did you, Isabeau? And although you start with plenty of heart, it leaves you slowly, like a disinterested lover." A ribald comment rang out, much to the enjoyment of Julius's men. He held up a hand to quiet them. "Gentlemen, please. We are speaking of my sister here. But I'll agree there's not a man among you who would lose interest in the intoxicating Mistress Blythe, save, perhaps, for my lord Kilwylie."

The barb hit its mark, and Sir George stiffened beside me. It was a petty and cowardly thing to attack the most decorated knight in Scotland while he was helpless to defend his character, and it irked me that Julius was thoroughly enjoying himself. "I could teach you to attain perfection, Isabeau, if you would let me," he said, looking straight at me. "But I doubt my sister will let me, nor will she welcome me, I'll wager, once she learns that I've come to lighten her coffers a measure."

It was this remark, offered so flippantly, announcing a bold intent of robbery on the house of a nobleman—by the nobleman's own son and heir—that caused the King's Guard to rebel. While Sir George stayed, diligently guarding me, chaos broke loose around us. Steel clashed against wooden chair legs; silver and pewter goblets drove hard against cuirass-covered bellies; platters, candleholders, and wooden bowls were all expertly employed, yet all to no avail. Small daggers and meat knives were no match for heavy swords. Julius, damn him, always came prepared.

"Stay where you are," he warned, "and no one will die an unnecessarily painful and highly imaginative death. I've not come here to practice all I've learned from the Turk just yet, although the Turk, my sweethearts, in case you were wondering, is indeed Master of all Cruelty. So do not try me. My needs are simple. I need to care for my men, because even an army composed of lawless mercenaries still requires the basic necessities of food, drink, shelter, and, yes, plenty of lively entertainment!" At this last addition his men gave a mighty cheer. The sound, magnified by the vaulted ceiling and solid stone walls, caused the panes of glass in the arched windows to shudder. He then gave the signal, and half his men started circling the room in search of loot.

Behind me Marion let out a gasp, and from the tone of it I knew that she too was filled with the same cold terror that gripped me; for there could be no doubt that these men, led by a self-proclaimed profligate, were as base and wild as they appeared.

"Please," I said, stepping in front of Sir George. This charade of Julius's had gone far enough for my taste. If he wanted money, I'd give it to him—anything to make him leave. But I would not stomach this shameful abuse any longer. Like Sir George, Julius was an expert at exploiting weakness; he had been a mere youth when his schemes had induced the entire county to a civil war in which a king had died. That he had chosen to resurface in Blythe Hall on the day of my homecoming, just as Sir George had, was no coincidence or accident. Unfortunately, it appeared as if the only one surprised by my arrival had been dear Hendrick. "Please," I said again, "all of you, if you'll just be still." Yet my words had little effect.

Julius was approaching, his golden face smiling as his men cut purses off belts and searched fingers for rings. They took jeweled brooches and raided the silver, shoving goblets, candelabras, and platters into sacks. And still Julius was smiling. I stood speechless as he approached, forgetting everything, remembering only that this madman was my brother, my own mother's son. Dear God, what had happened to him? I realized in that moment that perhaps I had never really known him, and watching him now, a man with squandered gifts, I couldn't help but feel anger at the delusion that had been his demise.

My heart ached for him.

I took a step forward and offered my hand in a gesture I hoped would reach him. I could see that Julius was not expecting this, and he faltered slightly. But then a look crossed his eyes that I once knew. As if governed by some ancient reflex, his hand tentatively lifted to mine. With silent appeal I urged him closer, until our hands were nearly touching. And then, with less than an inch between our hesitant fingers, I found myself reeling backward, the air knocked from my lungs as I hit the solid, rain-dampened wall of Sir George's torso. Before I could utter a word of protest, I found myself in a grip so engulfing that it could have put a carpenter's vise to shame.

Julius, clearly not expecting the suddenness of Sir George's action, pulled to a halt, his cornflower-blue eyes attacking the man with a look that was utterly terrifying. Expertly, and with barely a break in his stride, he brought it under control, and the sardonic twist of the lips returned. "Douglas," he said with a smile that was never meant to reach his eyes, "my lord Kilwylie, while you've made your intentions regarding my sister painstakingly clear to everyone in the room, I'm astonished that you would so boldly, and forcefully, molest her right out in the open. Sweet merciful Jesus, what sort of lechery do you intend to perpetrate under my father's roof?" He winked at Marion, the sudden playfulness belying the danger that lurked so close to the surface. Although I could not see Marion, I could definitely hear her sigh. "And who is this lovely young creature next to Hendrick that no one has bothered to introduce me to? You must forgive Sir George his manners," he said to my friend. "Douglases lack them as a rule."

"She's my cousin, Marion Boyd, you dolt!" Sir George sneered. "Stop playing games, Blythe. Tell us why you're really here." His grip on me was tight yet protective, and I could feel the heat from his body penetrate the thick damask of my gown. Although I half wished he would let me go, I could not deny that he felt, and smelled, rather wonderful.

"I thought I had already made that perfectly clear?"

"Robbery?" Sir George scoffed, condescension thick in his voice.

"When you say it like that, it sounds rather trite. Yes, robbery . . . for now. And I would greatly appreciate you un-handing my sister."

Sir George, I realized, had no intention of letting me go. Instead his grip on me tightened. "Not while you and your men are inside these walls. Your sister is the very reason I live and breathe. I have come, I had hoped, to convince her of it."

Julius's eyes flew wide in humorous shock. "Really! My, my. And have you, in fact, convinced her of it? I only ask because she looks rather pale and unwell. I believe that for her sake alone you should let her go, Douglas."

"So you can cause her further harm?" he shot back. "I think not."

The two men, now the center of attention, squared off in some primal contest, the likes of which frightened me. Like a hungry predator assessing the measure of its prey, Julius never took his eyes off Sir George.

"Please," I uttered, and placed my hands on the stubborn arms. I pushed against them, stating that it was all right, that no harm could possibly befall me with so many witnesses. Yet Sir George would not be moved.

Julius, challenging the young lord with his mirthless blue stare, shifted suddenly and with a relenting smile replied, "Very well. If she *really* means that much to you, I shall let you keep her . . . in exchange, of course, for your purse."

"What?" I cried in disbelief. Yet this sudden outburst, jus-tified though it was, drew the attention of my amoral sibling, and just as the downy blond head turned to me with a grin that begged to be taught a lesson, Sir George, shifting me to one arm, pulled the other from the depths of his cape—holding a sword.

Sir George still wore his sword!

In a flash of cold steel the blade shot out swinging for Julius's unguarded body. Although dulled by strong drink, he still managed to jump back, drawing his blade as he did so. But even he couldn't move quickly enough. The sword sliced through his fine leather doublet before he could parry. A gasp escaped my lips when I saw what Sir George had done—a clean cut across his stomach, not deep but enough to draw blood. And with sickening realization I understood that he had no intention of stopping there. Still grasping me tightly, Sir George went on the attack.

With artful fluidity, Julius parried Lord Kilwylie's blows, but it was plain to see that he was not attacking.

"Are you mad?" Julius cried, his sword arm a rapid machine of deflection. Some of his men, watching from the edge of the makeshift circle that surrounded us, looked eager to come to his aid, but he would not let them. "Stay back, all of you! Douglas, for the love of God and all that's holy, let go my sister! She won't love you any less, I'll wager."

"Drop your sword and I'll consider it."

Julius, letting out a nasal *humph*, raised a sardonic brow. "And let you skewer me? I'd rather not. I happen to value my life a bit more than you give me credit for."

"Keep your sword, I keep your sister."

Backing away yet still holding his sword at the ready, Julius replied gently, "And I will not fight you while you hold the girl. Not overly chivalrous of you to use a young virgin as your shield, but on a grasping and desperate level I must commend you. Well played," he said pleasantly. "Very well, let us call this a stalemate. But you do realize you cannot hold Isabeau forever."

"Oh, but I intend to." The words, spoken as a taunt, had a dark and chilling ring to them. I then felt his warm lips brush against the top of my head and realized, as a tingling sensation swept through my body, that even had I wanted to, I could not escape his grasp.

"Marriage?" Julius interjected with a cheerfully chiding ring to his voice. "Do you propose marriage?" He let out a hearty laugh. "Oh, that's rich. Virgin Mother and all the saints in heaven! May God have mercy on you then." Although I had similar thoughts on the matter, Julius's laughter irked me a great deal more than Sir George's proclaimed desire to wed.

Still pressed like an oatcake against Lord Kilwylie's heaving body, and realizing that unless something happened soon, this absurd little standoff could go on indefinitely, I untied the heavy purse dangling from Sir George's belt; after all, it was what Julius had come for. Thankfully the knight was entirely unaware of my roving hands, his thoughts and focus being elsewhere. I could feel how Julius's mirth unnerved him, and he was desperately trying to land another blow as, prancing ever out of sword thrust, Julius guffawed like a drunken halfwit. The laughter stopped, however, when the coin-laden sack hit his tender, bloodstained stomach.

"There," I said, thoroughly disgusted with the lot of them. "Take that and leave. All of you!"

His golden brow rose as appreciation lit his bright blue eyes. And then Julius looked at Sir George. An ironic grin touched his lips as he opened the fine leather pouch. Sir George, still holding me tightly, watched in deathlike stillness. After a mocking glance at the contents of the purse, Julius finally pulled from its depths a folded piece of paper. The broken red seal was familiar. "Here," he said, walking over to Hendrick. "This, I believe, belongs to you."

Hendrick took the note as Julius winked again at Marion.

"I sleep with my windows open," she remarked, as if a simpleton.

"A fine habit indeed," replied my brother with a simpleton's smile. His gaze lingered over her in a bold disregard for propriety. He swayed slightly, from alcohol or the cut across his stomach, I didn't know—likely both—and then, abruptly, he turned and called out to the Great Hall: "Gentlemen, the secret of being a good guest is to know when you have overstayed your welcome, and I believe we have reached the very limit of ours. Thank you, sister dear, for the entertainment. 'Tis been an age; we should really get together more often."

"Once every four years is more than enough," I said. But to this he just smiled and signaled for his men to retreat.

It was neatly done, a maneuver of swift military efficiency that swept through the hall with austere silence. Julius, his men, and all our silver were gone.

"There." I let out a breath. "Now, if you're quite finished, perhaps you would release me." It was not a question but a request. Yet Sir George, and his arms, remained steadfast.

"My dear angel, not just yet. Not until I've explained." It was then that I noticed he was looking not at me but at Hendrick, whose pale eyes, hard as pond ice, were shooting daggers at him.

Chapter 4

NOCTURNAL BLUNDERS

IF MARION HAD BEEN HUNGRY FOR ENTERTAINMENT, then she had gotten plenty of it. The enjoyable pastimes of music, poetry, dancing, and flirting seemed rather dull compared with being robbed by a notorious outlaw—right under my own roof—and with the King's Guard and the highly trained army of a nobleman helpless to do anything but watch. Unfortunately, the notorious outlaw was my brother, my own flesh and blood. That he had been drunk was small comfort; that he had chosen to rob his ancestral home was an insult too deep to comprehend. And dear Marion. Where once she had been excited by the notion of an encounter with Julius, even she could not have been prepared for the debasing assault suffered in the Great Hall this evening. She had been rendered speechless, her thoughts distant, and she had even given up her attempt to seduce the noble Sir Matthew. Noticing this change in her demeanor, I had put her to bed myself, in my old room, and made her drink a mug of spiced wine while a hot brick traveled her cold sheets. Seeing to all the comforts I could, I then left her in the care of her servant, although hesitantly, and with the promise of kinder pursuits on the morrow. Traveling the dimly lit corridors back to my own chambers, I silently prayed she would not send word of this to her father, or wish to return home sooner than planned.

Although I was disturbed by this change in Marion, I was, on some level, grateful for her awestruck silence. Because tonight at Blythe Hall the gates of hell had been thrown open and Lucifer's favorite son had come to call on me, illustrating quite thoroughly that even with the protection of the greatest knight in Scotland, Blythe Hall was still vulnerable. Poor Sir George. His *armour proper* had taken quite a blow, and because of it he was still here—a somewhat humbled, self-imposed guard before my bedchamber door.

"Will that be all, my lady?" Seraphina asked, finishing her nighttime ministrations and gently setting down the brush. Her round face with its high, rosy cheeks smiled at me through the large gilded mirror that had once belonged to my mother. Mme. Seraphina, bless her, was a short, plump, stalwart, no-nonsense kind of woman who had come from France many years ago to accompany another young noblewoman to this same desolate castle. Then, when Julius was born, she had been his nurse, and after five years with him—after all her nerves had been frayed and her hair turned white—I was born. Mme. Seraphina, possessing a mother's love yet knowing her own limitations, claimed that my birth, however devastating it had been for the rest of the family, had been a godsend for her. This, I knew, was a sad untruth. I had taken the life of my mother, something I believed Julius and my father had never fully forgiven me for. Yet Julius had been kind to me when I was a child, and I remembered the kindness of my father as well, until he built his little chapel in the tower room.

It was Mme. Seraphina who held our family together. She

was the one who had given us our love of music. And she had been in the Great Hall this evening when I had played the little harp. She had also witnessed the sad debacle that took place afterward. That she still loved Julius there could be no doubt; he was my mother's son, and it was clear on her stoic face that he had broken her heart too.

I smiled softly back at her. "Thank you. And I think that will be all . . . unless you can persuade our large friend outside the door that he's not needed."

"I've already tried, my dear, but to no avail. If he were a smaller man, I'd persuade him with a firedog or the poker," replied my wary governess, her jovial face now grim and bristling with indignation. Bless her, but Seraphina was a diligent guardian, and she could never pretend to like a man of Sir George's reputation. "But I'm afraid," she continued, "that with that thick hide of his, it would only serve to make him testy. And I've enough experience to know that it would never do to get a man that size testy. I count it a blessing he's been humbled; he'd be a fool to step beyond the threshold this night. But we'll bolt the door all the same." And her full, ruddy cheeks dimpled in consternation as she marched to the doorway, her heavy skirts swishing around her plump ankles.

"Do as ye please. I'm not budging," came a deep, plaintive voice from the other side of the door. Seraphina stopped midstride and looked askance at me. The voice continued. "I have laid myself at your feet, Isabeau, my love. I have offered my body for your protection, the very gesture of which I believe has escaped you. And how many times will you have me say that I am truly sorry?"

Still seated, I turned to the door and replied to the stout oaken slab: "I understand your fear of my brother, and I believe I've already accepted your apology. However, what I haven't fully accepted is the fact that you used *my body* for *your protection*! Please explain to me again, if you can, where in your Chivalric Code—your rules of Knightly Honor—it is written to use the woman you proclaim to love as a human shield." I rolled my eyes as much in exasperation as in disgust; Seraphina shook her head slowly in conspiratorial deprecation.

We were no sooner finished with our silent disparagement when the door burst open, startling us both. There, filling the immense door frame, stood the magnificent Sir George Douglas, every dark, brooding, bedraggled inch of him. The sight of such a man reduced to a self-chastised wretch caused a measure of pity to wash through me. I was not without feelings for this man, but neither was I pleased with his actions. He had professed that he did not fear Julius, but it could only be fear that had caused him to act so irrationally. As it was, I was not in the mood to argue. It had been late even before I went to see to the comforts of all my guests. One would think that the offer of a private room and the promise of a warm bed would be welcomed, but Sir George had chosen instead to sleep on the hard floor outside my door. The ostensible reason was his noble concern for my protection; the real reason, I believed, was guilt. I had tried to explain that I was safer in Blythe Hall at this moment than I had ever been at Haddington. Besides our own men, we had two small armies: Sir Matthew's men, who were now billeted in the Great Hall, and his own, who were given the entire second floor of the tower. Guards had been doubled in the gatehouse, thanks to Julius, and sentries walked the battlements as well as the courtyards. No one was getting into Blythe Hall this night. And Sir George, try as he might, was not going to linger in my bedchamber.

In contrast to the afternoon, his eyes were soft and pleading, his brown curls, now dry, tousled endearingly about his head as he implored, "Must you cling to that one horrible little instance? 'Tis as I told you before, Isabeau; you were never in any real danger."

I was overtired, and this statement, delivered so glibly,

caused my blood to boil. "Never in any *real* danger?" I sprang
to my feet. "Are you so gravely depleted of common sense?
Have you suffered one too many blows to the head? Forgive
me for my concern, but you were conducting a sword fight
with my brother while pressing me to your body like a fleshy,
ill-fitting breastplate! Unless my eyes deceived me, you were
using real swords. How was I not in any *real* danger?"

"You were not ill-fitting at all, my dear," he said, attempting to diffuse my anger. "In fact, I think you'll agree that you
fit rather nicely." I was incredulous. He was making light of
the situation, and my jaw went slack at the remark. I looked at
Seraphina for guidance, and bless her, she motioned to the
fireplace across the room, asking with her eyes, *Shall I grab
the firedog now?* I gave a small shake of my head and brought
my focus back to Sir George.

"I hope, for your sake, that you're not trying to tell me you
used a deadly confrontation with my brother as an excuse to
get me into your arms . . . again."

His green eyes looked entirely guileless as he said, "I have
been trying for quite some time now, Isabeau. After our first
intoxicating encounter in that dark little corner of Linlithgow,
I cannot get you out of my mind. Forgive me, but I am like a
man possessed."

His mention of that night in Linlithgow Palace evoked the
memory, and suddenly, quite against my will, I was there, a
young woman fresh from the priory at the king's request. I
had engaged Sir George in conversation earlier that day, but I
had not expected him to be waiting for me in the corridor, or
to have taken my hand and pulled me into the darkened corner as he had, where his soft and eager lips felt free to explore
my own. I was appalled by his boldness, but I never expected
that his musky, leather-and-ale scent would have affected me
so, or that I would so thoroughly respond to his kisses. It had
taken nearly all my resolve, and the fortuitous arrival of Tam,
my dear groom, to pry him off me. I shook my head to expel

the memory. "I was on my way to bed," I stated tersely. "You surprised me and took advantage of my sleep-addled mind."

"If you'll remember correctly, I believe you were quite thoroughly awakened," he offered in a tone that implied what we both already knew. Anger and shame welled within me, and I struggled mightily to keep it in check. Yet Sir George was a perceptive man, and he added softly, "Some call me an impulsive man, and that night I was. Impulse, not intelligence, drove me to wait in the darkness by your chamber door. Had I been thinking correctly, I would have never done it, but I was not thinking correctly. What I was thinking, if it makes any difference, was that I could not let the night end without tasting you. And taste you I did, but instead of satiating a need, it only ignited my hunger, and ever since that night I have been driven to want more. Don't look at me like that, Isabeau! Don't pretend you don't feel it too. I have come here to make amends for my past behavior, yes. And although I have ached to have you in my arms again, what happened tonight—holding you in the manner I had—was not just another drunken attempt to fondle you but a very real attempt to protect you as well as Blythe Hall."

The notion was absurd, yet nonetheless the thought of his recent affront to my person—the desperate embrace, the masculine scent that clouded my thoughts, the heat of his body and the hardness of it against my own—had elicited a rush of such hot-blooded emotion, I was quite disturbed by it. I looked at him again and knew, without question, that Sir George Douglas had a powerful hold over me. To my knowledge he had never had any trouble convincing any woman of his undeniable charms before, and in fact, as I recalled he had quite a list of conquests already attached to his name. It was part of the reason I had resisted him so thoroughly, not wanting to be another; the other part was too entangled in the painful memories of my brother to understand. But he *was* compelling . . .

A cough, overly loud and obviously forced, coming from the direction of the diligent Seraphina pulled me back to my senses. I was still looking at Sir George, but the smile had gone from my lips, and they tightened still more as I proclaimed: "You drew your sword!"

He smiled in response and spoke gently, if not a little condescendingly. "My dear, gentle lamb, you forget: I knew your brother very well at one time. In spite of what you might think—regardless of the steel slashing about—Julius would never harm a hair on your head, especially in a room full of witnesses."

"You knew my brother once, but you certainly don't know him now. Nobody does. It's been four years, Sir George. I wanted the chance to talk with him . . . to make him see the foolishness of what he was about. But I never got that chance because you grabbed me and drew your sword, encouraging him to shred me to ribbons."

He shook his head slowly, his face fraught with concern. "Is that really what you think? Then again, I must beg your forgiveness. I knew you would never understand my motives, but that was the risk I had to take. I knew he was coming here, Isabeau. I knew when the first rumors of his arrival were whispered in the corners of the most disreputable of places that he would eventually seek you out—you who are so good and gentle, who are so kind that you are blinded by your own endearing naïveté. And that is exactly the reason you should not be here alone. One cannot bargain with the insane. One does not reason with the devil. Your brother is a dangerous, unprincipled man. Holding you in the manner that I had was not chivalrous, but it was the only way I could gain leverage . . . to wrest the grasp of power from him, and it worked."

He was right, it had worked. Yet his actions had unnerved me. I crossed my arms and glared. "You should have at least let me speak with him."

"And what?" he replied softly. "Risk kidnapping? Did it

ever cross your mind that you are, without doubt, the most valuable object in this old ruin?" And then Sir George started forward.

"Valuable?" I uttered, my eyes never leaving his. I was feeling suddenly flushed and a little ill. Mme. Seraphina, aware of my unease, jumped to her duty.

"You'll stay right there, young man." Her cheerful, round face darkened impressively; add to that her girth and implacable stance, and she would have put a mastiff to shame. Sir George, thankfully, had the presence of mind to obey, yet he continued to address me.

"You do understand that with King James as your guardian Julius could demand the world and he'd pay it? Did you think it would be prudent to risk that? If you won't think of yourself, Isabeau, if you won't acknowledge that Julius is a lost cause, a murderous outlaw, a man whose very life was forfeit the moment he stepped onto these shores, then at least think of your country."

"My country?" I uttered. "But I love my country."

"I know you do. Why else would you risk so much to come here? I know you do, my dear lass," he repeated softly, mesmerizingly, and began walking toward me again, sidestepping Seraphina and keeping her at arm's length while perfectly ignoring the warning in her eyes. "And that is why I had to take you in hand before Julius did. Do you understand?" He was standing directly before me, his splendid green eyes imploring my face, my lips, my heaving bosom, before finally settling back on my eyes. His large, battle-calloused hands took hold of mine, and I felt again his undeniable power.

"I know you don't want to believe it, but your brother is the worst kind of enemy to have." His gentle voice softened the harsh words he wished me to hear. "Julius is at once brilliant and charming; he draws you in like a moth to a flame— a dance of seduction so alluring you'll risk anything just to bask in his aura. I know. I was one of those who fell under his spell. But his heart, Isabeau, is as twisted and cold as the devil's own, and he'd as soon as cut out your heart and eat it as he would kiss your hand. How cunning he is; how quick his men are to follow him. He has a natural gift for leadership but an unnatural hunger to wield his influence over those he leads. Any one of those poor wretches who now follow him would gladly lay down his life if he but asked it. And he will ask it, Isabeau. Mark my words; he will ask it before he is done here. And he will win many souls for Satan. Time has not healed Julius, my poor, dear little angel; it has only made his hunger greater."

As Sir George spoke—as his eyes held mine—I realized I was shaking. Like an oncoming storm, the shaking began with subtle tremors, stirring my body with a gentle, enlivening wave, yet as I held the knight's huge hands the tremors grew in strength, until my teeth rattled in my head. It was Seraphina who finally broke his powerful hold by yanking me away.

Clutching me firmly in her protective arms, she chided the knight with more passion than I had seen her display in a long while. "You are frightening the child! You speak of my lady's brother, and the other soul she prays for nightly. She has witnessed for herself already what kind of man Julius is without hearing stories from you. Can you not see how it weighs heavy on her heart? And before you malign Master Julius," she said, still using my brother's hereditary title, "you might wish to explain how it was he found you in possession of the king's message."

Sir George's eyes widened at this charge, yet his disarming smile remained. "My dear madame, I make no excuses for intercepting the messenger. As I explained to Hendrick, I recognized the man. I have been keeping an eye on my lands in Teviotdale knowing that Julius was about, and when I saw the messenger coming, riding along the Kelso road, I had a feeling he was proclaiming the return of Isabeau. I was overjoyed when I saw that it was addressed to Hendrick, and told the lad I'd deliver the message myself, as I was going that way. A couple of groats in the lad's hand, and the letter was mine. I would have delivered it too if my men and I weren't so brutally set upon by the English when we were." He turned to me. "You must know, Isabeau, how anxious I was to have a word with you away from the eyes and ears of the king and his court. You have had a most diligent guardian in James, so diligent that even your most ardent admirers have had to admire you from afar."

Still shaken by his allure, I replied from the safety of Seraphina's arms, "I don't think you've ever been very far."

His response to this was a brilliant grin, and then he threw his head back and laughed. His laughter, deep and rich, echoed through the large chamber, bouncing off tapestry and tester bed alike. It was infectious, and I did all I could to suppress a smile. "You know me surprisingly well, Isabeau, my elusive dove, and that alone gives me reason to hope. I think you will find, if you'll allow yourself to give me a chance, that I can be a charming ally." The word *ally* was said with subtle mischief to make me understand his real meaning, and it suddenly reminded me of the king's request that I find a suitable husband or one would be found for me.

"You jump to conclusions," I said plainly, guiding him toward the door, "for I have never considered you an enemy. And if you wish me to consider you as anything at all, you'll let me get some sleep. I doubt it has occurred to you, but I'm spectacularly tired."

"Forgive me. I forgot for a moment that you've been in the company of Marion these last few days. A dear lass, but insufferably wearing." His eyes widened in a knowing manner. In spite of myself I smiled.

"It might possibly run in the family," I said half-teasingly as I steered him past the doorway. "Now, if you'll be so good as to let me retire, and if I make it through the night without incident, mishap, or molestation, we shall begin tomorrow with a new understanding of one another."

"Isabeau," he uttered plaintively through the swiftly narrowing crack. "I find that insulting with me before your door."

The door closed and I threw the bolt, grinning a little. "Sleep well, Sir George."

᷀᷁

Although thoroughly exhausted, my body limp with the lack of will or desire to move, I could not sleep. It was the wee hours of the night. The castle, filled with so many rambunctious men, all of them riled by the recent assault to their pride, had quieted down. I should have been among them, sleeping soundly if not peacefully, yet instead I found myself flat on my back, motionless in the giant bed that had belonged to my father, with the fine gossamer curtains fashioned by my mother's own hand drawn close. I was in a familial cocoon, surrounded by the strong and poignant memory of my parents, only one of whom I had the pleasure to know, yet both were now gone. The thought that I lay on the very bed I was conceived in haunted me a little, and as the stump of the taper guttered in the holder, throwing its wan yellow light against the curtains, I thought of them both—the legendary beauty whose life was cut short in childbirth and the man whose love for her was so great that it drove him insane. When the first tear trickled down my cheek I did nothing to stop it. And then, as if a floodgate had opened after a deluge, all the sorrow I had kept in check for so long came upon me, doubling in virulence with the realization that I had never cried for them before now. How long I lay in this strange and haunted bed dampening the coverlet with my tears I couldn't say, but once this bout of sorrow and self-pity played out, leaving me with no more tears to shed, I felt a little better and thought sleep would finally come.

But in this, again, I was wrong.

Frightfully unfettered, my restless mind turned next to the two men who most occupied it, the alluring dark knight holding vigil at my door and the golden predator who was my brother, now prowling the verdant glens of Blythemuir with his ravenous pack. Let loose upon the countryside, Julius and his men, like a cloud of insatiable locusts, would leave nothing but waste and desolation in their wake. Sir George Douglas possessed the will to stop him, but by inhabiting my castle he would be just as devastating—only on a more personal level. What was I to do? How was I to handle these two warring men while keeping my promise to Blythe Hall and her people? Mme. Seraphina liked to proclaim, as devout women often will, that angels watched over me. It was a great pity that I didn't believe in angels, despite the family legend and to the chagrin of my governess, because for the first time in my life I believed that a little divine counsel couldn't go amiss. But I knew, firsthand, just how dangerous such whimsical beliefs could be.

Perhaps it was this suggestion of angels and divine beings that invoked his memory again. I really couldn't say. All I knew was that for the second time in the same day I was filled with a vision of a man not only physically perfect but possessing something much deeper, something radiant and pure. I had the feeling one gets when standing in the full, glorious rays of the sun. He was the essence of light, this stranger, the embodiment of virtue and honor. And yet there was a powerful virility about him that rendered me breathless. The face, which could have been attributed to a Roman god, was strong and noble, with perfect symmetry from aquiline nose to firm jaw complete with chin dimple. Yet it was the eyes—like two unblemished sapphires peering from beneath a golden brow—that positively smoldered with passion and palpable desire. Even in this odd fantasy of mine it was hard to peer directly into them, yet when I did I believed I finally understood what a powerful allure physical love must be. The man from my vision did not speak, but I knew he felt my desire, which was as raw and unfettered as his own. This knowledge caused my body to suddenly erupt in a burst of tingling. From my head to my toes, every fiber of my being became alive, every sense heightened. And when it finally subsided, he followed me into my dreams, and there he lived, awakening my soul, igniting a fire within me that I feared only he had the power to quench.

ॐ

It was only when I felt the body in bed next to me that I began to understand that something was not right. At first it seemed the most natural thing in the world, a living extension of my dream where the elusive being, half angel, half warrior (yet undeniably all male), was fulfilling the more carnal desires he had awakened. Love pulsated through me, along with a yearning that went beyond my understanding. The man in my dream knew what I wanted even if I could not put it into words; his own emotions were so entwined with mine that I didn't know where he ended and I began. And so, when I felt the body easing its way into my bed, I subconsciously assumed my dream had become real. I believe I let out a small noise of surprise when his cold skin pressed against the thin fabric of my nightdress, yet his breath was hot and sweet against my cheek. He murmured something in a tone that was as soothing as it was sensual. I had no idea what he said, but my body responded for me and snuggled into him, inviting him to put his arm around me. This he did, and spoke once more. This time I heard exactly what he said, and no shock could have been greater or more thoroughly disturbing.

"Dear God," the expletive burst from his lips in a hot, breathy whisper. "What a wanton you are. Now warm me up, my sweet, nubile young vixen. I've come at last and have thought of little else but your delicious body writhing in pleasure against my own. Not even the great danger to myself—"

"Julius!" I cried, as every horrified fiber of my being exploded, causing me to slap his roving hand away as I simultaneously bolted out of the bed.

At the sound of my voice he jumped as well—as if being burned by hot oil. And in the darkness, his outline just visible against the fine curtains fashioned by our mother's own hand, he cried: "Holy virgins afire! What the hell are *you* doing *here*?!"

"What the hell are *you* doing here?!" I spat back, fully awake and aghast. "This is my bedchamber, Julius! And . . . and you are in *my* bed!"

"This is not your bedchamber, Isabeau! Your bedchamber's down"—he thrust out a finger and waggled it—"there. And what the devil do you mean by leaving your window open?"

"I always sleep with my window open!" I informed him, leveling a menacing glare at his shadowy figure. "And let me tell you that an open window is by no means an invitation to enter somebody's bed. Dear heavens, Julius, have you no shame? You're my own brother, for mercy's sake." The mere thought of his touch made me unspeakably queasy, dirty even. Thankfully he was as disgusted by it as I was, for I saw his body shiver in revulsion.

"I had no intention of getting into your bed, Isabeau!" His reply was heated, his tone a harsh whisper. "I may have many undesirable habits, but incest, you'll be happy to know, is not one of them."

This, in truth, was a slight relief, but it still didn't change the fact that he—a dangerous and partially clad outlaw—had gotten into my bed. Taking a deep breath to calm my nerves, I reached for the candle on the nightstand and paused to light it so that I could better see him. Enveloped in the cocoon of the large tester bed, the scant light, trapped and reflected in the fine gossamer of the curtains, caught his hair and made it appear a golden halo atop a face far too handsome for his own good. His only piece of clothing, as he stood across from me seething, was a long, loose-fitting shirt of expensive linen. It was open at the throat, revealing a sleek, finely muscled neck that melded into a well-formed, work-hardened chest.

"Whose bed did you think you were getting into?" I asked pointedly.

"That is none of your business," he replied crisply, his lips curling ever so slightly with smugness.

I glared at him. "Very well. Don't answer. But I would like to know how you got in here in the first place?"

"That is also none of your business."

"Oh, but I think that it is my business, brother dear, as this is my castle now. You ought to have that cleaned and bandaged, you know," I added, pointing to the blood-encrusted rip in his linen that bisected the flat plane of his stomach and revealed the cut he had received at the hand of Sir George.

He glanced down to where I pointed. "This little scratch? I'm fine. I heal like a mangled pup." He looked up and twisted his expressive mouth again, only this time there was palpable malice in the grin. "Call me Rondo, but somehow I always manage to bounce back from the brink of death." I ignored the painful barb.

"Rondo's dead, Julius, and I'll thank you to leave my dog out of this."

"I'm sorry to hear it. He was quite the little miracle. Yet had I known I would offend your sensibilities, or agitate such painful memories, I would have changed. Then again, had I known you'd be here, I would not have come at all."

"I'm relieved to hear it," I said in a voice thick with sarcasm. "I can clearly sleep peacefully now knowing that you've broken into my home twice in the same day but haven't come to ravish me. And here I was just beginning to feel safe, with two armies patrolling the grounds and Sir George sleeping before my door."

"Sir George? He's sleeping outside your door?" His look

was comically scandalized as he glanced in the general direction, although the bed curtains obstructed his view. He chuckled softly.

"Yes. I'm glad you find it so amusing."

"Oh, it is," he said, and attempted to quell his unstable mirth. "By God, it is. Tell me, did he, by chance, insinuate that I would attempt to kidnap you and then ransom you back to the king?"

"Insinuate, no. Insist, yes," I replied evenly, my eyes never leaving his. "And . . . well, are you?"

His response was a short burst of stifled laughter. "Heavens, no! I mean, at least not tonight. Truthfully, and I think you'll agree with me here, it was the farthest thing from my mind." He was filled with effervescent mirth, and it caused me to wonder if he was still drunk. "Oh God, he's good . . . the ass!"

"Forgive me for believing it was a real concern." My reply was petulant, but in my defense, I was greatly unnerved.

His brows momentarily rose in amusement. "All right, I forgive you. And to ease your little, overtroubled mind once again, sister dear, just as in the case of incest, kidnapping is a currency I don't trade in. Does it relieve you to hear it?"

"No," I stated truthfully. "Not at all. Because you attempted kidnap once—with the boy king."

To this he had no answer. After a long, contemplative stare he said, "Forgive me. I shall rephrase my answer: kidnapping is a currency I don't trade in *any longer.* Is that better? Is that what you wanted to hear?"

"I want to hear the truth for once," I demanded, my mind aswirl with contrary emotions—disdain, compassion, frustration, and forgiveness. But Julius was a stubborn soul whose motives had never been other than his own.

"The trouble with Truth, my dear, is that it is something quite different to all parties involved. What is truth? What is falsehood? What is it that one wants to believe? Truth can be as elusive as the fabled unicorn, and just as tricky to pin down. Even with solid evidence—take the spiral horn, for example— regardless of the fact that I know of no one who's actually seen a unicorn, 'tis easier to believe it exists rather than explain the real creature that wears such a prong. Truth gets mired in falsehood. I would tell it to you, but even I wouldn't be fool enough to believe it. So, for the sake of argument, let's just leave it like this: unlike your life, mine has been a wee less charmed."

"Excuse me?" Julius always had a tendency to be prolix, and I was slightly confused and a little affronted. "My life has never been . . . ," I began, but stopped when I saw the look in his eyes. It was the same cold, accusing glare from that day long ago—the day our father went mad. It was there but for the space of a breath or two, and then, like a mercurial wind, it vanished and he smiled. "But let us not dwell on a past we cannot change," he said with a pretense of benevolence. "Let us begin anew. Let us live in the moment, and I find at this moment I'm wondering who it was you were expecting when I climbed into your bed?"

"What?" I blurted, then stared at him. "What . . . kind of question is that?"

"Oh, come now, Isabeau," he said, and sat back down on the bed. His tone was infuriating, his looks cool and fresh as morning dew. Then, in a preposterous show of burning inter- est, he fluffed and rearranged some pillows, leaned back, and crossed his arms. "You may deceive others," he continued pleasantly, "but don't play the coy innocent with me. I wasn't lying when I said you'd grown into a real beauty. And I know a thing or two about young women your age, especially young, convent-bred women. Deny it if you must, but you know as well as I that you were as hot, primed, and ready to explode as Orban's great gun sitting at the gates of Constan- tinople, sister dear."

Inflamed, and more than a little outraged, I replied: "I

don't pretend to know what you're talking about. Obviously your lively imagination has run away with you—again. Get out of my bed!"

"I'm comfortable. And I'm not the one credited with a lively imagination." Under the soft glow of the single flame, his eyes widened, making his meaning perfectly clear.

Still standing between bed and curtain, shaking slightly while attempting to quell every nerve in my body that was threatening to spring to life at the memory of the erotic vision, I glowered at him. "I was asleep! And . . . and there's no one! I wasn't even dreaming of anything remotely like you're suggesting. And anyway, how could my thoughts have even wandered where your mind so easily jumps?" I yanked the pillow from under his head. He sat up, still amused.

"Your thoughts may not have gone there, my dear, but your body certainly did. But not to worry"—he waved a hand nonchalantly in the air—"unless the man you were expecting was Lord Kill-Me-Now."

Sir George Douglas. The thought never crossed my mind, but it was easier to explain away a real man than a mere dream. I hugged the pillow to my body as I challenged, "And what if it was?"

He grinned, but his eyes darkened dangerously. "Then I would have to kill him. He's already been the ruin of one Blythe. I will not stand idly by and watch him be the ruin of another." I hugged the pillow even tighter at this statement, for although Sir George had his moments, he was, at heart, a good and decent man. And besides, I found that I rather liked him. Julius, however, had a flair for the dramatic, along with a tongue in his head that did little but cause trouble and infuriate. That he had a valid reason to dislike Sir George was evident. They had, at one time, been friends, yet in the end it was Sir George who came forward with the evidence that nearly sent Julius to the gallows. But one could hardly blame Sir George, for he was merely trying to save a kingdom, whereas

Julius had been trying to overthrow it. And then it hit me, the sudden, sinking feeling of why he was really here.

"Julius," I said, sitting on the edge of the bed. "Why have you come back now? Am I to believe it's just some cruel twist of fate that brings you here . . . on the very day I return home?"

"People, I find, give Fate far too much credit. Would you believe that I missed you?" he offered softly.

"I believe you've missed a great many things, brother, including Scotland. But you had no right to open this evening's festivities with a campaign of humiliation against me and your former king."

"And?" he prompted, his head tilted, eyebrows raised. "Go ahead, say it! Georgie Douglas, my lord Kilwylie! You'll have to excuse my theatrics; I was spectacularly drunk at the time." His lips twisted into a grin of sardonic amusement. "And, if you'll recall, it was my lord Kilwylie who began the spectacle of the night, bursting into the hall and flinging his heart at your feet. I was perfectly content with the meal and the music, until he carried his performance too far. 'Tis rank bad manners to mock a person in his own home. The man was sorely in need of a verbal thrashing."

"So," I began, looking skeptically at him, "are you trying to make me believe that you were coming to my defense?"

"I'm not trying to make you believe anything. You've proven time and again that you're perfectly content believing what you like."

While I attempted to process this accusation, he grabbed the pillow from my arms and thrust it back under his head. His arms were crossed and he was looking overly relaxed when I finally replied, "That's not true. And you're right about Sir George, he did go too far, but his life is not forfeit. He's also a nobleman and a knight of Scotland. Yet more important, *he* wasn't trying to rob me."

"I wasn't trying either. I succeeded." A gloriously smug grin lit his face.

I ached to hit him. Instead I yanked the pillow away again. He wasn't expecting it and cracked his overinflated head against the bed frame. "Are you utterly mad?" I said. "If you were in need of money so desperately, couldn't you have just sent a message or something?"

"And forgo the pleasure of seeing you and Sir George together in the same room?" he replied cheerfully, rubbing his head. "Why, I've paid good money to see lesser spectacles."

"*Get out*," I said, seething. I had suffered enough of him and his wicked tongue for one day. "Get out of my castle, or I swear I will call the guards!"

He moved quickly, with the grace of a cat, and before I knew it my trembling hands were cradled in his irritatingly steady ones. Julius had remarkable hands, long-fingered and elegant, yet I could see that they were marred by fine silvery scars, speaking of untold hardships suffered after his exile. And there was something else too: a ring. Feeling the coolness of the gold band on his middle finger, my hand stilled. I looked at Julius; his animated face was void of all expression. And then, slowly, I turned his hand over. The sight of the ring took the breath from me, for it was the Blythe Angel, the signet ring of our father, with the motto JE SUIS PROTÉGÉ written in reverse beneath the winged warrior. Our eyes met and held. It was then that I saw, for the second time in my life, a look in Julius that caused my heart to ache. It was a naked vulnerability that he had worked hard to conceal beneath a mask of indifference. But it was there now, as we both beheld our father's ring, in a look suffused with all the pain, hope, and loss I had ever felt. Julius was a master at the art of deception; yet even he could not deceive me this time.

"Isabeau," he uttered, and for once there was no irksome grin or ironic sneer on his face as he spoke. "I was going to speak with you later, but since my little nocturnal blunder, I shall tell you now. I have not come here to dredge up the past, if that is your concern. I have returned to protect the future of our race, and in order to do that, I'm going to need your help."

"What are you talking about?" I said, watching him carefully, for I half believed the knock on his head had done some real damage.

"It's late. I'm late, and it's far too complicated to explain now. The truth is that I have come to ask for your help. No, wait, that's a lie too. I believe we can help each other," he corrected, and offered a forced smile.

"Really? How so?" I was utterly befuddled, and I believed he was a little as well.

"I need you to help me find somebody, and in return I will help you maintain peace and appearances here."

"What? I don't need . . ."

He let go of my hand to hold up a cautioning finger, stopping my protest.

And then I had another sinking feeling. "You wouldn't, by any chance, be thinking of blackmailing me?" Unfortunately the use of blackmail was all too common in the Borders.

"Don't be silly." He waved off my suggestion. "I'm simply offering my help in return for yours. I'm quite anxious to help, really. After all, I have a band of idle mercenaries, remember?"

"And if I don't help you?"

"Again, I have a band of idle mercenaries." He smiled sweetly. "I would hate to make you look the fool."

"You are blackmailing me!" I cried, and yanked my hands from his. "My own bloody brother has come home to blackmail me. I'm certain I've never heard the like. Well, let me save you the trouble, brother. If it's Sir George you want, I know where he is. You're welcome to him. Just do me the courtesy of leaving my castle before you conduct your ugly business."

The mirth, the air of insouciance, returned, and he replied,

"God as my witness, I wish it were that simple! But no, the man I'm seeking, Isabeau, is a very elusive being. Do you understand me?"

It wasn't the words he spoke so much as the manner in which he spoke them that made the hair on the back of my neck stand on end.

"Ah," he uttered, studying me intently. "I believe you have guessed it."

"No." I shook my head, refusing to believe him. "No. You have not come here for that."

"Oh, but I have. I have returned because I have need of something only you can find. I have need of an angel, my dear. And what better place to find such a creature than within the walls of our unchancy home, this monument built by the mad to worship the divine: Blythe Hall."

Chapter 5

THE ALTAR
OF ANGELS

ALTHOUGH I LIKED TO THINK THAT I HAD MANY COM-
mendable qualities, I was, by nature, a stubborn and prideful
person. The good sisters at Haddington had stumbled upon this
sinful defect in my character a time or two and, bless their misguided hearts, had tried to correct it. Yet eventually even they
recognized a lost cause when they saw one; for I would not suffer being made to look the fool by anyone, and I certainly would
not do so now at the hands of my estranged brother.

And Julius was planning to do just that. Like a sickening
wave of nausea it had hit me, as I stood listening to his ludicrous demand, that he had amassed and flaunted his merry
band of outlaws for a reason far more devious than I had at
first imagined. It was for my benefit that he and his men had
rendered the cream of the King's Guard helpless in the Great
Hall. It was for my benefit that Sir George had been exposed
for intercepting the king's messenger, regardless of his more
personal motives. Julius, like the consummate manipulator he

was, had been subtly letting me know who was really in control of Blythe Hall and the people of Blythemuir. And he would do his utmost to shatter all the confidence I had worked so hard to build in defense of the family madness by reducing me to a crazy woman who chased after angels. It was, I had to admit, maniacally brilliant.

I was seething with this new wave of hurt and anger. How was I to manage anything if I couldn't even manage my own affairs? It was shameful enough knowing I was being played, yet I somehow found it even more humiliating to learn, in the manner I had, that Julius had infiltrated my home a second time—in the space of mere hours—just so he could satisfy his lust. In truth, there were a good many women in the neighborhood who would likely have welcomed him; he had a bit of a history in these parts. Some women, I had even heard though hardly believed, found debased outlaws such as Julius to be particularly appealing. These were definitely the weak-willed, morally deficient sort, the favorite prey of one such as my brother. Yet still, given all this, the fact that he had chosen to practice his vile sport in my castle—which was doubly guarded, no less—was not just another slap in the face but the height of irreverence.

It was then that I noticed the room had grown suddenly quiet; his near-silent footfalls had all but vanished. I had promised not to watch him leave, but I could listen, and I strained to hear the direction in which he headed as he slipped from the room in silk-clad feet. I assumed he would not venture toward the room where Mme. Seraphina slept, nor would he head out the door and risk waking Sir George, although Julius would have reveled in doing just that. No, I believed his only choice, having had another objective this night, would be to slip out the high window the way he had come. In this, however, I was wrong. I distinctly heard him head in the direction of the solar, but there was no sound of a door opening. I sat up, crawled to the end of the bed, and lifted the curtain. The room, awash with moonlight streaming through the open window along with the effervescent scent of dewy grass, was empty; however, the door to the solar stood wide open. I eased myself off the bed and silently made for the door. The big room, with its plush furniture, bookcases, and settle by the fireplace, was vacant; both doors, the one opening onto the hallway and the other leading to the laird's study, were locked. Julius had quite literally vanished.

Dejected, and more than a little frustrated, I went back to bed, where I consciously fought to control my breathing, for my lungs, heaving as though I had just run across the unforgiving moors, threatened to explode with the anger building inside me. I had learned over the years to master my emotions, to temper them as a lady ought to, pushing aside messy, unnecessary feelings that got in the way of common sense and clear thinking. But I could not quell this flood of white-hot rage. It was too raw and powerful, even for my great abilities; that fact alone angered me all the more. Yet with this impotent rage I experienced an equal amount of sorrow, and this I found to be just as devastating. I collapsed onto the bed, burying my streaming face in the coverlet, muffling my anguished sobs in the thick quilted folds of linen and down, so that no one would hear me—so that no one would see how low he had brought me. After years spent living a fiction of self-preserving denial, I was finally made to accept the dark and spiteful nature of my brother. Julius, with all his God-given gifts—the keen intellect, the athleticism, the winsome smile, the rapier wit—had squandered them all in his perverse desire to expose and exploit weakness. And he had come to expose and exploit mine. Like a long-forgotten nightmare, he had resurfaced, hell-bent on punishing me for that day long ago, that day he had never fully forgiven me for. The day I convinced our father that I conversed with angels.

❧

It had always been said that our father had the strength of ten men in battle, for he, like the five other Lord Blythes before him, was a guardian of the kingdom of Scotland. He had been a man renowned far and wide, on both sides of the border, for his vast intelligence, his ability to prosper and even flourish in a troubled land, his keen observations and wise counsel, and the quiet strength with which he led those who followed him. He was a man who garnered the respect of his king, a loyal man and a brave one, and he had always been a good father. But the man who finally emerged from the long-forgotten tower room, after weeks of self-imposed isolation, could have been a stranger, so greatly was he altered. During his mad vigil he had allowed no one but Mme. Seraphina to enter, and ate only enough to sustain him. So it came as quite a shock when we first saw him, a man once gifted with graceful movements and a powerful frame; for he had emerged grossly diminished in girth and haltingly timid. His hair, the mane of thick, tawny curls, had lost its luster and hung in lank ropes at his shoulders, heavily streaked with gray. But it was his eyes, those wise, intelligent pools of ocean blue, that my memory has never shaken. My father's eyes had always sparkled with life and mischief, but on that first day I spoke with him after he emerged from his sanctuary, I saw how they had changed— how the spark had altered—only to be replaced with a burning desire for something that could never be attained on earth. Even then I understood that he was straddling two worlds, hanging onto life with but a toehold in reality and one foot already firmly planted in the ever-after, the mental leap already made in an attempt to be with her once again.

Having never met my mother, I never fully understood the hold she had on him, but he would talk of her often. He especially delighted in telling me stories of her, of how beautiful she was, how kind she was, what a good mother she had been to Julius. And then he would tell me that she was a good mother to me too, for she watched over me, always, because she was an angel. By the time I was six I wanted to believe my father's words, for by then I had grown quite jealous knowing that Julius, and just about everyone else in Blythemuir, had known her. I wanted to know her too, and not just in stories. That's when I ventured for the first time up the many flights of stairs that led into the old peel tower. The tower was still in use, but no one lived in it anymore, not since the Great Hall and adjoining wing of apartments had been built. But I had learned from Mme. Seraphina that my mother had lived in the tower for a time, twice as a matter of fact, because she had chosen the highest room for her birth chamber. When I questioned the logic in this, not knowing much about birthing at the time, she assured me it was a usual practice, for the tower room was the highest place in the entire castle, and therefore closest to God. I liked hearing this, and it made perfect sense, for if my mother really was an angel, then naturally she'd want to be close to God. I believed the stories I was told, and when I discovered the room, fitted with a magnificent stained-glass window and still containing a large bed, painted chests, and beautiful clothes of the finest fabrics, though hopelessly covered in dust, I believed she still lived there. It was my little secret, going to the tower room, and when I'd play in her clothes, or rummage through her chest, or slip on a pair of her exquisitely beaded slippers, I imagined she was with me. I imagined that she would sit and talk with me as I played. In my imagination she was an angel, and sometimes she would bring the little winged boys with her, but they could be naughty. And I never called her Mum; I didn't call her much of anything for that matter, because I hadn't needed to. In my mind she was the white lady: a pure spirit.

However imaginative I was, the sad truth of it all was that my mother had been gone a long while. She had died in childbirth. It was, as everyone knew, the risk one took when entering the marriage bed, and if truth be told, it was partly the reason I was cautious to enter myself. But most men, after losing wives in such ways, replaced them soon enough. Our father never did. And all the women clamoring to be the next

Lady Blythe eventually gave up trying and went away. Her death had affected him in a way I could never imagine and, as a child, hardly understood. Yet up until that day, our father had been an exemplary parent. That was why we didn't understand his refusal to see us during his isolation. And when, weeks later, we were finally summoned, Julius and I, who had once been everything to him, seemed little more than physical reminders of a distant, shadowy past. Alone in the tower room, haunted by memories and convinced of miracles that never were, he had a new objective in life, for he clung to the belief that our mother had been, and still was, an angel.

I remember when he told us of his revelation. We had been brought to his apartment, the same opulent chambers I had taken as my own. He had been sitting at the desk in his room talking softly with Hendrick, a great pile of books and papers strewn on the table before him. At the sound of our arrival he turned from the conversation. That's when we saw he had been holding Rondo in his lap—Rondo, the little collie pup he had surprised me with after the spring shearing. The puppy had endured some rough handling by the wicked Englishmen but had fully recovered, and because of it he held a peculiar fascination for our father. The dog grew excited at the sight of us, yet our father didn't let him down. Instead he sent Hendrick and Mme. Seraphina from the room, for what he was about to tell us was for our ears alone.

Lord Blythe was convinced he had witnessed two miracles, the first occurring the day I was born, while the second, and most recent—the vision he experienced in the tower room— had been too fresh in all our minds to contemplate. He brushed over this recent miracle with a strategic lack of detail, for his real purpose in bringing us to his chambers was to explain, as he had never before, the mysterious circumstances surrounding our mother's death. I remember sitting close to Julius on the cushioned settle, my hand clasped tightly around his, for there was a desperate elation about our father as he spoke that unnerved me. I knew Julius could feel it too, for I saw how his eyes, narrowed in a look of guarded inquiry, followed him as he paced before the hearth, clinging to the little puppy in the same way a mighty ship clings to a small anchor. And we had good reason to be frightened; for the story he told us revealed the depths of his madness.

I was reminded again that there is good reason men are not normally privy to the mysteries of the birth chamber. While no one would dispute a man's brave nature or his ability to remain strong and focused in the heat of battle whilst fighting alongside his men, impervious to the blood and death moans of dying comrades, the same cannot be said when the woman he cares for goes into labor. First, there's the matter of an heir, which is no small trifling, especially for a lord. Second, when a woman's pain elevates to the unthinkable horror it does in the last stages of the ordeal, there is no sword to wield, no enemy to battle but for time and the unknown. A man in the birth chamber is helpless to do aught but watch, and it fair drives him, and everyone around him, insane, or so I've been told. That's why the secrets and struggles of birthing are reserved for midwives and the womenfolk of a household, and my mother's birthing had been no different. In her eighth month she had taken to her birth chamber in the old tower room, just as she had with Julius. And when her pains had started on that day in late October, my father, thankfully, was well outside the castle walls working alongside our tenants to bring in the fall harvest. However, when word reached him that his wife was laboring to bring me into the world, he rode home at once and waited in the Great Hall, pacing and fashing away like a skittish horse, until he could see her.

He told us that at first everything appeared normal, for my mother had brought Julius into the world with little trouble and it was assumed it would be the same for me. It was Seraphina who came to tell him the news, shortly after midnight. There was no midwife by then, for the birth had gone well and she had already left. Lady Blythe had a healthy daughter; but there was something amiss—something untold in the elderly woman's eyes.

When he spoke to us of how our mother had looked when he first saw her, lying in the big bed propped up on pillows and holding the swaddled bundle that was me gently in her arms, I half believed he still saw her. He told us of the joy that radiated from her lovely face and the peacefulness that had settled around her, entirely belying the painful struggle she had just gone through. His heart stopped, he said, with that first glimpse of us together, and he went to her side so that he could look upon my face. But here he stopped his narration.

Standing before us as Julius and I sat pressed together on the settle, he suddenly dropped to one knee so that his eyes were level with our own. He must have sensed that we were somehow frightened by this interview, for his demeanor changed and his gaze grew soft, almost pleading. He put Rondo down, and I could tell he chose his next words carefully. "I dinnae ken how else to explain it, my wee hearts," he said softly, "but the moment I crossed thon threshold, I saw the light."

He meant for his words to be taken literally, for, according to our father, a strange glow came from directly behind our mother—as if her head were blocking a source of light so that only soft, luminous wisps could be seen fluttering around her solid form. As she sat silhouetted by this strange halo, he assumed that the light was coming from a window. But he then realized that this was impossible, as all the great windows of the birth chamber had been covered with heavy, embroidered cloth, as custom dictated; it was a precaution against evil. And he was quick to assure us that no evil had entered the room, only this extraordinary light that fell across both mother and child.

Seeing that he was standing tentatively near the door, my mother had beckoned him closer, offering him the bundle in her arms—their newborn child. He did as she wished, and they talked softly then, expressing great joy of my birth. They stayed like that for a while, sitting together on the bed, holding hands with heads pressed close as they watched me sleep, until, as my father explained, he felt her hand go cold. It was late October, and there was a chill in the air. A brazier had been lit and gave off some heat, but still, another quilt or two wouldn't go amiss, he thought, and went to fetch them out of the chest at the end of the bed—until her voice stopped him.

"William, there's no need," she whispered. "I'll be gone soon, my love."

The chill that had reached her hands gripped his heart, for her words, shocking to the ears, had become at once weak and distant, and filled with terrible regret. He looked up and saw tears as brilliant as diamonds well up in her eyes. He dropped the quilts and ran back to her, falling to his knees beside her and taking her cold hands in his. "No . . . ," he uttered. "No, Angelica. Ye are fine. Ye are fine!" he reiterated with passion. "The wee lass is fine. Stop talking nonsense."

"Oh, William . . ." At the sound of his name he looked into her eyes. His heart stopped. "My soul, never you fret. It is my time, but we shall not be parted forever."

Those were the last words she spoke.

My father had seen the face of death many times, for he was a warrior, but the death of my mother was unlike any other he had ever witnessed. Her body, which had appeared so young and vibrant moments ago, began to fade as the soft light behind her grew in intensity. Then, as if out of the pages of the Old Testament, a ray of this now brilliant flame shot heavenward, only to be blocked by the high vaulted ceiling. But this was not an impediment for such a light. He explained how the polished oak beams shimmered and wavered until they became translucent—as if they had melted away. Although he was stricken with a paralyzing mixture of terror and awe, he could not pull his eyes from it. Then, with the roof thus opened to reveal the cold night sky above, he saw two radiant forms. They appeared to be young men, he said, and they were profound beyond words in their beauty and purity. They came down into the room on the burst of light that connected them to our mother. At once he knew what they were, and suddenly, as if a sharp crack of lightning had pierced his overwrought brain, he understood what they had come for.

Stupefied, while still holding on to my mother's hand and with me nestled in the crook of his arm, he watched in disbelief as his wife left her physical body. He described to us a feeling of reeling joy, while at the same time his cheeks ran with an unheeded flow of tears. His conflicting emotions caused his insides to churn away like a roiling sea, for the woman he had lived for and loved had passed before his very eyes—without warning—leaving her lovely body like some old, discarded cocoon. And she had emerged from it a radiant being of ineffable beauty and grace. What was more, like the two perfect incorporeal beings that had come for her, she too had wings of shimmering light.

Our father, newly come from his self-imposed isolation and with eyes touched by an unearthly zeal, pulled from inside his shirt a piece of folded cloth that had been kept close to his heart. We watched as he gently unfolded it with all the care and tenderness he might use with an ancient manuscript. Once it was opened, I saw that it contained a lone white feather. Mesmerized, I reached for the feather, because I too had found one like it in the old tower room once. But just as my father brought it closer for me to inspect, Julius slapped my hand away.

"You daft old fool!" he had cried, jumping to his feet. "That's a swan's feather! How dare you tell us such lies! How dare you fill our heads with such addled, barmy fantasies! Isa's a child and knows little better, but I am not a child, and I will not be placated by your deranged fairy tales. You lock yourself in the tower for months, and this is the best you can do?" There was derision not only in his voice but in his eyes, his brilliant blue eyes. I could tell that it broke my father's heart to see it.

"Julius, my son . . . ," he pleaded softly.

"She's dead!" he spat with brutal finality. "The sooner you accept that, the sooner we can all get on with our lives. But I, for one, will not stay here and watch you crumble and decay like a battered and besieged old keep." After a sad shake of his head, he turned his back on us and stalked out of the room. Lord Blythe made no move to stop him.

"I believe you, Father," I uttered, touching his sleeve. His eyes, raw with pain, came back to mine. He attempted a smile, but his lips failed to obey. And how could they? His son thought him mad. Maybe he was, but at that moment I wanted nothing more than to believe that his story was true. Because I loved him.

But it wasn't true.

Julius had been right. My brother was fortunate to have had our mother for five short years, and her death had been just as hard on him. But the true cause of her sudden departure, as everyone commonly understood it, was a latent hemorrhaging that the midwife had failed to detect, not a timely appearance of angels. It was easier for our father to believe his story, and for the most part, it had been a harmless belief . . . until the day he was convinced that she had come to him again.

The Blythes as a race, as many God-fearing Christians do, embraced angels and angelic lore, but our father, the sixth Lord Blythe, elevated this gentle fascination to an obsession. It was as if he was out to prove something, not only to himself but to his disenchanted son. The day after that odd interview, Julius left for Hume Castle to serve Sir Alexander, the Master of Hume. He was driven to separate himself from his father while furthering his education and completing his training in the military arts. My father was driven as well, but his aim was entirely different, for he was determined to scour Europe in search of angels.

Those were lonely years for me. I was not yet at the convent, and aside from sporadic visits from Julius, and the odd occasion when my father was home from his travels or serving the king, I was left in the care of Mme. Seraphina and Hendrick. It was during those years, however, when my father slowly began to transform the old tower room into a thing of true wonder. Works collected and commissioned from the most gifted artists across Europe—from Flanders to Florence—graced the walls with what some believed were the most breathtaking depictions of angels Europe had ever seen. The ceiling had been reworked and fitted with a dome that was painted like the sky, only with cherubs playing amongst the fluffy white clouds. An oculus had been cut into the center of this dome in tribute to the magnificent pantheon in Rome, or so he explained. However, his reason for this opening, which he fitted with a roundel of Venetian glass, was a much simpler one. It was a window to heaven, an open invitation to the angels who had once come for my mother to do so again. The last treasure he added to the tower room was a magnificent gilded altarpiece. It took the longest to create and was a staggering work of artistic beauty. And with this last piece added, the room became not only his sanctuary but a shrine dedicated to the worshipping of these heavenly hosts.

While some, particularly King James III, believed that building a shrine to elusive biblical beings was a noble and worthy way to spend a lifetime, others abhorred it, no one more so than the collector's own son. Julius had always been a bright, precocious boy. By the age of twelve he had plumbed the depths of his tutors at Blythe Hall. He was gifted, anyone could see it. His untrammeled genius had a tendency to embrace wilder pursuits, but he was under the practiced hand of a good and industrious nobleman who worked him tirelessly. There were times, however, when the three of us found ourselves at home living under the same roof. We were a family, of course, but one riven by a harmless madness. On some level, Lord Blythe understood this and made every attempt to soothe some of the hurt and anger that the young Master of Blythe bore so close to the surface. But if we were left too long together, tempers would flare. Loud, angry arguments ensued, and in the end Lord Blythe would not be moved on any account to give up his desperate search for angels, because, as he believed, he was very close to unlocking the secret. For Julius, a young man bursting with energy, intellect, and a contemptuous sort of pride, visits with his father were as futile as they were frustrating, especially so because he was the one who suffered publicly for our father's madness. To me both men were kind, but it was never again the same as it had been before. I let my father believe that I understood his need to talk with angels, because I didn't want to break his heart like Julius had. For this weakness, and for the incident that had sparked the whole shameful debacle to begin with, Julius could never fully forgive me.

Then, finally, like a mild wind after a bitter winter, a noticeable change occurred between father and son. It came years later, around 1486. That was the year the altarpiece had been installed in the chapel, the Altar of Angels, he had called it. That was the year I was sent to Stirling to serve briefly at the court of Queen Margaret. Julius spent a good deal of time in Stirling himself, for Sir Alexander Hume, his lord, was the Keeper of Stirling Castle. It was there that I met Marion and her older cousin, George Douglas, who was Julius's particular friend at the time. It was also there that I first met the king, although he was James, Duke of Rothesay, back then, and the oldest of the queen's three sons. It was no secret, even upon my arrival, that Julius was a favorite of the household, especially worshipped by the young princes, James in particular. Yet after only six fascinating months of service on my part, the queen suddenly took ill and died. The princes were sent to the castle in Edinburgh to live with their father, while Marion and I were sent to Haddington to live at the convent. My father was back in Scotland by the end of that year, for the king had need of him, and he was one of the few noblemen the king trusted.

Although a kind man, James III was not a revered ruler. Throughout his reign his policies and throne were constantly threatened by powerful nobles as well as members of his own family—the late Alexander, Duke of Albany (his own brother), being a particularly sharp thorn in his side. The result of this weakening authority and political sabotage by the country's powerful, self-seeking noblemen was that the king took to surrounding himself with common men, particularly musicians, poets, artisans, and architects. My father was one of the few exceptions. Most felt this was because of Lord Blythe's peculiar madness and not because of his loyalty. I believed it too until I learned from Julius—on one fine day when he had come to Haddington to entertain us with music, wild stories, and the latest gossip from court, as he often did—that it was something quite different altogether.

It came out during a private conversation held in the prioress's apartments. I was pleased to see how well my brother looked, how mature he had grown under Sir Alexander's patient guidance. I could see that he had thrown aside his childish ways and was finally ready to fill the role he was born to play, and his skills as a knight (and, if truth be told, with the fair sex) were already growing legendary. But there was something else too. He had just come from court after spending time with the king and our father. And it was in low tones that he convinced me that he finally understood our father's obsession with angels.

"I don't believe you," I offered with a grin, for I believed he was baiting me again; Julius loved to bait me, especially in conversations regarding heavenly beings.

"Oh, but you should, sister dear," he replied with a like grin. It was then that I saw the spark of excitement bright in his eyes. "You should believe me," he continued softly, "because it's not just angels, Isabeau. Ever since that day I thought it was. I could never understand it; he was absolutely unhinged. I thought the man had been flogging himself silly chasing after something that just doesn't exist. But now I understand what he was trying to tell me all along. Oh no, Isabeau," he said, placing his hands firmly on my shoulders, forcing me to look up into his eyes. They were still bright but deadly serious. "It's not just angels our father has been chasing after all these years. Angels, you see, have become a metaphor for something greater . . . something much, much greater."

It was never explained to me what exactly the Blythe men were up to. Perhaps I didn't really wish to know, for there seemed to hang about them a subtle air that spoke of a deeper, more desperate pursuit. In truth, I was just relieved to see that they had finally been reconciled. After our visit in Haddington, Julius left the Master of Hume to serve our father at Blythe Hall. I was pleased to see that they were beginning to recapture that special bond that had once been so strong between them. Yet soon the rumors began, hinting that Julius too had become touched by the madness.

And then came that terrible year when the king and his nobles were further divided by policy, particularly his threatened alliance with England. King James was not only seeking for himself an English wife, but he intended to find suitable matches for his younger sons as well, solidifying the bond between our two fractious countries for good. This did not sit well with the nobles, especially the powerful Borders family of Hume, who hated the English and who were no friends of the king's. Trouble was brewing in Scotland. My father had always been loyal to the crown; Julius still revered his old master, Sir Alexander Hume. That was the year my father received a note of safe conduct from the king to go to England. He took Julius with him. Sir Archibald Douglas, fifth Earl of Angus and a powerful ally of the Earl of Hume, also went to England on a mission of his own, taking his nephew Sir George Douglas, Lord Kilwylie, with him. My father never returned from England. According to Julius he was still alive when they parted ways; but I could see the hurt in my brother's eyes as he told me how our father was driven to find the last missing piece of the mystery he had been in search of all these years, even if it meant killing himself in the process. He had gone straight from England to the Continent, with barely a word of explanation as to why. Over the years I received a few letters from him, but they had stopped a long time ago.

Julius returned from England to pursue the inglorious path he had chosen. He was a loose cannon—a dangerous and highly trained instrument of war that had been left without direction. He fell back into step with Hume and had been instrumental in supplanting the king in order to replace the king's son on the throne. Yet it was soon found out that he had been hatching a lucrative plot of his own that involved selling the soon-to-be king to his enemies in England, leaving the throne of Scotland open for the taking. And Julius stood to gain a fortune in lands and titles from his new master. But for his timely escape, my brother would be dead. And I really thought he had died, drawn to the same heartbreaking fate as our father.

I had been wrong. For just as the keeping of Blythe Hall fell to me, Julius had returned to make me suffer for all the pain I had inadvertently caused him—because of that one horrible day in the tower room long ago. And he was using blackmail to do it.

෴

I distinctly smelled fish. It wasn't just any fish, but a particularly odiferous sort, and it made no sense at all, coming to the surface as I was from a deep, obliterating sleep. The thought did flash through my mind that I was dreaming. But the smell was so pungent, the evocation so real, and my mind as blank as a virgin sheet of parchment, that I was inclined to believe I hadn't been dreaming of anything at all. Yet I most definitely smelled fish. Only when the voice accompanying the smell spoke did I know for a certainty that I was not dreaming.

"M'lady. M'lady," came Tam's soft yet insistent urging. I cracked an eye open. "Och, there ye are," he said cheerily and displayed a broad smile, one much too bright for so early in the morning. He then, unbelievably, proceeded to wave a little platter under my nose. The smell was beyond stomach-churning. "Look," he beamed proudly. "I caught ye a fine brown trout. Old Hendrick said as I could drop a line in the river, and so I did. Nothing like a breakfast of properly seasoned river meat tae face what you've got on your plate just now, aye?" His boyish features were attempting something on the order of sagelike wisdom—an intuitive knowing—which looked absurdly unnatural on the smooth, freckle-dusted skin.

I wanted to laugh but knew better. Instead I said, "I'm afraid that what I've got on my plate just now doesn't smell anything like a trout."

He raised a copper brow at this. "Oh, aye, it's a trout."

"It's not fresh then. You couldn't possibly have caught that today. It's likely been rotting in your saddlebag since we left Edinburgh."

"*It was not*," he insisted softly, scrunching up his nose and looking highly offended. "I just caught it! You're only confused by the herbs and whatnot I used to season it with."

"Herbs and whatnot? Please tell me you didn't cook it yourself as well."

"Of course I did! And ye'd do well tae not mock me, for the herbs I used are the ones what ward off evil." This last little tidbit, and one that from the smell of it seemed entirely true, was punctuated by a nod that shook the disheveled auburn curls.

"Evil?" I repeated, propping myself a little higher on the

bed to get a better look at said fish. A dead eye peered at me from the confines of the slightly charred head. It was the only part of the fish visible, for the rest was covered in what appeared to be a stinky plaster of mud, moss, weeds, chopped cabbage leaves, chunks of onion, garlic, and, I believed, coarsely ground pepper. The poor fish looked as disgusted as I was. "The only thing evil within these castle walls, Tam, is— I'm sorry to say—this fish." I offered a polite smile before pushing the platter away. Tam was, at heart, a dear lad, but frightfully misguided. He had a reverence for pagan superstitions that bordered on irksome. Yet he was harmless enough, and even at times highly entertaining. And he did have a way of seeming to anticipate my needs even before I understood what they were, for he was a gangly, nimble sort of lad who possessed exceptional hearing and always seemed to know what was afoot. However, in the wee hours of the morning I knew for a certainty that I did not need a dubiously seasoned, highly suspect fish.

Tam, however, was also tenacious, and now set the platter on my lap. I held up a hand to stop him. "Sorry, Tam. The fish was a kind gesture on your part, and I thank you for thinking of me. But I'm not particularly hungry just now. If you'll please set the platter over there, I'll be sure to see that it doesn't go to waste." This was not a lie. Although I had no intention of eating it myself, I was certain a dog could be found that would. I smiled.

"I'm no' daft or simple, in spite of what ye may think. Ye really need tae eat this, m'lady."

"Really?" I said. I was not used to my groom ordering me around. "And why would that be?"

"You need tae eat this because it'll give ye the strength ye need tae deal with that man."

"Ah, I see." And I believed that I did, for *evil* was a word not bandied about lightly by Tam. "And by *that man* I assume you are referring to Master Julius."

"No." He gave a grave shake of his head. I frowned. "Sir
George Douglas, m'lady. I'm referring tae Sir George. The ingrate's gone into the tower."

"Ingrate?" I repeated, frowning slightly. "Tam, please, he's
a nobleman. Wait. Do you mean to tell me he's . . . he's not
sleeping outside my door?"

"M'lady," he said softly, soothingly. No one could deny
that his voice was particularly calming. "But for yourself and
Mistress Marion, the entire castle's been up and about for
hours. Ye can hardly expect a man like Sir George tae sit at
your feet and grovel all day like a besotted hound."

I reached beyond his shoulder and threw back the curtain.
Sure enough, sunlight streamed in from the tall arched windows, bringing with it a mild midmorning breeze. "I expected
no such thing," I replied, unable to hide the mild irritation in
my voice. "And what do you mean he's in the tower?"

"Not just the tower. I've been watching him. He's been
wandering the corridors and climbing the stairways since well
before dawn."

"I don't wonder. He couldn't have been comfortable on
the floor. He was just looking for a better place to sleep,
Tam."

"Sleep? Och, he dinnae look like he was in the mood for
sleep. No, he's searching for something."

I gave the boyish face a mildly reproving glance. "What
could he possibly be searching for in this old castle?" Yet the
words had no sooner left my lips than a disturbing thought
struck me.

"Indeed," said Tam, reading the look on my face. "But he's
no' searching any longer. He's found it. And he's bound and
determined tae break down the door and see it for himself."

᪥

Never was a fish so unpalatable, but I ate the required few
bites in order to leave my bed. Once Tam was satisfied, I

hastily dressed and followed him down the stairs and out the main doorway opening onto the upper bailey. It was definitely midmorning, for the courtyard was alive with the bustle of servants going about their daily business, weaving their way around our boisterous, armored visitors, who were engaging in lively pursuits of their own. Dice, cards, even a chess set had made its appearance under the gentle morning sun. And much to my chagrin, a group appearing to be made up entirely of Sir George's men had gotten a hold of two roosters and were in the process of baiting the old birds, riling them up into a cacophony of flapping wings and sinister crows. Nothing good could come of that, I knew, and doubted very much that Hendrick would want to lose a perfectly good bird in the name of amusement.

"Put those birds down!" I cried, marching toward the tower in the wake of my very determined groom. At the sound of my voice, the men did throw the birds down, and then they closed up the circle so that all I could see was their broad backs. My jaw dropped. Glowering, I was about to change direction until Tam pulled me forward.

"Best let my lord Kilwylie handle that."

"Right," I said, seeing the soundness of his advice. A group of Sir Matthew's men waved at us. I waved back. At least they were employed in honest work, polishing their boots and sharpening their swords.

Tam had not been lying. Sir George was already standing inside my father's chapel when we found him. The full colored light from the vast windows reflected off his highly polished cuirass and dazzled the hilt of his sword. The heavy door that had been locked these many years was hanging off its hinges, the wood of the casement in splinters.

"What . . . have you done?" I gasped, bringing my hand over my mouth. I was unwilling to step beyond the threshold, for my heart was beating with an unnatural fury. It had been years since I had laid eyes on this room, and many more since

I dared step on the floor. It was, in a sense, the lodestone of my youth—a room so intricately tangled with my personal history that it still cast a perverse and frightful hold over me, not the least because it was the legacy of my father. Seeing it so, violated by this brash and obtrusive visitor, caused my heart to ache and my whole body to tremble with another uncharacteristic surge of rage. I feared I was becoming an angry person, so familiar had the heady rush of irritation begun to feel. But Blythe Hall was mine to protect now, and Sir George had just pierced the very heart of it.

At the sound of my voice the huge knight turned, and the full force of his magnificent green gaze settled on me. My sudden outburst had startled him, for although his eyes were wide and penetrating, his face still held that look of wonder that the room—this remarkable and strange little chapel—never failed to evoke. For it was literally (as it had been designed to be) like crossing over from earth into the realm of heaven—a small, wondrous portal where man could dwell and converse for a few moments with God's own angels. I could see that Sir George, a man who had been on the hunt for something, had not been expecting this. Seeing him gazing at me in speechless awe, seeming utterly humbled by the sheer magnitude of the creation that surrounded him, I felt the anger that had been coursing inside me fizzle away, and a small, begrudging smile surface.

It took a moment for this change to register on the face of Lord Kilwylie, for the room had such a hold on him. But then, seeing that I was not about to charge him with fists flailing, however insignificant they might be, his face changed too, and the charmer's smile appeared.

"Isabeau . . . forgive me," he uttered, his brazen gaze containing for the first time a look of contrition. It was unsettling, and I was sorry it didn't last more than a moment, for as quickly as it came, it passed, and was replaced with a more familiar gaze. His beautiful dark head tilted as his hand, slightly unsteady, beckoned me to join him. "Come, my gentle Lady of Blythe; come stand beside me and let us marvel upon this heavenly masterpiece together."

The sound of my name, whispered in such a way, had a disquieting effect, and I found myself drawn to him, and the room, regardless of the trepidation that warned me against it.

And then Tam laid a gentle hand on my shoulder.

It was this touch, calming and crystallizing, from the young man who cared for my horses—who accompanied me on all my outings and who was so good to Mme. Seraphina—that finally brought me back to my senses. I ignored Sir George's compelling invitation while consciously reviving my anger. "This . . . this," I began, shaking slightly, "is a sacred place, Sir George, and one that is off limits to all but family. You must come out at once!"

"Again, I beg your forgiveness," he said, and his smile faded as his hand dropped to his side. He turned his back on the room and walked toward us, but stopped well short of the threshold. "Isabeau," he said, his face suffused with contrition. "It was never my wish for you to be angry with me. 'Tis just that I've heard rumors of this place for so long. I wanted to see it for myself."

"You should have asked first instead of breaking down the door."

He smiled then, kindly yet condescendingly, as the hint of a stifled chuckle escaped his lips. "And would you, my dear, have opened it for me if I had?"

He knew the answer to this, as he had always known it, yet it didn't justify the fact that he had kicked in the door. "Sir George," I said at last, fighting the frustration and helplessness that crept into my voice. "There are things here you should not meddle with. This room, sir, is one of those things."

"But there, my sweet, I believe you are wrong. Do you not know that there is a sculpture here by Donatello, a painting

by Bellini, and three from Botticelli, not to mention the spectacular triptych by the Fleming Van der Goes? Such treasures
should not be tucked away at the top of an old keep, hidden
behind a locked door."

"They were my father's treasures, sir, and they remain hidden behind a locked door because that was his wish. And I intend to honor his memory by keeping it that way."

"So you do know about them?" he questioned, and saw
that I did. "Isabeau, what a mysterious creature you are.
Come. Please, my dear? I want nothing more than for you to
come and tell me about this room."

Sir George, standing to his full towering height and looking splendid surrounded by the glory of the room, did not
move, did not take a step in my direction, but stood very still
as he extended once again his large and capable hand. Inexplicably I felt a welling desire to join him, to take his hand and
gaze once again upon all that was left of the memory of my father. In my mind's eye I recalled each and every exquisite
piece hanging on the walls, placed on pedestals, or gracing the
unique altarpiece. It was a room charged with emotion, for
these were my father's treasures, these works were how he
measured his days. It had been from the start his objective to
transform the very place that had transformed him, and each
work reflected the secret in his heart that drove him. For me
each painting, brilliant with its pigmented oils and cleverly
placed brushstrokes, the gilded and bejeweled icons looking
on from above, the playful cherubs in the clouds, or the marble statues that had been chipped and coaxed to reveal the divine being within, were little more than blasphemy, for this
room with its mesmerizing décor was the glittering harlot that
had finally and inexorably lured my family away.

And yet the attraction of the room, and the madness that
spawned it, was hard to ignore.

There flashed before my eyes for the briefest moment that
image again: the golden man of my vision. My heart came

alive, beating with something stronger than anger. I was quite unsettled by it, until I looked once more at Sir George. Unlike Julius, he was not a man who hid his feelings or toyed with the feelings of others, nor was he pure like the man from my vision. But he was a man, and he made no secret as to what he wanted. His hand was still extended, his eyes beckoning. Why not join him? I thought. For God's sake, why not? What harm could it do? It was just a room; he was just a man. My foot stirred and I took a step. That's when Tam's voice whispered in my ear: "Dinnae forget about the sheep."

The sheep? It was an odd thing for the young man to whisper, and it caught me off guard. What sheep? Whose sheep? And then it registered exactly what he was talking about. My sheep!

I looked at my groom with mouth agape. "Dear heavens," I uttered, and took a small step backward. "Sir George," I said, suddenly turning to the dashing Lord Kilwylie. "I'm very sorry, but I don't have time to tell you about this room, and even if I did, I'm afraid I wouldn't be able to tell you much. This was my father's collection; it has little, if anything, to do with me. However, what does matter to me is finding my livestock. The men are still loitering about the castle." I motioned feebly beyond the chapel room to the far window, where, below in the vast courtyards, both upper and lower, the men were entertaining themselves. "There's a cockfight," I said, recalling the shameful display. He grinned. "My point is, sir, that it's late morning and no one has yet stirred. I have less than two days to find my sheep. Tam," I said, turning to the young man, "please ready our horses, and while you're at it, find Hendrick and tell him to send the carpenter up here to repair this door. Sir George, feel free to stay as long as you like. You'll have to excuse me, but I have an estate to run." I made a curtsey and turned to go; the sound of laughter stopped me.

Sir George Douglas, Lord Kilwylie, was laughing at me.

"Oh, sweetheart," he said, a smile lighting his strong, handsome face, "but I do intend to stay. However, not before I find and return your precious sheep. The reason I am here now, if truth be told, is because I wanted to see you before we left, and to lay before you once again my intentions." In three great strides of the powerful legs, tightly encased in fine blue hose, he was beside me, sweeping me up in his arms. "I beg that you will forgive me; for this place has a way of altering the senses, just as does the mistress who owns it. And I intend, Isabeau, to win you both." He then employed his lips to convince me, and I found myself very willing to accept them. But to my great surprise he stopped short. "Dear God!" he exclaimed and drew back ungallantly. "I'm sorry, but what the devil have you been eating? Your breath smells like a Sicilian cesspool festering under the hot Mediterranean sun."

My jaw dropped. Sir George gently, and very politely after such an ignoble slight, released me. He tried to smile, but his face was comically contorted. And then I looked beyond him to Tam. My groom was still there, pressed near the wall of the landing and peering at me with a smugly satisfied look affixed to his freckle-dusted face.

Damn him and his stinky little fish! There had never been any evil to ward off but for poor, dear, unsuspecting Sir George. Wisely, Tam turned and vanished down the stairs with a speed and lightness of foot that even the best of the king's spies would have killed to possess. Luckily for Tam, I was not nearly so quick.

Chapter 6
DISTURBING
REVELATIONS

AFTER ASSURING A SLIGHTLY PUT-OUT SIR GEORGE that I would indeed have my teeth shining and my mouth smelling of cloves by the time of his return, and after promising myself to have a word with my meddlesome groom, who had providently made himself scarce, I was still disquieted to find that the sight of Sir George standing in the center of my father's whimsical chapel, illuminated by the parti-colored light and with a look of sublime wonder transforming his strong, confident features, had affected me more than I liked to admit. To see such a holy place entered with violence, and then to view the transgressor in the midst of his transformation while he struggled to understand just what he had stumbled upon, moved me beyond words. And it caused me to wonder for the first time if the odd visions I'd been having ever since my arrival—the visions of the pure and breathtaking man—were somehow connected with this bold and unsettling knight.

Maybe I had been meant to see him, witnessing for myself this small but vulnerable chink in the steely armor of his pride, where the masterful image of an angel could render him speechless—and Sir George, to my knowledge, had never been speechless. Perhaps, just as the redemption of Blythe Hall was my destiny, maybe Sir George was too, and I was only now realizing it. Had he not always been there in the shadows waiting for me? Was not his past already intricately tangled with my brother's? I knew I had always judged him a little harshly as a result of the fate of Julius, and I was, admittedly, frightened of his raw, sensual masculinity. My only excuse for this was that for me, coming fresh from the convent as I had, a man like Lord Kilwylie was a shock to the senses—especially so because his spectacular and unapologetic gaze was artfully pitched to awaken deeply suppressed urges. He had a dark nature indeed; but I had been given a glimpse that suggested there was more to this brash, physical, hard-living man than he allowed the world to see. Perhaps he really did need something as simple as honest love to draw from him that perfect and pure being of my vision. He had asked me for it himself—a loving and gentle hand to guide him the rest of the way, he had said. There was never any doubt that Sir George Douglas knew very well the kind of man he was, just as he had some inkling of how I saw him. Perhaps it was time I grew up and threw aside my childish fears. Here was a fine man, from a noble family, who was willing to cast his fate with a family touched by madness, and even to protect me from it. Yet there was one more reason that perhaps surpassed all others, and that, quite simply, was that Sir George Douglas of Kilwylie, to my knowledge, was the only man in Scotland that Julius had reason to fear.

Within minutes of his departure from the tower room all the knights loitering in the courtyards—all the men-at-arms filling their idle time with cajolery and aimless pursuits—had packed up their belongings, strapped on their helmets, cuirasses, and sword belts, and ridden out of the castle gates in near silence contemplating their new objectives. For Sir George's men this meant tracking down and recapturing the sizable herd of livestock that had been missing for more than four days. It was a hard, physical task they were on. There were only two days left before the window of justice would close and our prized flock of sheep would be lost for good. Weigh this against the fact that if, by some miracle, they did succeed, they would not personally stand to gain anything for their efforts. No, the onus lay strictly on Lord Kilwylie, who was certain that the return of the Blythe flock meant the acceptance of the marriage proposal so publicly laid at my feet. A marriage proposal that, when viewed in the full light of day, seemed reasonable. I would accept Sir George's offer upon his successful return. If, however, he failed his mission, I would still likely accept him; after all, the people of Blythemuir deserved a strong leader, one who would protect them from the vicious cycle of retaliation, robbery, and murder that plagued our land. No one could doubt young Lord Kilwylie's ability as a military leader. But I would not think of that now, just as I would not entertain the thought that Sir George might fail.

With Sir George warmed and fed by the hopeful prospect of a wealthy and willing bride upon his successful return, Sir Matthew was driven by quite a different emotion. It was no less powerful, I believed, for during our brief interview he informed me that instead of returning to Edinburgh with his men, as the king expected him to do, he would employ them on a task of state and scour the distance from Blythemuir to Berwick in order to apprehend and punish my irreverent, outlawed brother. The events of the previoius night were still fresh in his mind, and he was visibly possessed by a determination to recover his stolen swords. I did ask if I might impose on him to recover my pilfered silver—but only if he had the chance. For this I was awarded a self-chastising smile.

It was Sir Matthew's great misfortune, however, that he

never asked me if I had any notion of where Julius and his men might be hiding. If he had, I might have felt obliged to offer the fact that I had seen him quite recently, and therefore he must be close by. I also might have revealed, if pressed, that Julius was, in fact, blackmailing me. But dear Sir Matthew wasn't thinking very clearly. There was a matter of pride, I believed, and a pressing need to repair what had so recently been wounded. He informed me that he would use a combination of instinct and logic to catch Julius, for he was a professional soldier, and this lethal combination had never failed him.

As I watched the King's Guard gallop somberly out the gate, fresh on the heels of the Kilwylie men and bent on retribution, I felt strangely relieved. It wasn't because of any false hope that they would catch Julius; it was because I knew for a fact that they wouldn't. It pleased me to know that, reprobate that he was, my brother defied all logic, and as for instincts, no mortal man could possibly compete with the devil.

With both small armies out the gates, joining our own men already on the Hot Trodd, and Julius gone to ground until God only knew when, I, thankfully, was finally able to let out my breath and turn my mind fully to the task I had undertaken: the managing of Blythe Hall.

Managing a castle was a bit more complicated than I had assumed. After having a word with Hendrick about the chapel, I in turn learned that the staff was already employed in putting the household to rights after yesterday's explosion of activity. There was an extensive list compiled of all our missing silver. Mutton Johnny, the head cook, came to complain about our near-empty larders and the state of the buttery. And I was treated to a particularly troubling account when three young women near my own age, Maggie Scott, eighteen, her sister Gwyneth, who was sixteen, and Kate Lindsey, seventeen (all three employed in the castle dairy), claimed that they were visited in the night by a very affectionate soldier, and might, in fact, be pregnant, although it was far too early to tell.

There were other problems too, most of these concerning poaching, the wool trade, and the new-sown fields.

My mind was aswirl after leaving Hendrick's office, and I headed to my own chambers wondering every step of the way what I had gotten myself into. It was there, in the solar, that I found Marion sitting with Mme. Seraphina at the table under the window. Marion had not yet dressed. She was lounging in a dressing gown of pale pink, her auburn hair tumbling down her back as she daintily plucked figs from a platter. Even in this state of undress she looked entirely more composed and better suited to the title of Lady of the Manor than me. The hem of my russet gown was caked in mud, my nerves were frayed, and I was seriously considering marrying a Douglas. Oh, how I envied her spoiled, self-centered nature.

"Isa!" she cried upon seeing me, the fig poised before her smiling mouth. "Oh, isn't it exciting? All the men have gone, my cousin after your sheep and Sir Matthew back to Edinburgh, and here we are, all alone on the edge of the world."

"Actually, Sir Matthew and his men have not yet gone back to Edinburgh. They're taking a little detour. And we are hardly alone; the English reside just over there," I said, gesturing to the window and the sweeping land beyond the Tweed. "But let us not dwell on that. How are you this morning?" I asked, and pulled over a chair to join them. "Did you sleep well? I hope so. You look positively glowing." This I remarked because she did, and it caused me to direct a quizzical grin at Seraphina. "Truthfully, I was afraid that all the commotion of last night, especially the shameful robbery, might have put you off, and that you'd be demanding to return to Edinburgh—you're not going to demand you return, are you?"

"Oh, of course not," she said with a barely concealed twinkle in her eye. Her hand, holding the half-eaten fig daintily aloft, made a sweeping gesture of the room. "And miss all this? I'd rather lounge about the halls of your drafty old castle—as your guest—than live at the palace and have to serve a middle-aged princess."

"Why, that's truthfully spoken, my dear," Seraphina commended her with a nod. Tolerant, although not entirely approving of Marion, Seraphina was quite used to her by now. Her round, jovial head tilted slightly as she added, "May I make another observation? I believe the last time Mistress Boyd looked this radiant was her birthday last when she danced with the king."

"Oh, I remember!" I said, picking up a warm saffron bun. It smelled wonderful, and I suddenly realized how hungry I was. I stuffed quite a bit more into my mouth than was proper and, still chewing, remarked: "You wore that crimson gown with the cream bodice and gold embroidery. I teased you about it, stating that you looked like one of the pope's cardinals, or a seasoned courtesan, rather than a proper lady-in-waiting. You certainly caught his eye that night, though. He may be painfully shy around women, but our dear Jamie was quite smitten."

"My uncle Archibald gave me that gown," she offered complacently.

"Really?" I said, and swallowed the remains of my mouthful. I set down the roll. "Old Bell-the-Cat? Why ever would he give you a gown like that?"

"So that Mistress Boyd would get noticed," Seraphina answered, smiling a little at Marion.

"But . . . that's ridiculous. Who wouldn't notice Marion?" I had a point, I believed, for in my opinion Marion Boyd was not a young woman to be overlooked—especially at the court of a young bachelor king who surrounded himself with men.

Seraphina patted my hand gently and with another kindly smile added, "With you in the room, dear, it's often hard for anybody else to be noticed."

With my face reddening, brow furrowing, and head shaking in open disagreement, I pulled my hand away and protested, "Oh, that's not true, Seraphina, not by a long shot!"

Marion, nibbling unconcernedly on another fig, stopped long enough to add, "Actually, it is, dear."

I don't know why, but that statement depressed me slightly, especially coming from the two women who mattered to me most. Yet if it really was true, or at least their opinions had some validation, it might be the reason for all the unwanted attention of late—and that dreaded list in possession of the king. I took another unladylike bite of the bun before noting my governess's quizzical gaze.

"I thought you already ate?"

"No," I replied.

"Did Tam not bring you a fish this morning?"

I stopped in midchew, recalling the unpleasant way my morning had begun. "Ah, yes," I uttered, "as a matter of fact he did." I swallowed. "But it wasn't cooked right. It was inedible, which reminds me, will you call for some cloves and cinnamon? A basin of water too, and some soap. My breath smells like a Sicilian cesspool, or so I've been told. And I could use a good wash."

Marion sniffed in my direction. "I'll have to agree with you. You do. My heavens, what on earth have you been up to?"

"You really don't want to know."

"Oh yes, I believe that I do." Her eyes, those large, peaty pools of curiosity, were wide with anticipatory delight. It was a reminder that Marion lived for my misadventures, and recalling my morning, I knew she would not be disappointed.

I waited until Seraphina left the room, for although Marion had no idea what was really going on, being eternally self-absorbed as she was, Seraphina was a good deal wiser. Her powers of observation were astute, but more important, she had another tool equally as effective: Tam. Obviously she knew about the fish, which meant she likely knew about Sir George's desire to find the Chapel of Angels. However, I was pretty confident she did not know about Julius and his nocturnal visit, and I thought it best to keep it that way. "All right," I said to Marion, "you are aware that your cousin wants to be the next Lord Blythe?"

"Very." She leaned in closer. "As I've been telling you, Isabeau, 'tis no secret."

"Yes, well, I believe I've convinced myself it would be in my best interest to marry him . . . if he successfully returns our sheep."

Her dark, perfectly sculpted brow lifted. "And if he fails?"

"If he fails," I repeated, looking levelly at her expectant face, "why, I'm not sure. Likely I'll do the same."

She swallowed and exclaimed, "My dear Isa . . . , that's . . . wonderful!"

"Is it?" I asked in breathy dismay. "Because I don't know if it is. I don't know much of anything anymore. I'm not thinking straight. I believe I'm desperate, because all I can think of is getting my sheep back, returning Blythe Hall to its former glory, and getting Julius out of Scotland before he gets himself killed. And speaking of Julius; somehow he entered the castle last night and possibly got three dairymaids pregnant. Hendrick says it's too early to tell yet. However, he's spiteful, is Julius. You'd never know it to look at him—all charm and entirely self-composed on the outside. But on the inside, in his heart, it's another matter. Since he can't be Lord Blythe, I think he's planning to overrun Blythemuir with an army of his own bastards—from the inside out—because he knows that I'll be responsible for every one of his misbegotten brats. He's bound and determined to ruin me yet!"

"That's . . . impossible," Marion said.

"Is it? He's Julius, Marion. He escaped death, returned

from a lifelong exile, broke into my castle, overthrew the King's Guard, and stole my silver. To him nothing is impossible!"

"Ummm, actually, dear, I believe it is." It was said quietly, seriously, accompanied by the nervous wringing of hands. Marion never wrung her hands. At the sight my heart began pounding in my ears.

"Marion . . . what is it?" I uttered, the cold fingers of fear creeping into my voice and down my spine. "What's happened?"

"Julius. He was with me."

"WHAT?" I cried. This news sent me reeling back on my chair, my arm narrowly missing the wine decanter that sat near Marion. "Oh God! He did not! Oh, no, no, no . . ." I lurched forward and leaned across the table. "Please tell me he did not do what I think he did."

"Well," she said, attempting, of all things, a smile. "I guess that depends on what you think he did?"

"You know very well what I think he did!" I was not amused. I did not wish to be toyed with.

Marion, finally showing mercy, demurred. "Of course, I do. I'm sorry." And then she averted her splendid dark eyes; the proud tilt of her head slipped downward, and a troubled hand began massaging the area just above her left brow. It was a moment before she had the courage to look at me again, admitting, "And he did exactly what you think he did."

"Holy merciful Mother of Christ!" I swore, unable to control the rage and anger that took me. Horrified, I brought my hand directly over my mouth, then removed it to utter: "Peter and all the saints in heaven, I am so sorry . . . so very sorry." I looked at her, attempting to make sense of what she was telling me as tears of remorse welled in my eyes. "My dearest friend," I said at last. "And under my own roof! It is unconscionable! Whatever have I done? What evil have I unleashed? I never should have brought you here. . . ." I held her wide, vacuous gaze with my own, vowing: "I will kill him myself for this vile insult. I will hunt him down like the indiscriminate hare he is—rutting in my warrens, breeding in my hills—and I will bring him to heel and crush him like no man has ever had the courage to do before."

"Perhaps . . ." It was Marion's voice that brought me back from my fantasy of violence. Her tone held no outrage, no remorse, but something more along the lines of gently reproving guilt. I looked up and saw a hint of a smile on her lips. "Perhaps ye missed the part where I told you that I invited him?"

I stared at her then, unmoving, watching closely to see if it was her pride that made the wild claim, or truth. By God, it was truth! "You . . . invited him?" I said, incredulity thick in my voice. I had known Marion a long time; she was a terrible flirt, but she was only a flirt. She was a noblewoman, after all, and, whether she liked it or not, her virginity carried great value. That she should so carelessly throw it away—and on my undeserving, profligate brother—was too great a tragedy to comprehend. And an even greater tragedy was that he had allowed it. Damn him to hell!

Marion's eyes narrowed. "Do not look at me like that, Isabeau!" she said firmly. "This is not the convent, my dear friend, and we're no longer little girls. I'm not ashamed of what I've done."

"Not ashamed? But you should be!"

"Why?" she challenged heatedly. "Because I fancy him—or because he's your brother?"

I stared at her impassioned face, noting the firm set of her jaw and the flashing eyes. Hers was not a look of a woman who'd been misused. And then I recalled how she had looked when I entered the room—she had been perfectly radiating happiness. I exhaled, feeling as if I had just been punched in the stomach. "I don't know," I answered truthfully. "But I believe your family has certain expectations of you. And I'm sorry; I wasn't even aware that you knew Julius."

"Well, I didn't know him. I mean, I met him—years ago when we were at the convent. Mostly I just knew of him . . . from my older sisters. He had quite a reputation, you know."

"I know."

"And now I *know* him too."

I closed my eyes, because looking at her glowing face was just too painful. Like myself, Marion was at an age where she should be married, but she wasn't. It certainly wasn't for a lack of suitors but because her family was a bit too ambitious, and Marion was a bit too beautiful. A dangerous combination any way one looked at it. She had been paraded in front of the young king for over a year now—they were cousins of a sort—and she had flirted with him shamelessly. Yet James had been too much the gentleman to take advantage of what the Boyds were offering, or perhaps he had just been too politically savvy. Julius was neither a gentleman nor politically savvy. He was an opportunist with the morals of a feral cat—another dangerous combination. And he had pounced on my flirtatious friend like the animal he was. The thought disgusted me. And then, struck with another thought—a more wistfully hopeful thought—I suggested, "Are you certain that it really happened? Could you have just been fantasizing that it happened because of all the excitement of the robbery? It's perfectly all right. You've a lively imagination," I added, trying not to think of myself and my own lively nocturnal visions. "What if you thought he was with you when he was really with the dairymaids?"

I'd never seen a brow arch with so much venom, or lips purse with so much disdain. "Are you quite finished?" she snarled. "I should be highly offended you even suggested such a thing! Unlike you, I know how to grab and hold a man's attention, Isabeau, and I did. I'm sorry you feel violated by the notion, but you're just going to have to accept it. I enjoy men. And I enjoyed your brother—several times as a matter of fact, if you're curious to know."

"I'm not," I said, closing my eyes while willing my anger to abate. "And I believe you. You've done a marvelous job of convincing me." I looked at her. "So, if Julius spent the night with you, then who molested the poor dairymaids?"

"Well, it certainly wasn't your brother. He stayed until well after dawn."

"After the sun was up? Are you certain?"

"I think I know very well what the term *dawn* means! I may not see a sunrise often, but I do know it happens every day—and quite early too." She lowered her voice and looked levelly at me. "For such a kind, gentle, forgiving soul, you've got an awfully negative opinion of your own brother."

"If you had a brother like mine, you would too," I replied, and stood to leave.

"Where are you going?"

"Hopefully to have a word with your lover."

She appeared amused by this. "And where do ye intend to find him? I've already searched, but a man like that comes and goes like a ghost." Marion, with a languid smile, shrugged and plucked a piece of cheese from the tray. "However, if ye do find him," she began, popping it into her mouth, "give him a wee kiss from me."

⸭

Marion and her glib attitude toward the improprieties that had taken place under my roof had me flustered, so flustered I nearly upset a basin of steaming water as I dashed out the door. The chambermaids, shepherded by Mme. Seraphina, had arrived. They had brought not only hot water and towels but clean hose, a freshly pressed gown of rose silk with slashed sleeves, along with a finely embroidered cream chemise to go with it. It was, admittedly, a far more respectable-looking ensemble than the kirtle and yesterday's hose I had thrown on this morning. But I had no time to wash and change, because the wily fox was close, so close I could almost smell him, and I would be damned if I didn't bring him to ground before he could bury me. I couldn't explain any of this to my governess; there was no time, and so, left with no choice, I matched her look of surprise, added a fleeting grimace of apology, and grabbed a handful of cloves from the bowl as I ran out the door.

Having pleasantly fresher breath, I began my hunt, questioning the staff, searching every room, chamber, and antechamber, combing the outbuildings, wandering the corridors and peering into every nook and cranny I came across, and still I came up empty-handed. Because the castle had been filled with so many men, all of them strangers, it was nearly impossible to determine whether Julius was among them. He was, after all, a master of disguise. However, there was one suspicious instance reported by two lads from the kitchens. It came from the Mackenzie brothers, Jerome and Brendon, and just like the boys, their story was suspect at best. The boys' father was one of the shepherds who had gone missing. The lads themselves had been shepherds as well until some incident occurred a month ago that landed them a year serving in the castle under the watchful eye of Hendrick and Mutton Johnny, the cook.

Since they had somewhat of a reputation for invention and tomfoolery, I found it hard to take their story seriously. But they looked sincere, even slightly shaken by what they had seen. Around dawn the boys had gone to the storerooms under the great hall for another cask of mead for our guests when they spied a white form running down the passageway. It was her, they insisted, crossing themselves. The white lady. At the mere mention of her name a wave of gooseflesh covered me, causing every hair to stand on end. I fought to remain calm, to breathe deeply and steadily as they began educating me on the apparition, for the white lady of Blythe Hall was now legend. And, according to this legend as told by Brendon and Jerome, the mere sight of her caused madness — why, didn't I know that the old laird had gone mad at the sight of her? It was at that point that I reminded them: "You do re-alize the old laird you speak of was my father?" It likely hadn't occurred to them, and they nodded apologetically.

"The young master went mad too," the taller boy, Jerome, offered softly.

"Yes, he did. And what about the young mistress?" I ques-tioned, looking levelly at them. "Do you have any comment there?"

"Ye?"

"Yes. Me. Am I also mad?"

"Umm . . ." Jerome looked to his slightly shorter, slightly ganglier brother and shrugged. "I . . . dinnae believe so?" It was apparent by the slight inflection on the word *so* that there might be a question there, a question I was not about to give them the satisfaction of answering. The boys next admitted that they didn't get a good look at this mysterious fleeting white form. It was traveling fast—a blur. Besides, they were in no mind to chase such a thing, for fear of going mad. But they did swear, after I posed the question, that it was definitely a lady, flowing gown, white kerchief, and all. They would know a lady when they saw one!

But the legend, the madness associated with it, and the sud-den appearance of the white lady wandering down a subter-ranean passageway in the hour following sunrise, smacked of Julius.

Hendrick and I inspected the passageways where the inci-dent occurred. But everywhere we looked there was nothing to indicate that Julius had ever been there. Perhaps he was a ghost, I mused, for his ability to appear and disappear wher-ever he liked, at my expense, was uncanny. But I knew very well he was no ghost. A ghost would have had more decency than to coerce my dearest friend into amoral, lustful acts, or so I liked to believe. However, I wasn't entirely certain about that either. In fact, I wasn't certain about anything anymore except that Julius wasn't in the castle.

Tam had my horse ready and waiting long before I got to the stables. I was alone. Only Hendrick knew what I was about, and I had appealed to him to let me solve this problem on my own. Begrudgingly he agreed. Tam, however, being my groom, was a thorn I could not so easily shake, and truthfully, although he created terrible mischief at times, he was a good companion. He even apologized for the fish incident and made the feeble excuse that he was only trying to help. He promised to keep his nose out of my personal affairs in the future. Tam was sincere, and I believed him.

We rode under an azure sky dappled with fleecy white clouds. The clouds, like fat, contented little sheep, made me think of the animals we had lost and the devastation that would come because of it. Could we buy more? How long and how much would it take to rebuild the numbers we once had? Would we be able to fulfill the demand of the carders, spinners, and weavers who depended on us? Or would they turn elsewhere? Would our men turn elsewhere and steal what had been taken from them? As we rode over the gentle hills, skirting newly planted fields and orchards in full bloom, heading instead into the heather where the tender grasses and succulent wildflowers that fattened our sheep grew, I folded my hands, entangling them in the reins, and prayed.

There was so much I didn't know, there were so many forces at work against me, that I felt entirely overwhelmed. And, most distressingly, there was that small voice in the back of my head—a voice echoed by Sir George and my brother— suggesting that I was not cut out for this—this untamed life. Last night, mere hours after my arrival, each man had made his point. One was blackmailing me into engaging the madness that had destroyed him; the other only wished to be the Laird of Blythe Hall. I wasn't even certain what I wanted anymore, or how I was to govern my people when I could barely govern myself. I rode beside Tam, my head full, my heart heavy, as I prayed for guidance and strength.

I prayed to God, to Jesus, and to Saint Jude, the patron saint of hopeless causes. I was born on his feast day; I thought it appropriate. And then I prayed to my mother, hoping she would listen from wherever she was, hoping she would hear me. It was during that silent prayer, composed from atop a walking horse, that something marvelous and totally unexpected happened: the sun came out from behind a cloud and illuminated the land. Although this in itself was not unusual, for the sun had made an appearance many times since I'd left the castle, this time it was somehow different—brighter, more luminous. The peaty brown Tweed, snaking along peacefully in the valley below, weaving around the distant castle, was transformed—appearing as if it were a river of spectacularly cut diamonds. Every ray of sun that touched the surface exploded in a burst of prismatic light, igniting the countryside. My eye caught the tower room, high above the castle walls. The magnificent stained-glass window stood out from the grayness of the stone, depicting Saint Matthew the Evangelist, with wings, carved out of magnificent jewels from the Orient.

With effort I pulled my gaze away and turned to face the hills. Purple moor grass and bell heather shimmered like a thousand ells of the finest satin unrolling before us, interwoven with delicate splashes of white and yellow atop a foundation of living green. The wind, infused with the heady perfume of spring, stirred from the north like a mighty breath and carried on its gentle fingers a shower of white petals. It was like a dream, a vivid yet surreal dream where everything was familiar and foreign at once. But I was very aware that I was not dreaming. And then came the warmth, gentle yet absolute, and it filled me, penetrating all the way to my bones. Every sense I possessed was heightened; every nerve in my body tingled. I felt alive, I felt invincible, and I wanted this feeling to last. I needed it to last. I needed it in order to face what lay before me, and so I closed my eyes, tilting my face toward the sun. I was soaking up every drop of it.

That was when I saw him—the golden man from my vision: my dream, my angel.

The clearness of the image, the subtle detail, the intensity behind the smile, startled me. And then came a pang of longing so primal, so sudden, that I was forced to open my eyes as the cool air rushed into my lungs. I looked at Tam. He was beside me, a gentle smile on his lips as his hair, peppered with apple blossoms, fluttered on the soft breeze. His boyish face looked innocent enough, yet I had the strangest feeling he had been inside my head—that he had seen what I had seen. I blushed at the thought and noted that the world looked normal once again.

❧

Though I was still no closer to finding Julius, the fresh air had done wonders for my nerves, and I found I was less oppressed by the thought of him lying in wait nearby. The truth was, the land surrounding Blythe Hall unfolded in every direction, twisting and undulating between trickling burns and turgid rivers, rife with forested hills, hidden glades, petulant bogs, and the high, sweeping trackless expanse of the moors. It was a land where a thousand head of sheep or cattle could disappear, becoming entirely hidden from the population that traversed it daily. It was a land that championed the intrepid outlaw, warm and protective as a mother's embrace. Julius knew this land, and he had chosen his hiding place wisely. I was a fool to think I could find him when the best of Roxburghshire had failed. He was likely across the border; perhaps he even owned land there—a homecoming gift from Mother England. It would be ironic, and Julius, above all else, loved irony. I was not about to cross the Tweed. My brother would come to me when he was ready. And when he came I would be ready as well.

Smiling, resolved, I turned my sights instead to the forested hillsides we were approaching, where white birch, steadfast

pine, and stolid oak sprang from the ground like tenacious gi-
ants, and where the old peel tower, built in the time of David
I, and fallen to ruin after the turbulent years of Robert the
Bruce, could just be seen poking a wobbly parapet above the
canopy of green. Crumbling and moss-covered, it still stood
guard over the cleared and rolling glens of Blythemuir, where
the timber-and-thatch homes of the shepherds were to be
found.

Tam and I cantered silently along a narrow, winding road,
our horses' footfalls muffled by a blanket of leaves and soft
needles. The going was steep in places, and there were times
when the trees resembled a battalion of bare-legged soldiers,
the lower branches and bark having been stripped by hungry
deer. And then the forest thinned, and we found ourselves
thrust upon the open, wind-scoured lip of a great hill. The old
peel tower sat crumbling deep in the shadow of the trees to
our right, while before us the land fell away in a breathtaking
view of verdant green bisected by the silvery trail of a burn as
it tumbled and careened to the marshy edge of a little lake.
Whitewashed cottages, split-rail folds, and rambling shearing
sheds belonging to the men who husbanded our sheep dotted
the edge of the meadow. It was a strategic location. Every cottar would have a commanding view of the greening sward
where the sheep and other livestock should have been idly fattening. However, at the moment it was eerily void of grazing
animals. I glanced at Tam. He shrugged and started down the
well-worn path to the nearest cottage.

The cottage, quaint and with a puffing chimney, belonged
to Jacob Mackenzie, head shepherd, who had been reported
missing. His wife had passed away a while ago, and his two
sons, Jerome and Brendon, were busy working in the castle
kitchens and spinning tales of madness and the white woman
of Blythe Hall. By all accounts the cottage should have been
empty, but someone was definitely at home. I smelled dinner.
Severely overcooked mutton, by my guess, with a side of

burnt bannocks and drying wool. Yet these smells, sharp and pungent as they were, sparked a memory, and suddenly I had visions of being a little girl again—happy, carefree—visiting these cottages with my father. I had loved coming here. Visits always meant kindness, warmth, and laughter—and that was even before the spirits started to flow. My father had been a good laird to his people. But it had been a long time since I had been here, and I was suddenly struck with the fear that I would not be remembered.

Tam, dismounting swiftly, was in the process of helping me down when a young woman burst out the door. We both stopped, riveted and a little frightened by the sight. The woman was petite; the baby in her arms was not. It was a child of astounding girth with chubby legs kicking, roly-poly arms flailing, all the while attempting to swallow one of its sizable fists. The front of its little, rumpled gown was awash in drool. Not two steps behind this poor, tiny woman was a stream of dirt-smudged youngsters—four children in all—the oldest of whom appeared to be four or five. The young woman I recognized instantly. She was Katherine Kerr, and she was just two years older than me.

"Why, angels save me!" she exclaimed, a huge smile splitting her drawn and tired face. The children gathered around her, peering up at us from the safety of her skirts and hopelessly stained apron. The baby, impervious to everything, continued to try to eat its fist. "Could it be true? I had heard a rumor from those daft, devil-spawn stepsons of mine, but I'd no' believe it if I hadn't seen it for myself. Mistress Isabeau, you've come home at last. And might I add, not a moment too soon."

I was already on the ground, Tam taking hold of both horses, when I returned the greeting. "Katherine Kerr, how good it is to see you again. But whatever are you doing here, and with all these . . . fairy folk?"

"Kerr? Dear heavens, I haven't been called Katherine Kerr

for an age." She rolled her eyes as if it was a great joke. "I'm Kat Mackenzie now, and these wee fairy folk are my children."

❧

Kat Mackenzie, the mythically prolific second wife of Jacob and stepmother to the two mischievous kitchen lads, ushered us into her home for some refreshments. The smell inside was a bit overwhelming at first, which was reasonable when one understood that only one of the four children could use the chamber pot successfully. Yet aside from the smell, I was taken aback by the change in Katherine, and her ability to placate four busy little creatures while ladling stringy mutton out of the blackened pot. She was more than happy to share her meal with us, as she was the burden that weighed so heavily on all the women of Blythemuir; for all the men had gone missing with the sheep. "I dinnae ken what we're tae do?" she decried, plopping the chubby baby on my lap. "Wee Jacob's teething, so dinnae put your fingers too close to his mouth, aye?" she warned, and placed a wooden block in the baby's fist. Turning her full attention to the hearth where the supper pot dangled on a hook before a screen of drying nappies and tiny homespun shirts, doublets, gowns, and hose, she continued. "They've been missing for days. Just vanished, they did. There's nae sign of 'em anywhere. If the weavers of Galashiels hear of this, we'll be ruined. 'Tis unholy, I tell ye! 'Tis the work of the devil!"

"It is odd," I agreed, pulling my head away. Wee Jacob, a surprisingly heavy, yet undeniably cute little squirming bundle with a shock of curly brown hair and the round blue eyes of his mother, was trying to feed me his wooden block. "But it's not the work of the devil, just a clever reiver. And don't worry about the weavers just yet. We'll find the flock soon enough," I offered cheerily, gently pushing the block away and hoping I sounded more confident than I felt. "Besides our own men," I began, "Sir George Douglas has gone out on our cause, and the king's personal guard is keeping an eye out for them as well. We've the best men in Scotland searching the countryside. They'll find them."

She placed the bowls on the table, then stood with hands on hips. "Do ye suppose," she began, her dark head slightly askew, her eyes focusing beyond me to a spot somewhere in the distance, "that Master Julius could be behind this?"

I nearly dropped the baby. With a speed remarkable for her tiny size, she plucked him off my lap. I looked at her and asked: "Why . . . what do you know of Julius?"

"Oh," she said wistfully, "what any of us know of the young master, I suppose."

"But why would you think he'd be behind something like this?" I asked cautiously.

"Well, because he's returned, of course. He always was the jaunty one."

"How do you know he's returned?"

"Humm?" she replied, as if she hadn't heard me.

"I asked how you knew that Julius has returned. Julius is an outlaw. He's not supposed to step foot in Scotland under forfeit of his life."

"Aye, I ken that." She sat down next to me holding the gurgling baby in her lap a bit tightly. Wee Jacob protested, but Kat just held him tighter. She then glanced over at the corner where Tam was still entertaining the children. "And I ken he's returned," she finally said, her voice lowered to a whisper. "Because I saw him."

"What? When?" That beautiful feeling of peaceful calm that had carried me here began to fade, slowly being replaced with that rage that was becoming all too customary.

She shrugged. "I dinnae ken, perhaps four or five days ago."

"Where did you see him?"

"He came here, when Jacob was gone. We used to be . . . well, ye must have realized we were . . ."

I held up a hand to stop her. "No need to dredge up foolish mistakes of the past on my account. If you'll just please tell me where he is, I'd be grateful."

She looked genuinely surprised by this. "Why, I thought ye knew. I thought ye knew because I thought he was staying at the castle." The look on her face changed then, and she uttered a very tentative "Ye willnae mention this to Jacob, will ye?"

⁓

With bellies full and thoughts clouded once again by the mention of Julius, Tam and I left the cottars of Blythemuir as the sun was making its descent in the western sky. The brightness of day had come off the land, and the heather-covered hills were dappled with the long shadows of trees and rocks, and the great flocks of birds heading to their evening roosts. To the east the tips of the tall pines were gilded with soft light as they caught the last rays of the fading sun. It was a breathtaking spectacle, and it was a pity I couldn't fully enjoy it. If Julius had been in Blythemuir five days earlier, then he had not ridden with us from Edinburgh. That was a slight relief. Knowing that he was visiting his old paramours again was not. It was infuriating, especially after learning of his dalliance with Marion that morning. I was consumed with anger, and I'm sorry to think that I had searched the faces of all Katherine Mackenzie's children to see if there was any echo of Julius in them. Thankfully there was not. At least nothing I could see, but I was no expert in the sordid matters of cuckoldry. At any rate, Jacob Mackenzie had no reason to suspect his children were other than his children, and wouldn't hear differently from me.

"Tam, do you suppose it could be true . . . what Katherine

had said about Julius hiding in Blythe Hall—right under our noses?"

Tam, riding with the loose-limbed ease of one born in the saddle, looked at me in a thoughtful sort of way. "Well, 'twould be just about the most brilliant piece of chicanery if it were true; but I highly doubt 'tis true . . . unless Master Julius is a powerful wizard. In that case he could ha' sent the sheep and all the shepherds to the underworld, and could, in fact, be wandering the corridors of Blythe as a cat . . . or mouse, though probably a cat. He sounds smarter than one what would transfigure into a wee mouse. But a cat, no one would notice an extra cat slinking about."

"Tam, please, this is no time for nonsense."

"Oh, 'tis no nonsense, m'lady. I've heard it done by an old woman in Skye once. She cast her soul into her familiar, which was her cat. The townsfolk suspected as much, for she always knew what was afoot; she always knew the towns-folk's darkest secrets without ever being told. So one day, they see her old cat skulkin' in a corner, watching them with its big glowing eyes. So, they set a trap for the beast and kill it. The next day they find the old lady dead. Mistress Isabeau, I've never met your brother, so I canna say for myself, but is he, by chance, a wizard?" The lad looked distressingly hopeful.

"No! Of course not," I chided, trying to expunge the thought of the poor old lady and her dead cat from my mind. It was a terrible story, and a terrible tale to tell upon the gloaming moor. I had no idea where Tam came up with such tripe. "In spite of what you've been told and what you obvi-ously believe, there are no such things as wizards and witches with magical powers, Tam. It is the hard truth, and I hate to be the one to dash all your hopes. But my brother is just a man, just a devious, amoral man."

Dark brows rose above the twinkling blue eyes as he replied, "If ye say so. But mind what I said about the sheep

and the shepherds? For the de'il can charm like no other, and
everyone kens he's a hunger for the new-sprung lamb."

We rode in silence after that short exchange, for my mind,
thanks to Tam, was turning on all manner of dark thoughts.
The sun had dipped below the horizon, making everything
look a bit more sinister. Behind every boulder lurked the
devil; behind every tree was a beastly creature ready to devour
me. Every birdcall was a banshee; every skittering noise was a
wild-eyed demon. As the shadows moved in closer, I was
growing more and more uneasy. It was small comfort that the
castle was in sight, for we still had to make it through the
gates. I took a few deep breaths, knowing my common sense
was spiraling away from me under Tam's daft suggestions.
There are no such things as banshees, I told myself; there are
no such things as demons, or angels for that matter. Man is a
fabulous creature of invention, and I'm a fool. My heart was
nearly settled, slowing to a normal pace, when a truly chilling
sound hit my ears.

It was the sound of a lone horse racing across the fields.

The rider was barreling down at an alarming rate. Tam
quickly reined in and spun his mount around, placing himself
in front of me. I sat still, watching as the horseman, cloaked in
black, raced toward us on a demon steed. We were unarmed.
We were unprotected. I was in my own country and felt no
need of such things. I was indeed a fool.

"Speaking of the devil," I said quietly, as a numbing wave
of regret washed over me. "And I had such high hopes of re-
deeming this place."

"Wheesht!" Tam hissed. "That is no devil, m'lady. That is a
man."

"Look again," I said. "That is a man on a fine horse—
a horse much too fine for the likes of any around here. That is
Julius; that is the devil." I crossed my arms and waited.

"Actually," said Tam, watching intently as the rider approached, "I recognize thon horse."

"The horse? Really?" With arms still crossed, I made a little noise of disbelief.

"Aye, the horse," he repeated, and looked back at me. "For unless your brother is bold enough tae steal a horse from the royal stables, I'd say that's no' your brother."

"And I've learned, quite recently actually, never to underestimate my brother." I leaned in to get a better look at horse and rider. It was growing dark, but not so dark I couldn't see. They were drawing nearer; the horse, a powerful black beast of fine lineage, ate up the ground like a child on a fair day eats sugary comfits—without heed, without remorse. The man was fearless.

Tam stood steadfast, his thin shoulders squared to the oncoming rider; his skinny body and shaggy little bog trotter, or, as he referred to it, a fine Galloway pony, were all that stood between the barreling rider and me. Understandably I was growing nervous. And then a rogue gust of wind lifted the hood off the rider's face as one last ray of light touched his features. Shock constricted my throat. "Oh dear," I uttered. "Oh, dear Lord!" My heart was racing again. "How can that be? That is *not* my brother! Oh God! Oh, dear heavens above! That is . . ." I looked at Tam, unable to finish my sentence.

My groom, with a self-satisfied grimace on his boyish face, finished softly, "Aye, that'll be the king."

Chapter 7
A ROYAL PAWN

THE SUDDEN APPEARANCE OF THE KING RACING toward Blythe Hall in the fading light of day meant that something horrible had happened—perhaps Edinburgh was aflame, or the English had invaded by sea and were raping and ransacking up and down the coast. The cream of his guard had been sent with me, and as far as he knew, they were still at Blythe Hall. Yet it didn't make any sense. A messenger would be sent—not the king. The king should never be left to travel alone. Yet here he was, and there was no apparent emergency to speak of, save one.

James Stewart, King of Scotland, not yet twenty years of age and without any issue whatsoever to the throne should he perish—not even an illegitimate one—had apparently evaded the many watchful eyes that surrounded him and stolen off on his own private adventure, riding incognito through his realm like a prince of romance. He had not so much as a groom with him. He was entirely alone, pretending to be a common traveler, dressed in the stout fustian of the working man, complete with baggy hose and well-worn riding boots. And, to his credit, he looked the common man, but no common man ever looked so elated—so full of life, so bursting with joy to be riding through bog and over moorland. Nor did a common man, I'd venture to guess, ride a beast so impressively bred.

"Isabeau! Tam!" he cried with hearty delight, pulling up fast before his mighty charger bowled us over. His cheeks were flushed with cold and excitement; his rich brown hair, worn long and unbound, was wild about his head, and his dark blue eyes were positively incandescent. "How timely that we should meet here, and on the threshold of your own castle! It has only been days, but I've missed you, Isabeau."

I looked at him, looked around him, then back at him again. It was unbelievable. "Your Highness," I said, bowing my head, as did Tam. "I . . . have missed you too."

"Please," he urged in a lowered voice. "I am not the king here. Call me Jamie. And I must apologize. I would have been here sooner if I hadn't happened by a shepherd's hut at midday. The shepherd wasn't in, of course, but the goodwife was, and she plied me with curds and bannock and a jug of their best mead." He leaned in, his face radiating an unquenchable joy. "I felt obliged to stay and natter awhile. She was full of well-meaning advice, she was, and most complimentary when describing the virtues of the king." This last comment was punctuated by a meaningful widening of the eyes.

"Really?" I breathed with a touch of skepticism. I was unsure of what else to say, for the whole notion of the king dining incognito at some cottar's hut was utterly surreal. I cast a helpless glance at Tam. I knew my groom to be very fond of the king; he had worked in the royal stables. James was quite fond of Tam as well and had given him, as a gift, to my household. I was expecting Tam to have a little more sense about him than his former master seemed to possess. Yet in this I was wrong. Tam, sitting on his stout little pony, met my ques-

tioning gaze. His shoulders slowly rose to the level of his ear-
lobes as his mouth split in an irritating grin of boyish delight.
I turned back to the king. "And . . . how is the country, sire?
Are we . . . at war?"

"Jamie," he corrected with slight impatience. And then:
"At war? Lord, I hope not!" He was still in high spirits—his
grin matching my groom's—yet the question was a serious
one. And James took matters of Scotland seriously. His smile
faded as he offered, "Unless Angus has rekindled his friendship with old Henry again, in retaliation for what I had to do
at Tantallon, then no, we are at peace. But as I've already discussed with you, Isabeau, I blame myself for Angus's turn of
heart. He was my guardian. He acted as regent during my mi-
nority. He loved me. He deserved better." And although he
spoke of Sir Archibald Douglas and his recent treachery, in his
words I caught the echo of another, older devastation: *Julius
was my friend. I worshipped him. He promised to protect me.
What did I do wrong?* Both men had meant the world to the
young king. Both had betrayed him. And it was Sir George
Douglas, Angus's nephew, who brought to light the misdeeds
of my brother, and possibly even his uncle, the Earl of Angus,
solidifying his unwavering status as Scotland's hero.

I felt the king's disappointment as acutely as if it were my
own. My throat tightened a measure, and I wanted to cry out:
You did nothing! Men are but feckless, thankless creatures
driven by greed and avarice. Harden your heart, my king.
Live and learn. Yet instead I caught myself placating him with
"You were but a boy. How were you to know you'd offend
old Angus by giving Lord Hume Wardenship of the East
March? By the way, I heard tell he acted like a spoilt child.
Men who hold titles should not act like coddled children."

"Still, I should have known." His voice was grave and
plaintive. After he paused for the slightest moment's reflection, however, a soft, wistful smile appeared on his lips. "I
know now."

"Indeed," I concurred, unable to hide the hint of sadness in my voice. "You know better now."

"Ahem, sire?" It was Tam, young, eager, and void of any emotion but for curiosity, who pulled us back to the present. "If I may, m'lord?" His auburn curls flopped forward, indicating that a bow was attempted, before he launched right in with "If Edinburgh's safe, and there's nay great emergency, an' auld Angus is brooding in peace, why have ye come here? Surely ye dinnae leave just tae sneak away for a pint o' mead and some quiet natter with an auld crone?"

James raised a brow. "Old crone? Whatever gave ye that impression, Tam? And the mead was very fine, very fine indeed." His grin was a little unstable, his eyes a little too bright. Yet when he saw that we were not partaking in his quiet mischief, his smile slowly faded. The expressive brows pulled together, the regal head tilted, and he uttered a probing "You are teasing, correct? For you must have received my messenger?"

"Messenger?" I heard myself repeating the word as a burst of cold dread shot down my spine. "You . . . sent a messenger?"

"Aye. Days ago. It was in the same missive I sent to Hendrick alerting him that you and Mistress Boyd were set to arrive."

"*That* message?" My voice nearly failed me as I recalled how *that* message had been intercepted by Sir George. But I had seen that message. Although I had been furious with Sir George for intercepting it, making our arrival a total surprise to Hendrick and the entire castle, I was fairly certain it did not contain one mention of a possible royal visit. "Are you certain you included other information in that message? Could it have been in another?"

"My dear Isabeau, you know me too well to doubt that I am a man of my word. Yes, I sent a messenger. And the missive he carried spelled it all out, how you were to arrive followed a day later by me." He paused, then added as if as an afterthought, "You were aware that my aunt arranged for this?"

"What? Princess Margaret?" My voice was too loud, but in my defense I was utterly taken aback by the notion. I fought for control over my thoughts as well as my vocal cords. "Princess Margaret arranged for you, the King of Scotland, to ride through this ... this dangerous, thief-infested land alone?" I asked with a bit more aplomb.

To my surprise he reddened and looked mildly abashed. "Ah, yes and no. So I see you were not aware. But how can that be? Hendrick did receive my message?"

"He did. It was a bit late, though. And it was delivered by Sir George Douglas, not a royal messenger. Sir George admitted to intercepting the messenger because it was his wish to bring the good news himself. Why did you say 'yes and no'?"

The king, deep in thought, raised a brow and clarified. "Yes, my aunt arranged for me to sneak away. No, I was not to travel alone. I had a small guard. So, Kilwylie's here?" He seemed to find this highly interesting and turned his intense gaze on me. "At Blythe Hall ... Excellent! I should have known he wouldn't wait a moment longer than he need. Still, he should not have interfered with my messenger."

"You suspected Lord Kilwylie would come here?" It was more than curious. "Why did you not mention this to me before I left? And what do you mean, you had a small guard? Where are they?"

"Really, Isabeau, 'tis good to be surprised every now and again. I thought you'd welcome a surprise containing the likes of Sir George. He's a good man. And, if you must know, my guard's in Linlithgow. It was a deceitful act of misdirection on my part. Yet for the sake of my own modesty, and a firm belief that I should be able to ride through my own country unmolested, I contrived to make this journey alone. I had done very well too, until recently." He delivered a look that was suspiciously sarcastic. "Alas, do not look so alarmed," he chided softly, his minor irritation swallowed by the heady adventure he was on. "Do not give a thought to my safety, for I shall be in fine company for the return trip. My guard is still here."

On my lips was affixed a smile, of the kind that served me well in the convent, yet in the hollow of my chest I could feel my heart stop. Sir Matthew and his men! Only the dear Lord knew where they were at the moment, yet it certainly was not at Blythe Hall. And it was certainly not the time to tell the king. "Ah, yes. Yes, they are. Of course!" I lied, and it scared me how easily the falsehood slipped off my tongue. I would have to repent for it, of course. I would work on that later. "You sent your guard with *us* knowing they would be returning with *you*. At least *that* was smart thinking." What on earth was I to do? I cast a helpless glance at Tam.

"That was only part of the reason, Isabeau," Jamie replied, his eyes softening, his voice level yet earnest. "I would have never let you leave without knowing the kingdom's best men were guarding you."

This sentiment—the way it was said—had a measurable effect on me. My wooden smile became genuine, and the fear, doubt, and confusion that had welled up at the sight of him so far from his throne receded, becoming as trivial as the quiet whispers of the great ladies at court. I even let myself believe that I was glad that he was here, appearing as if by magic on this unruly border to help me sort out my compounding issues. James Stewart, the fourth of that name and King of Scotland, was a brilliant, gallant, very capable young man. And then sanity came to me again, urged along by Tam's practical, piercing gaze. He was entirely correct to bring me back in hand, for we had another, greater problem this night. Why was the King of Scotland allowed to escape the many watchful eyes that protected him? Why was there no mention of his visit in the message brought by Sir George? And what would compel him to travel alone to such a wild stretch of country in the first place?

The answer, like a virulent sickness, hit me; for there could be no possible reason save one: Julius.

The thought sent a wave of cold, prickly sweat across my skin, dampening my chemise and beading on my brow. I cast my eyes to the east, where the forest grew high on the ridge. It was dark; the trees were a brooding shadow. Yet I knew he was out there; I could feel his eyes on me.

Julius knew that Sir George had intercepted the king's message; he had been driven to exploit that fact. But it wasn't the king's message.

The King's Guard had been led away on a merry chase; Sir George and his men were hunting phantom sheep. Blythe Hall was empty but for the household staff, Hendrick, and two frightfully inexperienced noblewomen. It was as if some twisted genius was playing a game of chess with our lives, systematically eliminating all the obstacles until nothing stood in his way. And now the board was nearly clear, leaving only the king, a poorly defended castle, and a handful of pawns. The machinations, the plotting, the scheming—it was terrifyingly brilliant.

It was the hallmark of Julius. And he had men—an army of idle mercenaries he had called them. His men would be in the hills, melding with the darkness, moving like shadows. They would already know that the king had arrived.

That James had been allowed to arrive unmolested I took as a warning to me. This was, after all, a game. The great performance of the robbery had set the stage, and now the cat was merely toying with the mouse to prolong the sport. The king was in my care. Should I fail to do as Julius wished, the nation would suffer. It was, perhaps, fitting payback for his failed schemes. But I could not let him succeed.

The king, thankfully, was too elated by his newfound freedom to be aware that anything was amiss. Tam, however, had long picked up on my thoughts. Like the invaluable groom he was, he employed his boyish charm as he casually brought his mount around to flank the king. Thus surrounded by our paltry bodies, we urged him toward the gates of Blythe, noting that the torches had already been lit.

"Sire, let me be the first to welcome you to Blythe Hall," I said with a grim sort of cheer before turning my gaze to the archway where the warrior-angel stood in relief, illuminated from below by torchlight. The outstretched wings, the graceful head looking downward, the mighty sword held aloft and ready to strike, were all fully lit and glowing like an ominous beacon; the words *I am protected* rang loud in my ears. Please, Lord, I uttered fervently, let it be so. I looked back at Jamie Stewart, noting that he too was held captive by the sight. "I beg you excuse us if we appear to be a bit unprepared for your visit. There's been quite a spell of excitement since our arrival yesterday, and your sudden appearance this night will be unparalleled, I should think. However, know that I shall do all in my power to see that your stay is a memorable one. Now, before we pass through those gates, would you mind very much telling us why it is that Princess Margaret has arranged for the king to escape his court in order to come to a forlorn place like Blythe Hall?"

৶৹

While it was true that to be a king required great responsibility, it was also true that to have such great responsibility thrust upon one's shoulders meant that one was seldom ever allowed to be alone. James was the jewel of our country; through his veins coursed the blood of ancient kings, and because of his birth order and impressive lineage he was honored with a staff of servants who never left his side. He explained that he could not even use the chamber pot without two courtiers assisting him—one to hand him a piece of towel, the other to cover and carry the royal eliminations away. I thought him joking at first but could see that he wasn't. Of course he had been groomed for this life, being raised a prince, so the attention came as no surprise. Yet he was a modest man by nature, and there were certain things—certain pressing urges—he yearned to indulge. And he wished to indulge them without the entire palace knowing, as they were certain to know eventually.

"Marion?" I repeated, my head hurting slightly as I attempted to comprehend what was unfolding beneath my roof, and feeling somewhat deflated that I hadn't even considered this possibility myself. We were sitting alone in my solar, warming ourselves with mulled wine and a soft, crackling fire as the king attempted to spill his story. Hendrick, upon being apprised of our visitor's identity, had stood in ineffable silence, for there were no words to describe such an honor—such a calamity. Hendrick understood the situation perfectly; it meant another bout of furious activity to ready the castle as best we could. James, having never been to Blythe Hall before, was gracious in his praise, yet even a blind man could see that his thoughts were occupied elsewhere. And when Hendrick fibbed and explained that Sir Matthew and the Guard had left with Sir George and his small army on an errand, the king showed little interest. Julius, due to some tacit agreement, was never mentioned.

"Aye, Marion," James reiterated, turning a healthy shade of pink as he spoke her name. "I've been getting pressure of late. Ye know, I mean, I'm a man. I should be doing these things. My subjects are talking. I need to sire a bastard or two to stop the chatter."

"I say, let them talk," I suggested, the pall of gloom hanging thick in my voice. "Bastards are highly overrated. So, Mistress Boyd is the reason you're here."

"Aye," he conceded, his tone invoking the image of a man being swept away on a current too powerful to fight.

"And you don't mean to marry her."

"Ye know I can't, even should I be so inclined. I won't mistreat her, Isabeau, if that's what you think. I would never do such a thing! I know she is dear to you, but you must also know that royal mistresses are . . . well, there's no shame in it. It's not like being a common . . . I mean, 'tis a position of honor."

"Honor? You will lavish favors on her family," I stated.

"Yes. Of course."

"Let me ask you something else: Is it a coincidence that her uncle is Sir Archibald Douglas, Lord Angus? Is this an olive branch after your siege at Tantallon?"

He paused before answering. A soft, reflective smile appeared on his lips as he said, "'Tis not a coincidence, but a benefit. I am entirely taken with her, Isabeau. I have a kingdom to run, but all I can think of is Marion. Do you understand?" His dark eyes were intense yet tempered with hope.

"No. I don't think I do, but if that's how you feel—?"

"Aunt Margaret understood," he said, cutting in while clutching his goblet as if it were all that was keeping him upright. His eyes were glued to the soft, mesmerizing flames of the fire. Of course Aunt Margaret would understand, I thought smugly. She had once, in her youth, been contracted to marry the English king's brother-in-law, Earl Rivers. But Margaret never left Scotland, nor did she ever marry. She had an illegitimate child instead. James continued. "She saw an opportunity, sent Marion here with you, and told me . . . Do you think . . . I mean, will she agree?" He turned his head to look at me. "She's such a beautiful, spirited creature, and there are many who feel as I do . . ."

I touched his hand to stop him. Here was a man who had no equal in the tiltyard, a man of vast learning and devout nature, a man who held the reins to a kingdom yet was as timid and chaste as myself in matters of the heart. And he had poured out his heart to me. How could I tell him that Julius had beaten him to his heart's desire—arriving a day before him, an outlaw, a reprobate, a hedonistic debaucher of women who cared not a fig for poor Marion? And how could I tell him that Marion had invited such base attention, knowing what Julius was, and would keep doing so if not stopped?

"You are the king," was all I said. "And were you not, there still would be no question. You are a good man, James, and you have risked too much in coming here already. Now, I will not hear another word." I stood to go. "You are here. Marion is here, and there are very few others. Now is your time, my dear friend. And I do wish you happiness. Please, accept these chambers for as long as you care to stay. Now, if you'll excuse me, I must change, for we have a royal visitor in our household." I smiled, turned to go, then stopped, thinking on something else. "In the spirit of adventure, and in keeping with your yearning for the common experience, I believe we shall dine on pewter and wood instead of silver tonight, if that is all right with you?"

"Oh, that would be grand." His grin was endearingly genuine.

"Good," I replied, and allowed a small bubble of relief to break the surface of my ocean of worries. One less embarrassment to explain.

"And thank you, Isabeau," James said, standing to face me. He took my hands in his, the soft glow of the fire casting half his face in a golden hue, while the other half lay hidden in shadow. "For listening to me. Nobody listens to me like you do."

ॐ

Dinner, although held in the Great Hall, was a comparatively quiet affair—when one recalled the day before. There was still plenty of pageantry, for this was, in essence, a courting feast, served upon platters of pewter and wood, and eaten on fresh-baked trenchers of bread. No one complained. The subtle theme, as concocted by the rushed Mutton Johnny, appeared, unbelievably, to be breasts. The rather intimate feast opened with a plate containing the small, tender breasts of squab, done to a turn and, no doubt, hastily gathered from the dovecote. Next, a dish of the slightly larger, plumper breast of chicken—likely the maimed combatants of the courtyard—stewed and glistening under a rose water glaze. Turnips were cut in half and roasted with carrot nubs plucked in the middle. Cabbage appeared much the same, only larger, and a bit saggy. There was a breast of swan, stuffed to bursting with herbs and grapes, and finally, a dish of poached pears, dusted with cinnamon and topped with tart cherry nipples. Mildly erotic theme aside, I had little appetite for any of it, given all that weighed on my mind, yet every now and then I felt the annoying urge to giggle. Mme. Seraphina's lively comments didn't help matters any; Hendrick, I believed, was merely thankful that food appeared at all, under the circumstances, and the incorrigible Mackenzie brothers, making trip after trip from the kitchens, had cleverly titled everything, purely for their own entertainment. The king, thankfully, was oblivious to all, for his eyes never left Marion.

Marion, having heard of the king's intentions from my own lips, looked nothing less than stunning in a satin gown of pale butter yellow. Her hair, glossy after a thousand brushstrokes, had been loosely contained in a woven caul studded with tiny diamonds and seed pearls that fell well below her shoulders. Her neck, slender and white, appeared far too fragile to support the chain of emeralds she wore. The contrast was striking, as was her choice to wear her gown low, showing a good deal of creamy skin and the swell of her firm, round breasts. The good sisters of Haddington would have never approved. The king, however, did.

Marion was no fool. While admitting that her appetites were somewhat on the order of my brother's where sexual intrigue was involved, she knew that the young king was the ultimate prize, and she did appear genuine in her affection for him. "Really, Isabeau, you took all you learned at the convent to heart. Life is meant to be lived, not meticulously planned and then tucked away until all your bucks are in a row. And the king, he is a buck without equal."

"I believe the saying is ducks—all your ducks in a row," I said, stopping the brush in my hand to look at her reflection in the little mirror.

She made a disparaging face back at me. "See what I mean? Bucks, stags, rutting bulls—start thinking along those lines. You must jump when an opportunity arises, Isabeau, or you will miss it all."

"Yes. Thank you for that bit of sage advice. However, I believe if you jump too often, you'll run the risk of scaring the bucks away." I smiled oversweetly at her reflection.

"Humm," she said, pretending to think. "Interesting. However, I stand firm on my original premise, which is that if you never jump at all, the bucks will stop coming around altogether."

I laughed then. Marion and I were as different as two friends could be, in temperament, looks, and especially our attitudes concerning the opposite sex. Yet it was this same vivacious and palpable hunger of hers that I found so compelling, likely because it was so tempered in me. In turn, my stolid attitude helped balance out her earthly impulses, or at least I had hoped so. "All right," I acquiesced. "But did you have to jump at Julius? Could you have just, for the sake of decency, passed on that opportunity?"

Marion let out a small sigh and turned. Her face was composed, her snapping eyes softened by reflection, and her hand, warm and gentle, came over mine. "I know he's your brother. I know all that lies between you two, for I am your dearest friend. But I am not sorry, Isa, nor do I regret my actions. I shall never forget him."

"It was only one night!" I said. "For the sake of the king, I think you can forget one night!"

Her lips curled, and in them was a hint of mischief. "Oh, Isa, there are many *knights* I'd gladly forget, but not this last one. And because of it the king, who is so like you in many ways, will be very well served by me, never you fret. I do hope, for your sake, *you* take a chance on one of these knights, Lord Kilwylie in particular. You may balk now and cite scripture, but one cannot experience heaven through the written word alone. You may think me a trollop, and perhaps you're right, but what I experienced last night would put heaven to shame."

My hand came over my mouth. "Oh, Marion, that's blasphemy!"

"I know. But it's also the truth."

Her words, her look of sublime wonder, still plagued me as I poked at the little squab with my knife. It was so fragile, so insubstantial, and yet I found it overwhelming. This feeling was compounded by James, who ate of the little morsels with thoughtless zeal, for he had worked up a hearty appetite racing through the countryside as salacious thoughts of the lovely Mistress Boyd clouded his better judgment. Just how far his judgment was impaired became apparent by the anecdotes he shared with us, namely, the shepherd's hut incident, the questionable tavern near Dalkeith, the band of roving tinkers in Lauderdale, and a wayside traveler who introduced himself as Bugger Billy. At least he'd had the good sense not to dally there.

Marion, who mere hours earlier had attempted to woo Sir Matthew, and succeeded with my brother, was now employing all her skills to unrivaled perfection. She hung on the king's every word, offering a trill of laughter when appropriate and a coy compliment when encouragement was needed. The food before her became an artist's palate of seduction, and she toyed with it in such a manner as to make Hendrick choke on his wine, and the Mackenzie brothers to gawk in a most unseemly way. Mme. Seraphina even fell speechless a time or two, and I grew hot thinking that I should not be here, at my own table. Marion had no problem eating; I had no appetite for any of it. And it was with a sinking heart that I realized this was the role she had been groomed for—the role of royal mistress. It was as good as signed and sealed in triplicate, as far as I was concerned.

"More wine, m'lady?" It was Jerome, standing behind me. I shook my head. The wine came regardless, as did a low whisper in my ear. "Tam says that's the king. Is it true?" I nodded and took a hearty sip. "I thought he'd be taller, and wearin' a crown."

"He's just a man, same as you," I said flatly, then felt obliged to add, "only decidedly more refined, and with a far vaster wit and intelligence. And he's not the king here, Jerome. Don't address him as sire or Your Grace; an obsequious m'lord will do."

"Oh, indeed," he uttered, spellbound by the young king. My goblet was topped off once more. As the elder Mackenzie brother stood behind me studying the king, I studied the rosy liquid in my cup. Perhaps it was a sign from God, for the wine kept coming no matter how I tried to stop it; the words *drink up* echoed through me. *Drink up and release your troubles to me!* I eagerly obeyed. Two poached pears appeared on my plate as if by magic. "You'll be wantin' a nipple tart or two t' go with all that, or perhaps some succulent, sugared-mound of swan?"

"I'm fine, Jerome. Thank you." I drained my cup and motioned for more.

"Is that not so, Isabeau? Isabeau?" It was the king. His penetrating gaze was focused on me. Unfortunately my focus was on my cup, and Jerome, I saw, was eyeing the poached pear in a manner that didn't appear entirely proper.

"Excuse me?" I hurriedly replied, shifting my focus.

"Your father's chapel. It is said to be a thing of wonder."

"Oh, the chapel. Yes. Yes, it is, if you like that sort of thing."

"But I do," he said, holding me with a mildly chastising look. "I'd like you to take me there. You must know how I long to see it."

I set my goblet down and met his direct gaze. "Now? You wish to see it now? Is it not a bit late to be wandering around a strange castle?"

His eyes traveled from the goblet before me to my unsteady gaze. "It is your castle, so it's not at all strange."

"That may be, but are we not eating?"

"We were. But supper's over, Isabeau." The king stood and came before me, hand outstretched. I hastily scanned the table. The meal did appear to be over. "Come," he said softly. "Take my hand and show me to this chapel of yours. Tonight we shall pray for our fathers together."

I looked to Mme. Seraphina. She nodded while resting a hand on Marion. I understood. I was to oblige the king, while she prepared Marion to receive him. I closed my eyes, taking a moment to steady myself. "Very well," I acquiesced, focusing on the king. "But I think I should warn you, Jamie, I'm not really in the mood to pray."

❧

With flambeau held high before him, Tam led the way up the tower stairs. The light cast menacing shadows on the thick stone walls, and the pace of my heart increased with every step closer to the room in question. It didn't help matters any that my head was reeling slightly from the wine. The king, like a child about to discover an ancient treasure, was breathing heavily behind me. I could feel the rush of anticipation in his every breath, his every footfall tempered but eager. Such was not the case for me, and I silently cursed myself for overindulging. It seldom happened. I was always in control, yet I feared I was careening toward a precipice from which I would never recover. I couldn't entirely explain it, but my fear was real. My heart was a prime indicator of it. And lurking in the shadows, pushing me ever closer to the edge, was my brother.

The king was utterly unaware that Julius had surfaced. Perhaps it was wrong of us not to tell him, but why tell him? He was here now, and looking forward to entering that last bastion of manhood—choosing his partner with care—even losing sleep over the decision, and finally blazing the very same trail Julius had explored a day earlier. This little visit to the chapel in the middle of the night was just a mild distraction before the main event. We should be doing this in the morning; we shouldn't be doing this at all. But I was not a coward. And it would never do to show any signs of this weakness in front of the king. I schooled my racing thoughts and kept my eyes on the broad yet bony shoulders of my groom.

A large sheet of black cloth had been hung before the chapel door, a reminder of Sir George's earlier visit. It was the type of cloth one hung during a time of mourning. Perhaps it was all Hendrick could find. I was shaking, staring at the impending black barrier as if it were a portal to another realm. It was just a doorway, I told myself, and over the threshold was just another room. Tam, watching me intently, asked the question with his eyes. I nodded and he slipped inside, taking the flambeau with him. The landing went black, the cloth swallowed all light from the flame, and my heart beat away with a rapidity I feared would break it.

"Are you frightened?" the king whispered, holding my hand in the darkness.

"No," I replied too quickly.

"But you're shaking."

"Oh? That'll be the wine. I drank too much." My eyes were closed; I was trying to focus on what lay beyond the curtain.

"Wine," he repeated, and let out a soft chuckle. "I've never known it to make a body shake?"

"Indeed, but this is no ordinary wine."

Without warning, without a sound, the cloth was drawn aside, revealing the candlelit crowning jewel of Blythe. The king, caught entirely by surprise, was rendered speechless. And then he squeezed my hand and pulled me inside with him.

There was an undeniable power in the room. Whether it was imagined or real—real in the sense that a residual essence, trapped behind each brushstroke or chisel cut, oozed forth with a palpable energy—I could not say. But this was not an ordinary room, and the king had felt it too. It had been an age since I'd stood on this floor, and doing so now ignited something in me, something both fearful and reverent. Thankfully, James was too preoccupied to notice, and his eyes, wide and unflinching, were desperately attempting to absorb all the elements that comprised this unlikely place. He had a good understanding of art—much better than I did, in fact—and his tutors had instructed him well on the master artists of the day. But James also possessed a preternatural sensitivity, one that belied his prowess in the tiltyard and his levelheaded approach in matters of state. And the room, with its astounding works of art, domed ceiling, and oculus opening to the night sky, clearly took his breath away. "In all my life," he said, turning to me, "in all the places I have been, I have never beheld anything so . . . so . . . ." His grip on my hand was uncomfortably tight, yet I squeezed back just as tightly, a gesture of understanding.

"Words fail. I know. Even your talented makars could not capture what this place is."

"How . . . ?" the king uttered, his eyes still hungrily devouring the flame-gilded color, the heavenly imagery.

"You'll have heard the story of my father, I'm sure. He thought my mother an angel, literally. This was his shrine to her."

Catching the tinge of derision in my voice, the king turned, his deep-blue eyes swimming with moisture as he pleaded, "Oh, Isabeau, dear Isabeau, you must forgive us men—you who are so pure, so logical. Put a sword in our hand and we conquer the world, but put a beautiful woman before us and we fall to our knees, forgetting even our own name. Your father was no fool. No fool could create a vision this perfect, this sublime. This room speaks of a love I can hardly imagine, an intensity so raw, a passion so visceral, that I can barely comprehend it. Why . . . why have you kept it from the world?"

It was a good question. There was a fine line between obsessive passion and sheer madness. Luckily I still had control of my head, or I might have blurted out the thought. Instead I chose to give a painfully simple answer. "Because it doesn't belong to the world," I said. "In truth, it doesn't even belong to me."

He accepted this explanation with the graciousness that defined his character. Yet understanding as he was, there passed behind his eyes a flicker of something dark and troubling. We had been friends a long time, which meant that he knew I was adept at reading his moods, and his mood had definitely changed. "I told you the reason I am here, and it is the truth. But I haven't told you everything." He let go of my hand and stood for a moment in silence before looking to Tam. The young man bowed and quietly slipped over to the other side of the curtain. Now the king drew his attention back to me. "You know that you are as dear to me as a sister, and because of it I have given great consideration to your future."

As he spoke these words my head became light while at the same time an aching hollowness gripped my stomach. I knew what he was going to say; perhaps it was the reason I had been so fearful to begin with.

"If I believed that there was someone who held your interest, it would have made my decision easier, for you must believe I truly want you to be happy. But sometimes, Isabeau, the path to happiness must be pointed out, and I, as your guardian and your friend, have taken it upon myself to nudge you over that first bump. I have already settled the matter."

"It is Lord Kilwylie, isn't it?" I said, feeling that hum, that subtle vibration take hold.

"He is a good man. And he cares for you deeply. And as your husband he will make amends for being the one who . . ."

Who ruined my family? Who saved the nation? It was true that Sir George shared a common past with Julius, but the only real hesitation I felt at the moment regarding Sir George was a personal one—a tantalizing fear that he would devour me in a way I could not even comprehend. I smiled softly and said, "That was a long time ago, James. I don't blame Sir George for what he did."

"I know you don't. You are remarkable in that way. I only hesitate because now he will bear the title Lord Blythe. This chapel will be his."

It was my turn to take his hand. "My dear king, my dear friend, this chapel will never be his, just as it can never be mine, but I gladly give him Blythe Hall and all its myriad of problems. So, you have agreed on a marriage contract, and yet he still attempted to win me over?" The thought was oddly endearing.

"'Tis already signed," he admitted, blushing a little. "And 'tis a very generous contract at that. I would have told you the day I signed it, but Kilwylie begged me to tell no one. It was his wish to win you over without my help." He smiled a little then. "All men are vain, Isabeau. Sir George is no different. Forgive him, for he's never been faced with the challenge of a woman like you before. Women usually fall at his—"

"I know," I said, gently cutting him off. "The truth is that I might have too. I believe that's what frightened me most. He's been very persistent."

"But, Isabeau," he said softly, "there is no need to be frightened any longer."

Yet I was frightened. My heart hammered away at the mere thought of the man, but I knew better than to question royal judgment. James had thought deeply about this decision, and the intensity of his gaze as he watched me process this news and all its implications expressed honest concern. That a king should express such concern over my affairs was touching, and the truth was that he had found me a good and highly respected husband. "Sir George will make a fine Lord Blythe," I said at last, and with conviction. "But you'll forgive me, I'm sure, if I don't fall at his feet when he returns. He's courting me as we speak. I rather like it. And I think, for the sake of his pride, I shall keep this little meeting a secret."

"Very wise," he said, grinning broadly. "And I can't tell you how it lightens my heart to hear that Blythe Hall will have a welcomed and worthy lord. I admit that I was a bit fearful."

"Fearful? You?"

"Very. It does happen, you know. Not often, thankfully, only when dealing in matters that are very dear to me. And you are dear to me, Isabeau."

"You have no reason to be afraid. I've always trusted you. And I trust you in this. I just hope Lord Kilwylie knows what he's getting himself into. Come now, James, let us kneel before the altar. You have a big night ahead of you, and I suddenly have the urge to pray."

It was while kneeling before the magnificent altar, head bent in prayer, eyes closed in supplication, that I felt a hand on my left shoulder. It was solid, its grip firm as it gave me a little comforting squeeze.

My heart stopped.

My eyes flew open, and I looked to my right at James, for he was the only other person in the room. He was still beside me, deep in prayer. It was this knowledge—this vision of him praying—that sent a burst of white-hot prickles traveling down my spine. The feeling was familiar. And I knew before I turned my head what I would find. Fear gripped me then, because I didn't want to go mad.

But I feared I was, because there was no one on the other side of me—nothing but a lone white feather.

Chapter 8
OVER-
INDULGENCE

AGAIN I SILENTLY CURSED MYSELF FOR OVERINDULG-
ing in wine. It was making me sleepy and maudlin by turns. I
didn't want to be sleepy or maudlin, yet still I held a cup in
my hand. My only excuse was that it was a marvelous panacea
for fear; for I was afraid. The thought of Sir George Douglas
as my husband terrified me, but it was nothing compared with
the madness Julius had unleashed upon Blythe Hall. And then
there was the possibility that I too might be going mad.

It was well after midnight. After giving over the laird's
chambers to the king and his mistress, I returned to the room
I had known as a child. I sat in a corner beside the fireplace,
motionless, melding with the shadows as my eyes held the
empty bed across the room. The familiar smell, the trundle
bed and piled quilts, was like a lullaby, luring me slowly to my
childhood nest of pale pink and creamy white surrounded by
curtains of heather purple and spring green. There was a real

promise of an obliterating sleep there. But I would not go. Not yet.

I tossed back the remaining wine and set the mug down on the hearth, careful not to crush the feather. The fire had been banked for the night; Mme. Seraphina had seen me to bed herself, yet here I was, wide awake and staring at the pristine white, impossibly downy feather that had shaken me to the core. Nothing on earth could be more harmless. The rational part of me understood this. But what the rational part of me could not deny was that this harmless little bit of bird down was the link to every memory I had of the tower room—every memory I had of things I didn't believe in anymore or wished to forget. There was a time when finding such a feather meant happiness. It was a token that appeared when the white lady had gone. I had a box where I put such feathers, which I kept in the old chest at the foot of my bed. My father had also understood the significance of this. His was the last feather the room had given over. It was the tangible sign he had been looking for, and it had spurred him on a quest that drove him to madness. Was it happening again? I prayed not.

I told no one of it, especially not the king. He had other matters on his mind—pressing matters that had led him across the country. I thought of him now as I had left him, standing on the threshold of the laird's chambers looking both excited and nervous at once. His visit to the chapel had served its purpose; he had unburdened his head to me and his heart to God, as often happened when we were together. Yet tonight there still hung about him a vulnerability that touched one's soul. He was the King of Scotland, yet his title held little comfort. He was young, his remarkable confidence absurdly frangible as he contemplated what lay beyond the door. I of all people understood his trepidation, and because of it, all I could offer by way of encouragement was a watery smile and a tepid "Good evening." What I didn't say, what I should have said, was that he had nothing to fear. Marion would see to it that all went well.

I thought about how furious I had been with her and her cavalier attitude toward love—how desperately she sought it and, once in her grasp, how easily she had given it—yet now, staring at the bed she had so recently shared with my brother, I forgave her everything. Who was I to cast judgment on a friend? She was right; we were two vastly different people. I had spent so long learning to govern my thoughts and emotions that I had grown afraid of where they might take me should I give in to them. Marion had no such qualms. She jumped at life; she toyed with it; she flirted with impropriety, and was now in the arms of the king, guiding him expertly through this definitive rite of manhood. I picked up the feather, now rosy from the soft glow of the embers, and slowly twirled it between thumb and finger, letting the gentle tingling take hold. I wished them happiness, I truly did. Yet I knew, as they must know, that it would not last. Marion would always love the king, but he would not marry her. And I would marry a man I did not love, because that was my duty. It made no difference that my heart belonged to a vision—to a being that did not live in this world. I knew it was madness. It made no sense. And try as I might, I could not deny the truth of it, not here at Blythe Hall.

I had felt it the moment I arrived. It was compelling; it was reaching out to me invoking visions so real that the line between heaven and earth became blurred. And now tonight I had received the solid evidence that drew one into the illusion. Only it wasn't an illusion. Julius had known my secret, and he would push me to the edge to expose it, knowing I could not fight it forever. My father was a strong man, and he had cracked; I was not nearly as strong.

I set the feather down and put both hands on the little bow resting across my lap. It was a short bow, an old weapon that my father had given to me when he taught me how to shoot. I hadn't touched it for an age, but I needed it now. I needed it to protect my king. I needed it to protect my castle. But mostly I needed it to protect my sanity, for I knew that Julius, like a feral cat coming around for a dish of cream, could not resist a free meal. He would visit this room before the night was out, and I would be waiting for him.

My will was strong, but the allure of the madness was stronger. Invoked by the touch of the feather, he came to me again, my golden man. I closed my eyes, giving in to the emotions I had kept in check for so long. My head was swimming with the dulling effects of wine; it was easy to give in. I released my heart from my body, willing it to go where it must. Cut loose, it was no secret where it went, it went to the one who owned the other half. His smile was glorious, his emotions pure, and I longed to gaze upon his face forever, afraid I might never see anything so perfect again. I reveled in the feel of his breath as it gently caressed my cheek. He was speaking to me. He was telling me something private—a great secret that could only be understood by us. His smile faded. He said it again, slowly this time and in a voice vaguely familiar. I finally understood what he was saying; he was urging me to wake up.

My eyes flew open only to see a man standing before me. He was leaning against the solid post of the bed, his shadowed body just visible in the glimmer of the slumbering fire. He moved slightly; light fell across his hair and half his face, revealing the golden color, the sardonic grin. I grabbed my bow, put the nock of the arrow in the bowstring, and pulled the cord back in one fluid motion. The grin grew broader.

"You're getting clever."

"You're getting predictable," I replied, and pointed the tip of my arrow at the level of his heart.

"If you could only hold your liquor," he said, indicating the empty mug. He picked it up and tipped it; one glistening drop fell out, and he tossed it back onto the hearth. "You might have pulled it off." I drew the bowstring farther; the telltale creak of stressed wood wiped the grin from his face. He tilted his head and squinted. "A fully barbed arrow? How very naughty of you. Did you fletch it yourself?"

"No."

"Well, that's small comfort. I must tell you, the decoy of pillows was a good move. I came to it like a deer at a salt lick. The snoring was also authentic, but coming from the wrong direction. However, I shall leave you to your nocturnal hunting if you'll leave me to mine. Just kindly point me in the direction of your lovely friend, and I'll be on my way."

"She's with the king."

"The king?" he parroted, and laughed. "Dear God! I can barely understand your petulance, but I accept it. However, you seem to be under the impression that I did something wrong here. Surely you must know that your little friend is adventurous? I was invited. I behaved in the manner she wished me to. There's no need to lie on her behalf."

It was my turn to smile. "I'm not lying. She's with the king."

"I beg to differ, sister dear. Your lovely friend cannot be with the king because the king is in Linlithgow."

My smile faded. I fought to keep up appearances, just as I fought to keep the bowstring taut. "Come now, brother, I'm not the idiot you believe me to be. I know the king is not in Linlithgow, just as you do."

"You're wrong. I don't think you an idiot, I think you presumptuous. In example, you presume I will believe your lie."

"It's not a lie!" My reply was terse, but I was tired, and my arm was beginning to shake under the stress of the bow. "You arranged for it. It was all part of your evil plan. Well, he's here, and now he's doing . . . well, you know what he's doing—the point is he's doing it with Marion." It was my turn to mimic the sardonic grin. I felt oddly triumphant as I added, "You never thought of that, did you?"

"No," he replied, and crossed his arms. He settled back against the bedpost. "It was never a consideration." On his face was a look of consternation, whether from his foiled sexual exploits or the news of the king's arrival, I couldn't tell. My arm trembled and burned; my fingers hurt from the cutting bite of the cord, but I would not ease up. Julius, always infuriating, knew this and appeared to revel in taking his sweet time as he pondered what I was telling him. His graceful hand moved to caress his chin; his eyes, staring into my own, turned suddenly inscrutable, and the room fell silent but for my slightly labored breathing. He waited, knowing I was in pain, knowing my arm was screaming for a respite—a dangerous thing to do for a man on the other end of a barbed arrow. He was remarkably unflinching as he lowered his hand and asked, "Are you, in fact, telling me that James is here, now?"

I exhaled with purpose. "Yes! And I . . . don't believe . . . you don't . . . know that . . . already!"

"Ease up on the bowstring, Isabeau. If you really wished to shoot me, you would have done so by now." I broke under his infernal hubris. With an angered grunt and a piercing stare I let fly the arrow. It slammed into the bedpost with lethal force, a mere hand's width above his head. He never flinched. A grim smile appeared as he offered coolly, "The fact that you didn't fletch your own arrow suggests it flies true. I knew you didn't have it in you to kill me."

"An insult and a compliment rolled into one. I'm flattered. But let me clarify, I don't mean to kill you *yet.*"

"I'm relieved to hear it." His tone was pleasant and slightly mocking. "Shake out your arm. Go on. It'll feel better. So," he said, shifting away from the bedpost. He paused to glance at how close I came to ending his life, raised an appreciative brow, and continued, "If I'm to believe your little story, you're insisting that James Stewart is here—at this very moment—in Blythe Hall. That, my dear, is impossible."

I found the manner in which he spoke confounding, for his tone was lightly weighted with sarcasm—as if he didn't believe me. I knew him to be a great dissembler, but what could he possibly gain by feigning ignorance? Yet the better question might be, what did he have to lose? "Let's pretend for a moment that I believe you," I said at last. "Why do you think the king is in Linlithgow?"

"Very well, I shall play your little game. Pretend that I have spies, and my spies tell me the king left Edinburgh early this morning, riding with a small retinue heading for the palace there."

It was unbelievable. And he was correct. James told me himself that he had managed to slip away from his Guard, sending them ahead to Linlithgow, where the court would shortly follow, while he traveled to Blythe Hall alone. Yet all I could think of to say was, "Why do you have spies watching the king?"

"We were playing pretend, remember? You're breaking the rules. Don't break the rules, Isabeau."

I set the bow down, entirely forgetting my reason for wanting it in the first place, and stood. Slowly I walked toward him, demanding, "Why are you watching the king, Julius?"

"Assume that I believe you. The mere fact that he's here, if, in fact, he *is* here, should tell you that I'm not watching the king." His look of innocence was infuriating, and only slightly convincing.

"Stop it!" I said at last, having had enough of it. "I'm not playing *pretend*, Julius. He *is* here! I'm not lying. What reason would I possibly have to lie to you about this?"

"You're right," he agreed, and after a moment's reflection all artifice, all caprice left his face. "You have many gifts, Isabeau," he added softly, "but lying, unfortunately, was never one of them."

The chilling levelness with which he spoke startled me

more than I would have liked to admit, prompting me to ask, "Are you telling me that you really didn't know he was here? You really didn't plan for this to happen—you, an outlaw and a traitor?"

His face darkened menacingly. "You have a bad habit of giving me far too much credit. No. I did not plan for this. But somebody did. What was his reason for coming? Did he give one?"

"Yes. It was Marion. He . . . he's very attracted to her."

"Marion?" Wan light flickered across his face.

"The woman you debauched last night?"

"I know her name," he snapped, and then his face stilled as a flash of a thought crossed his eyes. "She's Lord Kill-Me-Now's cousin, isn't she?"

"Yes, she is. Julius, what's going on here?"

"What's going on here, you ask?" His voice was soft yet his countenance was mockingly quizzical. "Oh, Isabeau," he uttered, and his lips twisted into a grin of heart-stopping cruelty. "Why, something exquisitely diabolical."

His words were like a vise on my heart, constricting painfully with each rising beat. Ignoring my fear, or because of it, he walked past me, picked up a brick of peat, and tossed it onto the glowing embers. There came a hiss of protest and a plume of black smoke. He knelt down and, employing the bellows, coaxed the nascent flame. "Think of it," he said, staring into the fire as he worked. I studied the familiar profile, watching how the growing light played along his classic features. His hair, flattened on the crown, had gone to curl at the ends, and appeared for a moment a glowing halo as the light caught it. But the look was deceiving, for here was no angel. He turned to me, facing away from the golden light. His features were once more cast in shadow. "The King's Guard is out hunting renegades. Kill-Me-Now has gone over the border to lift sheep. And you are here all alone, virtually unprotected, while the King of Scotland is so busy rutting your pretty little friend that he cannot begin to comprehend the danger he's in."

Julius made no secret that he knew very well what was going on. I glanced at my bow lying next to him; he slowly shook his head. Knowing it was of little use to me now, I crossed my arms and glared. "I'm painfully aware of what's going on. I should have put that arrow through your heart."

"And you believe that would solve all your problems?" He let out a soft, mirthless chuckle.

"I believe it wouldn't hurt. And another thing, Sir George is not lifting sheep; he's retrieving mine—as a favor to me. He loves me."

He set down the bellows and stood. "Of course he does, sweetheart; you're the key to the treasure room he cannot unlock. But you're wrong about the sheep. Georgie will certainly return bearing sheep, but they won't be yours."

I could not hide the anger in my voice. "How are you so sure?"

"Oh, Isabeau, what a sweet, gullible creature you are. 'Tis a pity I had to leave during your formative years. I could have taught you so much. Very well, if you must know, Lord Kill-Me-Now cannot return your sheep because I have them."

"You *what*? *You* stole my sheep?"

"Our sheep," he corrected. "And I didn't steal them. Douglas did. I merely took them back."

"What? Are you trying to make me believe that Sir George stole my sheep?"

"Our sheep. Yes. Truthfully, I was hoping to get there first, but he beat me to it. However, he's painfully predictable."

"Wait. What are you saying? Are you actually suggesting that *both* you and Sir George stole my sheep?"

"Aren't you listening? Why is it so hard for you to understand this? Douglas arranged for the sheep to be stolen. 'Tis not an uncommon ploy. A beautiful damsel is in distress because her livestock goes missing and with it her livelihood. The handsome knight, who wishes to win the heart of said beautiful damsel, suddenly appears on her doorstep and bravely volunteers to retrieve her missing sheep—at great peril to himself. But there's really no peril, just a little chicanery. Handsome knight trots off into the sunset, lies low for a day or two, rolls in the dirt, musses up his clothing, and then returns to the poor, desperate damsel with sheep in tow. It's a heartwarming reunion. Our dear damsel throws herself into her hero's awaiting arms and offers him whatever he wishes in return—silver, sustenance, her body. Our brave knight, of course, will want all three in an attempt to sate his insatiable hungers. But he won't get them, not on my watch—because I have the sheep. You won't, I'll wager, throw yourself at my feet."

It was unbelievable. I stared at him with mouth agape, sputtering, "You . . . you stole my sheep?! *And my silver?!*"

"*Borrowed* is the term I prefer. You seem to have overlooked the fact that I'm doing you an enormous favor here."

"Favor?" I sneered, very close to tears. Feeling helpless, I grabbed a pillow and hugged it tightly, as if it were an anchor keeping me from losing my sanity. "You think stealing my livestock and killing the good men of Blythemuir a favor? Did it ever occur to you that I'm a grown woman and perfectly able to fight my own battles?"

"Aye, you're a woman, but you cannot fight the likes of Sir George Douglas. He will eat you whole."

"I don't want to fight him, Julius!" I cried, and threw my pillow at him. He caught it and walked slowly toward me. "Don't you understand?" I hissed. "I do not wish to fight Sir George because I am to marry him!"

"I know," he said softly, standing over me. He gave me the pillow and eased himself onto the bed beside me. "I am here, in part, to see that you don't."

"It is the king's wish," I added helplessly.

"I will handle the king. And I shall return your sheep in the morning to prove my point. The silver, I'm afraid, is tied up at the moment. Kill-Me-Now will also return claiming he has your flock shall multiply before you—quite a miraculous feat, and one not entirely inappropriate for a place protected by angels. However, the former owners of Lord Kill-Me-Now's offering are certain to want recompense and will come storming the castle. It has the makings of quite an exciting day."

"The king? Julius, you are not to go near the king! I cannot allow that."

"The king is not safe here, Isabeau. You know that yourself. You would kill me before letting any harm befall James. I give you my word I won't go near him. I shall simply put the fear of God into the King's Guard. I imagine they'll be horrified when they find James here, alone."

"Why should I believe you?"

He gave a short, joyless laugh. "You really have no choice, do you? And if you've ever had a care for me, you will keep searching for my elusive friend. He will reveal his true identity only to you. Don't fight it, Isabeau. Don't fight what we are. We're a cursed race, and the sooner you embrace the truth, the better off you'll be."

෴

My head was pounding as I sat in the music room playing my little harp for the ebullient king and his shining new paramour, Marion Boyd. Apparently, unlike my own night, theirs had been magical—they were a couple transformed, and they whispered, giggled, and held hands as I was made to suffer their overbright company, in an overbright room with the full light of the midmorning sun beating on my aching body. Of sleep, I had gotten precious little, but I was taking a page from my brother's own book of deviancy and put on a convincing performance of placid Mistress of the Manor. It would never do to let anyone know of Julius's recent visit, or the many worries that ran wild in my mind.

Mme. Seraphina, however, did not live to such a great age by being as jolly and kindhearted as she appeared. Underneath the warm, motherly exterior was a mind as shrewd as a fox at the horn. She had seen the carelessly discarded mug on the hearth and had smelled it; she had taken note of the deadly bow on the floor by the chair, and she was particularly interested in the arrow still stuck in the post of the bed. "Oh, I see you were at the archery again. A fine shot, if not a rather close target." Her white brow rose with approbation, yet her eyes, round as coins, were not so easily diverted. She sat next to me on the bed, her penetrating blue stare fixed on the feather still clutched in my sleepy hand. I had no idea how it had gotten there, yet there was a look about her that suggested she did. Her rosy cheeks, soft and fragile as old parchment, expanded in accordance with her smile. And then she asked sweetly, "Tell me, dear, is it a coincidence that your arrow is a hair's breadth above the height of your brother?"

It wasn't a coincidence, and had I imbibed a little more wine, he might still be leaning against the pole, only with the aid of said arrow. I forced a smile and answered, "Purely a coincidence." She handed me a cup of tea then. It was a sweet, calming blend of herbs and honey that was much more pleasant than anything Tam would have forced down my gullet.

My fingers worked the strings with little thought and little heart. I knew this, yet I didn't much care because the inside of my head felt like a turbulent sea—only with two sets of waves rolling in from opposite directions, and coming to crash on the harried beach of my nerves with double strength. The truth was, I didn't know what to believe anymore, or even who to believe. The only thing I knew for certain was that the king was here—besotted, unguarded, unaware—and that I would protect his life with my own if it came to that. I prayed it wouldn't come to that. Yet just the fact that I was out of bed, sitting before the vast windows, dressed in a costly gown of spectacular pale blue silk, smelling of lavender and rose water, my hair coiffed to perfection, and my smile belying the pounding in my head, spoke volumes of my dedication to my cause if to no one else but me.

Before last night I had been certain that Julius was behind the suspicious sudden appearance of the king. He was, quite spectacularly, the logical culprit. Yet there was something about his manner that made me believe he was truly ignorant that the king had, in fact, turned up at Blythe Hall. Perhaps it was the knowledge that he had been watching the king, and that the king had escaped the notice of his spies? Yet the mere fact that he had been watching the king did not bode well. Why was he watching the king? Why was he trying to make me believe that Sir George was hatching a diabolical plan? Clearly he had qualms about my impending marriage to the man who had revealed him as a traitor. Yet the fact remained that Sir George was a hero of Scotland, and a man in very high favor with the king. And this favor was not about to diminish now that his cousin was the royal mistress.

Was it jealousy that drove him—jealousy that Sir George Douglas was soon to become Lord Blythe? Or was he protecting some secret? For he and my father had been the guardians of many secrets, of that I was certain, including the driving impetus behind the magnificent Chapel of Angels. The explanation that made the most sense, however, was the obvious one: Julius was mad. And to a madman without allegiance, direction, or a god, nothing would avenge his twisted soul so much as forcing me to embrace that same consuming affliction. According to my brother, an angel held the key to his salvation, and only I had the ability to find this angel. I wanted no part of it. I wanted no part of any of it. Yet I could not deny, in my heart of hearts, that there was something deeply alluring here, something that played upon the imagination, blurring the fine line between reality and madness.

"Isabeau, are you listening? I'm asking if you can play something a little more lively than that dour piece of religious drivel. The day is glorious! The birds are singing! And we have no wish to be reminded of pain and suffering. We are in love! Play us a French love song."

I stopped plucking the strings and looked at Marion. She was sitting on the window seat nearly on top of James, looking particularly lovely with a new string of white pearls around her slender neck that complemented her high color and flashing brown eyes. Her hand, elegantly grasping a tiny, sugared strawberry, was poised before the king's lips, yet going no farther. James, to my amazement, was entirely focused on this little berry—as if nothing else existed—and looking more like a lapdog than a fearless ruler of men. Mme. Seraphina, assiduously attacking a pair of hose with her mending needle, glanced up and rolled her eyes.

"Let me see . . . French love songs . . . ," I said, and pretended to think on this ridiculous request—ridiculous because I didn't feel much like taking requests at all. My head was pounding. I *was* in pain. I *was* suffering. Yet being the gracious hostess I was aiming to be, I replied sweetly, "Um, I don't believe I know any, except for those containing cautionary tales aimed at pretty young maidens who are tricked into lustful acts by conniving courtiers. Those seem to be very popular these days. However, that perhaps is not exactly appropriate either. And really, a proper love song should be played on the lute. I don't much feel like playing the lute."

James looked at me and grinned. Mme. Seraphina dropped her needle, then cleared her throat as she bent to retrieve it.

"Very well, I could make something up, I suppose." I thought for a moment, then began to pluck out a tune, sweet of melody and a wee bit livelier than a death lament. It was going rather well, I believed, yet I was only a few measures into it when the door to the room burst open and Tam fell in, his face flushed, his voice excited as he cried: "M'lady! Sire?" He paused, gave a curious look, and threw his head forward. "M'lady Boyd, ma'am." He paused again to catch his breath.

"They're here! The sheep have been found, and ye'll never guess what's happened to them or who's bringing 'em in."

I set down the harp and ran to the window, answering in a hopeful tone as I looked back at him, "Is it Sir George?"

"Nay. Not him."

The gates were opening. A long, velvety black nose poked through, followed shortly by drooping spiral horns. Then, as if a great press of water burst through an ill-constructed dam, the gates crashed open and a sea of white, skinny little bodies began filling the lower bailey. I gasped, for here were my sheep, although somebody had clipped all their wool. It was incredible! It was unbelievable! It was downright diabolical! I looked beyond the walls and saw the entire flock, moving cloudlike in wispy strands of fifty or sixty closely shorn beasts. They came through the sloping pastures near the river and onto the bridge as men on horseback guided them home. For the life of me I could not make out whose men they were. "Dear heavens above, what has happened to my sheep? This has the mark of Julius all over it. That devil! Oh, certainly he'll return my livestock now that he's deprived them of any value. God damn him! God damn his twisted soul to hell!" I swore, unable to conceal the derision that consumed me. Ignoring the general pall of incredulity that hung in the air at my wicked blasphemy, I could not ignore the king's look of horrified ecstasy at the name that so glibly rolled off my tongue. The string of blasphemy would be forgiven; uttering Julius's name had been a terrible mistake.

"Julius?" James repeated. "You think this is the work of Julius?" He sat up and stilled the hand that was ready to feed him yet another sugared berry. His glossy brown hair, worn shoulder-length, looked wild as it swirled about his face; his jaw was set in such a way that no one could deny the power and purpose of this man, yet when our eyes met, I saw question in them—and raw anger, and something very like wounded pride. And underneath it, subtle as a petrel over a stormy sea, I recognized the heartbreaking vulnerability that drove it all. I recognized it because it was a reflection of what lay in my own fragile heart. I had no choice but to look away.

Tam, observing us in the manner with which he might look at a horse for soundness, replied levelly, "Aye. It could be him, if Julius is a piratical-looking gent with a gold earring and the tongue of an Italian in his head, then aye! And he's with the shepherds too. Nearly all of 'em. They're a wee worse for wear, but they're a-singin' and a-grinnin' so, ye can hardly credit it."

⊰⊱

Leaving Marion in the company of Seraphina, James and I followed Tam into the courtyard. Once there I instantly recognized the man Tam had alluded to as the Italian. He was one of Julius's men, an absurdly fine-looking gentleman who at once appeared refined and utterly lethal. He possessed the same build as my brother, elegant and lean, only this man was his shadow, dark where Julius was light, with glossy black hair, olive skin, and the soft eyes of a spaniel. I found him slightly disarming, especially when he smiled. He had a mesmerizing smile. And he was smiling now as he looked down on me from the height of his saddle. I had to remind myself that the last time I had seen him he had been in my hall stealing my silver.

"Signorina," he began in honeyed tones, his lips poised in a wry grin, while his eyes beheld me in such a way that I actually checked to see if my clothes were still on, for I felt I must be naked. "It is with my master's compliments that I return what is yours. He asks that you have no ill will and begs me give you this." He handed me a note. I reached for it, yet the man held it a moment longer, allowing his eyes to linger over my face. I yanked the note away.

"And *who* is your master?" demanded James, exuding a regal air. "Where is he now?" I placed a hand on the king's arm, a subtle reminder that he must not make his identity known.

The Italian smiled, and with measured effrontery replied, "Signor, in this world there is only one man worthy enough for me to call master. He is neither a god nor a king, but a man who goes by the name of Blythe."

James looked at me, his brow furrowed in puzzlement and anger. He turned back to the Italian and demanded again, "And where is he, this man you call Blythe?"

"Ah," the Italian began, and shrugged his leather-clad shoulders in a manner that was both wistful and subtly shrewd. "Like the wind, he moves in all directions and is hard to pin down. I can hardly say from one moment to the next."

James, unused to such treatment, looked as if he was about to throttle the man. I held tightly to his arm and changed the subject. "Where have you been hiding my sheep?" I asked, seething. "And what power on God's green earth gave you the right to take their wool?"

"Beautiful signorina, I regret to tell you that it is not for me to say. I am only charged with delivering your beasts."

"And what about my wool?"

"The sheep were growing irritable. They enjoy using their horns. It needed to be done."

"Are you going to return my wool as well, or are you keeping it to line your fetid little nest in the brambles of hell?"

The Italian grinned. "Such spirit! Such imagination! Yet you forget, wool grows back. You have your sheep, and you have your men. It is infinitely better than not having them at all."

"You're right," I said, and shot him a basilisk stare. "Forgive me. I forgot for a moment that I can just ask my men. My men will tell me everything I need to know. And you can tell my brother that if he values his life at all, he'd best leave Scotland before the day is out."

"It is sound advice, and well-meaning. However, as I'm

sure you must know, my master answers to no one. Your advice will fall on deaf ears, signorina. And as for your men, your gentle shepherds, you may ask, but do not be hard on them if they cannot answer. But let us have a try, shall we?" He was clearly enjoying some great secret as he motioned to a man. To my surprise the man who came forward was Jacob Mackenzie, Kat's husband.

I studied him closely. He stared back at me, squinted, and then, opening his brown eyes unnaturally wide, cried: "Isabeau Blythe! Why, bless m'soul. Whatever are ye doing here, lass?"

"I'm . . . I am living here now, as Lady of the Manor."

"Och, that's chust grand!" he exclaimed. In a sweeping gesture of gratitude, he threw his head back to the heavens, and then he tumbled off his horse, taking a sheep or two to the ground with him. The sheep bleated and, employing a bit of horn, squirmed free. Jacob Mackenzie did not move. He was out cold.

"Is this man drunk?" I demanded of the Italian.

"Very likely so," was his infuriating reply.

"Are they all drunk?"

His dark, compelling eyes narrowed as if he was deep in thought. "They most probably are. And they were blindfolded a good deal of the time—and there may or may not have been drugs, although probably there was." He offered one last smile, displaying beautifully white teeth, and one last piece of advice. "Read the note," he said, and then he turned his horse. He wove his way through sheep and shepherd alike with the skill of a born reiver, and was out the gates as the beasts were still moving in. There was really no point in stopping him, even if, by any account, we could have.

ॐ

"Let me see the note again. What does he mean by this? And why the devil did you not tell me of Julius's return the moment I arrived?"

We were alone, sequestered in my father's solar. Hendrick was in the hall attempting to sober up the shepherds. Tam, with the help of Mutton Johnny and the Mackenzie brothers, was rounding up all able-bodied souls to help remove the sheep from the courtyard and return them to their folds. Seraphina thought it best to take Marion in hand, gently, lest she lose her head and start babbling about Julius. And I was left to deal with the king as he paced nervously before the fire. I left my seat at the window and walked over to him, placing my hand on his arm. He stopped pacing.

"Would you have turned around and gone home if I had?" I asked gently. "Julius showed up two days ago. It was the first I had seen him since . . ." I was about to say, his trial, but instead just said, "the day he left. Besides, if you'll remember, I had no idea you were planning a visit to Blythe Hall." Then, filling with anxious fear, I upbraided softly, "In the name of God, why did you have to come gallivanting to the Border-lands now, James—and without your guard?"

His face hardened, his lips pressed into a firm line of con-sternation. Like me, James did not like being scrutinized, nor did he tolerate very well being criticized for his past lapses in judgment. "I already told you," he replied curtly. "I will not say it again. But understand, Isabeau, that I do not regret coming here one bit. And what is more, I arrived unharmed." This last remark was punctuated by an arrogant lift of his brows.

"For that we are all grateful, my lord," I replied sincerely, and removed my hand from his arm. I turned once again to the window.

"I know you're angry with me, Isa, but still, would it not have been prudent of you to mention that Julius was back— before your sheep arrived today? You might have dropped me a little hint of it last night when we went to visit your father's magnificent chapel."

"And cause you added mental distress moments before

you were to . . ." I stopped, changed course, and added, "Besides, you dropped your *little* news on me regarding Sir George Douglas. Forgive me if I was a bit distracted."

He came beside me. "I'm sorry. I should have waited. But I had no idea anything was amiss."

"James . . ." I turned to face him. "Can I ask you something? Do you trust Sir George? I mean, implicitly?"

"Of course. Of course I do, or I would never have agreed to your marriage. Why do you ask?"

"I only ask because Julius indicated that Sir George was the one who lifted my sheep in the first place."

He smiled then, as if I was simple. "Really? Then how was it Julius's men had them and brought them back?"

"Because Julius retook them, or so he said."

He held up the note and read: "*I have upheld my end of the bargain. I've told you what will happen next. If you value the life of your king, you will do as I have asked. Embrace what you are, Isabeau. Do this one thing for me.*" He crumpled the note, crossed the room, and tossed it onto the fire. "It sounds an awful lot like blackmail to me. He returns the sheep; you do as he asks. By the way, what *does* he ask?"

"'Tis rather personal," I replied, and watched the paper burn. Out of the corner of my eye I caught the familiar, probing gaze. "What I mean is," I said, giving him my full attention, "that I'd rather not say."

"I am your king; my life is at stake here, or so your brother claims. I believe I have a right to know what he asks of you."

I considered what he said; I considered what the note said, and realized that there really was no point in reticence. A small, joyless laugh escaped my lips as I conceded, "Very well. If you must know, my brother has asked me to find him an angel. Apparently he believes me capable of the task."

James froze; his entire body stood motionless as he held me under an inscrutable gaze. And then he put forth the one question I feared might come. "And . . . and are you, Isa-beau?"

My breath escaped in a violent burst of irritation, and I crossed my arms, holding them tightly to my chest. "Of course not! And don't be so quick to believe such absurd notions. Julius is mad."

"Yes. But . . . why?"

"Why is he mad? Or why ask of me something I cannot do?"

"Why ask?"

"Well, that's just the point, isn't it? I don't know why. My personal belief is that by requesting I do this thing, he will succeed in pushing me to the edge of madness—along with him."

"I knew Julius once, as did you. Do you really believe him mad?"

"Oh yes. Brilliantly so. Which makes him all the more dangerous. But again, I keep asking myself, why is he here now? And why is he trying to make me believe that Sir George might not quite be what he appears?"

"That's simple," James said, and sat on the cushion of the window embrasure. "Revenge. Surely you realize he has to malign the man who ruined him? Yet being Julius, he must also realize that any attempt to slander such a great name would be futile. Perhaps that's why he wishes to ruin your credibility, and if he succeeds in getting you to believe him, why, then he will turn you against Sir George. Julius, out of spite alone, would not want Kilwylie holding the title that should have been his. By God . . . it's a brilliant plan!" he exclaimed, his eyes bright with bitter admiration. And then he caught himself, and tempered his emotions. "And finding me here, with naught but a few kitchen lads at the gates—"

"Please," I said, unwilling to let him finish. "Do not think of it."

"But I must, and should God see that I survive this madness, I swear I will never let him leave Scotland alive."

I looked at him. He was serious, yet I knew that should he ever come face-to-face with the viper, he would believe every gilded word dripping off the forked tongue. Unfortunately, I knew I was little different. And just to appease that cold and withered place in my heart that still held a glimmer of hope for my brother, I decided to play the devil's advocate. "But," I uttered, sitting gently beside him, "what if Julius has a point? What if Sir George is not everything he appears? Certainly no one could argue the man's bravery or his service to his country. But don't you find it a bit odd that both men descend on Blythe Hall the same day I returned home—only to engage in some sort of twisted power struggle? And odder still is the fact that you are here as well."

Only because it was me, I believed, did he consider this, although he found it to be execrably distasteful. "Isabeau, my appearance here is purely coincidental; it has nothing to do with Julius or George. And what happened all those years ago I have struggled to put behind me, and so should you. I was made to believe that my father was my enemy; I was made to believe that your brother was my friend."

"I know. You wear an iron chain around your waist so that you will always remember the price of your throne. And I have fashioned one around my heart as a reminder of what I have lost."

"Dear Isabeau," he said, and laid a hand over mine. "Do you remember how you insisted I cover the iron links with fabric so it would not chafe? Would I only had a solution for you to ease the pain you still carry. Look at us. What a fine pair we make, both of us tortured by a past we cannot change, nor can we forget. You must take heart that you were an innocent bystander in the calamity that beset your father and brother; I, however, played a willing part in my father's death. Julius may have tried to sell me to the English, but I allowed my father to be killed by his own rebellious noblemen. We were children; I have tried to come to terms with it, just as have you. I have prayed. I have received absolution from Pope Innocent VIII. I have embraced the Observantine friars—in my mother's honor, yet I am not at all convinced God has forgiven me of my sins. The one thing he has done, to lighten my heart, is that he sent me you. You may not be able to summon an angel at will, but to me you are an angel, Isabeau; for how could I have borne all those years without your friendship? There is no greater truth than that. And now we find ourselves here, no longer children but two burgeoning adults, on the eve of yet another calamity. You know I will fight to the death before I let Scotland be torn asunder by a grasping madman. Yet if we are to survive here at all, I believe our only hope lies in the hands of Sir George and Sir Matthew. Let us pray they come soon."

I stepped back to better look him in the eye. "I was afraid to tell you yesterday the true whereabouts of your Guard. They are not with Lord Kilwylie. Sir Matthew and his men left yesterday in search of Julius. Julius knows where they are, or so he made me believe. He implied he would bring them back, just as he said that Sir George would return bearing more sheep. But if Julius is correct about Sir George?"

He closed his eyes, and in that instant—as the color drained from his young, princely face—I caught a glimpse of the weight he carried. "If Julius is correct," he breathed, "then God help us all."

Chapter 9
THE MASTER

THE ITALIAN WALKED DOWN THE LONG, DARK PASSAGE-way carrying before him a sputtering taper. He moved with the ghostly elegance of a man used to surreptitious dealings, his footfalls muffled, his breathing measured, until at last he spied the pale light in the distance seeping from the doorway. He knew it would be left open a crack, for the master was expecting him, and he thought once again how ingenious it all was. He stood before the door, blew out the candle, and gave a solid knock.

With a groan the heavy oak gave way under his knuckles and opened further, allowing him a view of the remarkable room. It was quite large and spacious. The ceiling was not very high, but it was vaulted and held up by a span of stone arches mirroring the eight points of a compass. The vaults were supported by thick stone pillars set into walls of large, rectangular slabs of yellowish stone, much like all the castles in these parts. The furnishings were quite costly, and on the floor was a thick carpet he placed as Syrian. Yet what he found most interesting was that the room was circular, which meant no corners for the devil to hide in. The thought made him smile. Air moved imperceptibly through the room, drawn by the low fire that no one on the outside would be able to detect. This unlikely chamber, carved out of stone and earth, and hidden from sight and all the senses, had been painstakingly thought out, and he had never seen its like; for in the city where he grew up such things were impossible. He understood it held a treasure, although not the material kind he preferred. The riches here were of a different nature, written in the scrolls that sat in the walls like bees incubating in a honeycomb, or the wooden cases where the musty old books and leather-bound parchment were kept. There were also maps here of places he had never heard of, and of seas he had never sailed. And then there were the odd drawings, kept in a drawer, of things both frightful and glorious. The master sometimes slept here, for there was a pallet near the hearth cloaked in rumpled blankets, and beside it on the floor was a gown that looked suspiciously like a woman's. Yet he knew better, for Julius Blythe would never bring a woman here—to a place far beyond the comprehensive abilities of the fair sex. But it would, he mused, make quite the love bower. And with this thought he stepped into the room.

The master, sitting at a heavy desk built into the curvature of the wall, did not flinch. He remained unmoving, bent over some fascinating scribble contained on a scroll or some ancient piece of parchment. It was hard to tell, for the desk was cluttered with books, papers, ink bottles, a half-eaten bannock, a lump of stale cheese, and an assortment of pewter mugs. The flame from an old oil lamp illuminated his hair, making it appear a shimmering halo of soft curls, while his shoulders, rounded with the slightest hint of fatigue, strained against the white fabric of his shirt. He was reading again, as he had been nearly every quiet moment since they had arrived. The man was tireless; his energy seemed born of dark sources, for it flowed in abundance and gave life to the razor-sharp wit that both lashed and caressed those who fell under it. Yet even a titan will weaken, just as every man had his limit, and this man was swiftly approaching his. Darkly amused by this thought, and feeling quite brave, he came softly behind the master and said very near his ear, "By the gods, your sister is exquisite! The other night, in the hall, it was far too dark to see her clearly, but today, with the full light of the sun falling on her lovely face, her cheeks flushed with anger, her aqua eyes—I never knew such a color to exist!—flashing daggers, and that hair . . . Oh, that hair! Far prettier than your flea-infested mop. I could bathe in that hair."

The master's muscular back straightened, the linen of his fine shirt eased, and his golden head came up. "Dear Dante," began the master. "Your mother was a whore. You were raised in a brothel." His chair slowly scraped over cold stone, and in a moment the hooded eyes were staring into the Italian's. "And when I found you, you were bloodied, and broken, and chained to the bench of a Turkish galley. Given all that, what makes you think I would possibly let you pursue your current train of thought?"

"Possibly because you were chained next to me?" said the Italian, offering a disarming grin.

"True," replied the Master of Blythe. He folded his hands and created a steeple with his forefingers, which he placed gently against his pursed lips, as if deep in thought. The fingers slowly lowered. "But again, I harken back to your humble beginnings."

"My father was the Doge of Venice . . . or possibly a cardinal, it was unclear, but certainly both are great men."

The master gave a soft chuckle. "If I were to make a guess at your dubious parentage, I'd wager you were the spawn of an ambitious Medici banker, solely on the observation that your gift of numeracy is unholy."

"Maybe," replied the Italian, "but still, I prefer to think of my father as the Doge of Venice."

"My dear Dante, think whatever you like; I prefer not to think of my father at all."

Dante smiled at this and replied not unkindly, "You forget. I know what a convincing liar you are." He looked beyond the master to the table before him, where he saw what had held the man's attention. It was a magnificent illumination of an archangel, surrounded by shafts of holy light as he descended from the heavens with wings unfurled. And then he read the Latin inscription beneath: CADO ANGELUS. Correction: this was no archangel; this was a fallen angel.

"Your recreational preferences astound me. Women fall at your feet, and yet you are here, in your cave, deciphering ancient chicken scratch. What joy, what physical elation can you possibly get from studying such as that?" He motioned to the drawing.

The master sat back and raised a brow in wry amusement. "If you would lift your head out of the brothel every now and again, you might realize that there are other varieties of elation besides physical. And, if you must know, I've had my fill of women for the moment. Ancient chicken scratch on parchment is easier to decipher than the mind of a woman. Tell me, Dante," said Julius Blythe, deftly changing the subject, "in your humble opinion, what do you think the secret of immortality is worth?"

Dante, taking the proffered chair, grinned. "So, you *are* working. You had me worried for a moment. Very well, I shall tell you. The value, my friend, is incalculable, because immortality is impossible."

"Is it? Yet for ages men have sought immortality, believing the secret to such unobtainable treasures to be found in a stone created of base metals that would turn other base metals, such as lead, to gold—the sorcerer's stone, or the philosopher's stone if you like. The thought behind it is really quite just, for if gold is the purest substance on earth and it never tarnishes, the mortal mind that unlocks the secret of this remarkable transmutation must therefore be rewarded with infinite knowledge, infinite wealth, and, of course, immortality. Yet in the history of man it has never been achieved. Why?"

"I told you why, but you weren't listening." Dante feigned a look of impatience. "Very well, I shall tell you again. It hasn't happened yet, because such a thing is impossible."

"That appears, by all accounts, to be true. But only because immortality is not attained through a stone."

"And you know this—you, the broken, reprobate son of a Scottish nobleman?"

"You know it too, Dante. As a Venetian you were made to witness every year your doge wedding the sea in an ancient and elaborate ritual. But is it possible to marry something that is not human and not of the opposite sex?"

Dante frowned. He didn't like it when people questioned the ways of his native city. "The doge marries the sea because it is tradition. The sea is the lifeblood of the Venetian people," he answered plainly. "It is out of reverence. To us the sea is as bountiful as she is beautiful."

"And sometimes she is a hard, cruel bitch. My point is that it takes a tremendous leap of faith to believe that a man can marry an element as powerful as the sea. It's presumptuous; it's irreverent, and yet it is very likely the reason you yourself believe you sprang from his loins as well."

"He's a very virile man, the doge. How else does one keep pace with an insatiable mistress like the sea?"

The Master of Blythe chuckled at this, displaying the source of his mesmerizing charm—his smile. He poured a glass of wine from a decanter and handed it to the young Italian. "Marrying the sea is, in itself, a subtle display of man's quest for immortality, for the sea, dear Dante, unlike the man elected as the Doge of Venice, is without end." The master took a drink, and so did Dante. "What is your opinion?"

Dante, savoring the dark red liquid as it caressed his parched throat, did not reply at once. It had been a busy morning; he was tired, and the wine was superb. He pretended to think for a moment, his dark eyes glancing to the ceiling for inspiration. At last he smiled and replied, "My opinion is that you need to lie with a woman."

The master, with the fine lines of exhaustion just visible on his face, gave a sigh of exasperation, as a mildly disappointed parent might do. "Forgive me," he said, "I've been caught up in personal matters. You have come, I hope, to tell me how your delivery went."

Dante tossed back the last of his wine. "Under the circumstances, I believe it went rather well. Although your sister was displeased to learn that her sheep have lost their wool."

"I imagine she was." The thought made him smile. "You'll be happy to know I've received word from Berwick. The silver is standing surety for the cargo, and Sir Andrew Wood is ready to set sail on the *Yellow Caravel.*" He reached behind him and pulled a sheet of paper from beneath the scroll he had been studying. "Here," he said, handing it to Dante. "These are the ledgers, with the first column indicating the current rate for a bale of raw wool in Antwerp—not bad. More than enough to secure the cargo coming from Cyprus. The second column is the projected percentages of exchange in the larger European markets for our Cypriot cargo, reaching a 300 percent profit. Thanks to the Turks and their institutionalized destruction of Rhodesian sugar refineries, we can ask whatever we like. Europe, dear Dante, has an insatiable sweet tooth."

As Dante studied the sheet, a slow smile appeared on his lips. "These are good."

"They're beyond good," Julius proclaimed, mirroring the Italian's smile.

"And here I thought we left our lucrative trade on the Continent to come here, spend money, live like kings, and wreak havoc on all your old friends, particularly him," he said, a mischievous gleam in his eye as he pointed to the illumination of the fallen angel.

Julius glanced over his shoulder and then turned back to the Italian. He smiled, knowing what he meant. "He's not fallen yet, but God knows I'm going to try. He once told me he believed there was no temptation on earth that could make him fall from God's grace. However, you know I love nothing more than testing such heavenly paragons."

"And you plan to test him. How?"

"Dear Dante, use your imagination."

Dante, staring into the cerulean eyes of the man before him, suddenly understood. "Your sister," he concluded, and grinned. "Oh, that's cruel—even for you!"

"Cruel? I guess that depends on your definition of *cruel*. My scheme, however, is not without variables."

"Isabeau, for one," Dante remarked appreciatively. "She's willful. She hates you. And there are plenty of other men to distract her. Why do you think she will look at him," he said, gesturing to the magnificent illumination, "any differently than she looks at me?"

"Because, whereas your pleasing looks may fool most women, my friend, beneath it all you're just a piratical reprobate with the morals of an alley cat. Our friend is not."

"But she may like piratical reprobates," he offered hopefully. "She likes your friend Kilwylie."

"Only because she has so little choice," replied the master, remarkably calm. "I'm merely expanding the stagnant pool of inbred locals."

"And you believe he will come, our friend?"

"I have it on good authority that he will, yes."

"Your vast network of spies tell you this?"

"My spies, I'm learning, are not all that reliable. And in this case they wouldn't know where to begin to look, for unlike you and me, our friend does not slink down hallways or lurk in shadows and dark places. He walks in rays of sunlight. Rainbows form overhead when he's near, and his path is sweetened with the perfume of a thousand rose petals, because he only walks on rose petals," the master said mockingly. "People, dear Dante, are afraid to look directly into the path of the sun; people are tired of rainbows. My sister, with her lively imagination, is not one of them, thankfully. When the air smells of rose petals, we'll know he's arrived. However, I fear we're running out of time, because Douglas, the cunning bastard, is doing his utmost to destroy me. And speaking of Douglas, what do we know?"

"There's been no word of him as of yet. And I haven't heard from Fergie Shaw either, although it's likely too soon. I sent Will Crichton the moment I received your message regarding Sir Matthew and the Guard."

"Excellent. Will's our fastest rider and knows these hills as well as myself and old Fergie Shaw. We should get to Sir Matthew before Douglas does," he said, then paused, his brows drawn in concern. "Let me know the moment Will arrives?"

"Of course."

"One more thing. You say the sheep have all been delivered soundly, and will soon be fattening upon the greening sward, but did you happen to see the king?"

"If he's a man of good height, athletic build, hair that is neither brown nor red, with penetrating eyes and a chafing manner, and standing far too close to your lovely sister, then yes, I believe I did."

"Oddly enough that description fits him like an expensive glove," Julius answered reflectively. "But do take heart, for the king is not interested in my sister the way you think. He's interested in Marion Boyd, if Isabeau is to be believed."

"That pretty little signorina with the welcoming eyes and the lips that promise untold pleasures?"

"Ah, you know her too. I take no comfort in that thought." It was an honest reply, and one that made Dante grin. "And the shepherds, will they talk?"

"Oh, they won't talk. They've been paid and sworn to secrecy. My guess is that by the end of the week they'll all be begging to come back here, wherever here is."

"Good work. Now, return to the men. I shall be with you all shortly. And about the women, it's time to swear them to secrecy as well. Pay them accordingly and have them discreetly taken back to Kelso."

"The whores? Must we? So soon? But the men so enjoy their company," he stated plainly, in a fleeting attempt to change the master's mind.

Julius took the empty glass from the Italian's hands and said in a tone of irrevocable finality: "Dante."

With a sigh of resignation, the young man stood. "Very well, my lord," he replied, "I shall do as you ask."

"And do not linger," added Julius Blythe, watching his second in command walk to the door.

The Italian turned back to the room with a mischievous twinkle in his eye. "Sir," he said theatrically, bringing a hand over his heart. "Like you, I never linger."

Chapter 10
RETURN OF
THE KNIGHT

JAMES'S WORDS HAD SHAKEN ME TO THE CORE, AND I could not dispel the cold fear that seemed my constant companion. I found it irksome how fear and anger—such counterproductive emotions—were dominating my better judgment. In spite of my headstrong tendencies, I believed myself to be a pleasant person and quite good company, yet I was wearing on even my own patience. I was beginning to doubt nearly everything I believed as truth, including my own sanity; for how else could I explain my visions or the fact that yesterday I had truly wanted to kill my brother? Even now I had no reason to give credence to a word Julius said, especially after his debacle in the hall and his unremorseful debauchery of Marion. He was a shifty creature—a man with the charmer's smile who courted danger and dined with the devil—and he had violated everything the name Blythe stood for. Given all that, I still could not kill him. I doubted I could even wound him. Because the Julius of my childhood—

valiant, kind, spirited—I still loved. It gave me no right, however, to trust the man he had become. Yet deep down, in that empty and dark place within my heart, I knew I wanted to do just that. Perhaps it was the mere force of his personality. More likely it was my inveterate longing for redemption, for redemption was the key to a good story. But Julius was not the hero of any story. He was real, and he was terrible. And he was up to no good. Still, I wanted to believe he was not entirely evil. And yet, on the other side of that same coin lurked another distasteful conundrum. If what Julius had been hinting about Sir George was correct, then the ramifications were greater than I could fathom. Sir George was connected, powerful, and utterly trusted by the king. If he meant to do harm, it would be on a grand scale. But what could he possibly gain by harming the king . . . or me? Truthfully, I didn't know him well enough to even venture a guess.

Perhaps that was the real problem nibbling away at me like so many ravenous mice in the larder. Perhaps that was the real source of my fear and anger. Sir George was largely a stranger to me. Yet no one could deny that he was a commanding man of fine looks and dark sensuality, and if I was being utterly truthful, I would admit that I had never been immune to his charms. In fact, I found that I rather liked the man, in spite of his once intimate connection to Julius. He had been right to do what he did regarding my brother—for the good of the country. And maybe he did feel he had earned the right to be the next Lord Blythe; maybe he did feel some sense of responsibility toward me. And just maybe he truly did love me. Whatever governed the motives of Sir George, he had come to Blythe Hall in search of me. Julius had come to thwart him. Yet I couldn't shake the feeling that both men were looking for something more.

With our marriage, Lord Kilwylie would gain Blythe Hall and her title, just as I would be Lady Isabeau Douglas of Blythe and Kilwylie. Admittedly, Blythe Hall wasn't the largest or wealthiest estate in the kingdom, but it did hold a strategic place along the border. In my opinion it was a precarious bargain, and Sir George would have no choice but to be a guardian of Scotland—a hard, thankless job. He would also have me as a wife, which might also prove to be a hard, thankless job. But that was cruel. I shouldn't think such things. The king had thought long and hard about my welfare, and he believed Sir George the best man for the position. I would not disappoint him.

The most logical answer to what was really going on was the one James had suggested. Julius had returned to seek revenge on the man who had ruined him. It made sense. Julius somehow knew Sir George was heading to Blythe Hall, and he had intended to make him look the fool, just as he had intended to humiliate me and poison my mind against his enemy. Julius had robbed me; Sir George had used me as a shield in a sword fight. Sir George apologized and professed his love; Julius didn't apologize and was attempting blackmail. Julius was nudging me toward madness; James had revealed that Sir George had negotiated a marriage contract behind my back. Clearly both men were no angels, but now was not the time to complain and deliberate. The king was in danger, sitting like a fish in a barrel here at Blythe Hall. The wisest thing to do was not to believe anybody, for surely someone was lying. And I would know the answer soon enough; I would know the answer when Sir George returned. Truthfully, I didn't know which thought turned my stomach more.

After my brother's Italian lackey left—the fact that he had an Italian working for him was puzzling in its own right—the castle was a perfect beehive of activity. The sheep, after a good deal of hard work by a couple of men, some boys, and a few dogs, had finally been removed from within the castle walls and were on their way to the pastures of Blythemuir to graze. The shepherds, lying on benches in the hall as if awakening from a long night's sleep, had been revived to the best of Hendrick's ability, but by all accounts they were an interesting case. And all ten men were still frightfully woozy from their ordeal. They were fed, made to drink tepid milk, and ordered to walk around the room until they sobered or purged. Yet given all Hendrick's wise ministrations, they still could not tell us much about what had happened to them over the past five days other than the fact that they were in some kind of glorious dream world with shadowy references to Greek orgies.

This, of course, piqued everyone's interest, including Marion's, who had a fondness for classical tales and loved nothing more than a good story of Roman or Greek (she wasn't picky) debauchery. Interesting as it was, however, this did cause me to ask Hendrick, rather discreetly, if those certain places in Kelso, Coldstream, even Jedburgh had been checked. Unfortunately, I was frightfully unaware of just how many places there were like that. However, as Hendrick explained prosaically, there were none to his knowledge that could possibly fit the shepherds' description—on this side of the border. The fact was, we had very few able-bodied men left, and the king's safety, however tenuous it was, was far more important than sending any more men beyond the bounds of Blythemuir to hunt for Julius. Chances were, he would snap them up, putting the odds in his favor that much more—if, in fact, he was the one bent on doing the king harm. The result of our precarious predicament left little choice as to the course of action to be taken. We would do what I was painfully good at doing: pretending everything was just fine.

Mme. Seraphina was a godsend. During the trying events of the morning and all through the messy aftermath of the drunken shepherds and misguided sheep, she had skillfully maneuvered Marion back to the solar, where she could keep her from asking too many importunate questions about Julius. For although Marion was securely engaged with the king in both body and mind, we suspected that my brother had managed to steal a bit of her heart. For both their protection it was in Marion's best interest that she be kept well clear of Julius and his machinations if at all possible. When, after reining in my wild nerves and careening fear, I came to join them, a genuine bubble of amusement rose within me, and I almost smiled. For there, sitting before the tall arched windows with a plate of oatcakes and what I imagined to be very strong spiced wine on the table between them, was my aged governess discussing with Marion the latest fashions in France, with a most serene and engaging voice.

Seraphina had spent her youth in France, as had my mother, and it was her habit not to talk of her native country. She was also not one to care overmuch about outer garments other than that they be clean and tidy, for she was a woman who fashioned and dressed the soul. "Anyone," Seraphina often proclaimed, "with enough silver can slap on the finest double-cut velvet and prance about like a queen, but the road to heaven is not so easily won, and no amount of silver or double-cut velvet can open the gates of eternal paradise like a clean conscience and a pure heart can." They were undoubtedly wise words if not a bit disheartening for a young girl newly come to court, but such was the mien of Seraphina. And that's why this conversation tickled me the way it did. The fabrics, gowns, shoes, and headdresses she was describing in great detail to my friend could not have been called anything remotely like the latest in courtly fashion, yet Marion seemed entranced, captivated by her every word. ". . . And I marveled at her poulaines of red velvet ending in points at least the length of the foot itself, with little silver bells sewn on the tips, and her gown was woven with real gold thread, so she shimmered like the flame of a candle as she walked."

"Oh," I heard Marion utter dreamily, "I should like a gown of gold cloth."

"I know you would, dear." Seraphina smiled and sat back

in her chair, cradling her goblet of wine between her plump hands. "Wouldn't we all?"

"I thought poulaines went out of fashion a good thirty or forty years ago?" I said, coming to join them. "A highly impractical shoe—far too impractical for us Scots at any rate. I've heard tell of French knights who, after some hideous battle, had to chop the points off their poulaines before they could run from their enemy. Why is it the French always run from the enemy?" I smiled at Seraphina and was awarded a disingenuous look of surprise.

"Oh? Well, perhaps you're right," conceded my governess with a look that showed the depth of her waning patience. "They're not at all the thing for a fighting man, I agree. But they look fine enough poking out from the hem of a gown spun with gold thread I should say—especially when bedecked with tiny silver bells." This last point was marked by a spectacularly wide-eyed gaze, which caused me to understand that the suggestion of silver bells was not a whimsical one. I wanted to smile but fought the urge and offered a small, barely perceptible nod instead. Bell the cat, indeed, for how else were the mice to know when the cat was on the prowl?

"Silver bells," repeated Marion with glossy-eyed wonder. "How charming! They would look quite nice, wouldn't they?"

"Would you like a pair, dear?" offered Mme. Seraphina. "I shall send the tailor to the cordwainer in Kelso and have him make you a pair directly."

"I'd like a pair too," I said. The subtle sarcasm in my voice was not lost on Seraphina. I hadn't needed to add—for my brother. One look at my face told Seraphina all she needed to know.

"I'm sure you would, dear," she replied with a smile, although her voice was void of any perceptible emotion. "But for now I believe a little wine would serve you better."

I gladly accepted the offered drink and sat down to join

them. Yet I had no sooner put the rim to my lips than the king walked through the door. The change in Marion was immediate. "Are we in danger?" she asked, coming alive at the sight of him.

"My dear," James began, and crossed the room to stand before her. He took her dainty little hands in his, and with a voice as gentle as a midsummer breeze asked, "Why ever would you think such a thing?" James, being a gallant young lover, had wanted Marion soundly kept in the solar to shield her from the dangers that lurked beyond the castle walls; we thought it best she remain there to keep her from speaking of Julius.

Marion smiled coyly. "Because you are wearing your great big sword."

"Ah," remarked the king, and laid a hand on the beautiful silver hilt of the ancestral weapon that hung at his side. "I am, aren't I? 'Tis only because of this talk of Julius. Isabeau told me he has been in the castle quite recently." At this mention of my brother I looked at Marion, begging her with my eyes not to say a word, for whatever had happened two nights earlier in my old chamber had affected her deeply, and the mere mention of my brother's name caused her eyes to smolder, her cheeks to go red, and her breathing to become deep and slightly irregular. It was happening now. My brother's name, combined with the visceral sense of danger—and quite possibly the wealth and power of the man standing before her— was like catnip to a kitten. Thank goodness the king didn't know her like I did, for he believed her excitement and high color were for him and him alone. Maybe they were. Who was I to doubt my dearest friend?

"And what about the sheep and all this talk of Roman orgies?" she asked sweetly, although her magnificent dark eyes, if truth be told, were boldly suggestive. "Do you believe Julius is responsible for this as well?"

The king swallowed and broke from her penetrating gaze

to look out the windows. "The man who returned them was one of Julius's men," he answered softly.

Marion brought her hand to the sword and gently laid it over the king's, stilling his roving fingers. His eyes came back to hers. "Surely returning Isabeau's sheep is not an act of treachery. Surely Julius does not mean us harm."

James, staring once again into her fathomless eyes, beheld her with a look of such raw tenderness that this time I had to look away. "You are entirely correct," I heard him say, and he unbuckled his sword belt.

⚶

I learned that it is hard to keep a young man of boundless energy and probing intelligence confined to a few secure rooms of a castle—especially when the man in question is overwrought with palpable sexual tension and the very real threat of danger to his person. James wanted to hunt—he was a man of action. Instead we confined him to the solar. We indulged in music, but no one was in the mood. We played chess, but neither Marion nor I was a fit opponent for him. Mme. Seraphina suggested he try his hand at needlework, believing busy hands would relax a restless mind. But the king, growing frustrated with the intricacies involved in making little stitches, finally tossed his frame, needle, and skein of thread out the window, an act only a king could get away with in the presence of Mme. Seraphina.

All polite conversation had been exhausted. Our meal was eaten in near silence. Finally, when the young man's agitation had grown unbearable, Marion stood, grabbed him by the hand, and pulled him into the bedchamber. No one commented; no one so much as exchanged a knowing look . . . even though it was only midafternoon. I retired as well, but only to the top floor of the castle from where a small winding staircase led to the battlements.

I hadn't walked along the battlements for an age, and it felt odd that I should do so now. There was no one up here, for no men were to be spared, and so I walked along the rooftops looking in all directions. It was, in spite of the troubling events of the morning, quite a beautiful day. I stood for a moment gazing out over the gentle roll of the budding orchards to the far hills, where the top of the crumbling old peel tower could just be seen poking through, and to where the verdant fields on the other side of the hills were welcoming home our tired sheep. I thought of Tam then, and the slightly devious Mackenzie brothers, who had accompanied him on the task. They were much the same age, I realized, and perhaps even cut from the same mold. Yet whereas Tam had the pressing responsibility of being my groom and, by default, the larger responsibility of my safety, Jerome and Brendon had only themselves to look after, and whatever menial tasks Mutton Johnny desired them to do. Therefore, it wasn't any wonder that they had not yet resurfaced. They were likely still visiting all the cottages, spreading the good news of the shepherds' return and celebrating with food and drink. Suddenly, selfishly, I wished I had gone with them. Nothing lifted the spirits like a genuine, heartfelt smile after so much worry.

A smile . . . What could bring a smile to my lips? I mused, resting my forearms on the cool ocher stone of a crenellation. I leaned forward and stared out over the land that for as far as the eye could see fell under my jurisdiction. Dear to me as Blythemuir was, the thought brought no great joy. And then, as I dwelled on happiness and the fleeting nature of joy, the answer sprang forth in a powerful yet evanescent vision. Like the idea of trapping an emotion in a word, or containing the spirit of an eagle in a feather, the essence of the man who filled my imagination was impossible to capture. He was a thought, an emotion, a glimpse of a dream unattainable. I felt a rush of joy followed swiftly by a pang of sorrow so acute that tears, first stinging the lining of my nose, began filling my eyes. I was happy and miserable at once, happy because he was my secret pleasure—a man ineffably sublime. And yet I was miserable because I knew he lived only in my imagination—miserable because Sir George, the man I was to marry, would eventually drive him away.

I had come to the battlements seeking solace, and I had succeeded only in making myself lower than I could have imagined. I was sulky, trying to recapture that frangible wisp that caused my heart to soar and made my future seem brighter even though dark clouds gathered on the horizon. I could hear men in the courtyard below, the shepherds were sobering up, yet my sight was still blurred by tears of frustration and a feeling of hopeless destitution. I kept my head to the hills, not wishing to see the men my brother had abused. It was then that I caught a flash of light on the edge of my watery vision. It came again and again, and it was a moment before I dried my eyes in order to discover its source.

My breath caught in my throat at the sight. It was Sir George and his men, the banner of Kilwylie flying before them as they raced toward Blythe Hall. They rode in one cohesive unit and moved with brutal elegance as they crested a distant hill and veered toward the castle gates, sunlight bouncing off their polished helmets like sparks from a Catherine wheel. The martial sounds of jostling armor and straining leather accompanied them as they came three abreast up the road that ran between new-sown fields and flowering orchards. Clods of black earth exploded beneath furious hooves, while delicate blossoms of pink and white fell on the mail-covered bodies like fairy-tale snow. It was a scene both serene and violent, and it caused my heart to ache and my soul to bleed, for Sir George and his warriors had returned empty-handed.

Empty-handed they might be, but even I could see that they rode with urgency, and it was this, above all, that gave me a start. I pushed aside my own sorrows for that small, fading ember of hope I had fought to keep alive—even against my better judgment. I had wanted to believe in Julius even though I knew perfectly well what he was. And now, the appearance of Sir George was the final, abrupt ending to a long and heart-wrenching chapter in my life. Julius had lied, and Sir George was the harbinger of the evil he was about to unleash.

With a flood of grief only slightly outweighed by a sense of urgency, I turned from the incoming army and shouted down to the courtyard: "Open the gates! Open the gates! Sir George has come." Yet as soon as I gave the order I realized that the men in the gatehouse were infinitely more prepared to receive Lord Kilwylie than was I.

᪡

Like a plague of ravaging locusts, the news Sir George had brought to the gates of Blythe spread unchecked through the castle and lay waste to everyone's hopes. The king, after being roused from his chambers by my insistent knocking — I thought it best to knock even though I possessed a key — stood beside me in the courtyard, along with Hendrick, as an incredulous Lord Kilwylie delivered his incredible news.

"Your Highness? Your Highness!" he said, his spectacular green eyes wide and unblinking as he dismounted his horse and fell to one knee before his sovereign. He looked up into the face of the young king — a face that was remarkably calm yet filled with high color — and uttered with rapt disbelief, "Dear God, how is it possible that you are here . . . now?" It seemed, by all accounts, that Sir George was every bit as perplexed by the king's sudden appearance in the Borders as Julius had been. Yet Julius, unlike Sir George, I knew to be a gifted actor.

"I sent a message," the king replied, motioning for the knight to stand. "It was not, however, received." James cast me a look that implicated my brother as the source of this inconvenience.

"Forgive me, Your Highness, for I am guilty of intercepting a message myself," Sir George confessed, and looked gently upon Hendrick. "But the message in my possession never mentioned that you'd be coming to Blythe Hall as well; it detailed only the movements of the lovely Lady Blythe, whom, as you know, I have a reason to watch." He paused, looked at me, and said, "Julius must have intercepted and changed the original note."

With a flash of rising anger, I nodded.

He continued, looking at James. "Your presence here grieves me all the more, for the news I have to deliver takes on a more dire aspect, as it concerns your safety directly. Lady Blythe, I assume, has told you of the return of her notorious brother. I saw him myself a few days ago, when I arrived here to win the heart of the woman who has captured my imagination, and whom you, in your infinite grace and wisdom, have granted me permission to marry."

He looked to me as he spoke these last words; a deep and penetrating smile appeared on his lips as he revealed to me the real reason for his visit. His gaze was as intimate as it was heated; I did not look away. I did not have the freedom to look away any longer. Instead I gave a small smile in return and replied, "I know the reason for your visit. The king has told me of it himself."

"He has?" uttered Sir George. It was no secret that he was pleased by this and gave a small deferential nod to the king. "I am glad you know, Isabeau, so that you will better understand when I say that Blythe Hall is not safe for either of you—my king, whom I have sworn to protect, and you, the woman I'm to marry. It pains me to tell you this, but yesterday, after having no luck tracking your sheep, we doubled back across the Tweed, continuing north of Berwick. We knew Sir Matthew and his men had passed that way, hot on the trail of Julius and his men. We followed them deep into the Lammermuir Hills, where we discovered, early this morning, that they had all been slaughtered in what appeared to be an ambush."

"What?" the king cried, wrought with terror and disbelief. "My Guard . . . has been . . . slaughtered?"

"Aye, my lord, every one of them is dead, including the venerable Sir Matthew."

At this unbelievable news James crossed himself, as did Hendrick, yet I could not move, paralyzed by the thought of the King's Guard—all those fine and noble men—slaughtered by my brother's hand. I could not believe it. I could not believe Julius would ever do anything so terrible as to set upon the very men who guarded the king—men he had fought beside in his youth—and mercilessly kill them. And yet, somewhere in the back of my wildly racing mind, I knew that he, out of anyone, possessed the will and the cunning to do it. Had he not tormented Sir Matthew in my own hall? Had he not deprived the Guard of their swords and valuables? He had, of course, given the weapons back, but then, like a cat toying with a callow mouse, he had lured them across the wooded Merse and into the desolate stretches of the Lammermuir Hills, a landscape he knew intimately, and one where he could spring his horrible trap on those less versed in the precarious geography of the area. The thought curdled my stomach and pressed upon my soul a weight that I knew could never be lifted.

"Isabeau, do you understand what I'm saying?" I felt Sir George's hands on my shoulders before I realized he was speaking to me. His mere touch gave me a jolt, and my focus was immediately drawn to him. "Without the extra protection of the Guard, the king is vulnerable here. We have too few men to defend the castle properly, and Julius will know how to breach these walls to get what he wants, of that I'm certain. There's no time to waste, my dear. We must leave at once."

"What? Leave? But . . . but I don't want to leave," I heard myself protesting. I stepped back, moving beyond his reach. "And we have men—your men, my men, and the shepherds have returned." I looked to Hendrick for support. His gaze, however, was fixed on Sir George.

"The shepherds have returned?"

"Yes," I replied, but failed to add the small detail about Julius's men returning them. "They have returned with the sheep."

Sir George looked around the bailey and stopped when he spied an archway under the timber-covered gallery near the stables. It was there that the shepherds had gathered. His piercing gaze settled on them. The shepherds, so recently gaining a foothold on sobriety, shrank further beneath the timbers under Lord Kilwylie's harsh scrutiny. He chuckled then, and it rankled more than I would have liked. "Your shepherds," he said, "will be slaughtered like lambs before a lion. To Julius these men are mere excrement from the animals they husband and will be squashed beneath his boot and soundly kicked aside. Do not be difficult, my dear. If you care for these men, send them into the hills, where they'll be safe, with their women and children, for if they tarry here, they will certainly fall to the same fate as the King's Guard."

It was an ominous warning, and one that didn't entirely make sense. Why would Julius bother returning these men if he meant to kill them? Even I knew that to defend a castle was easier than attacking one, and any extra able-bodied men, shepherds or not, would put up a good fight. Julius was vain, but even vanity must have limits. I looked at the man I was to marry and replied, "I appreciate your concern for my men, and what you're saying is undoubtedly correct. But perhaps we are being a bit rash here. We cannot possibly make it to Edinburgh or even Linlithgow before nightfall. And if we seek shelter along the way, we'll be even more vulnerable to an attack, I should think." This time I looked to James for support, but the news of the slaughter had shaken him greatly, and his gaze, like Hendrick's, was fixed on the huge knight.

"Edinburgh? Linlithgow?" Sir George repeated, mildly amused by my alarm. I found his tone a bit condescending.

"My dear, you are a treasure," he continued, "yet I must confess that I'm relieved to find that you are no prodigy in the military arts like your brother. Of course the risk of whisking the king back to Edinburgh with only my men and his retinue to guard against an attack from Julius would be too great. Julius is likely expecting us to do that very thing, and that is why we must leave immediately for Teviotdale and my stronghold of Kilwylie."

"Kilwylie," James repeated with both question and reflection in his voice. And then, thinking on it, he added, "We could make it to Kilwylie." He looked at Sir George, a man who stood a good head taller, was substantially broader, and thick with muscle, and yet compared with the regal manner of the young king this physical superiority seemed somehow insubstantial. "To Kilwylie we shall go then. Hendrick," he said, turning to the steward, "would you please apprise Marion and Mme. Seraphina of our plans. We must leave at once. For Sir George is correct—any man who can slaughter the cream of my Guard can breach the walls of his own castle. We are not safe here. Marion and Isabeau are not safe here, and their lives shall not be placed in jeopardy on my account. It is me he is after, and were I not encumbered with the fate of a kingdom on my shoulders, I would gladly meet him on the field and settle this old score as honor dictates. But I find I do not have that luxury. Much to the dismay of my Privy Council, I have no wife and therefore I have no issue to the throne. And my brother Ormond, dear soul though he be, would not relish the responsibility his new title would carry."

I stared at the king, jaw agape, and cried, "And you're just realizing this now!? You who rode alone through a wild and violent country rife with men who slaughter other men just so you could indulge in a tryst with Lord Kilwylie's cousin! I should think the thought would have crossed your mind long before this dire hour!"

"What? You are here alone?" Sir George, quick to pick up on the important point of my tirade, darkened alarmingly. "You have no men with you?"

"No," James answered unapologetically. "And since there is no hope of the other half of my Guard returning, it appears that I am entirely at your mercy. I make no excuses for my actions; they are what they are. The die has already been cast, my friends, and now we must choose the course that has the highest probability of a favorable outcome. It would be to remain here and wait for reinforcements, if I believed these walls could repel the likes of Julius Blythe long enough for them to come."

"They can't," I said, my ire rising. "He's been here—many times. I don't know how he does it. But James is not safe here if, in fact, it is the king Julius is after."

Both men looked at me, yet it was Sir George's cold, pellucid gaze that penetrated the very marrow of my bones. "He has been here? Since the night of your arrival?" His voice was demanding and filled with either fear or contempt, it was hard to tell which. Yet the intensity of his manner caused me to wonder whether it was raw concern for me or deep-seated hatred for Julius that affected him so. In my heart, in the space of a beat, I prayed it was not for me.

"Yes," I heard myself utter.

"By God, why? Did he . . . did he harm you or Marion in any way?"

I believe my heart stopped entirely at this question. Sir George, having exceptional insight into the nature of my brother, was hinting at reprehensible, incestuous behavior concerning me and common underhanded debauchery concerning Marion. I was not a great dissembler and could not hide the fact that his question angered me, partially because he was correct on one count. If I had been troubled by Marion's indiscretion concerning my brother, I knew better than to divulge her secret, for James Stewart, at times a brash and prideful young king, deserved to believe that the woman he had risked his life for was entirely his. And Marion deserved a little happiness, even though she knew it would not last forever. "No!" I heard myself rebuke. "He did nothing of the kind!"

"Then why risk slipping behind the walls of Blythe?"

"It was not for Marion, if that's what you think," said the king, stepping forward in her honor. "Marion is the reason I am here. She will return to Edinburgh the royal mistress," he added, knowing that Sir George would understand that his cousin's new position in the royal household would bring favor to the Douglas clan. "Perhaps she was the bait that lured me here; perhaps it was coincidence. It does not matter. Julius risked entering the castle to get to Isabeau, for he is poisoning her mind against you; he is attempting to drive her mad by insisting she find an angel."

"What?" uttered Sir George, and behind the probing green eyes I could see that the mad, errant quest did not seem so errant or mad to him. This realization, above all else, frightened me. "He has asked that you find an angel?" he repeated, and his gaze softened while his tone was gently rebuking.

"Yes, he did."

Sir George did not question the sanity of such a request, as I anticipated he would. His only response was, "Why?"

"I don't know why. He never told me."

"Very well," he said, as if satisfied with my answer. "It is best that we leave this place at once—for your own safety, for the king's, and for the realm of Scotland."

❧

It was odd, but I was unduly hesitant to leave my home. I had only just returned after long years away, and the few days I had spent at Blythe Hall were the most unnerving of my life. And yet there was something gnawing at my conscience, a dark and persistent knot of a thing that made me reluctant to leave. At first I thought it had to do with Tam, for he was still in Blythemuir. Importunate though he might be, he was, beyond a doubt, dear to me. Tam was not a warrior, or even very handy with a bow. But he was clever, and he was an invaluable servant. Most important, his mere presence gave me a sense of security. My feelings were mirrored by Seraphina, who asked that we wait until he returned, at which Sir George promised he'd send a few men to retrieve him and bring him safely to Kilwylie. Seraphina was not overly pleased by this, but it was the best Lord Kilwylie could offer. The shepherds were to return to their homes, pack up their women and children, and move the sheep into the hills. Hendrick would stay behind with the rest of the staff, as was his duty.

We were to move quickly, packing only the barest essentials to ensure swift, surreptitious travel. I knew it would be dark long before we arrived, and it would be cold. I ran to my room to retrieve my riding coat and a few personal belongings. When I came through the door I was startled to find two of the compromised milkmaids standing in my room staring at the arrow still stuck in the post of the bed. Both girls turned at the sound of my arrival. They had been charged with helping me pack.

"Did ye do that?" asked the maid named Maggie, motioning to the arrow with her head while her hands deftly folded a clean chemise.

"Unfortunately, yes."

"Was it because of that man, that big, braw, green-eyed knight in the courtyard?"

I smiled softly and replied, "Lord Kilwylie, do you mean? No. It would have killed him had I shot it at him. He's much taller than that."

"That knight is Lord Kilwylie?" There was incredulity in her voice, and then she cast a glance at the girl next to her. Both flushed with ill-concealed distress.

"It is. Why do you ask?" Although emotions were running

high in the castle, I found their behavior to be curious, and so I studied them closely.

"Jerome says Lord Kilwylie is tae be the next Lord Blythe. I dinnae ken *he* was Lord Kilwylie."

I assumed she was referring to Jerome Mackenzie of the kitchens, a young man who undoubtedly would be drawn to the fresh and wholesome beauty of this girl. "Well," I began, picking up a pair of hose and motioning for her to add it to the saddlebag on the bed. "Jerome would be correct. Is there a reason why this should upset you?"

"Nay," Maggie said, and looked to the brush in her hands, "there's nay reason." She thrust the object into the bag, and although she was trying to act as if nothing was amiss, her face was far too red to be anything like convincing. She picked up the saddlebag and handed it to me, along with my riding cloak. "Take care, m'lady," she said, and crossed herself. "Gwyneth and I shall say a prayer for ye." Yet before I could make sense of her distress, she grabbed the other maid by the hand and pulled her from the room. I watched them go, a feeling of extreme unease seizing my limbs. And then I went to retrieve what I had come for: the white feather.

With the feather placed directly over my breast and tucked safely beneath the many layers of my clothes, I rode out of the courtyard heading for the gatehouse. I would soon pass beneath the Angel of Blythe, heading for the lands of my future husband. The feather, small and inconsequential, gave me a small comfort, for I was on edge. I brought my hand over my heart, pressing the little feather tighter to my body, and took one last look at the tower. My eyes moved up the ocher stone, all the way to the room at the top, where beneath the steeply pitched roof sat the magnificent chapel my father had built with his own hands. I stared at the stained-glass window as a feeling of sorrow took me, and my head was filled once again with my brother's fervent, beseeching words: *And if you've*

*ever had a care for me, you will keep searching for my elusive
friend. He will reveal his true identity only to you. Don't fight
it, Isabeau, don't fight what we are. We're a cursed race, and
the sooner you embrace the truth, the better off you'll be.*

Suddenly I could not help but feel that somehow I had
failed, that somehow I had let down a force far greater than I
could comprehend. Tears of remorse blurred my vision as my
eyes remained glued to the high window. And then, as if in a
dream, I saw a light. The window, previously dark, was now
alive with color—as if illuminated from within by a bright
flame. I marveled at it; I was unable to take my eyes away.
And then it was gone. I gasped, realizing that it wasn't gone,
only changed, for the shadow of a man appeared in the window outlined by a halo of brilliant colored glass. It startled
me, for no one could be in the tower. And then the shadow
slowly changed, and this time I saw the shimmering, light-
gilded wings. I stopped breathing, stopped thinking, as heat
radiated through me from head to toe. For there, appearing in
a shrine built to honor heavenly beings, was an angel, the
angel my brother had begged me to find, and I could not help
but feel that I had abandoned it to a far darker fate than my
own.

Chapter 11
TAKING OF
THE PRIZE

IN THE OLD PEEL TOWER OF BLYTHEMUIR, IN THE
recently renovated room at the top of the turnpike stairs,
Julius Blythe lay on a cot staring out the gaping hole in the
roof he had purposely left unrepaired. He had tried to sleep
for an hour or two after working all night in his father's hidden chamber. He had come back to the tower in the late afternoon, shortly after his meeting with Dante, taking the ancient
subterranean route his ingenious predecessors had con-
structed, and whose existence remained a secret to all but a select few — the select few now including a thousand head of
sheep, who, he was fairly certain, would remain silent about
their recent escapade.

Like the old tower, the mine shafts and tunnels that connected it with the new had fallen into decay over the many
years it lay dormant. It had taken the better part of a month,
working surreptitiously, for he and his men to brace the
crumbling stone from the inside, making it livable, while tak-

ing pains not to alter its outward appearance. They had also inspected and made repairs to the complicated network of mine shafts and tunnels that ran through the hills and provided what any band of outlaws coveted: escape routes. For this he had Danny Cochrane to thank. Cochrane, whose father had renovated Stirling Castle, was a gifted architect in his own right as well as a master mason. He also had an egregious gambling problem and a mountain of debt to his name. His bellicose nature only added to this unsavory stew, and before long, once the law caught up with him, he had won himself a trip to the gallows. His sentence, however, was never able to be carried out—because Julius Blythe had intervened. This act of charity on the master's part was not out of any love for Cochrane, for the architect was a quarrelsome bastard at best. The master simply knew a good bargain when he saw one.

With a crumbling façade on the outside, and four floors of spacious, and slightly drafty, living quarters within, the old peel tower was a masterly and devious hideout—masterly because it was well equipped, and devious because it stood half a mile from the sheepfolds of Blythemuir, in plain view of the very castle that was to be harassed. Of course such activity around an abandoned tower, even in a sleepy little hamlet like Blythemuir, had drawn suspicion. A few cogs in the neighborhood had needed to be greased, and it was a huge credit to him that he knew just who those cogs were and what they required in order to keep from squeaking.

The shepherds, for example, comprising an entire tier of their own, were remarkably compliant when, abducted and blindfolded, they had been asked to shear the fleece from the animals in their care. They worked in shifts around the clock and had been rewarded handsomely for their efforts. He had personally seen to that. All that was asked when they saw they were to be released was that what had occurred in the Devil's Lair—for the level of profligacy and debauchery that had taken place was unparalleled in the whole of Scotland—stay in the Devil's Lair. When men were as compromised as the shepherds had been, it was easy to swear them to secrecy in exchange for secrecy. It was just one of the many currencies he enjoyed trading in. And now his hay wains of wool had left Berwick safely and without notice. It was just another small cog in a larger wheel that had been set in motion after that night in Venice, half a year ago, when hell had unleashed yet another demon for him to battle, and when the heavens had finally opened, urging him back to a land that had already once destroyed him.

This time, however, he had come prepared.

As he lay on his cot watching the clouds pass overhead, he filed away all that he had learned in his father's reading chamber, although he had not yet found what he was after. He had seen it once, the ancient document written in the time before the Great Flood that gave proof of the existence of remarkable things. Although it was only a copy, he had traced the original document back to the Council of Nicaea, when in AD 325 the Roman emperor Constantine had gathered together a council of bishops from the many flourishing and diverse Christian sects of the day in order to define and create from these a uniform Christian doctrine. The particular ancient text he was looking for, and one previously regarded in the time before Jesus as divine scripture, had been excluded. The reason was simple: it was too powerful. And yet, somehow, some renegade Christian scholar had understood this strange and cryptic text and made a copy of it, and this one copy had survived. It was this copy that held the secret of Blythe Hall; it also, by default, held the secret to immortality.

Long ago, in a moment of weakness, he had exchanged this secret for his life. His mistake had been that he had grown cocky, for after years of familial struggle and fervent denial, he had finally understood what his father had been trying to tell him, and this secret had given him an unholy strength. He believed himself impervious to danger, and this had allowed him to place trust where none should have ever been placed. He had believed that Sir George Douglas was his friend, only to learn too late that he was yet another demon sent to destroy him.

The wind had picked up, causing the clouds to move faster above him. He could hear the faint whinny of horses and of bleating sheep in the valley below. This caused a smile to appear on his lips almost of its own volition; for the recently shorn sheep had finally returned home. His men were billeted on the two floors below him, leaving the bottom floor for their mounts and armor. Like him, those who weren't employed on a task elsewhere were relaxing—playing dice, tarocco, backgammon; reading; taking refreshments—for they understood they were to have a busy night. They would need all their strength. He felt perfectly relaxed, and his mind was unwinding as the effects of the strong Turkish drink, *alqahwa*, slowly left his body. He sometimes used the drug as the Sufis did, the holy men who drank it to stay at prayer all night. It was a powerful stimulant, and it kept him from sleeping. Yet now he wanted to sleep, and he allowed his lids to close. It was possibly an hour—or mere moments—later that he was awakened by Dante.

"Julius," came the gentle tone flavored with an Italian accent. His eyes flew open, and he found himself staring not at the night sky but at a blue sky blocked by the dark and handsome face of his longtime companion. "Sir George has arrived at Blythe Hall." Julius sat up and rubbed a hand over his face. "But there is something wrong," Dante warned. "He has no sheep, and Sir Matthew has not returned with him."

The blue stare, grave and probing, held Dante's. "Have you heard from Will?" Will Crichton was their link between Fergie Shaw—the man in charge of a small detail currently harassing Sir Matthew—and headquarters.

"There's been no sign of him. There's no sign of anyone. I fear something has gone terribly wrong."

The master was up and pulling on his boots; his face, normally pulsing with color, was pale and ghostly white. "The king," he said, casting a cold and frightening look at Dante. The Venetian, having been on the receiving end of such a look a time or two, knew that nothing good could follow. He braced himself as the master continued. "Kilwylie knew James Stewart would come to Blythe all along. The message I exposed to Hendrick was not the original message he intercepted. He's known all along and didn't wish anyone else to know, the cunning bastard," the master added with a malevolent grin. "My friend plays a wicked game. He uses my sister as a shield. He uses his cousin as a lure. And now he is forcing me on a path to the gallows. He is forcing me to take the king."

"The king?" Dante replied, alarm seizing his fine features. "But why take the king? He is not part of our plans."

"Our plans have changed, dear Dante," said the master levelly, strapping on his sword belt. He shook his head in weary amusement and let out a sigh of resignation. "'Tis very simple. We take the king, because if we don't, Kilwylie will kill him, and I will carry the blame. The king must not be harmed. He must never be harmed. And now it is up to us to protect him."

This the Venetian understood, and he gave a grave nod. "Very well. But what about Isabeau?"

But the master didn't have time to answer his question, because at that moment a sound, frightfully incongruous with the peaceful, bucolic noises of the valley, wafted through the uncovered windows of the tower room and caused the hair on the back of his neck to stand on end. It was the sound of racing horses and jangling armor. With admirable conservation of movement he crossed to the window, where he was just in time to see two of Kilwylie's knights breaking from the forest with swords drawn. He looked down the valley, searching for their target. With a sinking heart he found it: three spindly shepherd boys laughing and chatting on a rise above the newly arrived flock. They had been much celebrated, he saw, and were sitting beside their horses eating and drinking the gifts the goodwives had bestowed on them. The poor bastards would never know what hit them. "Dear God," he uttered, his heart sinking, his hatred growing. His stomach turned to liquid as it often did before a battle, and he found he was unable to pull his eyes from the scene unfolding before him. "They're going to slaughter those boys."

Chapter 12
KILWYLIE
CASTLE

WE HAD BEEN TWO HOURS IN THE SADDLE, AND THE image of the angel, a dark and monochrome silhouette against a palette of color—was so firmly imprinted in my mind that every time I blinked I saw him on the inside of my eyelids. The truth was, he was perhaps clearer in my imagination than he had been in real life, for the tower room that contained the chapel was high up, nearly sixty feet aboveground to be exact, and rather hard to see. I had been leaving the castle, and I had been crying. Angels did not appear in tower windows. My mind had obviously been playing a trick on me, or perhaps I was truly going mad now that I had learned the hard and heart-wrenching truth about my brother. Julius really was the devil's spawn; was it any wonder I embraced visions of angels? Angels, regardless of whether or not I wished to believe in them, were infinitely easier to handle. Angels did not slaughter innocent men.

The thought of what had befallen Sir Matthew and his men

sickened me, as it had Marion and the king. The Guard comprised some of the best men Scotland had to offer, and their loss was a national tragedy. Marion was particularly shaken, yet she refused to believe that Julius had anything to do with it. It was an opinion she wisely voiced only to me, however, and I knew why. She had been seduced by the viper—had offered herself willingly to him—and now refused to acknowledge her prodigious lapse in judgment. She refused to believe that Julius was what he was.

Seraphina was little different, yet her denial was understandable. Julius was my mother's son, and therefore incapable of such wanton destruction. The news of the slaughter in the Lammermuir Hills had reduced her to a state I had not seen in many years, not since the first time Julius had waged his private war on the kingdom of Scotland. I knew that her heart bled on the inside, while on the outside she was but an inscrutable, emotionless shell. There was no spark behind her eyes, no life in her movements, and when she cautioned in a voice bereft of all timbre that we not leave Blythe Hall, I could not listen. Seraphina did not like Sir George Douglas any more than she liked any man who showed the slightest bit of interest in me. If she had had her way, I believed I would still have been in the convent—as a novice—preparing to take holy orders; for no man, in her opinion, would ever be good enough to be my husband. It was, on some level, an endearing quality in a governess—to place a higher value on her charge than perhaps that charge deserved. I was naïve; I had been cleverly kept that way, and I had never been encouraged to embrace marriage and all it entailed.

But that was before I came to Blythe Hall.

I knew I could never explain to her what it was that had changed in me. But I could no longer deny that I was a woman of warm flesh and pulsating blood, just as I could no longer deny that I yearned for something that went far beyond my comprehension. Perhaps Marion Boyd was to blame for this. Her joy in the opposite sex was not feigned. She understood men; she understood what they needed, and she took great pleasure from it. Who could deny that her beauty had grown even greater since she had entered the halls of Blythe? I wanted to know what Marion knew. I wanted to learn it from the man of my visions, but he was not real. Sir George was real, and he was beside me, and he knew what my brother was, just as I did. It was a tenuous bond at best, but it was a real bond, and one I believed I could work with. We had a common goal in protecting the king, and we had a common hatred of the man who was bent on destroying him. Many long and successful marriages were built on less. It was the only thought that kept me in my saddle, yet I would never admit as much to Mme. Seraphina.

Sir George, knowing how the events of the day had upset me, and that leaving Blythe Hall was not something I relished or even wished to do, was exceptionally kind. He had promised that we would return once James was safely ensconced in the Castle of Edinburgh and Julius was safely locked away in the tolbooth; we would return to Blythemuir and live as husband and wife. It was his wish; it was the wish of the king; and I was resolved to honor it. Sir George had even sent a small detachment of men to find Tam, knowing how worried I was about my groom. Tam was clever enough and could charm his way out of most trouble. But he was not a warrior. And he had never met the likes of Julius. If my brother got to him before the men of Kilwylie did ... but I didn't want to think of that.

We had passed the neighborhood of Jedburgh and were on the Hawick road heading toward Kilwylie. We had spoken little, for we were riding hard through a land crisscrossed by the mighty Tweed and the Teviot, and so many burns and streams and so much squelching bog land that it was impossible to stay dry. This was no leisurely trip, like the one taken from Edinburgh to Blythe Hall. Sir George pushed us, keep-

ing to the forest whenever possible, avoiding towns and set-
tlements as much as he could. James was used to such riding,
and he had come alive with the threat to his life. Marion and I
preferred a gentler pace, and Mme. Seraphina preferred not to
be in the saddle at all.

"Do you think," I said to Sir George, noting that the last
rays of the sun had dipped beyond the horizon, "that we
might stop for a rest? Surely we are halfway there by now?"

He turned, his stony face softening as he understood what
I was asking. "Dear God," he cursed mildly and reined in his
mount. "Look at you. You're shivering. What have I done? In
my haste to reach Kilwylie I've forgotten that we are in the
company of ladies."

"I'm fine," I assured him with a soft smile, although I really
wasn't. "However, I think Mme. Seraphina might be dead."

"I'm not dead," she replied testily from inside her fur-lined
cloak. "I only wish I was. We should have never left Blythe
Hall."

"We could leave you here," suggested Sir George, not unkindly. "We are not far from Jedburgh. I can have a few of my
men take you there and return for you in a couple of days."

"Take me and the young ladies," she said levelly. Marion
and James had come beside us, as our horses were taking a
much needed rest. "It is the king you need to protect. We only
serve to slow you down."

"Leave Isabeau?" Sir George replied, and although he was
speaking to Seraphina, he was looking at me. His eyes were
dark and unreadable in the gloaming, yet his voice was full of
heated intent. "I will not let Lady Isabeau out of my sight
again."

"That is a wise decision," James agreed, bravely airing his
opinion on the subject. And then, adopting a voice suffused
with authority, he addressed my governess. "Dear Seraphina,
you are a good and kind woman who has watched her charge
with unparalleled diligence, but we have asked too much of

you already. Take Sir George's offer. I shall personally guarantee the safety of both women."

"You may be the King of Scotland," Seraphina replied,
much to my horror, "but you are first a young man, and I
have witnessed for myself how you guarantee the safety of
Mistress Boyd. That is all very well and good, but you were
not charged by the lady's mother to guard her daughter. I will
ride to Kilwylie, even if it kills me!"

"Well then," said Sir George, smiling warmly, "have it your
way."

After a small reprieve, which I was eternally grateful for,
and which Marion insisted be longer, we mounted up and
continued on a course that would bring us to Sir George's
border stronghold. It was a dark night, moonless with patchy
clouds overhead, making it nearly impossible to see in the forest. The path through the woods was winding and narrow,
and there were times we were forced to proceed in single file.
Sir George was in the lead, and I silently marveled at how he
did it, navigating such a landscape in total darkness. I had
heard tales as a child, of course, mythical tales about men of
the Borders being able to move entire herds of cattle fifty
miles in the night without so much as a candle to guide their
way. Stealth and an innate knowledge of the land were required skills of a reiver. And I had little doubt that Sir George
had done his share of reiving in his youth. It was the one
thought that eased my mind a measure.

At night, in the forest, when one does not have the privi-
lege of sight, sound lives on its own. Above the muffled jangle
of harness and labored breathing, a rustle in a nearby bush
gave me a start. A twig snapped under an unseen weight and
caused the fine hairs on my skin to prickle and stand on end. I
had never been in the forest at night; it was a place avoided at
all costs, and I suddenly understood why.

Because at night the forest came alive with mysterious
creatures that shunned the light of day.

Wind rustled the nascent leaves overhead as the hoot of an owl pierced the impenetrable darkness. My horse pulled up, suddenly spooked by something unseen that had crossed the path in front of us. It capered sideways, pinning my leg against the trunk of a tree. I grabbed its mane and wound the coarse hairs tightly around my fingers. The horse reared, my leg came free, and I felt a hand hard on my thigh. A scream, primal and frightening, burst from my lungs as I kicked into the darkness. My foot hit something solid, and I kept screaming. So did Marion.

It happened at once, a burst of energy so confounding that it rattled the night and shocked the senses. Light exploded on the path in front of our party, casting Sir George in a daunting silhouette, broad-shouldered and poised for attack. At the same moment the blinding light came, men sprang from the woods, and the sound of clashing steel erupted behind me. I saw the shadow of a man beside me and gave another kick, this time so hard it sent him reeling backward, crashing in the bushes. I spun around to look for James and Marion. But I could not see a thing. It was dark as pitch behind me.

"Isabeau!" I heard Sir George cry. "Ride to me!" Up ahead, just beyond Sir George, was an opening where the forest ended and what appeared to be a great expanse of undulating grassland began. It was there that men with torches awaited us. It was a fiery gauntlet, yet behind me was a battle. Neither option was good. "Julius!" I cried then, seething with fear and anger, knowing he was behind it all. He was the animal in the dark that I dreaded most. The forest was thick with trees, cloaked by darkness and now host to a swarm of vicious, lawless men. I wanted to turn and race toward the king and Marion—and Mme. Seraphina, who had dropped somewhere far to the rear. I wanted to protect them, to carry them from the thick of the fighting and bring them toward the opening before me, where we might have a chance if we were lucky. Yet the majority of Lord Kilwylie's guard was with James, fighting for the king's life, and hopefully Marion's and Seraphina's as well. I would be just another body in the mix if I went to join them. And so, with tears streaming down my face and a welling of impotent anger coursing through my blood, I did the only thing I could do, I kicked my horse as hard as I could, heading for the men with the torches.

Sir George, after deflecting a blow from an attacker, lunged for the bridle of my horse as I careened past him, shooting out of the woods. The sudden jolt of his grasp whipped both our horses around, a move that drove us out of the path of an on-coming rider. It was a narrow miss. The rider had clearly been aiming for Sir George when I broke through. His blow went wide, yet I caught the hiss as the blade sliced through the air, mere inches from my body. The rider, foiled, disappeared in the trees. Sir George still held the reins of my horse as two more armed men fell on us, coming at the knight from both sides. I ducked low, on his order, hugging my horse's neck as his mighty sword fought them off. Sir George was a powerful man, and his sword packed a lethal force. But our attackers were no fools. They moved like ghosts in the night, light, shifty, and able to disappear into the darkness from which they had come. Nearly as soon as the attack began, it was over, the torches snuffed in the dewy grass. Julius had used the light to his advantage by momentarily blinding us, and now the light was out and Julius and his men were gone. The torches hissed on the open moor as the men of Kilwylie began to emerge.

It was dark again, and I sat beneath a patch of star-strewn sky waiting for my eyes to adjust. Sir George had dismounted and gone to fetch one of the discarded torches. The sound of steel on flint rang out, and within a few moments a torch had been lit. What the light revealed was truly surprising, because for all the mayhem and chaos that had occurred, it appeared that there were no casualties. The Kilwylie men were worse for wear, to be sure, with cuts and vivid red marks on their skin that would turn dark with bruising before the night was out. They had been roughly handled but had stood their ground. Mme. Seraphina also suffered, but her pain was caused by long hours in the saddle rather than any mistreatment by the attackers. As more torches were lit and more men emerged, it slowly became apparent what the attack had been all about. Sir George, riding to the entrance of the woods, held up his torch and called out the names of the two souls that were missing. He called again and was answered by a high, throaty whinny. A moment later two horses emerged. Their saddles were empty.

That was when Sir George started to laugh. His laughter bubbled forth, a low, mirthless rumble building to a crescendo of harsh, bitter irony. It chilled me to the bone.

"The devil," Sir George began in a voice that was deceptively gentle, "has been upon us this night, my dears, and God have mercy on the souls that have paid for my arrogance. In my haste to protect the life of my king, I have failed. Scotland is in mortal danger. The English have been waiting for a reason to pounce, and Julius Blythe, a treasonous outlaw and reprobate, has returned to give them one. I vow I will not rest until he is destroyed."

☙

If Blythe Hall was considered a bit whimsical for a border fortress, then Kilwylie Castle was a Spartan sentinel of daunting utility. The huge stone tower, built to withstand multiple attacks and lengthy sieges, stood on a small island surrounded by a great expanse of bog and marsh. There was nothing inviting or even remotely welcoming about Kilwylie Castle. It was a square, stone instrument of war, and I shuddered to think that it was soon to be my home as well. The walls of the fortress were underlit by wavering firelight, and my heart sank even lower when we came through the gates and into the bailey, where a crowd of horses, wagons, and armored men competed for space around the fires. Our party entered dirty, wet, cold, bone-weary, and morally defeated. I wasn't entirely sure Mme. Seraphina would ever recover from what we had gone through, or the consequences to come. For me, all I wanted was to be warm again, to fall into bed and cry myself to sleep, for the king and my dear friend had been abducted by my brother. It was the greatest insult yet to our family name, and it shamed me like nothing ever had before. I did not want to smile or mumble pleasantries to strangers, or feign empathy or gratitude to the retainers my future husband surrounded himself with. It was one of the first times in my life I could not pretend, or mimic a smile, and perhaps this showed on my face. Mme. Seraphina was carried from her horse by the two knights who guarded her and whisked into the castle without delay. I was still on my horse, numbly watching the activity around me yet not fully registering any of it, until Sir George lifted me down and gently led me up the stairs to the hall. The doors opened for the lord, and I took my first step inside the cold, stark walls of Kilwylie Castle.

Sir George, at my side, was silent. The madness after the brazen attack had passed, and a quiet, sober resolve had come over him. His servants, already on the move following the limp form of Seraphina, received yet more orders from their lord before he turned his attention to me. His liquid emerald eyes were inscrutable as he said, "I will get you something to eat and have a basin of water brought to your room. And then I will put you to bed. It has, I am sure, been a day beyond compare." Noting that I was shivering slightly, he put his hands on my arms and rubbed vigorously. Warmth penetrated the thick layers of my cloak, and I could feel my blood begin to move again. A soft smile crossed his lips, and to my astonishment, I answered in kind.

"Kilwylie!" A booming voice penetrated the hall from the next room. Sir George's hands stilled. The voice, deep, rich, and commanding, was one I recognized. "Get ye in here, lad, an' bring your wee prize. We've been waitin' a muckle lang time, and we've done drunk up your pitiful cellar."

Sir George, quick to school the flash of surprise and contempt that crossed his face, said calmly, "I see I have visitors. It is most importunate. Stay here, my dove. I shall be only a moment."

"That is your uncle," I said, for the voice of the Earl of Angus was hard to mistake. "And those are his men camping in the bailey, aren't they?"

"I forget at times how close you were to the king and his Privy Council. Yes, I believe Angus has come to pay me a visit."

"I shall go with you. He will be suspicious of my arrival, and we must break the news of Marion and the king gently. We should not cause undue alarm until we figure out how best to handle this situation." I started in the direction of the room where Angus and his friends were waiting.

Sir George grabbed my arm. "No. Do not go in there! My uncle is not alone, and he's likely deep in his cups by now. He's a coarse old fool and highly unfit for the company of a lady. You can see him tomorrow."

I looked at him, looked at his white-knuckled hand on my arm, and then back at his face again. I was not smiling, and neither was he. His face had grown hard and implacable. I was about to yank my arm away when the earl spoke again, this time from directly behind me. The first words from his mouth shook me to the core, and I could not peel my eyes from the face of Sir George as his uncle spoke.

"Jamie Stewart!" said Sir Archibald Douglas, the fifth Earl of Angus, "I ha' loved ye like a son, and never knew a better mind for thae cards, but I will nae stand being—"

"You're drunk!" cried Sir George.

I turned around, knowing he had mistaken me for another, and pulling the hood from my head, looked into the eyes of one of the most powerful men in Scotland—a man who had fallen from grace in recent years, a man who had once been the royal guardian of James Stewart but had lost influence to the Humes.

"Jesus God!" The words tumbled from his lips as if pulled unwillingly from within his ruddy, horror-stricken face. "Isabeau Blythe?" he uttered. It was then that I noticed that two other men stood behind him, two men I had never before seen—and who looked suspiciously like Englishmen. Although my mind was sluggish with exhaustion, it began churning, spewing a jumble of contrary thoughts and impossible conclusions. Nothing made any sense at all—nothing but for one small fact. The Earl of Angus, from his own admission, knew that the king was not in Linlithgow where he was supposed to be. He knew the king would be coming to Kilwylie. Suddenly I was visited by an odd clarity of thought and the urge to put on a convincing performance. My life, I believed, depended on it.

"Dear Lord Angus," I began, "I'm sorry to disappoint you. I'm not one of your card-playing, dice-gaming friends, but I am soon to be your niece, for the king has finally decided on my behalf, and I am to marry Lord Kilwylie." I smiled at the man still holding me tightly, and I believed it was convincing. "Isn't that just grand!"

"Och!" exclaimed the old earl. "Ye gave me a fright, lass! I thought the ghost of an auld chiel had come tae haunt me at last. 'Tis a rare dark night, and the stink from the bog of Kilwylie is said tae pickle the mind—or, perhaps 'tis the unholy gut-rot that passes for whisky around here? I forget which. Likely both. But come now, gi' your uncle a hug."

The earl was a big, powerful man, just like his nephew. And like his nephew, he had a frame that was muscled and hardened under sword and shield, and endless campaigns on the heather. Therefore, when his arms came around me for a hug, I had no misunderstanding about the power he had at his command. He could, should he wish, crush me like a bedbug.

I stepped away and made my excuse. "I would love to stay and catch up with you, and hear all the news of your family, but your nephew is a most anxious suitor, and in his zeal to bring me here, I'm afraid I have been pushed beyond my mortal limits." I smiled at Sir George and patted his hand, the one that still held me. "If you'll excuse me, I shall retire and leave you and your friends to your cards." The looks, the veiled secrecy that passed between all four men were not lost on me, although I did my utmost to feign ignorance. But something terribly chilling was to have taken place in Kilwylie Castle this night, of that I was sure. The presence of the two English agents—for that's what I believed them to be—in conjunction with the name James Stewart, only pointed to one thing: without a king on the throne of Scotland, and with money placed in the right hands, Henry of England would rule.

And then I thought of Julius and his hatred of Kilwylie. His appearance in the Borders suddenly made sense. It was his own greed that had driven his brazen attack and abduction of James (and Marion). That it prevented Kilwylie and Angus from reaping a huge reward only sweetened the deal. And it showed the brilliance of the English king, a man who had defeated Richard III, finally putting an end to the bloody conflict between Lancastrian and Yorkist. This Tudor king knew how to overthrow a nation, just as he knew how to pull the strings on the Scotsmen who were his puppets. Angus and Kilwylie were two of his puppets and likely offered English estates and a huge stake in the new government. Julius was simply offered revenge, and perhaps Blythe Hall.

I was now in the middle of a nightmare.

I was alone and defenseless, trapped in a tower and surrounded by a stinking bog while the king's enemies circled like sharks in a blood frenzy. I had known what Julius was; his involvement came as no surprise. But I had wanted to believe in the goodness and virtue of Sir George. He had the implicit trust of the king; he was the man I was betrothed to. And I wanted to laugh at the foolishness of letting myself fall for him—nearly becoming his willing lover. I had been right to suspect that I was only a pawn in a deadly game. Correction: Marion and I were the pawns, and we had been used to lure the king to the Borders in a gross attempt to exploit his weakness. And now he was gone, and Scotland was at the mercy of two madmen. God help us all.

⅌

I was not allowed to see where Seraphina was; Sir George would not abide that. I was told she had fallen ill on the ride and was now sleeping peacefully. It was best, he had said, that she not be disturbed. I was brought to a room on the floor above the Great Hall. It was a spacious chamber containing only a large bed, a chest, a chair near a glowing brazier, and a long, narrow window. The walls were bare, as was the floor. The smoldering peat did little for the chill in the air, and Sir George's silence did little for the tension that had grown between us.

I had been staring at the window—at the narrow strip of night sky that was visible—numb with foreboding, when I felt him come up behind me. I stilled at his touch, sensing his mood to be both dark and pensive. I held my breath, afraid to move, as he slowly pulled the cloak from my shoulders. Once the heavy weight fell away I wanted to turn but was stopped by the large hands holding my waist firmly. His silence was commanding. My heart fluttered away like the wings of a hummingbird, for I knew any plea or utterance I made would fall on deaf ears. The Lord of Kilwylie was testing me. If I knew what lay in his heart—what treachery and deceit he lived, what debauchery he was planning—I would not let him touch me. I knew! I knew and yet I had no choice but to let him touch me. Because James still lived, and as long as he lived there was still hope for Scotland, if not for me. And so I closed my eyes, attempting to stop the first tears of humiliation and self-loathing as he began untying the laces of my gown. I thought of Seraphina, and of Tam, and of how miserably I had failed everyone. Tam had never come, and I feared the worst for him. Even the vision of my angel had left me now.

My gown came off, falling to the floor in velvety waves of blue, and with it the white feather. My eyes held the feather as it fluttered to my feet, but I made no move to touch it. I stood still, unwilling to step beyond the circle of cloth; I felt naked and vulnerable in my thin chemise. His breath, light yet sporadic, was a measure of his arousal. As he took hold of my shoulders, it came warm and urgent against my neck. And then, with exquisite gentleness, he lifted my chin and raked the stubble of his hot cheek against the tender skin of my neck. He breathed deeply, taking in the scent of me, of my hair. His breath caught in his throat, and after a long pause he let it out, purposely slow. I felt him shudder. It was this, or perhaps the feel of warm air on my bare skin, that sent a wave of tingling throughout my body. My jeweled caul was his next conquest, and I felt him take the weight of my hair in his hands as it fell away. He stroked the fine strands with a gentleness that only served to make my heart pound harder, until he finally let it sift through his fingers like shimmering waves of golden wheat. I thought he was finished; I prayed he was finished, and took a deep breath to steel my nerves. But Lord Kilwylie was only beginning.

His fingers moved to the nape of my neck, and under my hair. His touch was soothing, unnervingly so, and I could feel my resolve dissipate like warm breath in cold air. My mind and body became two separate entities then. I knew I should fight him, and yet my body understood how useless that would be. Lord Kilwylie was powerful and confident, and he knew how the night would end; it didn't help my case any that a small moan escaped my lips. His fingers caressed my hair. His warm body pressed against mine. The heat of him was like a drug, and I found I could not resist this alluring comfort he offered. This gentleness of touch, this radiant heat, this dark and earthy scent that enveloped me, combined with the sheer physical presence of the man, worked as a powerful soporific. A pleasurable tingling hummed throughout my body, clouding my fear and apprehension while turning my overwrought limbs to jelly. Yet before I utterly crumpled against him, his fingers slowly began to close. Like the long crank of a carpenter's vise, his grip on my hair became firm and painful, and with a sudden tug I was forced around to face him. Body and mind, heaving with indignation, became one again.

With me pressed tightly to him, my head tilted painfully back to expose my neck, he breathed, "I marvel at your foresight in not mentioning James or Julius to my uncle. If he learned your brother was in Scotland, or what he has done to the king, he might be fool enough to go after him. He might be fool enough to use you as a hostage." It was a warning, one driven home by deceptively gentle lips.

"I wouldn't make a good hostage," I breathed, feeling both pain and pleasure as he trailed soft kisses along my neck. "Julius despises me."

"And yet he needs you," he whispered near my ear. "He needs you to find his angel. You said so yourself. It is the other reason he has returned."

I grabbed his doublet, pulling on him as hard as he was pulling on me. "I don't find angels! For anyone!" I let go. So did he.

"You are frightened," he said, his inflection one of mild satisfaction. "But what are you frightened of, I wonder?"

"I am frightened of many things," I replied honestly, attempting to stay calm, for although he had released his grip on my hair, I was still firmly in his embrace. "For instance, at the moment I'm frightened of what I'm feeling for you, and of how dangerous it is that we are left alone in this room together." I attempted a smile and pulled away. Thankfully, he let me go. "I think that until our nuptials take place it would be best if you kept to your own room."

His eyes, veiled by darkness, held mine. And then, suddenly, he laughed. It was hearty laughter, not brought about by madness, yet still, it was slightly unnerving. "That is very good advice," he said, "and I shall heed it, I promise. Yet I also promised that I would put you to bed, and I am not a man to break a promise." He walked over to the large piece of furniture that dominated the room and pulled back the covers. I looked at him, marveling at the change—thankful he no longer talked of Julius or angels—and obeyed. I was so tired, so tired I could barely think, and I crawled between the fine linen sheets. The bed was cold and I was covered by a thick layer of soft quilts tucked high under my chin with all the care of a tender parent. I shivered slightly, reveling in the knowledge that I would soon be warm. He sat beside me and smoothed my long hair. "It's been a long night for you, Isabeau. Yet for me it will be even longer. I must go now and placate my uncle and his friends, or I would be a most remiss host. I would far prefer to stay here with you." He bent to kiss me. It was slightly reminiscent of that night in the dark corridor of the palace, only he was gentler. "I shall return before dawn and join you," he said. "And I will make you understand once and for all that you have no reason to fear me."

"Join me?" I sat up, coming fully awake. "But you promised me you wouldn't, not until—"

"I promised no such thing," he said, cutting me off. "I only promised to keep to my own room. It's rather fortunate for me you are in it." He smiled, triumphant and smug, and stood to go. "I always keep my promise, Isabeau, and I promise to return. I promise to finish what I started here. I promise to hunt Julius down and kill him. And I promise that whatever secrets you are hiding will become my own. Do not fight me, Isabeau, my little dove. This is one battle you cannot win." He walked out the door, shutting it firmly behind him. Yet it was the sound of the key turning the lock that chilled me to the bone. It made me understand the truth of what had happened. I may have fooled the Earl of Angus, but I had not fooled his nephew. And for my stupidity—for my stupidity in leaving Blythe Hall—I would suffer.

※

I don't remember falling asleep, but I do remember waking, and my heart pounded with the thought of what I was to face when I did. The lock had been turned and Lord Kilwylie was about to enter. I tightened my grip on the fire poker hidden beneath the sheets. It had been all I could find in the stark room. It would take a good deal of strength to fell a man the size of Sir George; but what I lacked in strength I more than made up for in will. I would not be a prisoner if I could help it.

He approached the bed. My muscles tensed, waiting for the right moment to strike. I waited until he came directly over me, and then I waited a breath more.

"Isabeau. Isabeau, wake up." The words hung in the air as I threw back the covers. I sat up, fire poker in hand. The man gave a high-pitched yelp, even though I didn't touch him.

"Tam!" came my muffled cry. It was impossible. I had been certain I would never see him again. "How are you here? How did you know where to find me?"

"Easy. Lord Kilwylie's men came for me—with swords. They wanted to make sure I would never find ye again."

My hand came over my mouth at the thought. "Oh, dear Lord! They attacked you? He told me he would find you and bring you here. I began to suspect the worst when he locked me in this room. How did you escape?"

"I had help. The Mackenzie brothers may no' be so handy in the kitchens or even diligent shepherds for all that, but they're canny, and agile, and surprisingly accurate with a slingshot." He smiled. "And then some riders came and chased Kilwylie's men away."

"Riders? Who?"

"I don't know. Just riders. Likely broken men. We didn't stay tae chat. Come now," he said, heading for the door. "In less than an hour's time the crows will start crowin', and the dogs will start barkin', and the maids will start wakin', and Sir George will come tae find ye. I want tae be well clear of here before he puts us tae the horn."

"Puts us to the horn?" I replied, pulling on my gown. I gestured for Tam to lace me up. "He wouldn't. I'm no outlaw!"

"But I am," he said, finishing quickly. In one swift movement he grabbed my cloak off the floor and flung it around my shoulders. "And abducting the lord's betrothed carries a heavy price."

We slipped out the door and locked it. Tam had borrowed the key from Sir George, who was passed out drunk in the Great Hall with his uncle and a good number of the Kilwylie men. They had been at the cards all night. He started down the corridor toward the stairs, but I went the other way, stating that we had to find Mme. Seraphina. Tam stopped. "There's no time," he said gently.

I knew he was right, but I didn't want to hear it. "No. We must. We cannot leave her here!"

"Isabeau," he said, his boyish face gaunt and serious under the pale light of the wall sconces. I could also see that he had gone through more than he had let on. His left cheek was red and swollen, his doublet torn, and his hose muddied beyond repair. And the black circles under his eyes told me he hadn't slept in a long while. I knew how he felt. "I love the auld bird as much as ye do; she's my granny's dear friend. And if there were any way, I'd do all I could tae take her from here. But we need tae move fast. She's already gone through this once. She would no' want us tae put her through it again. She is your guardian, I understand that, and the closest thing ye have tae a mother. But I made her a promise once, and now I am keeping it."

Angry, heartbroken, tired, I gave a curt nod and slipped down the stairs behind him, reconciling myself to the fact that if we made it out of here alive, I would come back for her; because if we didn't make it out of here, she'd have no chance at all. We skirted the Great Hall, where the drunken men slumbered, and took the servant's entrance to the courtyard. Fog had settled in, and we waited until the sentry passed. We slinked along the wall, then ran behind a shed, where Jerome Mackenzie was waiting for us. I was relieved to see a rope ladder. I climbed over the wall and was helped on the other side by Brendon. When I saw that they had brought four horses with them, I was suddenly filled with gratefulness for these three young men. After suffering a great risk to their own lives they had ridden miles in the settling fog and darkness, over rolling hills and through daunting forest, to come save me. Kilwylie Castle was a fortress built to withstand long sieges and heavy artillery attacks, and these boys had slipped right in. I knew many grown men who would never attempt such a thing.

Once again I found myself back in the saddle. I stifled a moan. I was still tired and fretfully sore, and knew it was going to get much worse before it got any better. We rode silently into the fog; the only noise beyond the croaking of frogs and buzzing of insects was a slight sucking sound as the horses picked their way through the marsh surrounding the castle. Halfway through, Tam paused, took out Sir George's heavy key ring, and threw it into the darkness. Somewhere far off I heard them land with a wet thud. I felt a strange elation then, for I was now free of Sir George's grasp. I was going home, and if I could help it, he would never walk through the gates of Blythe Hall again.

Then the first rooster of the morning began to crow.

SIR GEORGE HAD NO NEED OF HIS HOUNDS; HE KNEW where we were headed. Dawn broke as we cleared the dense forest, and with the increasing warmth of the sun, the fog began to dissipate slowly. I had visions of men waking in a hall not far off, their drink-muddled heads beginning to clear as the castle came to life around them. It wouldn't be long until the lord of the castle, finding his heavy ring of keys missing, discovered what had happened. He would be in a rage, for he was a proud man, and one with a terrible secret. He would strap on his armor, buckle his sword belt, then choose his fastest mount and come find me. Tam, being a clever groom, had exchanged three spent mounts for four very fine horses from one of the Kilwylie horse breeders. Fresh horses, the fog, and a small head start were our only advantages. In the vales between the rolling hills the fog still lay thick, like a heavy blanket, and for this I was glad. It swallowed our party and made me believe I was invisible. But we could not hide in the fog forever, just as I couldn't ignore what was to come.

We rode hard. My body screamed with pain, for the saddle was jarring and I was not a warrior used to long hours on horseback. There were times I feared I wouldn't make it. I even had thoughts of stopping and hiding in the hills until he found me. It was in those times that I closed my eyes and prayed for strength; it was in those times that I took comfort from the image of the angel, a noble shadow against a palette of color. I could see it in my mind once again. This small detail gave me tremendous hope, and because of it I endured more than I ever believed I could.

Four miles from Blythe Hall we saw him. We had just crossed the Tweed below Kelso when we caught the glint of helmets on a distant hillside. Sir George had not come alone; he had brought an army. My heart sank, and for a moment my vision darkened at the edges. Although we had a chance of making it to Blythe Hall before being overtaken, we did not have men to fight an army. My companions knew this too, yet instead of adopting a defeatist attitude, as I was doing, they seemed to be inspired by the sight. Tam turned to me, a grim smile on his lips, and said, "He must ha' found his keys."

"He kicked down the door," replied Brendon. "Or got his army tae do it for 'em."

"Ye know what this means?" It was Jerome, his face bright with excitement. "It means we get tae test it."

"Test what?" I cried, spurring my poor horse to an even greater speed.

"Whether or no' the auld castle's protected. I mean, 'tis a bold claim."

"What?" I was horrified.

"An' no' only that," he continued as a frightening gleam appeared in his brown eyes. "Now I'll get tae dump a cauldron of boiling pitch on 'em. Do we hae pitch?"

"Yes, I think so. Why?"

"Why? For what he did tae my Maggie and her sister," he replied, his pleasant voice now gruff with anger. "I dinnae care a fig if he's a lord and the most decorated knight in a' Scotland. He's a coward an' a fool. Ye dinnae force favors from another man's woman. He thought he could get away with it, and he sent his men tae kill us. But we dinnae die so easily!"

"Maggie," I uttered, remembering the pretty maid and her sister Gwyneth. And then I recalled their horror at the thought of Sir George living at Blythe Hall. *He* was the man who had violated them on the night of my homecoming. I had blamed Julius, but it had been Sir George—a man who professed love for me and insisted on sleeping before my door! He hadn't been sleeping. The thought sickened me that much more, and I rode to Blythe Hall wanting a little revenge of my own.

"Open the gates!" I shouted as we tore up the soft earth leading to the gatehouse. The heavy doors were swung open before we reached the bridge, and we clamored on through, the army fast on our heels. I was oddly reminded of that day long ago when Julius had risked his life to save me. For a fleeting moment I believed I would see my father, standing in the courtyard waiting for us, and he would come to chide me for my foolishness. But it wasn't my father who came to me on this day, only a terrified Hendrick. He looked to the four of us, then behind us, his eyes full of question and heartache. Marion and the king were missing, that much was evident, but so was Mme. Seraphina.

Dear God, what had I done?

It happened as if the world had slowed down before my eyes. Everything became silent then as I scanned the courtyard around us. I took in everything—Hendrick beside me, talking urgently, guards dropping the heavy bolt on the gate behind us, a small girl holding a chicken, Mutton Johnny carrying a sack of flour on his shoulders, his small dark eyes staring at me as he walked past—but I didn't hear a sound. And I didn't feel anything. It was like a dream, and I slowly got off my horse and walked away.

To my great despair, I found myself alone in the tower room. It was the one room I had avoided ever since my return, not wanting to believe in such whimsical things as angels. My brother had tormented me with a task, and I had refused him. Yet now, as if reverting back to a simpler time when fears and sorrows were best dealt with by calling on some higher power, I found myself in the very room I had spent a lifetime running from, prostrate once again before the magnificent stained-glass saint, just as I was on that day long ago, with a puppy named Rondo in my arms. This was the room my mother had died in; it was the room that had driven my father mad. It was a shrine. It was a chapel. It was a collection of priceless art, and it was where I had come to deal with a hopelessness so vast that I thought I would never recover from it. I had abandoned my governess; I had lost my king and my best friend, and I had led the army of a traitor to the gates of Blythe Hall knowing that we were entirely unprotected.

I sat in the shadow of Saint Matthew the Evangelist and watched in awe, speechless, as sunlight, caught in the wings of the saint, burst onto the floor before me like a shattered rainbow. It was beautiful and mesmerizing, but it didn't change the fact that Sir George was coming for me. My gaze, wandering the room, took in the vaulted ceiling, where light came through the clear glass of the oculus. Around the opening the ceiling was painted like the heavens, complete with little winged cherubs who frolicked amongst the clouds. The walls, having been plastered and painted the same fathomless blue, were host to spectacular paintings depicting angels in every form, from warrior to guardian, and from every culture. Some were adorned with wings and halos, while others looked remarkably average. There were little carvings placed on pedestals and three masterly marble statues, life-sized, standing in the corners. My gaze finally settled on the altar, the magnificently gilded and embellished centerpiece of the room, because just above it stood the mighty archangel Michael, that notorious and utterly stunning warrior of God, at the head of his army of angels preparing to battle Satan and the fallen ones. He was awarded the center panel of the breathtaking triptych. On his right stood God's glorious mouthpiece, the golden and dulcet archangel Gabriel, announcing the resurrection of Christ; and on his left, that miraculous healer and fishing companion of Tobias, the boyishly adorable archangel Raphael. One had to admit it was a remarkable work of art. Done in the ancient Roman style of strong, symmetrical features, perfectly proportioned bodies thick with muscle, and flowing white tunics and hair, each archangel was the embodiment of earthly virility and heavenly perfection. And although they were mere depictions of biblical stories, heavily steeped in metaphor, I found I was a little breathless at the sight of them.

My attention, however, was soon diverted by a low rumbling that underlaid the gentle birdsong and soft clattering of servants in the courtyard below. I sprang to my feet and crossed to the open window, where I saw, beyond the walls of Blythe and to the west, a dark, shapeless mass of men and horses racing along the banks of the river Tweed. Without thought I ran to the altar and knelt before the center panel of the triptych, looking to the mighty archangel Michael, God's warrior. For I had no need of a messenger or a healer; I had need of the sword of God, and to him and him alone I would direct my plea.

"Oh, dear Lord," I breathed, knowing I was utterly mad yet staring at the archangel and thinking how easy it would be to become swept away in the cult of worshipping such entities, just as my father and brother before me had. And then, embracing the madness, I yelled to the heavens, "Why aren't men more like angels? I could love an angel, but I cannot love that man!" And then I laughed. It was mad laughter because I knew that men were not angels. They were flawed, and imperfect, and riddled with vice.

The sound of hooves was growing closer, and I realized I was shaking. I had escaped Kilwylie Castle and Sir George; and I was heartsick knowing that the king and Marion had not been so lucky. Julius had James, and he would sell him to Henry of England. Marion he would keep, I reflected darkly, for his amusement. I had nothing left to me now but a prayer, and I would not waste it on God any longer. I could not help but harken back to when my father began doing the very same thing. Well, I thought, if there was ever a time to start acting like my father's daughter, I supposed it would be now; and if calling on angels for salvation was the very height of desperation and madness, then at least they could say that it ran in the family.

"Michael," I began, falling to my knees. I looked into the determined eyes of the warrior while trying to ignore the building thunder as it approached the stronghold of my ancestors. And then I repeated as best I could the prayer I had heard many times before, a prayer that sprang from the lips of my father. "Commander of God's armies and minister of the divine glory, it is I, Isabeau Blythe. Unworthy though I am, I beseech you. Carry me this day under your wings of immortal glory. Give me the strength to face my enemies, namely, that bastard Sir George Douglas, although, technically, he's not really a bastard, but feel free to smite his hell-tarnished soul and send him back down to his maker, Lucifer—that most depraved of your fallen angels—if it pleases you . . . as I'm certain it will. I implore you; bolster me with your divine justice. Empower me with your righteous arms of steel. And, for the sake of God and my good name, valiantly guard my virtue from that storm of turpitude about to descend on my household!"

"My lady! My lady, they're here!" cried a frantic Hendrick. I looked up to see him standing in the doorway, only now his gray head was tilted, and his eyes, those piercing orbs of steely blue, were narrowed to mere slits of trenchant disapproval. "Holy saints afire! Tell me ye were no' just prayin' to thon wee winged men," he demanded sternly.

"Of course not!" I lied.

"Good. Because I thought ye had more sense than all that."

"And I do," I replied, rising to my feet and hoping to appear sane. "I was just looking for a bit of inspiration. It is a most enchanting room, after all, and one designed to be inspiring." I could feel my cheeks go red with shame.

"Aye," he replied slowly. "The lads told me how Sir George sent men tae kill them. They told me you were locked in a room. And they told me about Seraphina."

I closed my eyes, unable to look at the disappointment so clear on his face, and hung my head. "It was not my choice to leave her," I said, feeling terrible for what I had done. I had been rash in my decision to leave with Sir George. I had been afraid, and my fear had prevented me from thinking clearly. It was not a good trait for one who held the responsibility for an entire estate on her shoulders. "I will find a way to get her back."

"Ye did what ye had to do, m'lady," he said softly. He then lifted my chin with a gentle finger. "For a leader is often forced to make hard decisions. Had ye taken her, ye would never have returned home at all. And I'm glad you're home. I'm glad you're safe. I never liked that bastard Douglas."

"So . . . you're not angry with me?"

"Oh, I'm plenty angry with ye. But I'm also grateful you're safe. Now's no' the time for anger. Now's the time for clear thinking and smart action, for we've a bit of a problem on our hands." I nodded, filling with relief. "Well then," he said, looking at me with sobering seriousness. "What's your plan?"

This question implied that I had one, and I appreciated that. But I was no warrior; they didn't teach castle defense at the convent. Hendrick knew this; he was simply forcing me to embrace the role I had come here to play. Blythe Hall was my castle, and it was my job to defend it against the enemies of Scotland. And Sir George Douglas, my betrothed, fit that bill. I took a deep breath. "How many men have we got?"

"Men? Inside the walls at this very minute?" He thought a moment before replying, "Fifteen. Twenty including the carpenter's apprentice, the smithy's lad, the Mackenzie brothers, and young Tam."

"Tam's a man. Count him as a man."

"Very well, sixteen men and four lads; 'tis still twenty. Plus the women. They'll assist where needed."

"Make that twenty-one," I said, "counting me. I'm not a man, but I intend to fight." I could see this caused him to bristle, but he relented with a nod. "We need to get every man to the battlements. I want archers at the ready, bows, quivers of arrows, crossbows, buckets of boiling pitch, swords, halberds, lances, maces, and if we have any, I'd like some black powder and shot."

He raised a bushy brow. "Black powder? Shot? I think, for the now, we'll be fine with archers."

"How many men does Sir George have?"

"One hundred, or thereabouts."

"One hundred? He's brought more than just his personal guard?"

"He's brought a small army," replied Hendrick gravely. "May I ask a question?" I nodded. "Why would Douglas bring a small army here? He knows we've no' had a garrison since the lord left. I'm told the king's been taken by Julius, so why has he come here, after you, and not hunting Julius?"

I stilled at his question, unsure of how much to tell him. Then, knowing that Hendrick needed to hear the truth I replied softly, "He comes here with an army because he believes I have uncovered his plot to kidnap the king. Angus was at Kilwylie Castle. Angus was waiting for James Stewart."

"Oh, dear God," he uttered, and crossed himself.

"I am so sorry, Hendrick. I am so sorry." I didn't need to

tell him that today, within the walls of Blythe, I was fighting for my life. "Should Sir Douglas break through the gates, or scale the walls, I will bargain my life for all the lives in the castle. He need not know we've talked."

"He will never honor such a bargain!" he cried. "He sent men to murder innocent boys! Did you ever think that he was the one who killed Sir Matthew and his men! He will kill us all!" His entire body was shaking with fear and anger, and it broke my heart to know I was the cause of it.

"Hendrick," I said, suddenly grasping at a thought. "It was Sir George who brought us news of Sir Matthew's death; it's what caused us to leave Blythe Hall in the first place. But what if Sir Matthew is still alive? We have no proof, only the word of Sir George, and as greedy and self-serving as he is, I cannot bring myself to believe that even he would do something as desperately evil as . . . ." But I didn't finish. The thought was too horrific, and I needed a small glimmer of hope to cling to. "Sir Matthew and his men could still be out there looking for Julius."

"Aye," he agreed, although doubtfully.

"Whatever the truth is, now's not the time for anger. You said so yourself. What we need now is to get every man and boy on those walls," I said, sounding much braver than I felt. "I cannot promise victory, but I do promise to do everything in my power to protect the lives that have been placed under my care."

"Would that I had the strength of a hundred men tae fight for ye, my lady. Ye are an angel, and ye deserve so much better than this." With that he turned and stalked out the door. I cast the mighty archangel Michael one last, longing glance, and followed him, for Sir George was calling my name.

❧

I stood on the battlements above the gates breathing deeply, attempting to summon all my resolve, for I would not give up without a fight. But when I looked out on the raiders that had gathered beyond the bridge, my heart sank. Sir George had indeed brought a hundred men, and every one of them wore a breastplate and helmet; every one of them carried a shield and sword. Sir George, spying me, took off his helmet and, looking smug, rode his huge charger onto the bridge. He sat languidly on his horse—a beast that looked as if it could run another thirty miles easily—his glossy black hair fluttering in the wind. Behind him was his banner, a red heart on a field of white. It was not the romantic symbol of love it appeared but an icon to commemorate the deed of an ancestor who once carried Robert the Bruce's heart to Jerusalem. The man had been killed by the Moors while in Spain, and the heart was returned to Melrose Abbey. Not a glorious expedition, yet not enough to deter a Douglas from vaingloriously embracing the symbol.

"Come now, Isabeau, open the gate," he shouted. "Don't let's make this any more difficult than it has to be, sweetheart."

"Difficult? You think I'm the one being difficult? I would sooner put an arrow through your heart than ever let you touch me again!" His men laughed heartily at this, believing it to be a lover's quarrel. And they needed to believe it. I could not let on that it was anything different.

"Come now, sweetheart, anger doesn't suit you. I'm sorry for locking you in my room. I only did it for your protection. You're a gorgeous woman, Isabeau, and my home was filled with drunken men. It was my duty to protect you," he said, and brought his hand over his heart. "In hindsight, I should have given you a key. I was tired. I wasn't thinking clearly. And your kisses clouded my better judgment. Come, darling, unlock the gates. I promise to give you a key."

"I don't want your key!" I spat. This only made the men laugh harder. "And I'm staying right here!"

"Isabeau," he said, smiling up at me, sunlight dancing off

his piercing light eyes. There was no point in denying that he was a handsome man, or that, for a moment last night, I had been powerless against him. I did not want that to happen again. "Let me put it to you like this," he said, projecting his rich voice for all to hear. "You don't really have any choice in the matter. Your brother is an outlaw who has abducted the king. I am your betrothed; I am now your guardian, and it is my duty to guard you. And I cannot do that from down here. Open the gates."

"I believe you are missing the point, my lord. I do not want you as my husband. And I do not need a guardian. I am quite done with men!"

"Are you? What about that boy you ran away with—your groom, I believe? I will not abide my betrothed playing me false. Unlock these gates!" He was getting a bit testy, and I was sorry to think I enjoyed it.

"Tam is my groom and my friend. And I'm not the one playing you false. I know what you did to my dairymaids the night you pretended to be sleeping before my door. I am not unlocking the gates!" Tam and Hendrick were hauling up sheaves of arrows and placing them along the walls. The smell of warming pitch touched my nose. I looked apologetically at Tam; he smiled encouragingly in return.

"Oh, so you found out about that, did you?" Although he smiled to keep up appearances, his eyes darkened. I had put a chink in his armor. Sir George was a man used to getting his own way, and he didn't like being challenged by a woman. "Well, I'm sorry. I truly am. But it should ease your mind to know that I wasn't the first. And they didn't complain; in fact, your little maids mightily enjoyed themselves. I offered the same to you, but you locked me out of your room, if you'll remember." He smiled sweetly, innocently—as if his inability to master his urges was somehow my fault. It was preposterous! "Open the gates, my gentle dove, and you can judge for yourself if anyone was *mistreated.*" The men loved this. I wanted to put an arrow through his profligate heart.

"Are you really this dense, my lord? Don't you understand what I'm telling you? I shall make it plain for your simpleton's mind then. You are not welcome at Blythe Hall! Ever! Go home!"

"You forget," he said, and this time there was no hint of amusement in the compelling face, "I am to be the Lord of Blythe. It is a role I was born to play, my dove. I know the secrets you hide here, Isabeau. Nothing will keep me from them now. The King of Scotland has decreed it. This castle is as good as mine." For the life of me, I didn't know what secrets he was talking about, unless he was referring to the Chapel of Angels, which, in the wrong hands, could be sold off piecemeal for a sizable fortune. I would never let him do it! He had also mentioned the king, and nobody was fool enough to comment on what had happened to him. It was yet another worry that sickened me. I glared down at Sir George, silently cursing myself for being so foolish—for letting myself walk in the shadow of his seduction; for letting myself be lulled by the power of his mesmerizing gaze. He smiled back, drinking in my anger as a lover indulges in an aphrodisiac. The fine features sharpened, the tan skin darkened as blood coursed just below the surface, and his eyes burned like fiery emeralds. His desires were quite clear; it was the power of them that terrified me.

"You have two choices, my sweeting," he called up to me. "You can open the gates and be civil about this, or you can keep them locked and I will break them down. You cannot possibly think you can defend Blythe Hall with a couple of old men and shepherd boys. But if it amuses you, you're welcome to try. Then, after you've had your fun, why then, my little angel, then it will be my turn. And I can assure you that once you've experienced my idea of fun, you'll be wishing you had never left my room." His men, his built-in audience of well-paid retainers, wildly approved of this sentiment. The debased creatures. "I shall give you a moment to consider," he added, as if it were a great courtesy.

I was seething with anger and fear, and he knew it. He knew we had little chance against his might, just as he knew how to weaken my resolve. And then he went for the kill.

"Oh, I nearly forgot. Seraphina sends her regards. Such a feisty old bird! Such spirit! And I marvel at how a woman as fine and gentle as yourself could just cast her aside like that—a woman who has loved you and cared for you like a mother since your birth—without a backward glance. It chilled me to the bone, Isabeau—that you could just leave her without thought or care at Kilwylie Castle like you did."

His words were spears aimed at my heart, each one mortally painful, each one spurring a press of remorseful tears. This man was exquisitely cruel, and he enjoyed it.

"You know I have no use for an old woman." A grim yet thoughtful expression appeared on his face. "But I shall keep her. For you. If you ever wish to see her again, my gentle dove, you will stop acting so foolishly. It is time to grow up, Isabeau Blythe. Grow up and do the right thing for your shepherd boys and old men, even if you won't for your devoted governess. Grow up and open these gates."

He then cast me a look confirming my deepest fears. He had set down his sticks and stones and was now playing with a razor-edged sword. His knights fell silent behind him. The sparring between lovers had taken a dangerous turn, and they knew their lord was finished quibbling. Sir George had the devil's tongue, and he was stroking me with it, lulling me into believing he was counseling me to do the right thing. I wanted to put an end to it; I wanted to end it there and then, and so I reached down for my bow. But it wasn't there. In my haste I had left it in the chapel room.

I turned from the Lord of Kilwylie and left the gatehouse, tears streaming down my face, shaking uncontrollably. He believed I was going to open the gates, and maybe I should have. Because my prayer had not been answered; I had not been saved, and I was going back to my father's magnificent chapel for perhaps the last time.

❧

As soon as I crossed the threshold, I saw him. He was kneeling before the altar, golden head bent, gloved hands grasping the hilt of his mighty sword as he prayed in an aura of particolored light. I stopped, breathless. He turned when he heard me enter, and slowly began to rise. My heart stopped beating for the space of a second or two when I saw his face, because I found that I was staring into the eyes of the man from my vision. It was, to say the least, unbelievable. And even more unbelievable was that he was just as magnificent in real life as he had been in any dream. He too looked stunned to see me there—and I thought I caught a flash of recognition in his eyes. I gasped and stood unblinking as I watched him slowly unfurl to his full golden height. He was radiant and serene as any angel, beautiful, achingly so, and yet there was a hint of something wild and dangerous in his Viking dimensions. I caught the glint of a chain-mail hauberk under the rich surcoat of black that fell below his knees. The surcoat, with a small white cross over the left breast, was belted at the waist, and he gently placed the great sword he'd been holding back into the sheath that hung at his side. He didn't utter a sound as he stood looking at me, his heavenly blue eyes twinkling, his lips pulling to a disarming smile. I wanted to stay like that forever, staring into a face that represented to me everything good, and right, and hopeful in the world.

I had been a fool. I had been a fool of the worst kind. For I had avoided this chapel like the plague, believing it would turn me mad. And it had. But it was a glorious madness, a compelling madness, that enveloped me like a cocoon, and filled my every fiber with boundless joy. All thought left me.

I was no longer shaking with anger and fear, and the tears that fell from my eyes were born of vast and grateful relief. For outside stood the devil and his legions, but in here—in this odd little chapel—was an angel. My angel. And I knew that he had finally come to save me.

"I . . . I have dreamed of you," I finally uttered, standing as still as he was, while trying to ignore the sound of my name as Sir George bellowed from outside the walls.

"And I . . . ," he breathed, incredulity touching his strong, noble face. "I have dreamed of you." His voice was soft, and yet there was a richness to it that penetrated my bones. He then took off his gloves and stepped from the shaft of light that fell from the window. And when he stood before me, with great hesitation—as if he were about to touch the most fragile piece of glass—he lifted his mighty hands and cradled my face. His touch was like the crackle in the air before a lightning storm, and my body tingled with joy at the feel of him. I covered his hands with mine, holding him tightly as tears streamed unchecked down my face, and I knew that he felt it too—a connection stronger than anything I had ever known.

He closed his eyes and lifted his head to the heavens. No one could doubt the sincerity of the emotion that took him then—a look that was sublime and yet humbled—as if he had passed untold trials of hardship and was now finally home. I understood that look. I felt it too. And I didn't want to let go. It was a moment before either of us could speak. "I had no idea you would grow to be so lovely, Isabeau Blythe," he whispered, looking once again at my face. The sound of my name on his lips thrilled me. He knew who I was. And I believed I knew who he was.

"I'm not lovely," I corrected, smiling through my tears as he tried to dry them. "I'm crying, I'm filthy, I smell like horse, I haven't slept in days, and I'm sure my eyes are perfectly red and puffy. But thank you, Michael." And I smiled as I rolled his name off my tongue.

"Michael?" he repeated. His hands stilled. With a gentle pressure, he tilted my head to look him in the eye. "Who's Michael?"

I pressed his hands tightly, not wanting to lose his touch— the divine connection we had—and answered with question thick in my voice: *"You are?"* It was not my best moment, and I knew it.

This caused him to arch a golden brow while a frown replaced his look of wonder. "I am not Michael. My name is Gabriel."

"Gabriel?" I said, and we both took our hands away. It clicked then. In my desperation I had prayed to Michael, but in my dreams I saw Gabriel. Gabriel! Archangel of God. Dear God, I had been dreaming of, and fantasizing about, an archangel! I was certain it was a great sin, or the height of blasphemy. Likely both. My face flushed as I recalled my vivid dreams—how I had felt, what I had thought, what I had done! Dear God, I was worse than Julius! He at least limited his lust to human women. My heart could not be stilled as I cast a covert glance at Gabriel's oil likeness. Yes, there were some similarities: tall, broad-shouldered, golden as the sun. I could see no wings, but they could be hidden. Yet gentle Gabriel, glorious and breathtaking as he was, was not the incorporeal being I had called on, and that puzzled me.

And then I thought of Julius, and of the task he begged of me, and I knew this man before me had something to do with him. My heart sank at the thought, for how could Julius, debased outlaw and abductor of kings, be connected with this glorious sublime angel? And yet, and yet it made a modicum of sense, for Julius, like it or not, was my brother, and since stepping foot in Blythe Hall I had been having visions of the very being he was pressing me to find. But why?

"I am sorry," I uttered, seeing that I had startled him. I offered a watery smile.

"You do not remember me?" Gabriel asked, gentle question hanging in his eyes. "But how could you? You were just a little girl."

I thought of the little angels then, the two little boys. "I do," I said, my eyes locking with his. "You were in this room."

"Yes," he smiled, relief crossing his face. "Only it was much different then. I must tell you"—he cast a quick glance around the room—"this chapel is wondrous. Beyond compare. Your father is a remarkable man."

At the mention of my father my heart stopped for the second time. "My . . . father? You knew my father?"

"Yes. He's partly the reason I'm here."

"You are his messenger," I breathed. It was unbelievable, and entirely impossible . . . but not really. I looked around the room, absorbing each piece of the improbable shrine, and felt the bittersweet sting of tears. If anybody could have sent down an angel to save his children, it would have been my father. "Is he . . . ?"

"Concerned? Yes. Very, for you and for Julius. And I see I've come at the right time. Who is that obnoxious ass?" he asked, motioning with his head to the commotion outside. It was growing in intensity and getting hard to ignore. "And what the devil is he doing bellowing such atrocities to a lady?" He walked to the other side of the room and looked out the open window.

I stared at the archangel, so magnificently human in his earthly form yet somehow wholly divine. "That is Sir George Douglas, Lord Kilwylie. My betrothed."

"Kilwylie? Your betrothed!? Dear God, I *have* come at the right time! I feared I'd be too late. I ran into a bit of trouble on the way." He turned back into the room with a heart-stopping smile, a smile that lingered pleasantly over my form. "I take it you are not thrilled with the prospect?"

"Thrilled? I'm horrified."

"Excellent!"

"Excellent? I don't mean to be offensive, but what can you possibly do about it? We are pitifully understaffed here. I have no army. That man has an army, and they're about to break down the gates! While I have no doubt you can handle a sword, and I see that you have a very big sword, I believe, unless you are an epic warrior like Michael, commander of the heavenly hosts or something"—here I pointed to the panel of the triptych depicting Michael—"that we should run . . . if we can. If we stay, I'm afraid a man like Kilwylie would eat you alive."

He pulled back at this affront as his golden brows furrowed with something akin to indignation. There was no serenity about him now, only fierceness. "I . . . cannot . . . fight?" he bellowed. "And what, pray tell, makes you think I cannot fight!?"

I stared at him, stricken by this change. "I'm . . . sorry. I didn't mean to offend you. I'm not questioning your strength or your integrity here. In my opinion you have no equal. But . . . well, even you must know that you're not exactly known for your fighting, Gabriel." I crossed my arms and studied him. Again, I believed that I had said the wrong thing.

"Really?" He glowered and placed his large hands firmly on his hips. "Because I rather thought that I was."

His emotions were remarkably human, remarkably male, and I was silently amused by how he bristled when his honor was in question. I was also sorry to think that this little flare-up endeared him to me all the more. "Well," I said consolingly, "and perhaps you are where you come from, but things are different here. We are not battling Satan for souls. We are trying to prevent Lord Kilwylie from entering Blythe Hall." I cast him a nervous glance, for I had no wish at the moment to tell him why. "Our gates won't hold him forever."

"Maybe not. But we're inside the gates. And a fortress can be defended."

"Can you defend a fortress?" I asked, the merest glimmer of hope shining through.

"Can a popinjay sing, Mistress Blythe?"

"I don't know. Can it?"

"Only if it's been properly taught."

I thought about this for a minute, because I had never heard a popinjay sing. "So, are you saying that you can defend this castle, or cannot?" There was a loud crash that foretold of men charging the gate. He ran to the window and looked down at the chaos in the yard.

"Forgive me, but now is not the time to be arguing about this." He turned back into the room with a look I had seen many times. It was the cool, hard resolve of a warrior. "Stay here, Isabeau, and lock the doors." He made to leave. I stepped in his way.

"I've just found you. I have no desire to lose you. I don't want you to go out there," I said softly, hearing the fear and desperation in my voice.

This gave him pause, and his face suddenly softened along with his compelling sky-colored eyes. "And I have found you, Isabeau Blythe," he replied, and took my hands in his. "Half an hour ago, I thought I knew my mind. I believed I was content. But I now know why God has guided me here. I am God's warrior, and I am here to protect you. No fire bolts will fly from my sword, and I may not devastate with quite the same flair as your precious Michael. But I am here. I am all you have, and all I ask is that you put a little faith in me."

"I do," I breathed fervently. "I will! And Michael is not precious to me. I was just . . . desperate."

"Of course you were, my heart." He smiled and gave my hands a gentle squeeze. He cast one last glance out the window to where Sir George was still, very vocally, making his intentions known. "And I'll be back. But right now there's an insufferably rude nobleman who's begging for a swift lesson in manners and humility." He let go of my hands and went to retrieve his bow, which was resting beside my much smaller one. He was about to walk out the door when I stopped him once again. This time there could be no mistaking what I wanted. I threw my arms around him at the same time that he wrapped me in an embrace so tight I could hardly breathe. And then, just as in my dreams, he brought his lips to mine.

It was nothing like my dreams. It was nothing like I had ever experienced before. His lips were soft and warm, gentle yet urgent. His command over my senses was absolute, and yet there was nothing in him for me to fear, because he was honest, and pure, with a desire as great as my own. He held me tightly, as if I were his support in this world. I could not deny that he was mine, and I wanted him to know it. I ran my fingers through his thick golden hair, down the base of his powerful neck, over his broad, mail-covered shoulders, and down along the valley of his spine, reveling in the feel of him, the smell of him. He was all man; his skin held the essence of the wind, the heat of the sun, the tang of long grasses and cool, peaty streams. He tasted of salty oceans, of exotic spices, of musky, worn leather, and of the finest French wines. His response to my touch was maddening in its sweetness. His hands traveled the length of my back, over my hips, and around to my buttocks, where they stayed, caressing, pulling me closer as his lips became bolder, his kisses deeper. And then, suddenly, he let go.

"Dear God," he finally said, backing away as if I were a pariah. He was breathing heavily, yet instead of being fraught with passion as I was, his words sounded puzzlingly like remorse. "Dear God, I should not have done that. Forgive me," he uttered, his eyes looking troubled. "Forgive me." And without another look back he disappeared out the door.

I slumped to the floor of the chapel, the skirts of my gown pooling around me like a muddy fishpond, suddenly overcome. I felt heavy, disoriented, my mind reeling from the quicksilver emotions that coursed through me. And it was with real effort that I fought to collect my thoughts and my breath. What had just happened? What did I do? I had no answer. And that I found devastating.

Out in the courtyard I heard a commotion. Men cheered. Orders were given. And then came the rich voice of Gabriel, now fearsome in its anger, now terrifying in its pitch as he cried: "George Douglas of Kilwylie. It is I, Gabriel. You have a lot to answer for, and now you will answer to me!" A mighty cheer went up again, followed by a loud snap as many bowstrings released at the same time. The air filled with the sound of flying arrows racing across the sky.

I dried my eyes on the sleeve of my dirty gown, stood, and picked up my bow. There was a devil at the gates of Blythe who wanted me, and an angel inside who didn't. And there was a part of me that didn't care anymore who would win the day.

Chapter 14
NO REST FOR
THE WICKED

IT HAD BEEN A LONG NIGHT FOR JULIUS BLYTHE, LONG and arduous. He and his men had covered forty miles in the darkness, set a blind ambush, performed a daring raid, abducted the king and his consort, failed to abduct his sister, and failed to kill Kilwylie; at least they had lost none of their own. It wasn't a maneuver designed to last more than a minute or so, he knew. It had required a great deal of stealth and strategy, and as always with strategy, success relied on studied and projected behavior, chance, and caprice, and because of those variables they had been only 50 percent successful. He didn't like being 50 percent successful. He preferred 100 percent, and the god of caprice usually obliged. But it was Kilwylie he was dealing with here—a cunning devil if ever there was one. And the pity of it was that Kilwylie was the only enemy he had ever faced who had a thorough understanding of how his mind worked. That was the consequence of friendship, a lesson he learned four years ago.

He also hadn't planned on his sister being so feisty. He would have laid odds that she, out of all of them, would have been the easiest to pluck from a horse in the dead of night. Docile, angelic, malleable Isabeau. But he had failed. He had only had one chance, and he had failed. Kilwylie had guarded her closely and had almost gotten her killed. He released Seraphina then, the dear old woman, and deeply regretted sending her back to Kilwylie. She deeply regretted being released. But they both knew that without a diligent governess, Isabeau wouldn't stand a chance. He had promised that he would return for them both once the king had been secured.

As it was, their captives, frightened, tired, bound, gagged, and hooded, were too demoralized and exhausted to put up much of a fight, thank God. And by the time they wove silently through the forested hillside that surrounded their headquarters in the old peel tower, they were positively stupid with fatigue. He wasn't much better off himself, and he knew it. He had underestimated his old friend, and worse, he had underestimated the extent the man was prepared to go to in order to play this last and final game through to the end. He had witnessed Kilwylie's attempt to kill unarmed shepherd boys, a calamity narrowly averted. The sight had stunned him; it was a gutter move of the lowest kind, and yet he knew why Douglas had given the order. And it was this knowledge that chilled him most.

His head ached from lack of sleep, and his limbs had begun to feel sluggish and heavy. He was used to pushing himself hard. He had gone days without sleep before—days upon days of hard physical activity. With physical activity you could turn your mind off occasionally and fall into the rhythm of the movement. But there was no rhythm here, just an emotional drain that was beginning to wear him down. As he rode inside the crumbling walls of the tower, he gave a private sigh of relief. He thought of his bed then, his cold, empty bed on the top floor, and had a wistful image of himself sleeping there beneath the stars. But even he knew he wasn't for bed yet, for there was no rest for the wicked, especially when the wicked had two pressing interrogations to conduct.

The man standing guard in the tower opened the heavy door when he saw them. His face, shocked at first to see the two hooded captives, fell into a look of alarm. He was about to speak when Julius saw young Will Crichton, the messenger he had sent to Fergie Shaw, slumped against a wall in the corner. One look at the lad told him all he needed to know. His clothes were torn, his hair clumped with sweat, dirt, and dried blood, his gaunt face bruised, and his sword arm gingerly cradled. Julius nodded to the guard and dismounted. "How long has he been here?"

"Arrived two hours ago, my lord."

Julius handed his horse to his groom, and quietly gave Dante his orders. He then motioned to Clayton Hayes, their medico, who just above two hours ago had employed his deft hands in pulling Marion Boyd from her saddle, to tend to the boy. Clayton, spying young Will, had already dismounted and approached him. "I'll go get my tools," he said quietly, looking at the crude bandage soaked with blood. "I'll need to dose him."

Julius nodded. "Let me have a word with him first." He watched Clayton leave and awoke the boy.

"My lord," the boy uttered upon seeing him, alarm and urgency flooding his abused face.

"Hush now, lad." Julius, speaking softly, gently guided the young man up the stairs, while below, his men received their orders from Dante.

With great care Julius peeled the blood-encrusted clothes from the young man and laid him on his pallet. He noted the bruising on the body and knelt beside the boy, carefully removing the bandage on his arm to assess the wound. It was a deep gash, clear to the bone, and was still bleeding profusely. He placed his own hand firmly over the wound, feeling the warm blood pool beneath his palm. He then closed his eyes and gently squeezed. He could feel the boy relax beneath his touch; he could feel his pain dissipate as the blood began to slowly coagulate. Then Julius opened his eyes. He removed his hand, wiped it on the boy's discarded shirt, and tore a clean piece off for a bandage. This he secured tightly around the wound. "You've taken a beating, m'lad," he said softly, soothingly. "But 'tis nothing we cannot fix." He smiled and brushed a thick lock of red hair from the wet brow, staring into the deep-blue eyes as he did so. He was relieved to see that the boy was breathing easier. "Now then, if you're ready, Will, can you tell me what happened?"

It was a story that confirmed his worst fears. Will had found Fergie Shaw and his small detachment early in the morning. He had delivered the message and was planning to ride back to Blythemuir with the men, leading Sir Matthew on a merry chase back to the king. Their billet for the night was in sight of Sir Matthew's own, hidden in a thick grove of trees on a distant hillside. They had just broken camp when they saw Lord Kilwylie and his men racing toward the King's Guard. They were shocked to see Kilwylie, for he wasn't supposed to be north of Berwick.

Will's eyes filled with tears as he told the rest. "Kilwylie rode into Sir Matthew's camp early yesterday morning, all friendly, all helpful, and seemingly impatient tae tell Sir Matthew something. And then they dismounted, m'lord. Kilwylie's men dismounted, fully armed . . . and began slaughtering them all. When we figured out what was happening, we mounted and set on them, prepared tae kill every one of Kilwylie's bastards. But it was mayhem, sir, for Sir Matthew thought we were fighting him too. It was a three-way attack. I took a hit and went down. It was old Fergie who got me away. He got me away, m'lord, and begged I carry the message. 'Tell the master what happened here, Will,' he said, 'for nobody would believe it else.' I dinnae want tae leave, m'lord.

I dinnae want tae leave them!" Will uttered, tears streaming down his bruised face. "I dinnae want tae leave because I knew they were all going tae die!" He stopped then, and Julius held him as he sobbed. "Kilwylie slaughtered them all in a coldhearted, bloodcurdling display of shameful deceit!"

Clayton Hayes had come through the doorway with a sense of urgency, carrying strips of linen and his bulky leather case. But he pulled up short when he heard the boy's story. He looked at Julius; the master was holding the young man as he wept. Their eyes met and held. Clayton had been with the master for two years, and in that time he had never seen any-thing resembling fear in the eyes of Julius Blythe. It was partly the reason he had abandoned his rich patron, the Duke of Bourbon, for he had never met another soul like the young Master of Blythe. That he showed fear should have consoled him; for it meant this brash child of caprice and destruction was human. But it didn't. It only served to scare the hell out of him.

Julius nodded to the doctor and spoke one last, gentle word to the boy. "I'm glad you made it back, Will. You did the right thing by bringing this message. The good doctor's going to sew you up now, and then you're going to get some rest."

Julius Blythe walked out of the room, a hollow in the pit of his stomach, a chill in the space around his heart, for the full caliber of Sir George Douglas had been revealed, and he feared the price it would cost him in order to end the game.

ॐ

An hour later, after all the orders had been carried out, Dante took hold of the captive the master wished to interrogate first, still bound, gagged, and blindfolded, and brought her up to the master's chamber, just as he wished. The woman was tired, desperately so, but she still had fight in her once she realized she had been separated from her lover. She had kicked him, square in the shin, and had even tried to bite him through her hood. She was cursing him too, and quite colorfully, but the gag prevented him from understanding most of it. It was a pity. Feisty women with profane and venomous tongues in their heads greatly aroused him, and this little beauty was a particularly delicious treat. After a short, enlivening struggle he finally reached the landing and knocked on the door; the profane beauty tried to kick him again, and he smiled, a bit wistfully, knowing that she was about to be tamed by the master. And once they were tamed by the master, they were never really quite the same.

"Here we are, Mistress Boyd," Dante whispered softly near her hooded ear. "My advice, if you wish to see the morning, is to do as the master wishes. Bend to his every whim; feed his every desire; ignite the flame of lust, not anger. He's the devil to cross." And then, gently, he untied her hands and removed the hood from her head; the gag he did not touch.

She turned on him, anger and indignation flashing in her dark eyes, the words "hog-rutting ingrate"—or something very similar—coming from her sweet, muffled lips. And then her eyes fell on him. She stopped moving, and her mouth fell silent, for this was the first time Marion Boyd had gotten a good look at him. Her reaction was one he seldom tired of— on the face of a woman. When men looked at him like this, he killed them. But now, before the master's door, he invited it, fueled it, peering hungrily into the eyes that so desperately wished to excoriate him. He smiled and pulled her close; she did not fight him. Smiling still, he softly pressed the latch; the door clicked, and with a suddenness designed to shock, he pushed her inside the room.

Washed, freshly shaved, imperceptibly dosed, and immaculately dressed in a doublet of rich black velvet trimmed in gold, Julius Blythe stood leaning against the shadowed embrasure of the window and watched as Marion Boyd stumbled across the threshold. He made no move to steady her.

She was greatly agitated, and he knew why, for Dante did as he was told. The Venetian had shown himself to Marion, a young woman with an astounding hunger for passion. The result was as he expected: quick breathing; outrage, not anger; shoulders back; nose in the air—and, most tellingly, she had spun to face the door. It stood slightly ajar, revealing the space on the other side to be dark and empty. That she was facing the door caused mild relief. It told him what he needed to know, but he would put her through her paces nonetheless, and he would try to enjoy it.

It had been a long night; thirteen of his elite force had been mercilessly slaughtered. Sir Matthew, his old captain, had been ambushed and murdered as well, and the blame would fall on him. His mood was frighteningly dark, and alcohol had tempered it little. He knew it was unwise to have Kilwylie's minx of a cousin brought here—a woman who would not so much as put up a fight if he took her. And he wanted to take her, but not without a fight. He wanted to make her pay for the trouble she had caused them all. He thought of the king, who was now, at this very moment, being locked in a cell deep below the earth. He thought of Isabeau, and Kilwylie, and fought to expel the execrable vision that floated before his eyes. The bastard would use whatever means possible to bring him down—James, Isabeau, even his own pretty little cousin, who was now frothing with desire for her exotic, dark-eyed jailor. Her passions were fickle, and he would teach Mistress Marion Boyd a little lesson in loyalty.

He silently admired her as she slowly turned around: the proud tilt of her head, the fiery gaze, the palpable sexual titillation rising in her like a building tide. She was magnificent, like a prized mare coming into her first heat, and he could just understand why a young man like James Stewart had shirked his duty and his guard to ride forty miles through the heather. She pulled the gag from her mouth and looked wildly around the derelict room, her eyes trying to adjust to the low light.

He took one last sip from the mug and gently set it on the sill of the window. It was time to begin.

"I see you've met Dante," said the master, stepping silently from the shadows. The soft light from the brazier fell across his face, gilding the tips of his hair and dazzling the damascene trim of his dark clothing. The effect was deliberate. He watched her dark eyes as they fell on him. Her burning indignation slowly transmuted into warm appreciation and welcome relief. Her lips parted slightly as her body fell silent. Julius, silently amused, continued. "A most alarming young man, is he not? He was the property of a Turkish pirate when I found him. His striking male beauty had been a curse. The Turk regarded him much as you do right now—as an object of desire. Later, I caught that Turk and gave him to Dante. I watched as he slowly killed the man. I still have visions of the old pirate, on his knees, begging for a knife to end his life. He didn't get one. Dante had a lot of anger back then."

Her mouth, twisting into a grimace of distaste during his story, fell open in astonishment. "You're mad and offensive. First the gag and the hood, and now this—this horrible little story. This is no kind of greeting between two friends." Pique had now replaced the open invitation.

"Friends? Is that what we are? I don't think so, my dear. And I tell you this story purely as a favor to you, because if you were listening, you would understand that Dante's story is a cautionary tale of beauty. When he was younger, like you, he had used his beauty to get whatever he wished. There was no door in Venice that would not open for him, until the one day when he overstepped even his remarkable reach, and his enemies caught him and used his beauty against him. Take it from me, it nearly destroyed him. He has now learned to use the gifts God gave him for what they are. Dante has a brilliant mind; his male beauty is merely a distraction—a disarming weapon he uses when it serves him, or, at times, when it serves me."

"You're wrong if you think I'm remotely attracted to that ... that ... gutter boy! I know what you're doing, and you're wrong!" She was deathly tired and still reeling with emotion; tears suddenly appeared in her large pleading eyes. "I know you're angry with me," she stated, and moved closer to him. "But you must know that I had no choice? He is the king. I thought you were smart enough to understand that! And then you go and do something stupid and abduct me and torment me with your wicked Venetian toy! Well, Mr. Blythe, you've wasted your time."

He pulled up, astonished for a moment that she actually believed the abduction had been about her. There was no doubt in his mind then. Marion Boyd was no trained seductress; she was exactly the person she appeared to be—young, beautiful, spirited, and entirely self-absorbed. Her only crime was being related to George Douglas, and they had both used the poor thing enough already. "Be quiet and sit down, Marion," he said coldly, motioning to a chair by the brazier.

"I prefer to stand, thank you," she replied, endearingly defiant.

"Very well. There seems to be a little misunderstanding here. You seem to feel that I took my men, at great risk to their lives, and set an ambush specifically to abduct you. Did you ever think, for just one moment, that perhaps the king was the target here?"

"James? No, of course not!" It was plainly and confidently spoken.

"For God's sake, why not?"

"Because I *know* you, Julius Blythe," she whispered, looking unnervingly into his eyes through her tears. "I've known you *four* times now, and it was only half a night. I wanted to *know* you more, much more. And you wanted the same. There is no use denying it, Julius. We are made for each other," she told him firmly. He was disquieted to find that she was quite possibly correct. He would be a fool to deny that there was an attraction there—a physical attraction that was overpowering at times. But he was weak at the moment. He wasn't thinking straight. He was exhausted and slightly drunk. He fought to bring himself under control as Marion continued. "But we didn't have time to pursue our relationship. Your sister was perfectly horrified when she learned of it and wanted to kill you. I've never seen her so angry. She's dearer to me than any of my own sisters, you must understand, and I was willing to suffer her anger for you. But then James came. It was just as much a surprise to me as it was to you. Have the courtesy to at least believe me when I tell you that!"

"You really had no idea he was coming?" He stood perfectly still as he watched her.

"No. Why would I? I've been encouraging him at his own court for some time now, but to no avail—just a polite smile and a few kind words. He looked at no one. He was too shy and too comfortable in the company of Isabeau."

"Who suggested you encourage him?"

"Don't misunderstand the situation, Julius. I've always liked James. Who wouldn't want to be his mistress? His Privy Council is scouring the kingdoms of Europe to find a fitting wife for him. But there aren't any. They've been encouraging him, in the meantime, to take a mistress. Why not me? Being the royal mistress gives me power, a power I wouldn't otherwise have."

"A power to help your family rise above the Humes and the Hepburns, perhaps? Your uncle, the Earl of Angus, has slipped tremendously since the Humes and Hepburns have tightened their grasp on the young king. He must be angry."

She looked at him, sorrow touching her tired eyes, a prideful contempt in her voice. "You seem to think I have puppet masters pulling my strings. I find that mildly offensive. I'm a grown woman! I make my own decisions, and I am master of my heart; I choose whom to give it to. Angus and Kilwylie support me, but they do not dictate."

"Would either of them have reason to harm the king?"

"Not Georgie. He loves James."

"Who was it that suggested you go to Blythe Hall in the first place?" he asked, watching her closely.

"Why, Isabeau. She wanted me to come. I know Kilwylie's mad about her. He's always had his eye on Isabeau. He thought I might help convince her of it, should I travel to Blythe Hall. But you know Isabeau. She has very high ideals where men are concerned. She's the best person I know, although a wee stubborn, and she perfectly hates being told what to do. But her visions of men are truly skewed. She models them all after the king, and her father, and she is perfectly in love with chivalry. But ordinary men aren't like that," she said softly, dolefully, as she looked into his eyes, "are they, Julius?"

"No," he replied, wishing she was not standing so close. "You are wise beyond your years, my dear. Did Kilwylie know James planned to ride to Blythe Hall?"

"No," she said, and came even closer. She was mere inches from him now, so close he could smell the heady scent of her. The soft light caught the thick strands of auburn hair that framed her face and lit the silvery trail of tears that had rolled from her compelling eyes. She looked lovely, and vulnerable, as she uttered, "How could he? The only one who knew was Princess Margaret."

"Margaret?" The name invoked a vision of a regal, elegant, and willful woman, with a firm jaw and flame-colored hair. She was the king's aunt, and the youngest of the five children of the late King James II and Mary of Gueldres. Margaret, by her own design, had never married. He thought on this a moment, then asked, "Have you ever heard a rumor about George being Princess Margaret's lover?"

"Georgie's had many lovers at court. He's had many lovers at home. It is, unfortunately, the one flaw that prevents Isabeau from allowing herself to love him. But he would change for her," she said earnestly, as if she truly believed it. "He will change for her. I know he will."

"Men cannot be changed, Marion," he stated with cool detachment. "Women often make the mistake of believing they can change a man. It's simply not true. We are what our mothers and fathers have made us and what our tutors have failed to teach us; we are the memory of our experiences and echo the morals of our closest friends. Our malleable years are young, my dear. We are forged and hardened ever before the apron strings are cut. Isabeau, unfortunately, is much wiser in this one area than are you."

"Well, then Isabeau's going to be very unhappy, because James has given Kilwylie his consent to marry her."

"We're not here to talk of Isabeau," he said curtly. "We're here to talk of the king."

"James is a good man," she whispered as a hand reached up to caress his face. He let her touch him. He watched her lips, full and moist, making ready for what she knew must come next. But she was wrong. With cool detachment, the master stilled her hand with his.

"I'm glad you think the King of Scotland is a good man," he replied blandly, "because you're going to be locked in a room with him for quite a while."

"I could stay here," she offered almost pleadingly.

He raised a brow and smiled. "No. You cannot."

"If things had been different . . ."

"No," he said, and firmly removed her hand. "Do not finish that thought, because it's not true. To me, Marion, you were only a diversion—just one of many such diversions. But to the king you are a jewel. He believes you are his, and he must never know differently. It is wise for a woman to want to be valued. Be wise for once, Marion. The harsh truth is, my dear, that I value my horse a good deal higher than you."

Her jaw dropped. She shut it firmly and with bitter courage lifted her head and looked him in the eye. "You lie."

"Unfortunately, I don't. I need my horse. I don't need you. Are you so vain that you think you are the only one who has ever fallen at my feet and allowed me your secret pleasures? You simply made me an offer and I took it. We enjoyed each other's company—we amused ourselves, and that is all."

"It's not true . . . ," she averred, her eyes softening as she scanned his face for a hint of weakness. But he remained cold, golden, and unmoving, like a blasphemous idol—an idol she had worshipped.

"I'm afraid that it is true," he replied softly. "You mistook my lust for more than what it was, and you are too proud to let yourself believe it. Well, you best believe it. And my advice to you is this: learn discretion, my dear."

Her eyes narrowed as violent anger unfurled. "You're no better than an animal!" she said.

"I have never claimed to be anything else. You allowed your fantasy of me to cloud the truth of what I am. And what I am is far beyond redemption. Go back to the king, Marion. Value him like the jewel he is. And for the record, I brought you both here not out of any love for you, but because I am trying to save his life, and yours."

His words had cut her, deeply from the look of it, and he saw that she was crying. "I don't want anything from you! I hate you!" she seethed, as another large tear slipped down her cheek.

"I'm sorry to hear it," he replied with a stunning lack of emotion, and walked to the door. "Stay here," he ordered, and without another look back, he left her shattered and alone in the room.

Dante, melding with the darkness, was in the passageway resting against the wall. The moment he heard the door open he sprang to life. "That went well," he said, mildly cheerful, and a display of perfectly white teeth split his face.

Julius allowed himself a smile. "So, you heard the whole thing. Tell me, what did you think?"

"I think I don't like you telling my story to young women, especially when you leave out small details, like the fact that you were also owned by the same Turk and were treated little differently than me."

Julius's brows rose and his smile turned grim. "When one is telling cautionary tales to young women, it is best not to use oneself as an example. It has more impact that way."

"The impact appears questionable. I believe Mistress Boyd understands nothing but her own desires."

"I agree. Has the king been brought to my father's chamber?"

"Yes. He's got everything he needs—food, drink, oil for the lamps, armed guards outside the door. Still, he's less than pleased."

"I imagine so. Well, bring him Mistress Boyd to ease his mind, and give him my regards, will you? And, Dante, my dear incorrigible lad, do not toy with her. Keep in mind that Marion is a noblewoman, and she's had quite enough of men like you and me. Put the hood back on for her own good."

He gave a mild look of surprise and then nodded. "Very well. And do you wish to speak with the king?"

"Yes, but not now," he replied, and ran a hand over his tired face and through his recently tamed hair, mussing it up. "The cocks are beginning to crow, and I'm ready to drop. I'm for bed, and when you're done, you are too. I'm afraid we've got another long day ahead of us."

With hood and rope in hand, Dante stood. "Sleep well, m'lord," he said, and entered the master's room. Julius waited silently behind the door, listening. Marion spoke quietly to the young man but did not put up a fight. The door opened and Dante appeared with his docile prisoner, bound and hooded. There was no need for the gag. Dante cast one last look at the man he had hitched his wagon to over three long years ago; he had never regretted it since. He was the man who had saved his life, the man who would not let him die, even when he had tried to turn the knife on himself. Julius Blythe was a stubborn bastard, and could be a damned hard devil when he wished it, but he was brilliant. The man also had vision, and incredible luck, as well as an uncanny knack for courting trouble. It was true, he knew, that Julius Blythe valued little, but what he did value he treasured. And he had valued Dante. He was the first man who had ever bothered to look beyond the surface, and that one small act had changed the course of Dante's life. He might very well go to the gallows yet, he mused, but he would go in good company. Another grin, and he took the king's mistress in a firm but gentle hand and guided her down the steps.

Julius Blythe, tired and emotionally spent, slipped back inside his room and shut the door.

ॐ

They were all sleeping like the dead when, shortly after dawn, the sentries came in with the news; Lord Kilwylie was attacking Blythe Hall.

"He outnumbers us four to one," the master said, looking levelly at his men across the board as the cooks rushed to fill their bellies. Jugs of ale had been brought, and the smell of rashers and oat porridge filled the room. As soon as the news came, and was verified by himself, he woke the boys to light the fires and roused the cooks. It was a substantially smaller group of his elite force that now gathered in the hall, tired and hastily dressed. It had been a gruelling campaign so far, yet his men were used to such treatment. The presence of Kilwylie, however, was a surprise. It indicated that something truly fantastic had happened in the night, something he himself had not even believed. There was no reason for it except one: Isabeau had escaped Sir George's tight grasp and had made it home. But why? The last time he spoke with her, Isabeau had championed Kilwylie and had even admitted to liking him. There was no doubt that Kilwylie had poisoned her mind further against him by telling her that he was responsible for the slaughter of Sir Matthew and his men. He had learned that the night before. That was how Kilwylie had gotten Isabeau and the king to leave Blythe Hall. So why the change of heart now? What had happened? What had Kilwylie done to her?

"I have reason to believe my sister is at Blythe Hall now, with next to no means to sustain such an attack," Julius told them gravely. "If Kilwylie breaches those walls or gets inside the gates, we will have a devil of a time getting him out. As I said before, we will be outnumbered four to one. Although we'll have the slight advantage of attacking on his flank, it will not be an easy fight. And that is why I ask for volunteers, because I cannot guarantee a victory. No one will be thought less of if they wish to sit this one out. Think hard, gentlemen, and then raise your hand if you wish to join me."

The response was, of course, overwhelming. Dante didn't need time to think, and neither did most of his men. They were mercenaries without families. They loved a good fight, but what they loved even more was an entirely unfair fight with the odds vastly against them. Victory was sweeter then, and life was dearer, until the whiff of the next battle, when the whole cycle began again.

"Gentlemen, you honor me." Julius looked on them with a glorious smile, ordered more beer, unrolled a map on the table before him, and set down to business. "Danny, you'll go to the Mackenzie croft and call the shepherds to arms. Have them gather every able-bodied man they can find. The women and children of Blythemuir will be brought here. The sheep, I'm afraid, will have to fend for themselves." He looked down the length of the table to where his eyes met Dante's. "And Dante, I have something special for you. You will stay here, to safeguard the king." He could see his friend bristle at the order, and the men laughed at the Venetian's misfortune. "If I should fall, gentlemen, or something should go amiss, disperse immediately. Do not let yourselves be caught. And do not let Kilwylie near the king. James must be brought safely to Edinburgh. Any questions? All right, those are your orders, gentlemen. To arms!"

"I have a question," said Dante a while later, coming up behind the master as he swung into his saddle. He grabbed hold of the reins and stilled the master's horse. "It's cruel to leave me here alone with the women and children. I'd rather die with you."

"That's not a question," said Julius, not unkindly, "and you're not to be so lucky. Either I will kill Douglas today, or he will kill me. If I don't return, I'm relying on you to get the king back to Edinburgh safely. I'm relying on you to protect my sister and to find our old friend. In other words, I'm relying on you to take over where I left off."

Dante held the master's cornflower-blue gaze as his face, uncharacteristically, filled with concern. "I have never asked you, because I promised myself I wouldn't, but how do you even know he's coming? You've not seen him for years, and you've received no message that I know of."

The master paused, sitting on top of his powerful mount and staring at the armored silhouettes of his men as they rode out the open door of the tower, melding one by one with the bright light beyond. He took a deep breath and looked down at the one man in this world he would truly miss. "That night, in Venice," Julius replied quietly. "The night you sent me to your grandmother's brothel? The night I threatened to kill you?" Dante smiled wanly at the memory and nodded. "That night I saw my mother."

"Your mother's dead."

"I know. That's why I'm here."

Chapter 15

THE BATTLE
FOR
BLYTHE HALL

BLYTHE HALL WAS UNDER ATTACK, AND THE TWENTY men inside the walls were fighting like titans to see that the castle didn't fall. I had left the chapel, making a quick stop in the armory. All the hauberks and breastplates were too big and heavy, and there wasn't a shield or targe left that looked as if it could withstand the force of an arrow. I did, however, consider myself fortunate to find a battered old helmet, even if it did still emanate the pungent smell of sweat from the previous owner. Surrendering to practicality and prudence, I pulled it over my hopelessly tangled hair. My eye caught the worn leather of an old bracer, which I also borrowed and strapped on my left arm to protect from the bite of the bowstring. I planned, of course, to do a lot of shooting. I did own a rather nice pair of shooting gloves, but they were up in my room and I wasn't about to run up another flight of stairs.

So, dressed for battle as thoroughly as I could manage, I

picked up my bow and headed for the battlement above the gatehouse. Because that's where Gabriel—with his Viking stance, golden hair, and black surcoat fluttering in the wind—stood fighting like a demon-god. Arrows left his bow with astounding speed, three to one of any man there by my count. It was impressive. I believed I could beat it, and was going to give it one hell of a try. After all, this was my castle. And this was my battle.

When I got to the battlements, and to the defensive gallery where Gabriel stood beside the narrow opening, harassing the army of Sir George, I saw that Lord Kilwylie, slightly threatened by the alarming speed and accuracy of the arrows, had retreated to a healthier position. His men were also busy, I noted with a tinge of despair, stripping the branches off a good-sized tree they had felled. They were making a battering ram. Grimacing, I walked past four of our men who were attempting to make the job more difficult, and took up position beside Gabriel. In one fluid movement I strung my bow, nocked an arrow, took aim, and called out to Sir George. Gabriel, loosening his string a hair's breadth prematurely, spun to face me. Disbelief crossed his fair features, and then his eyes, bright and pure as the summer sky, narrowed with anger. He was about to speak, but Sir George beat him to it. "Is that you, my little dove?" Lord Kilwylie called out from atop his horse.

"It is me!"

"That helmet doesn't suit you! And I see you have a little helper. Where have you been hiding him, my dear?"

"Never mind about him! Come closer, my lord, so that I can put an arrow through your heart!" I cried.

"Tell your men to hold, and I'll be happy to play along."

"HOLD!" I cried down the line, and the archers, all in different stages of release, stilled their bows. They turned to me with questioning looks on their faces. Some were even smiling, but not Gabriel.

"What do you think you're doing?" he demanded, his voice rolling like thunder.

Looking at the magnificent archangel, I smiled sardonically. "What do I think I'm doing? I don't think. I'm going to shoot my lord Kilwylie through the heart. And don't you dare shoot your bow, or there'll be hell to pay." Angry and determined, I narrowed my eyes. And then, shifting my gaze to the man on the other side of the bridge, I called out, "Come to me, my lord. My men won't shoot."

Smiling, Sir George kicked his horse forward, eager to appease me. I looked at Gabriel and my anger rose. He still held his bow; his sight was true, and he was itching to loose an arrow into the man I had been contracted to marry. *I* deserved the right to shoot! And Gabriel was making it perfectly clear that he wanted to take it from me. Recalling the chapel and how I had been lulled into those warm, solid arms, and then dropped onto the floor like a sack of oats, I was, to say the least, infuriated. I cast him a glance and said with mock sweetness, "Did you hear me? Did you? Because I distinctly remember ordering you to lay down your bow. Lord Kilwylie is mine."

His face darkened as his eyes grew fierce, yet there was still a calmness about him that irked me. The man had impeccable control, and confidence. Unfortunately it only made him more attractive. "And I thought I told you to stay in the tower. That was also an order." Taking a page from my book, he offered a breathtaking smile of pure irony. It was, admittedly, disarming.

"Darling, are you still there? You've grown quiet. It's not like you. Have you, in fact, changed your mind?" Sir George's voice pulled me back.

I glowered at Gabriel. "And I don't listen to men who kiss me and then retch with remorse afterward!" I huffed, drew the cord, and loosened. "Are you merely a coward when it comes to women? Or do you prefer something else?"

Gabriel's hand stilled, the color drained from his face, and I watched his eyes as they followed the flight of my arrow, knowing it was heading straight for Sir George's black heart. His golden brows rose ever so slightly, and the eyes, like flawless aquamarines in the sunlight, could not suppress the approbation he felt when he saw that my aim was true. I turned my attention back to Sir George, and watched as he lifted his shield at the last second, to take the blow.

"That was brilliant, my darling!" he called out cheerily, waving his shield with my arrow stuck in the center of it. He pulled it out and tossed it aside. The men on both sides, with the exception of Gabriel, clapped in appreciation.

The archangel, with alarming speed, grabbed my bow and yanked it out of my hand. "You think this is about you?" he demanded.

"Isn't it? Isn't that why we're here now, fighting?" I gestured to Sir George and his army. "Unless he's got a bone to pick with you, which I highly doubt, this *is* about me!"

"Not this!" His voice was remarkably constrained as his face lost all semblance of the stoic calm that enveloped him like a cocoon. "I know what *this* is about!" He jerked his golden head toward Lord Kilwylie. "I'm talking about what just happened between us, in the chapel."

I paused, letting my jaw slacken as I attempted to process his words. It was then that I caught movement out of the corner of my eye and turned to see Tam. He was coming up the steps with a bucket of hot pitch, and Jerome Mackenzie was right behind him with another. Both young men had stopped, in mid-errand, with their eyes, amused and twinkling, glued to us. I was highly annoyed and shouted, "Get those up here, now!"

I looked back at Gabriel. He was still frightfully pale, only now a tinge of red appeared high on his cheekbones. He was looking at me, his chest heaving violently, and I was only slightly disturbed to find that a dark joy rose in me when I observed that whatever serenity he had arrived with was now completely shattered. I had gotten under his skin, and he had gotten under mine. "Are you trying to tell me," I said, giving him my sternest look, "that what happened back there isn't about me? Because I rather thought that it was." I was feeling the shame and indignation of it all over again. "I was yours," I hissed in a strained whisper. "From the first moment, I was completely and utterly yours. I have never given any man that gift. And you took it, and you reveled in it, and then dropped me faster than a piece of . . . of . . . plague-infested old linen!"

"No . . ." The word exploded from his mouth in a breath of mortification. "No." In his defense, he was rather convincing. "Oh, dear God! Is that what you think?" he asked, looking at me with disbelief, as if my reaction to his little rebuke was unfounded. "How . . . how could you even think such a thing?"

"How could I not!?" I shot back. "You were horrified by what happened. And then you . . . you just ran away."

"My God," he said. His voice was rasping and strained; his face expressed ineffable pain. "It wasn't like that. You've got it all wrong . . . so very wrong, Isabeau. God help me," he uttered as he tilted his head toward the heavens. And then his eyes closed, his splendid head came down, and he buried his grief-stricken face in his hands. I was completely speechless.

"My darling, are you still there?" came the cry of Sir George.

I closed my eyes then too, exasperated, and looked over the battlement. "What do you want now?" I shouted.

Unflinching atop his restless charger, and grinning rather smugly, he cried, "I want you to watch this, my darling!" Sir George waved ten of his men forward. To my horror they all had incendiaries—fire arrows. Gabriel, moving like a ghost, took aim through the opening and shot at the archers now in range. Sir George dropped his arm, and nine of the arrows flew, low and true, hitting the solid wood of the gates below us. Gabriel had struck one archer, but nine arrows had reached their target, exploding in flames as they hit.

Lord Kilwylie was trying to weaken the gates for his battering ram.

Gabriel turned and shouted for Tam and Jerome to put down the pitch, which would only make the fire worse, and start drawing water from the well. "Get as much water on those gates as you can," he told them. It was a job they had to do from the inside, as the battlements above the gatehouse overhung the wall by three feet, and the angle would make dumping buckets of water from the defensive gallery fruitless.

"Stand back, my little dove!" cried Sir George with a wide, maniacal grin, "and watch it burn." He made another signal, and a third of his men, most bearing torches, all of them armed with sword and crossbow, broke off and rode through the sprouting fields heading for the village of Blythemuir. "I'm laying waste to the countryside now, darling. It's time to rape and pillage! Be ready. I'll be coming for you soon!"

A cold terror filled me as I realized what Sir George was preparing to do. He was going after my people. He would make them pay for my resistance, and the mere thought of all those innocent crofters—all the shepherds and farmers, all the women and children—losing everything, including their lives, because of me was more than I was prepared to suffer. I stood motionless, watching as his men rode away, armor shimmering, ravenous torches bending to the light breeze. A feeling of helplessness swept through me then. My heart ached, and my limbs became too heavy to move.

The rest of Sir George's men had moved closer, and our archers, I believe, were taking advantage of that. I could hear Gabriel launching a near-continuous stream of arrows beside me and saw how many of Sir George's archers fell before they could launch their fire arrows. But Sir George's men were numerous, and overpowering, and soon the sky above us filled with fire. He was no longer aiming for the gates. They were already ablaze, and the black smoke billowing from the hungry flames was beginning to obstruct our view. Gabriel, dropping his bow, yanked me down, right as an arrow exploded through the black smoke, blazing a trail like a fiery comet, where my head had so recently been. Many such arrows came then.

"Get back to the tower, Isabeau!" Gabriel cried fervently. We were sitting pressed together against the thick wall of the battlement. I looked at him through my tears. I understood then that there was real concern on his face, but it was too late. It didn't matter now. "What happened . . . in the chapel," he said, "is not a discussion we're going to have here. It's too important, Isabeau. There's something you need to understand about me. Dear God, what's wrong?"

"We need," I said, hiccoughing, ". . . to open . . . the gates." I could feel myself shaking. "We need . . . to let . . . him in."

"Look at me," he demanded, and firmly held my face between his gloved hands, forcing me to look him in the eyes. He was a study of paradoxes: angel and warrior: confident and distraught, with a voice that was remarkably calming yet dire in its tone. "I will never let him touch you!" he said. "Do you understand that?"

"He's going to raze the countryside," I said tearfully. "He's going to kill the crofters!"

"That is the unfortunate face of war, my heart. And if you open these gates, it will only be worse, for everyone. We need to hang on here. It may look desperate, but it is often in the vastness of our desperation that the greatest miracles happen. Do not give up hope just yet. Do not stop looking for a miracle." His touch and his voice were like a balm to my nerves, and I could feel myself relax under his steady gaze and begin to think more clearly. I ignored Sir George and his stream of tormenting threats. I wanted only to stay beside Gabriel and bask in his strength and serenity. "Now please, please, Isabeau, take the women into the tower and wait there."

"May I propose a compromise?" I asked, wanting to obey him but knowing that every hand was needed. "I'm going to help put out the fires." This was not a question but a statement.

He saw what I was looking at. Stone didn't burn, and there was plenty of stone in Blythe Hall, but there were also buildings of wood and thatch in the lower bailey, including the stables. Sir George, having been inside the walls as a visitor, was now aiming for these targets, and many were already ablaze. Practicality won over pride, and Gabriel, with a grimace of understanding, relented.

༄

Like a rogue wave on a calm sea, I had been carried these last few hours by a surge of emotions ranging from paralyzing fear to ebullient happiness, from love to heartache, from hope to utter desolation, and just about everything in between. In all the commotion I had forgotten how tired I was, but I remembered soon enough as I began the physical task of drawing water from the well. Thankfully, I was not alone in this. I had Maggie, Gwyneth, and Katie beside me, the three dairymaids who had an axe to grind with my lord Kilwylie as well, along with two laundresses and three maidservants from the hall. We hoisted buckets of water and passed them in a line to the young men who threw them on the gates; for the gates were our greatest concern. But the water did little to help the situation there. It was too little and too slow. The half-foot-thick oak slabs were steaming as fire ate through the wood inch by inch from the other side, and at the top black scorch marks, like shriveled leeches, began to appear. The work was gruelling and dangerous. Incendiaries continued to fall from the sky, setting small fires in the lower bailey. The stables were already ablaze, and there was nothing we could do but move the horses to the upper bailey and hobble them near the hall. My body ached, my arms shook with fatigue, and I wished to

God I could make the chaos stop. Blythe Hall was burning, yet for every small fire we put out, four more had started. It was a Sisyphean task, frustrating and impossible. And the water on the gates was the equivalent of using a spoon to bail out a sinking ship. It only served to prolong the inevitable. But I would not give up until I dropped.

It was sometime later that I heard the cry from the battlements, indicating that a miracle had appeared on the horizon. A thought of Sir Matthew flashed in my mind, and I was certain it was he and the rest of the Guard that the men were cheering. Enlivened by hope, and cheered beyond reason, I dropped the bucket of water I had just drawn and ran to the steps, hoisting my dirt-smudged, soot-stained skirts to climb to the parapet and see this miracle for myself.

What I saw was not a miracle but another heartbreaking calamity unfolding outside the gates of Blythe Hall. The men on the battlements were not extolling the timely appearance of Sir Matthew and the Guard but another small army of knights, perhaps thirty or forty men in all, who were in hot pursuit of the torchbearers Lord Kilwylie had sent to Blythemuir. Their numbers had been drastically reduced; they were no longer carrying torches, and they rode through the fields like thwarted demons, heading straight for hell's favorite son, Lord Kilwylie, and the safety of his much larger army. The pursuers were well armed and highly skilled, and I knew at first glance who they were, for Julius on horseback was unmistakable. Quick, daring, and lithe as a red deer on the moors, he rode point, flying over the crest of the last hill with his band of helmeted and lightly armored mercenaries following closely behind him. They were shooting crossbows, and Kilwylie's raiders were falling like ripe apples in an autumn breeze. Gaining speed, Julius and his men were closing on the main body with the intent of trapping Kilwylie between them and Blythe Hall, with the river Tweed blocking one line of escape. It was a daring plan for forty men, and the heartbreak was that every rider he had with him appeared 100 percent committed, even as Kilwylie's arrows flew. There was a moment of chaos as the Kilwylie men crashed into their own army. And then came Julius and his men, full tilt, with swords drawn. The short siege turned into real battle then, where crossbow bolts pierced armor and broadswords hacked at limbs. And the archers on the battlements of Blythe Hall waited, with arrows nocked, until Kilwylie made that fatal slip.

But Kilwylie was a fox.

I found Gabriel not far from where I had left him. No longer above the gatehouse, due to the smoke and fire, he was now crouched on the stretch of wall that ran beside it, watching with the rest of the men, bows ready and waiting. "By God!" he exclaimed upon seeing me, his eyes alight with wonder. "Here is our miracle, Isabeau."

I looked at him, attempting to comprehend his joy while foreboding and sorrow battled for dominance in my heart. "That is no miracle," I said softly, heatedly. "That is Julius, my brother. And Sir George will kill him, right before my eyes, because Julius has abducted the king."

"What?"

"That is my brother!" I said again, with a little more force in my voice. I glanced at the battlefield with my heart in my throat, and pointed.

"I know Julius is your brother." The excitement that so recently filled his open, pleasant face was ebbing as a grim sort of irony took hold. "You have remarkable similarities, really," he added with an arched brow. He looked back to the battle, saw one of Kilwylie's men come within range, and shot his bow. The soldier fell. "But what I thought I heard you say," he began as he picked up another arrow and placed the nock on the cord, "was that he has abducted the king, which is impossible." He released again; another man fell.

"It's not impossible. You obviously don't know Julius."

"I don't mean to offend you, but I beg to differ. I know him quite well."

"Really? How interesting." As I talked he kept one eye on the fighting. "You appear here, materializing out of nowhere, invite my affection, reject it, storm into my courtyard, rally my men around you, and then call me a liar when I tell you my brother has abducted the king. I think, after just meeting me, that's a little rash, don't you?"

He shot again and turned to me, his crystal-blue eyes flashing. He was grinning. "I think I have already established that I have not rejected your affections. And I didn't call you a liar. I'm simply questioning your story." He grimaced, aimed, and drew the cord, bending the powerful yew to his will with the grace and speed of a master archer. He loosened, and another man, no doubt believing himself far beyond the reach of an arrow, fell to the ground.

"It's not a story," I said, marveling at his ability. The man was a machine, like a winding crossbow with expert precision, and infuriatingly, he kept at his work as we talked. I grabbed his arm. His arrow released and went wide. He exhaled forcefully, as if it was a great blow to his pride, and looked at me, none too pleased. "I was there," I said, staring boldly back at him. "I was with the king. We were riding through the forest at night, heading for Kilwylie Castle, when we were attacked."

He lifted a brow and picked up another arrow. "How do you know it was Julius?"

"Because the attack was quick, and well executed, and only the king and my friend, Marion Boyd, were missing when it was all over."

He stopped shooting and gave me his full attention. "You were on your way to Kilwylie Castle . . . with the King of Scotland?" His tone was skeptical. "How long ago was this?"

"Last night."

"Last night!?" I was gratified to see shock appear on his face. "And you're here, now?"

"Yes. Julius abducted the king shortly before I learned that Sir George and his uncle had the same notion. Angus was at Kilwylie Castle, with some English agents and a small army." A deep crease appeared on his smooth brow as he listened. His lips, firm, resolved, and wonderfully alluring, parted slightly as his focus shifted from me to an unseen distance beyond. He was thinking. He understood what I was trying to tell him, and he slid down against the thick stone of the battlement, pulling me with him. A gloved hand covered his eyes as he fully digested this information. "I overheard something I shouldn't have," I added, looking pointedly at him. His hand lowered, and his blue eyes locked on mine. "I pretended I didn't understand what Lord Angus had let slip. But clearly he had been expecting James Stewart, not me. Which really *was* impossible, because nobody knew the King of Scotland was here . . . at Blythe Hall."

"Here? The king was here? By God, why did he come here?"

I looked into his eyes, wanting to tell him but not quite knowing exactly how to put it—to hide away in bed with a woman? To indulge his private pleasure? None of it sounded very regal or flattering. Instead I smiled softly and added, "I shall tell you that and a great many other things, but this is not a conversation we should be having here." He mirrored my ghost of a smile and nodded. I continued. "Lord Kilwylie suspected I knew something and locked me in his room. I escaped before dawn and rode here. Hence the reason for the visit. My point in telling you this—and the reason I was so horrified at what you call a miracle—is that the King of Scotland is missing, Gabriel, along with my dearest friend, Marion Boyd of Nariston, and my brother is the only one who knows where they are."

He took hold of my shoulders. "Does anybody else know what you know . . . about Kilwylie?"

"Only Hendrick, my steward."

He looked down the row of archers and the swiftly dwindling stock of arrows to the end, where Hendrick stood shooting. "Very well," he replied. He took a deep, cleansing breath and then stood. "Thank you for telling me." He extended a hand to me and pulled me up beside him, steadying me with a firm grip. "Now, get back into the tower, Isabeau. And this time I mean it."

"Why? Where are you going?"

"I'm going to make sure your brother survives the day."

I watched in silence as he set down his bow, picked up a discarded helmet, and drew his sword. He was going to find a horse and join the battle. I shouted to him, bidding him to stop. It was a fool's errand to leave the safety of the walls now. Julius had entered the battlefield driven by hatred, by his need to destroy Sir George Douglas. They were two reckoning forces, entwined in a sadistic game of chess, in which no one, not even the king, was beyond their reach. It was up to Fate to intervene on my brother's behalf now, not Gabriel—not the warrior-angel God had sent to me. I cried his name again. He stopped and turned to look at me, blind determination in his gaze. It was a look that terrified me, for I knew what it meant. He looked at Hendrick. It was then that I realized that Hendrick was shouting too, only not at Gabriel. He was shouting to everyone, and pointing. Soon all the men on the battlements fell silent as they looked in the direction of Hendrick's alarm. Through the smoke, through the sound of steel hitting steel—as men cried and horses screamed—I turned to look as well.

It was a moment before I registered the enormity of what was unfolding before us, yet when I did, when I finally understood what it meant, I was paralyzed with fear. Out of the north came another army of warriors, greater than all the men on both sides put together. And they rode under the banner of Hume. It was Alexander, the second Lord Hume, our neighbor, Warden of the East March, a member of the king's Privy Council, Keeper of Stirling Castle, and devout protector of the realm. He was a man both Julius and Sir George had served under in their youth; he was also a victim of Julius's betrayal, and he had suffered personally because of it. Lord Hume came not to help the outlawed band of mercenaries that had abducted the young king. He came to enforce justice. He came to assist the young Lord of Kilwylie in his attempt to take Blythe Hall.

As Hume came barreling down on the battlefield, Julius must have understood what was happening. He was no longer the force that could turn the tide of the attack but the prime target. Watching with disbelief from the safety of the battlements, I had the nagging thought that Sir George Douglas—after failing to abduct the king, after learning of my flight, after realizing what I knew of his plans—had sent a messenger to Lord Hume apprising him of the situation, which simply and honestly was that Julius was back in Scotland and had, this time, successfully abducted the king.

Sir George had attacked Blythe Hall because he understood that what I knew would ruin him. He also knew that Julius could not stand by and watch it fall. Just as he knew that Lord Hume and his highly feared arm of the law would come and crush the outlawed rabble against *his* grasping, desperate sword. It hit me then, the lengths Lord Kilwylie would go to see Julius destroyed. The cold, aggressive calculations were chilling. And I realized, standing with my heart in my throat, that Sir George Douglas was about to make the final move in this twisted and lethal game both men had engaged in, perhaps long ago. It was then that something inside my tired, weary, heartsick head clicked and I saw what Julius had been trying to tell me all along. Damn Julius, I thought, as tears of remorse began to cloud my vision. Just like the consummate older brother he was, he had made me figure it out on my own.

It happened fast then. Seeing Lord Hume, Julius had given the order to his men to disperse, and many of them did, heading for the Tweed, where they'd risk drowning before being caught. But Julius could not escape. He saw that he was surrounded, caught between the devil and the law. Kilwylie was an old friend turned enemy; Lord Hume was an old master he had crossed. Julius, having little choice, quickly and efficiently chose the law, placing his life in the hands of the man who would, due to past charges and his latest affront to Scotland, ultimately hang him. It was, like throwing water on a burning door, prolonging the inevitable. But at least the law would give him a fair trial; at least Lord Hume would keep Julius safe until I could talk with him. With only a handful of men remaining, my brother rode to Lord Hume's army, where he and his depleted band of mercenaries made a show of dropping their weapons and raising their hands high in the air in the universal symbol of surrender. The battle had ended, and Sir George was victorious. But even he would not stop there.

He did not get the ultimate prize.

Seeing that Julius was putting himself under the protection of Lord Hume, Lord Kilwylie gave his last order. His men picked up the battering ram and made ready to knock down the gates.

I could hear Hendrick shouting orders at Gabriel, who stood beside me. "Get her out of here!" he cried. "Get her out of here! For God's sake take her away! Now!" Yet although I heard the desperation of his words, I could not move. My eyes held the field where Julius, defeated and weaponless, was riding toward Lord Hume with his hands in the air. I saw it then, a glint out of the corner of my eye, flying like a demon over the bloody green. A crossbow had been fired. I screamed at the same time that the bolt hit Julius in the back, piercing his steel cuirass. His body was thrown forward under the impact, and then he slumped, lifeless, across the neck of his powerful black charger. The horse capered under the impact, and Lord Hume, crying in outrage, dashed forward to retrieve him.

Tears coursed from my eyes unchecked as I stood in disbelief, staring at the lifeless form of my brother. And then, without warning, the world brightened and visions from a day long past—the day when the English had come to Blythe Hall—crossed before my eyes. I saw a blue sky. I felt a gentle wind that rustled the tall grass all around me. The Tweed, like a lazy blue snake, moved beneath the puffy clouds, threading its way to the sea; and I held a puppy. Joy filled me. And then I saw Julius, an untrammeled spirit that was one with the horse beneath him. My heart began to beat loudly, and I knew that it beat in time with another. I had no fear. I trusted completely. And I reached for the hand that reached for me. But I could not touch it. I could not reach it, and the hand, a hair's breadth from mine, moved slowly beyond my grasp. I screamed then. I screamed because I had lost my brother. I had lost my trust in him. And I had lost Blythe Hall. A white-hot and blinding pain struck my back between my shoulder blades and radiated outward. It was debilitating, absolute. The sunlight faded as darkness formed at the edge of my vision. There was a loud crash. Men shouted. Smoke filled my lungs. Hendrick was still screaming. "Gabriel, get her out of here!" And then I heard no more; because the darkness had finally come for me.

Chapter 16
THE
AWAKENING

I WAS IN PAIN. I DIDN'T REMEMBER WHY, BUT IT RADI-
ated through me with jarring force, and with a rhythm very
like a blacksmith's hammer on an anvil. My head was throb-
bing, because the pain that hit my bum shot to my skull, exploded, and then started again, in my bum. My thighs ached,
my feet were tormented with the numbing prickle reminiscent of a stroll through a nettle patch, and I doubted I could
move them, even if I tried. And then there was that pressure,
firm and binding, across my waist, that secured my back
against a hard and immoveable object. I wanted to open my
eyes. I tried, but the pain was too great, and I let out a moan
instead. The pressure across my waist tightened. "Hold on,"
said a voice near my ear. It was low yet harsh, and most desperately pleading. It was also slightly familiar. My mind,
mired in blackness and chivied with pulsating pain, fought to
make sense of it. Why was someone whispering to me? And
what in the name of heaven did I need to hold on to? A moan,

high and pathetic in its thinness, hit my ears. Pity filled me then; it was my nature to pity a creature so forlorn, until I realized, with a sinking heart, that the sound had come from me. The voice came again, this time with more desperation. "Hold on, Isabeau. Hold on, my heart."

I remembered the voice. My lips pulled into a smile as the face of the owner materialized in my mind, pushing away the darkness, challenging the tenacious webbing of pain like an intrepid maid with a feather duster. Broad, golden, noble, both divine and tangibly earthy, it was an inimitable combination and one that, in its purity, drove the pain from me. "Gabriel," I uttered, and opened my eyes. Expecting to see his face, I was stunned, for only impenetrable blackness filled the space before me. I felt a rising panic. I didn't know where I was or what was happening to me. I heard Gabriel, but I couldn't see him.

I shifted, pressing against the force that bound me. Yet instead of breaking free, I was gripped even tighter. My hands, suddenly coming awake, instinctively grabbed at the unrelenting binding. It was solid, like the trunk of an oak. And then I felt worn leather, as in the cuff of a glove, and thick wool, and a gap where the two materials met containing warm skin. I thrust my hand beneath the rugged wool, beneath a layer of soft linen, and ran it along a heavily muscled forearm that shivered slightly beneath my touch. The coarse hair stood on end, and I gently brushed my fingers over it, drawing a particular comfort from the solid feel of him. I understood then what was happening. We were on a horse; the pain that had roused me out of oblivion was in response to another long bout in the saddle—only Gabriel was holding me, keeping me upright. I brought my arms over his and held tightly. "Isabeau," he said in my ear, only this time there was no desperation or pleading, only a burst of relief. "You'll be awake?"

"I think I am. But I can't see a thing. What's happening?"

"We've been riding," he whispered, "in a very surreptitious

manner trying to put as much distance between ourselves and Blythe Hall before my poor horse drops from exhaustion. Dear Bodrum was ready to drop five miles ago." I felt him lean forward and pat the animal in question. And then, as he settled once again behind me, he lifted the hood off my head. A burst of cool air hit my face. "I'll ask your forgiveness for burying you inside my cloak," he said, and I felt his warm breath near my ear, "but it was for your own protection."

I marveled at the improbability of it all, for we were no longer inside the walls of a castle, and it was no longer daytime. It was night. I was on a horse—a powerful gray with a silvery black mane—that I didn't recognize, presumably Bodrum. I didn't know where we were but for the dull observation that we were riding along the marshy banks of a small lake, for the moon, rising in a sky with just the faintest hint of afterlight visible in the blue-black dome, was casting its reflection on the rippling water. It looked lonely, and isolated, and I suddenly felt a rising apprehension. It was then that I remembered the battle. It was then that I remembered Julius.

"Dear God, what happened?" I uttered, looking up at the firm jaw, now lightly dusted with golden stubble, that lay just above the top of my head. He did not look at me. Instead the arm around my waist tightened, as did the jaw. Met with this foreboding silence, I tried again. "At the castle . . . what happened?"

I felt the rise and fall of his powerful chest with every breath he took, and my question had made the breathing deeper and measurably forced. This was troubled silence, and it was the only answer he was willing to give. It confirmed my deepest fears. It was the last and final shred of self-preservation removed. A mere five days ago I had left Edinburgh with a dream of one day making the name of Blythe Hall ring with greatness again. In the short time since then I had been pushed to the edge of madness and beyond. I had been methodically stripped of everything I held dear. And now, on a cold and starry night, as we navigated the banks of a reedy little lake in the middle of nowhere, reality, like a ball of fire falling from the sky, came crashing down around me. The result was absolute devastation; the consequence was unalterable. I had no family left in this world. I had lost Blythe Hall, my inheritance. The pain of it shook me, and my tears, when they came, were unstoppable.

"Isabeau . . ." The sound of my name, suspended helplessly in the darkness, contained a naked pathos that matched, and resonated with, the void in my heart. This man, this divine being, was not trying to silence me, or to keep me from grieving my loss. A part of him understood it. A part of him shared my emptiness in a way that could only mean his connection was nearly as deep as my own. It was a thought that floated within me, not quite taking hold. I was further distracted as he lowered his head and placed his rough cheek next to mine, offering comfort, offering strength.

"They're all gone," I sobbed, falling completely apart. "My family. Their legacy. I've failed. Who will remember them now but me? I watched him kill . . . Oh God! I'm all alone . . ."

His arms, firm and gentle, held me closer. "You are not alone, Isabeau. You have never been alone," he whispered, boldly, heatedly, and with an undeniable desire. At first I didn't understand what he meant. But then, as with a seed planted too deeply, a small, pale shoot finally broke the surface, and I understood the truth in what he was saying. I was not alone. I had never been alone, because Gabriel had always been with me. And Julius, dear Julius, had understood this and tried to make me believe it as well. I thought of him then, forgiving him of everything—his waste and destruction, his brilliance and his unabashed profligacy—because of this one last gift. My sorrow slowly abated. My tears began to ebb. I leaned back, feeling Gabriel's warmth while gently brushing my cheek against his. I covered his arms, hugging them to my body and running my hands along the length of them as they grew bolder, straying from my waist. Our connection was spiritual, but there was an animal desire rising in him that my body instinctively responded to. It was palpable, visceral, becoming as insatiable as rampant fire, and I fed into him with a hunger to match his own.

Gabriel was my heart, my soul, my gift, and I would cherish him as he was meant to be cherished.

The horse, expertly trained and highly sensitive to the subtle movements of his master, moved slowly from the grassy bank of the lake and began to climb the dark, tree-covered slope of a hill. Bodrum wove his way patiently between the gnarled shadows of sparsely covered oak and the spindly scrub that clung to the hillside. His footing was sure, his instincts sharp as his master's, and when he reached a sheltered landing between rocky outcrop and the tall, conical shadows of ancient evergreens, he stopped, exhausted. Silent, yet breathing heavily, Gabriel swiftly alighted from the horse. I came next, assisted by his large, capable hands. They were slow to come away from my waist. I stood, languid and dreamlike on the soft ground, watching as he removed his gear, stripped the horse of saddle and bridle, and sent him off with a firm slap on the rump. Bodrum, steaming and silvery under the soft moonlight, threw his head, gave a throaty cry, and clamored down the hillside, disappearing into the night. Gabriel stood a moment watching the horse; his shoulders, covered by the black surcoat, were rising and falling with a building rhythm that had nothing to do with the arduous ride. My own heart was pounding just as fiercely as I stood watching him.

For a moment I feared that he would also run, now free of my touch. I understood that he wanted me; I had felt his desire as sharp and consuming as my own, but the memory of our last encounter in the chapel had made its mark. There was much about Gabriel I didn't understand. But I did know that

I could not suffer his rejection. Not now. My confidence had been manipulated and shattered under the hand of corrupt and careless men. My heart was as frangible as the translucent wing of a dragonfly. I was on the edge of utter desolation, but for the promise of something alive and pulsating I could not even name. I had let myself come close once—believing I had no choice—and the thought, as I stood breathless in the sheltered darkness, terrified me. Yet what terrified me even more was not finishing what we had started, for I feared that if he turned from me now, he would be gone forever. Resolute, and more determined than I had ever been, I walked up behind him. Sensing me, he turned, his face and the tips of his wild, pale hair gently illuminated by the full moon. I could not read his thoughts, but I could see the emotions that crossed his face. I had been correct in assuming that he wanted me, for he was fraught with passion, heaving with naked desire, yet he was clearly aggrieved by it. He was a man battling an inner demon I had no notion of, and it startled me more than I would have liked to admit. Did he think he would harm me? Did he think I would turn him away? I had no idea what he was thinking, and so, watching him closely, I took his hand, gently removed his glove, and pressed it against my heart. "Please," I said, "do not leave me. Not tonight."

His movements were swift and fierce. He took me in his arms, holding me as if he too was afraid I would disappear. He didn't speak; he didn't need to, because I knew this time that he was not going to run away. With both gloves now removed, he took my head between his hands and kissed me with astounding tenderness. He uttered my name. The sound of it caught in his throat, laying bare the sweet anguish that battled within him. It brought tears to my eyes to hear it, and I held him with even more desperation, trailing kisses from his lips, over and under his trembling jaw, and down the thick column of his throat, wanting him to know that whatever battle consumed him, he would not be fighting it alone.

My hands moved inside the heavy surcoat, and fumbled with the sword belt. When it finally came away, the weight of it shocked me, and it fell to the ground with a careless thud. He made no move to pick it up. He stood, with eyes large and wondrous, watching me. I ran my fingers over his haubergeon, the short-sleeved chain-mail shirt he still wore that fell a few inches short of midthigh. The steel links were warm and thick with the sharp tang of battle. With haste I tried to remove it but failed miserably. He was gently amused by this, and showed me the secret of removing a haubergeon.

Beneath his mail he wore a thick, quilted jupon or arming jacket. It was similar in length to the mail but fit him perfectly, and was secured with about twenty tiny buttons. As I attacked these with a driving purpose, I offered, "I suppose a nice, plain doublet and hose would be too much to ask?"

"I was wrong to think light armor would protect me," he answered softly, teasingly. But there was a tone of stinging truth in his voice. "I have never been so weak in my life. May God forgive me, but I am helpless under your touch."

With the last button undone, the jacket came away. "You fear that my touch weakens you? Perhaps you are looking at strength and weakness from the wrong angle?" I replied, breathing a bit heavily as I ran my hands along the fine linen shirt, warm from the heat of his skin. He was solid, and so finely made he could have been a work of art. "Close your eyes, Gabriel. Close your eyes and let me fill you with a strength you have never known."

Helpless, perhaps even weakened, he did as he was told, and tilted his head toward the star-strewn heavens. My fingers, restless with anticipation, snaked beneath the barrier of his shirt. At the instant of my touch, a burst of air escaped his lips and his warm flesh moved beneath my fingertips with the light and frenetic flutter of a butterfly's wings. I realized then that I was trembling too. Unable to stop—unable to resist— I allowed my unsteady hands to explore every inch of his hard, sarsenet-smooth torso. Growing bolder, driven by an insatiable need, I felt alive and vibrant, and willed him to feel the exquisite energy that coursed through my veins. I pulled off the confining cambric and pressed my lips to him, kissing, tasting, teasing. His pulse was quick beneath my touch, and it beat with the pounding force of a war drum.

Unable to stand the assault, he crushed me to him, and I felt, for the first time, the urgency of his need. My hands slowly trailed down his back, following his spine until it disappeared beneath his close-fitting hose. They were of soft leather, and they accentuated the firm and supple roundness of his backside. My hands lingered here as he kissed me, and I gently, very gently, pulled him to me, holding his straining hardness against the softness of my body. His reaction was instant. He stopped kissing me, straightened, and, breathing as if he had just run a mile uphill, motioned for me to be still. I watched in silence as he turned from me, the bare muscles of his back straining under the pale moonlight. He bent to pick up his bedroll, which lay beside Bodrum's saddle. He brought it to a sheltered spot and unfurled it over a nest of soft pine needles. He then came back to me, scooped me up in his arms, and gently placed me on the makeshift bed. It felt like heaven, and I pulled him down beside me.

I lay motionless, watching as he undressed me. He had about as little knowledge of women's clothing as I had of men's, and I found his ignorance deeply endearing, yet he unraveled the mystery artfully, slowly, and with rapt anticipation. "You are even more exquisite than in my dreams," he breathed softly when he had finished. He looked upon my naked body with a heated tenderness that left me breathless.

"You've dreamed of me naked?" His response to this was a mildly abashed look. I smiled and reached up to stroke his cheek. "I'm relieved to hear it, because you're not alone there."

"You've dreamed of me naked?" he asked; the thought surprised and pleased him.

"Mostly naked," I admitted, feeling the blood rise to my cheeks. "But there were places even my extraordinary imagination was afraid to go."

"And is your extraordinary imagination afraid to go there now?"

"My imagination, like my body, is yearning for completion. I want what you want, Gabriel. I want my dream to live," I implored him, staring into his glistening night-dark eyes. "I want to give it voice and revel in the miracle that you are really here." I threaded my fingers through his hair, each strand no longer than a few inches. It fell around his head, soft and buoyant, lying in curls at the nape of his neck and enhancing the symmetrical lines of his face. He felt wonderful. He felt perfect. And then I pulled his head to me.

"God forgive me," he breathed, struggling to remove the last impediment. With my fervent help his hose came away, revealing the last of his magnificent body. "God forgive me, but it's going to be quick, love, and I'm hopelessly powerless to do aught about it. But I promise," he uttered, trailing soft, hungry kisses over my cheek, earlobe, and down the side of my neck, "that before this night is out I will worship you, with every ounce left in me, until you beg me, convincingly, that you can take no more."

❧

I awoke once again to the smell of fish, only this time my stomach was growling with anticipation, and the voice, softly calling my name, brought a smile of pure delight to my lips. "It can't be morning already," I said, stretching lazily. I opened my eyes and basked, unashamedly, in the radiance of the face looking down on me. "I feel as if I've just gone to sleep."

"Well, that's not far from the truth. And I'm mortally sorry about it, but we've to keep moving. You really must get up." I looked closely at him. He did look mortally sorry—highly

troubled would be more on the mark, and it gave me a sobering shock, especially after last night. He was already dressed;
I saw that his leather hose were the color of freshly ground
cinnamon, and his jupon was sky blue, matching the color
of his eyes. He had made a fire over which two fish were
cooking. They smelled heavenly. I also noted that Bodrum, a
beautiful dappled gray, had returned and was now happily
munching on whatever treat happened to be in his feed bag. I
sat up, holding tightly the thick surcoat that had served as our
blanket, and felt the euphoria of my recent memories slowly
leaving me.

"I caught some fish, and I had these in my pack," he said,
and handed me a leather sack. The sight caused a lump to rise
in my throat, for the sack contained the delicate pale-orange
flesh of dried apricots; the golden egg of the sun, Hendrick
had called them. They were an exotic delicacy and my father's
favorite. "It's not a feast," he added, misinterpreting my silence. "I wish I could offer you more, but it'll have to do."

I drew my eyes from the apricots and looked again at his
face. "You didn't sleep, did you?" He affected a wan smile and
slowly shook his head. "Is it because you're mortally sorry?"
I could not hide the pain in my voice, and he flinched when he
heard it.

"No!" his response shot out, fast and sharp as the crack of
a whip. And then his brows drew together, and his face grew
pallid with remorse. "Not about that." He exhaled with force,
ran a hand through his sleep-tousled hair, and, when he was
done with this mental flagellation, looked me square in the
eye. "Yes, about that. God damn it, Isabeau! It's not what you
think! Christ help me, but it's so horribly complicated."

"I'll tell you what," I said gently, evenly, all the while
silently fighting the gut-wrenching fear that I was about to
lose him too. I didn't even know who or what Gabriel was—
man or divine being—but I knew that I could not lose him.
Not now. Not after last night. Not after a lifetime of looking

for him. I kept my eyes steady, focusing on his implacable troubled stare. "I'm going to get up. I'm going to wash in the lake. I'm going to put on my clothes, and then we're going to eat those fish of yours. And while we're eating, Gabriel, you and I are going to have a little discussion, because the look in your eyes is positively killing me."

I left the shelter of the little bower, naked but for the great surcoat pulled around me, and silently shaking. The scent of our lovemaking clung to the heavy coat as it clung to me, thick, sleepy, evoking feelings and images too powerful to suppress. Draping my dirty gown over my arm I began grabbing at the heads of delicate wildflowers that sprouted from the tall weeds as I walked past. To these I added some fresh evergreen needles and crushed the whole of it between a handful of gravelly sand. On the rocky bank of the lake I threw off Gabriel's coat, knelt, and added a few drops of water to make a pungent, earthy paste. And then I proceeded to rub it all over my body and through my hair, scouring my skin until I was nearly raw—until the scent of our lovemaking was gone.

The small lake was still as glass under the foggy grayness of dawn. But for a few waterfowl, there was not a soul around. It was a quiet and lonely little lake hidden in a verdant glen. And there was a beauty to it, a solemn beauty. I felt as alone as the lake then; we were maudlin kindred spirits. I walked into the frigid water, welcoming the sting of it, welcoming the shock of the icy liquid against my warm skin. My shivering became more pronounced, for it now had a physical purpose. I fought the urge to turn from the tormenting element and plunged ahead, until I finally dove in.

I knew he was watching me, and I didn't care. The water, coaxing my body to numbness, felt alive and invigorating, and I delighted in it, because it was so contrary to the fading warmth of Gabriel. Not until I was chilled to the bone did I leave the sanctuary of the lake. I stood on the rocky bank, dripping in the cool morning air and feeling remarkably clear-headed. And with a deep, cleansing inhalation I turned my eyes to the screen of evergreens.

The sight of Gabriel took the breath from me. He was just visible in the clearing, kneeling before his mighty sword with both hands tightly grasping the hilt. Before this makeshift cross his effulgent head was bent, and there was a violent desperation in his posture that melted my shivering heart. There was something visible in Gabriel that I had never before seen. It was the golden aura that seemed to surround him, dispelling the gray fog—the gossamer wisps of a halo near his head, the shimmering traces of evanescent wings. They were not physical, these things, and they were not unfamiliar to me. I had seen these before, when I was a child all alone in the tower room. They were the trappings of the white lady, the ghostly entity I knew to be my mother. And Gabriel had them too. I could hear his prayer then, not so much in words but in feelings. It hit me with a force so explosive, so powerful, that I could not stop the tears from coming to my eyes. I could not understand the conflict in his heart, because I had no reference for it. But I did understand that this was a cause worth fighting for; here was a ray of hope in a dark and desolate world. I breathed then, quick and deep, as if a weight had lifted from my chest, and with that sensation came the familiar and comforting scent of wild roses. Although I had never really met her, I knew it was her scent. Maybe it was his too. Imbued with a fighting spirit, I pulled on my dirty clothes and walked back up the hill.

৬⊙

"The whole puzzling crux of the matter is, Isabeau, that I have made a vow before God. To him I have pledged my life, and I have broken it." Gabriel, sitting close to me on the bedroll, cross-legged, knees touching as we faced each other, thoughtlessly picked at the tender white flesh of his fish. He took a paltry nibble. "I came here to help you, to protect you, and what do I do? I not only defiled you, a beautiful, helpless young virgin, but I fear that in doing so I have damned my eternal soul to hell."

This was a surprise. I had not been defiled, and I certainly wasn't helpless, but I didn't immediately contradict him, as was my nature, because the pain on his face as he voiced this fear—defiling helpless virgins or not—was heartbreaking. He truly believed that because of his one moment of weakness, which I had encouraged, he had damned his soul. And yet, odd as it sounded, it brought to mind a story Seraphina had once told me. Dear Seraphina had delighted in angelic lore, and was a veritable font of knowledge on the subject. There was one tale in particular she had told me quite often. It was like a fairy tale, really, one used to lure an unwilling child to bed. And it was the one story in her impressive arsenal that always worked. Of course Seraphina spun it with great detail whenever she told it, to evoke powerful emotions. But the heart of it was very simple. An angel, of a celestial division referred to as a watcher, became enamored with a beautiful human woman he had been watching. Over time he became so enthralled with this enchanting creature that he left his place in the heavens, forsaking his duty and his supreme commander, God, to come to earth, assume the form of a mortal, and become the husband of the woman he had fallen for. The angel, by forsaking God and his own divine nature in order to love a human woman, had been shunned from the kingdom of heaven and was forever damned to walk the earth. I looked at Gabriel, a sinking feeling in my heart, and yet, selfishly, I still wanted to be the woman he had fallen for—the woman he would spend the rest of his days with. I offered a soft smile. "If it's any comfort to you, I was not defiled. Something as beautiful and as spiritual as we have shared cannot possibly fit that term."

This caused a reluctant curl of his taut lips. "You misunderstand me. The pain I feel is in no way because of you. I would not trade what we shared last night for all the riches on earth and heaven. But . . . my point is," he said, looking sternly at the tin plate in his lap, "it should never have happened."

I had been eating my fish, and quite ravenously too, for I was starving. Yet his words suddenly quelled my appetite. "Why?" I said, and swallowed forcefully. My mouth had gone suddenly dry. "Is it because you feel that in loving me you have lost the promise of heaven?"

He raised a brow at this, and then it fell as his forehead creased with troubled thought. "Something like that, I suppose," he replied.

I set my plate down and gently touched his hand. "Gabriel, I think I know what's going on here; I think I understand your torment. It's a very unusual one, isn't it?" His face, recently pinched with emotion, transformed into an expression that might be interpreted as curiously skeptical. Encouraged, I continued. "I know that you love me, deeply. You can attempt to deny it, but your efforts would be in vain. I wouldn't believe you."

"I have no wish to deny it!" he said with fervor. "It's true." His eyes, an impossibly vibrant blue, were wide and searching, and utterly heart-melting.

"Good," I said, and felt a modicum of relief. Emboldened, I straightened up and squared to him, ready to plunge ahead. "I understood that ours was not a common attraction from the very first moment I saw you. And when you admitted to having visions of me—and quite personal ones at that—it all made sense. I have been seeing you as well, in wonderful visions that I understood were too perfect to be real. I almost gave up any hope of ever finding you. But I did find you. And that's what makes it so extraordinary."

"It is extraordinary," he agreed, yet he was far from happy about it. "And you have always been far too perfect for me.

That's why my dreams were pure fantasy. Fantasy because I knew *this*"—he motioned to me and himself—"could never really happen."

"But it did happen!" I said, slightly confused. "It happened quite a few times, if you'll remember. And I think, unless I heard wrong, that it was, um . . . nothing like in your dreams. But the visions, well, I've never experienced anything like them before. I have to admit that over the years, Gabriel, going through everything that I have, I had begun to lose faith. And I certainly didn't believe in angels. But when I saw you in my father's chapel, kneeling before the altar, appearing at my very darkest hour, something quite marvelous happened. And it happened again, just a moment ago when I came back from the lake. I believe again," I offered softly. "Because of you my faith has been restored. And while I admit that things have not turned out the way I wished they would have, God has at least given us this gift. He has thrust us together for a purpose. Don't you see? So why then must you feel that our love is a sin?"

"Maybe, in part, because it isn't God who has thrust us together, Isabeau. It is your brother."

"What?" I uttered in disbelief. "Julius?"

He nodded. His look was convincing, and I thought on this, my eyes moving to the distant lake as I recalled my brother's attempts to push me to the edge of madness.

"Sure, he may have planted the suggestion in my mind," I said, looking back at him. "He did, after all, practically demand that I look for an angel. But he certainly couldn't have known about my visions. They were entirely personal . . . and very private." And then I stopped. I looked hard at him. "But you knew Julius, didn't you? And you said that you knew my father? I remember."

He gave a weary nod.

"But how can that be? My father's dead, and my brother

was missing for years. Tell me, Gabriel, what are you? Are you an angel, or are you—"

"Angel?" he said, aghast. "Dear God, Isabeau, I am no angel! Is that what you believe I am?"

I was stunned. My jaw hung slack as I looked at him, utterly stricken with disbelief. It wasn't possible. I knew what I saw. "But," I tried to argue, "you didn't deny it. In the chapel, you didn't deny it!"

"Because I thought you were speaking in metaphor," he said warily, his eyes betraying the slightest glimmer of fear.

"Metaphor? Why would I speak in metaphor?"

"I don't know." He shrugged. "People do it. For instance, your brother does it all the time. I thought it was just your mannerism. I found it charming. And slightly amusing. Besides, if you'll remember, I was thoroughly disarmed by your beauty. But I swear I really had no idea you believed me to be something God knows I'm not."

It didn't make sense. And yet, at the heart of it, it made entirely too much sense. How could he really be an angel? I was such a fool! "But . . . ," I said levelly, attempting to rationalize my mistake, "you *are* Gabriel, aren't you?"

"Yes. That is my name."

"Can you not see the confusion there? I was told, by Julius no less, that if I prayed for an angel, then you'd appear. I did. I prayed for an angel. I prayed for Michael because I was just that desperate, and when I came back you were there, standing in my chapel—looking like a warrior-angel! Don't look at me like that! It's perfectly logical to believe, if you're taught to believe, that angels appear when you summon them."

"Heaven help me! But you're a Blythe through and through, aren't you, my dear." A bubble of subdued laughter, tempered further by derision, escaped his lips. "And Julius was just that wicked to force you into looking for me, making you believe I was what you needed most—knowing that when you found me, I'd be helpless against you. He knows my weakness, and he obviously knows yours. And by God if he didn't exploit us both for his own twisted and sadistic pleasure! I didn't want to believe it, but he really is the devil's spawn!" Although he looked a little peaked before, his sanguine coloring had come back with a vengeance.

"Well, you obviously do know Julius, and rather well, I see," I offered, angered and defenseless, and utterly mind-boggled. I had just witnessed my pride being stripped from me—as a result of my own admissions—and had learned that my most recent debacle was just another elaborate scheme concocted in the mind of my brother, who, as fate would have it, had been shot in the back before he could fully enjoy the fruit of his labors. There was a sweet and bitter irony there, yet my mind was too overwhelmed to fully acknowledge it. "Of course you are no angel," I said at last. "How could I be so foolish to even think that you were something divine, when you're so clearly governed by transparent male emotions? Angels do not exist," I stated flatly, angrily—as much for myself as for him. I felt anew the pain of having let myself believe it, and cursed my fragile and gullible soul. "So who are you then, Gabriel?" I demanded curtly. "You said you knew me. You are familiar with my family. How?"

"You don't remember, do you?" His eyes were bright yet hooded with caution, and, perhaps sorrow. "I thought that you did. You said you did."

"When I thought you were an angel I imagined that you were one of the little boys . . ." Catching myself, knowing I was looking the fool, I dropped the thought. His eyes never left my face as I spoke, and I watched as his beautiful head tilted gently to the side. It was utterly disarming. Something Julius might do. I had resolved to be adult about this, placing personal emotions far from my thoughts, yet I found it nearly impossible. "The truth of it," I said at last, exhaling softly, "is that you were very familiar to me. I knew you the moment I saw you—but only because of my dreams."

He took my balled fists in his hands, warm, large, and heavily calloused, and then gave me a look of heart-stopping sweetness. "And I knew you too, but not only from my dreams. Julius and I served Lord Hume together. You don't remember, but I have met you, many times in fact. I was lucky enough to visit Blythe Hall with Julius on a few occasions. I even accompanied him to Haddington—perhaps a dozen or so times. You were young," he said, pretending it didn't matter, although we both were acutely aware that it did. "You were much too busy to take notice of me, but I noticed you. And Julius alone understood my attraction to his beautiful, young, high-spirited, and charmingly naïve little sister."

"Gabriel St. Clair!" I cried, squeezing his hands tightly— smiling, remembering. It hit me with the force of a driving wind, sweeping through me, filling me with memories and visions of the young man he had once been. Tall, lean to the point of thinness, broad-shouldered, and incredibly well mannered, Gabriel St. Clair had been my brother's silent shadow. He was a companion so loyal that he seldom left Julius's side. He had also been terribly shy, as I recalled, and I couldn't, for the life of me, remember if we had ever exchanged more than a few words. And, in my defense, he had changed a great deal. His face had been sharper, his body leaner, and his hair had been more of an umber shade rather than the golden color of winter wheat it now was; but his smile and his eyes were definitely the same.

"Gabriel," I said, filling with ineffable joy and squeezing his hands even tighter. "Why did you never speak of this to me? You believe you never made an impression on me, but you couldn't have been further from the truth. I have always liked you! And as a woman I have dreamed of you." These last words were spoken softly, caressed with the sacredness they deserved. "I've had visions of you so exquisite that I was left in tears. That was the reason I believed you to be an angel. It was too perfect. My image of you was too perfect. And the joy of it is that you are not perfect, Gabriel. You're a real man: a knight. Julius may have toyed with us, but why excoriate him for it? We have been given a rare gift. Why shouldn't we be together? Where is the sin in wanting that?"

"There is no sin in that, Isabeau, my heart," he said, his eyes wide and liquid as mine. He pulled me into his embrace and, holding me tightly, uttered, "And there is no sin in believing in angels either. Forgive me for mocking you; forgive me for putting you through all this. Listen to me," he demanded softly, seeing that I was very near tears. The effects of the lake were wearing off. I was desperately tired and hadn't seen a proper bed in a long while. I dearly wished to know what was going on but feared that once I did I would not have the strength to accept it. I gave him my full attention regardless, because he deserved at least that much. "Listen to me," he said again, this time in a harsh and sorrowful whisper. "Listen and I will tell you everything your brother has left out."

ॐ

The man holding me, whom I had honestly mistaken for an angel, was indeed a warrior of God. He was a warrior-knight, to be more specific, and one who served the noble and holy order of Saint John of Jerusalem, in Rhodes, a strict monastic fighting order. It also meant, in short, that he lived as a monk.

"*You* are a *Hospitaller*?!" I uttered, using the common name the order went by. I sat up, pulling away from his embrace as my hands covered my open mouth. "Dear heavens preserve us!" I breathed, stupefied; for the shock of his identity could not have been greater, nor the knowledge that I had defiled—quite soundly and thoroughly as I recalled—a member of the holy brethren. I looked at his surcoat, at the symmetrical white, eight-pointed cross over the left breast—eight points symbolizing the Beatitudes of Jesus' Sermon on the Mount: the four arms of the cross representing the cardinal virtues of prudence, justice, fortitude, and temperance. Wanting to believe him my guardian angel, I had failed to comprehend that small detail. "It all makes sense now," I said, thinking of his odd behavior. "It makes sense . . . dear God! It makes no sense at all!" I concluded with a frown.

"Please, don't look at me like that, Isabeau."

"But I feel perfectly wretched about this too, if it's any consolation. I swear," I said, looking him bravely in the eye, "had I any idea of the level of your commitment to God, I would not have pressed you so hard." I raked my hands through my tangled wet hair, remembering. "I was shameless!" I said, horrified, and then hugged myself as vivid details of our night together flashed before my eyes. "Perfectly shameless! Dear God, I was no better than a twopenny wanton!" I was coming utterly unraveled. "And for once in my life I have actually succeeded in surpassing the deprecatory heights of Marion Boyd! It's a feat I thought impossible, but I did it! At least Marion goes after morally unfettered men— and kings! The man I seduce, body and soul, is shackled to God . . . Oh God, what have I done?" I whimpered, and then, frustration hitting me like an arrow through the heart, I cried to the heavens: "Why must life be so wretchedly unfair?!"

Throughout my tirade Gabriel had remained perfectly still as he watched me. Then, unable to take any more, he closed his eyes. His pain was truly my pain, and it was the last and most devastating deception my brother had foisted on me yet—correction: had foisted on us. I now understood what Gabriel had been trying so hard to tell me. "Please, please, forgive me," I uttered at last, looking upon his angelic face. I grabbed the sleeves of his jupon. He opened his eyes, and I saw how bloodshot and wet they were. We were both beyond consolation. "Please forgive me, Gabriel."

"By God, there's nothing to forgive!" he uttered harshly,

almost defensively, as unshed tears continued to pool in his eyes. "Don't you understand that I wanted this too—that I've always wanted this?" His voice was thick with emotion, and I watched, heartbroken, as the first tear slipped from his swollen eyes.

Men like Gabriel never cried.

"I do know that," I whispered sincerely, and took him in my arms, knowing that I was the source of his sorrows, knowing that I was the cause of his tears. They continued to fall, and as I wiped them away with trembling fingers I asked, "But why, Gabriel, if you have always wanted this did you become a Hospitaller? Why not just find me, and tell me how you felt before leaving Scotland? I would have taken you out of hand, had you done so."

This made him smile, genuinely, and it lifted my heart to see it. But then, as quickly as it came, the smile faded. "I couldn't come to you," he said, his eyes moist, his face serious. "It would have been impossible, and Julius knew it. And the reason is because unlike your brother, I didn't have the luxury of a legitimate pedigree. I may have the surname of St. Clair, but only because my mother insisted. She was a young Norwegian woman who was brought to serve the house of Lord William St. Clair when his Norwegian holdings in Orkney and the Shetlands were taken from him and ceded to the crown. That was when James III married Princess Margaret of Denmark, you'll recall. The gift of the Orkneys and the Shetlands were part of her dowry. Sir William, as hereditary earl of the Orkneys, had always paid homage to the Norwegian kings as well as his Scottish sovereign. My mother was the daughter of a minor Norwegian nobleman, and when Sir William lost his earldom—a bitter pill for him to swallow— she was what one might term a consolation prize.

"My father was old," he continued, "well into his late fifties when I was born. My mother was very young. But I know he valued her greatly. He could never acknowledge me, being married to Lady Janet at the time, but he did allow me his name. My mother insisted on it. However, I don't remember her very well. She died in childbirth when I was three, and I was sent from the big house in Blackfriars' Wynd to live at Rosslyn. Sir William was kind to me, gave me a fine education, and shortly before he died, put me in the service of Lord Hume. That was where I met Julius, and I must tell you what a perfect friend for a lost, lonely boy he was. I loved him like a brother. I worshipped the ground he walked on until about five years ago, when we had a falling-out. I told him my intentions of becoming a Hospitaller then. And he mocked me for it as I have never been mocked before. I took my vows shortly thereafter and have never broken them . . . until last night."

I could feel my cheeks grow hot under his gaze. "I'm sorry," was all I could think to say.

"I'm not," he said. He was breathing easier now, and there was a wild elation in his eyes as he looked at me. "Truthfully, I'm not at all." And then, just as the words left his mouth, his head shot up, and he looked suspiciously around. Cautioning me to be quiet, he stood.

It was then that we heard the baying of a hound. It was far off yet, but its effect was immediate. Bodrum's head lifted in alarm at nearly the same time Gabriel reached for me. "Quick, it may be nothing, but we need to move. Perhaps I forgot to tell you yesterday," he said, bending to pick up the bedroll, "but just after some cowardly bastard shot your brother in the back, Sir George broke down the gates of Blythe Hall, intent on capturing you. And I'm laying odds that the man who broke down the gates was the same man who shot your brother."

"Sir George!" The name filled me with a sudden terror and shattered our private moment.

With the swiftness of long-ingrained military precision, Gabriel broke camp. After securing our meager belongings to

Bodrum, he swung effortlessly into the saddle, then reached down for me. "I'm pulling you up behind me. I don't trust myself the other way," he said, and gave a wry smile. Seated behind him I tentatively held to his waist, feeling at once awkward and shy. Giving Bodrum a nudge, he grabbed my hands with his and held them tightly. "I may be a monk, Isabeau," he said as we started down the hill, "but I'm a man first, and it is with a man's heart and soul that I love you. Never forget that. I made the mistake of losing my head last night, and God forgive me, if pressed I'll likely do it again. I'm now yours to do with as you will. I'm eternally damned. Perhaps I've been from the start, but now I have you. And as long as I live and breathe, I will let no other man touch you again."

Chapter 17

A KNIGHT DETAINED

SIR ALEXANDER, THE SECOND LORD HUME, HAVING JUST received that title from his deceased grandfather, was in his mid-forties, trim, ambitious, and still covered with dust from the road he had recently traveled. He was tired, and fractious, and wanted nothing more than to see his bed, yet duty required him to sit at his desk and attempt to scribble out a cogent report of the troubling incident at Blythe Hall. He had come at the tail end of the fracas, bidden by a messenger of Lord Kilwylie's who claimed that Julius Blythe, setting his brazen foot on Scottish soil, had kidnapped King James and had him imprisoned in Blythe's ancestral home. Kilwylie's man also had claimed that Blythe was holding his sister, the lovely Mistress Isabeau, captive, along with Kilwylie's own cousin, the fetching Mistress Marion Boyd—both young women, according to Kilwylie, having recently left the king's court. Isabeau and Marion were friends of his wife, and he thought he should have known if they had left court. It was a wild, audacious claim, and only a fraction of it had been substantiated.

In truth, he had never heard so much as a rumor that Julius Blythe was back in Scotland. It was something he should have known if it were true. Yet not one man in his diverse network of spies had ever mentioned a word on the subject. Also, the claim that young Jamie Stewart, the King of Scotland, had been abducted was just ludicrous. He, Alexander, was Keeper of Stirling Castle and guardian of the king's younger brothers. He knew their movements. James could not, by any stretch of the imagination, be in the Borders! And yet there was a compelling reason to want to believe Kilwylie; and it was his duty, as Warden of the East Marches, to look into such claims, wild or sobering.

As fate would have it, he had just returned to Hume Castle after an interesting few days chasing reivers all the way to Carlisle. Ironically, his recent movements were in response to a matter concerning the stolen Blythemuir livestock. However, twenty-five miles into the chase they realized they had been following a reiving band of Armstrongs, and not, apparently, the men who had taken the Blythemuir sheep. They knew this because the Armstrong rogues had amassed a sizable herd of English cattle, which they had cleverly hidden in Eskdale, hoping to wait out the legal duration of the Trodd. Their hopes, however, had been dashed, and the Armstrong rogues were now locked up in Carlisle awaiting trial. Sir Alexander and his men had returned home, still no closer to the mystery of the missing Blythemuir sheep. And they had barely polished the dust off their boots when Kilwylie's man came with the summons. He remembered how grateful he was that his army was only required to travel as far as his neighbor's castle. How naïve he had been this morning. For given all that the messenger claimed, Sir Alexander still had not been prepared to see the face of Julius Blythe. It was a shock—a surprising shock that was linked to a web of deeply buried and thoroughly suppressed emotions. They had all, of course, resurfaced in that first instant.

As Lord Hume scribbled his report, his messenger sat patiently beside him nursing a mug of ale. Alexander paused, thought on a word, stuck the quill into the ink pot, and then scratched some more—until he heard the first echoing chord. The quill stopped. The men looked at each other.

The sound, pure in its sweetness, thin and light as a nightdress of the finest gossamer, tickled the tunnels under the Great Hall and wafted up through the chimney. "That sounds like a lute," remarked the messenger prosaically. "Where's it comin' from, d'ye suppose?"

Sir Alexander, his brow creased in consternation, gently placed the quill in its holder and sat back. "That'll be coming from the dungeon."

"The dungeon? Why would music be comin' from doon there?"

It was a good question, and one he didn't feel much like answering, but he did. "Very likely because I'm a gullible old fool." This he remarked as he laced his hands together, preparing to listen.

When Julius Blythe had been taken into custody, along with nine of his rough men, he had been less than healthy. The outlaw had surrendered, knowing he was trapped, and somehow a rogue crossbow bolt had still found its mark. He had not been pleased about that. The bolt had done severe damage, piercing the steel plates of the young man's jack, and striking with enough force to render the lad unconscious. It was a cheap shot. Luckily, the wound was not particularly lethal, striking the right shoulder blade and lodging in the bone. Had it been an inch lower, it would have been a different story. It was not the only wound suffered. Julius Blythe had blocked a few other blows with his body. After the bolt had been removed, and the other wounds seen to, the young miscreant had been placed in an isolated cell, away from his men. He had been lying facedown in the straw, bloody, bruised, and just barely conscious, when he made the odd request. It was only because of perverse curiosity, and none of the surging memories from four years earlier, that Sir Alexander had complied. Sir Alexander, hooked and reeled like a brown trout into a maelstrom of problems, had turned from the dungeon and ordered his jailor to deliver an old instrument, knowing the lad could scarcely do anything but look at it. He had even smiled then, thinking what a torment that would be. But he wasn't smiling now. Once again, it seemed the young Master of Blythe was going to make him look the fool.

The first song was a light, haunting lament, played the way only a man with too much idle time on his hands can play. Julius had been a great courtier, as he recalled, and his practiced artistry had never left him wanting for company, male or female. The effort, slightly detached yet coolly defiant, must have caused Blythe incredible discomfort. Lord Hume, with a smug look of satisfaction animating the creases of his face, picked up his quill and continued to write.

The songs continued as well.

His quill moved with greater effort.

The beat picked up pace.

The messenger began tapping his foot. And Sir Alexander, pausing in his difficult narrative, was visited by a long-forgotten memory of a smoky tavern across the border: a table strewn with half-empty tankards and pitchers of ale; lively, plump, painted women; platters overflowing with rich food; and a golden-headed young knight with a lute who, with seamless artistry, had brought them all to tears. He steadied his hand and fought to ignore the music.

But the songs grew louder and bolder.

And then the singing started.

It started out light and a bit shaky. But after a song or two the halls of Hume echoed with a tenor so pure, and with a range so astounding, it was almost blasphemous. The servants stopped working to listen; for the songs this gilded popinjay, this profane Orpheus, sang were quite unique. The lute was strummed with a vigor Sir Alexander had never before heard, the notes clever and interesting. It was like the beat of a heart, pumping, surging—coursing through the veins with a growing intensity. It brought to mind the way a man feels standing on the edge of a field in the seconds before a great battle. It was the way a man feels in the throes of an unfettered and raging passion. Building, pulsating, unstoppable. The voice continued, this time singing joyfully, jauntily, irreverently. He was a master of metaphors, was Julius Blythe. Double entendres rolled off his tongue thick and sweet as honey. He sang of sun-dappled meadows and cool, bubbling streams, of frolicking water nymphs and of bathing virgins desperately seeking to shirk the title. These were no battle songs; these were the songs he feared most. And the prisoners, locked in the dungeon with him, were clapping in time with the frenetic rhythm, urging this brash child of mayhem and profligacy on. This was the Julius Blythe he remembered so vividly, the boy who had his mother's angelic beauty and his father's raw cunning. It was a lethal combination if ever there was one. And he had learned, firsthand, just how lethal.

The bawdy song, thankfully, ended. The castle erupted in loud cheers and voracious clapping. Sir Alexander, shaken, slammed his quill on the desk, utterly ruining his report and the quill. With a speed and abruptness that belied his harrowing day, he pushed his chair back and jumped to his feet. "Come!" he called to his courier and his guard, and stalked off, making a beeline for the dungeon.

॰୭

The dungeon of Hume Castle, damp, ill-lit, and musty, was not a pretty place. In fact the word *dungeon* was too generous to describe the collection of small, damp, thick-walled, iron-gated cells that when not in use were often employed as additional storage for the overflowing cellars of Hume. When built they had not been intended for long-term use. They were primarily a holding pen for the rough men of the Borders, and on a quiet week the prison was blessedly still. But it hadn't been a quiet week. And the prison now rang with the robust voices of fourteen men, ten from Blythemuir and four lads from across the border. Sir Alexander walked down the narrow passage with a purpose, yet the sound of his riding boots clicking against the damp stone were all but drowned out as the prisoners sang yet another bawdy ballad. The lyrics of this one, bouncing from floor to wall in a deafening echo, were so lewd that he cringed at the imagery the words evoked. And he was disquieted to find, as he walked toward his prisoner, that he was halfway to a state of full arousal. Damn Julius Blythe! Thoughts of his lovely young wife, Nichole, suddenly clouded his vision. At the moment she was ensconced in their lavish town house in Edinburgh awaiting him, and he sorely wished he were with her, and not here in this fetid midden of sweat, blood, and vomit. He shook his head, fighting to expunge from his mind the visions that encouraged his embarrassing state. He summoned his outrage, focused on blood and vomit, and stood before the iron bars that harbored the mangled form of Julius Blythe.

The guards cried out their order. Voices trailed off as the lute fell silent. And Sir Alexander stood peering into the dark cell, heaving like a callow colt. "How is it," he began in a voice gripped with disdain, "that you, after being shot in the back and used like a hacking butt, can sit against that wall?"

"Sheer force of will, my lord," came a calm voice from the shadows. "Notice that I am not standing. Music, Sir Alexander, is reputed to soothe the soul, and yet I find, when properly played, that my soul awakens, my pulse quickens, and every fiber in my body comes alive. Lie to me. Tell me you are unmoved. Tell me you are not thinking of your delicious young wife right now, sound asleep and dreaming of rose petals and white ponies with long, flowing manes. Let her sleep peacefully, my lord. For this music I play is gimcrack and illusion. In short, 'tis a devil's panacea. But you know that already, don't you?"

"Only too well," he breathed, and stared at the limp, elegant hand, spent and resting on the cold stone, still gripping the neck of the instrument. It was the only thing visible in the dark cell.

"I'm glad you've come," said the Master of Blythe softly. His breathing was controlled yet shallow. It was a sign of pain, and it pleased Alexander to know that this man was feeling plenty of it. "I was beginning to think," continued the measured voice, "that you would make me go on and on until my repertoire repeated, and I fear the men wouldn't abide that."

"You knew I would come?" It was the height of presumption.

"Why else would I ask for the golden horn?" Although he could not see his face, Sir Alexander could feel Blythe's wry, sardonic grin penetrate the darkness.

"What is it you want, Blythe? You were entirely reticent earlier, no thanks to that arrow in your back. By the way, how's that feeling?"

"Like every arrow in the back feels, I imagine. Shamefaced, apologetic, thoroughly embarrassed it wasn't properly aimed. I've seen men, blind stumbling drunk, kick a pebble through a dung heap with more success. 'Tis a tough cross to bear, is the arrow in the back that has failed."

"You wanted the arrow to succeed?" Lord Hume asked with mild interest.

"No. I simply mock it because it failed, and because it failed I'm here to mock it . . . or, more specifically, the cowardly shooter."

"No one claims to have made the shot."

"Of course they wouldn't have," said the dulcet voice mockingly. "'Tis not the type of shot one wishes to claim, or even remember."

"But you'll remember it," said Lord Hume with gentle savagery, "for a little while longer yet. Sir George'll be happy to hear how well you're recovering. He wanted desperately to make you speak, you know. He would have killed you had I let him. Perhaps I should have let him."

"But you forbade him because you are a merciful and kind-hearted soul." This time there was no mockery evident in the gentle voice.

"And you've exploited that fact very well tonight. Why must you always be so horrid, Julius? Why can't you behave like other men?"

"Because there is no virtue in behaving like other men, if by other men you mean Georgie Douglas. Like the shame-faced arrow, it is the cross that I bear. But I shall try to behave better, if not for my own sake, then for yours. Tell me, Alexander," he said, "did you ever think when I was on trial that I was telling the truth?"

"No man wanted to believe you more than I. And that's the truth of it. You had more promise than any man I've ever met, and you forced me to stand aside and watch you sell your gifts like cheap baubles to the hussies in the hedgerow. There was too much evidence against you. A signed document from King Henry. The promise of English estates in exchange for an unspecified delivery. And then there was the fact that the day before the decisive battle you were found leaving Stirling Castle in the dead of night with the prince disguised as your groom."

"Do you remember what I told you? My defense for taking the prince?"

"Refresh my memory."

"I was taking him to meet his father. Nearly all his life his father had kept him like a prisoner at Stirling, afraid the

prophecy would come true. It had been years since James had
even seen his father. His younger brother was embraced by
the king, given titles and a marriage contract to an English
bride, while James was publicly overlooked. I do not regret
taking Stirling Castle, or fighting to make the Duke of Rothesay king. But I did regret the fact that he was never allowed to
meet with his father in person during the rising, and lay his
demands on the table before him, king to king. I was simply
arranging such a meeting."

"On a ship in the Forth estuary belonging to Captain
Andrew Wood," remarked Lord Hume.

"Yes."

"He was one of King James's most ardent supporters at the
time."

"So was my father, but he was out of the country. Of
James's supporters in Scotland, I believed Captain Wood to be
the fairest."

"But he denied any knowledge of the meeting, if you'll remember."

"I remember. That was after the prophecy was fulfilled and
the king was murdered trying to escape the battlefield. He had
been heading for Sir Andrew's ship at the time and never made
it thanks to one of our men. James never wanted his father to
die."

"Death is the price of a crown, Julius!" Sir Alexander
barked, swiftly losing patience. "You were as naïve as wee
Jamie if ye believed that it could be any other way."

"I was naïve," remarked the master, and rolled his head in
the direction of the speaker. It was enough for the scant light
to illuminate half the face and the familiar profile—strong,
classical, with a tragic elegance about it that left one momentarily breathless. Although he knew Blythe had remarkable
control over his voice, Lord Hume could now better understand what the effort had cost him. The smooth skin, pulled
taut over the fine bones, was now white as parchment and

glistening with sweat. Droplets fat as rainwater ran down his cheek and off the gold-floss curls that now hung in limp ropes against the finely shaped head. His eyes, normally a wry and mocking shade of blue, were wide and guileless in the half-light, sunken in the livid mask that ran from eye socket to jaw. There was no smile on his lips now: no challenge in the large, fever-bright eyes. "I have learned my lesson," he said softly.

"You have learned too little too late, Julius Blythe," replied Sir Alexander, heartsick and weary. "I have experienced your charm firsthand, and I have been burned by your lies so that I thought I might never recover. Your biggest mistake yet was coming home. You should have stayed on the Continent, where you were safe. Because tomorrow I intend to let Sir George have his way with you."

The finely shaped lips, moist with sweat, pulled into a smile of beatific wonder. "What? And forgo the pleasure of torturing me yourself? Please, you of all people deserve a pound of my flesh. And I shall willingly give it . . . if you do for me just one thing."

"You wish to bargain with me!?" Sir Alexander's voice was loud and incredulous.

"Yes. Isn't that what men do? Murder kings. Topple nations. Strike bargains."

Sir Alexander let out a low, mirthless laugh. "Indeed, but you, my brash young fool, are in no position to bargain!"

"But I believe that I am. You see, Sir George was correct on one count. He led you on a merry chase believing that my sister and Mistress Marion Boyd were being held captive at Blythe Hall. It's how he got you to help him storm the castle. But once the gates were breached, you discovered that the castle, but for a few loyal servants, was empty. The truth is, Isabeau is far away, having fled the unwanted affections of Georgie Douglas. It was simply his insufferable pride that made him attack Blythe Hall in the first place. Never fear for Isabeau; she's in good hands. Marion, however, is another story. At this very moment she's being held captive with the king, in a place where no one will ever find them. I know this is because I have them both. If Douglas had put his hands on me, I would have been dead before the truth of this terrible matter got out, and you would have never seen James again. What I'm offering you now is your king and the Boyd lass safely returned, and all I ask in exchange is for these men—these gentle shepherds of Blythemuir—to be set free. They did nothing wrong. Their castle was being attacked by Kilwylie, and I asked them to join me in defending it. There is no crime in that."

Sir Alexander thought on this and knew it was largely correct. Hendrick, the trustworthy steward of Blythe Hall for these many years, had said as much himself. But Hendrick was not a lord, and Julius Blythe was an outlaw. "You expect me to believe you have the King of Scotland? Why should I believe you?"

"Because you know me capable of it. Why else would I have returned if not to finish what I started four years ago? You can hardly think the food, weather, and fine hospitality were enough to draw me back—at considerable risk to my life. But you don't have to take my word for it. Kilwylie will as good as tell you himself tomorrow. Because he will come back here at the first light of dawn and finish what his arrow could not. If you let him into this cell, he will kill me, and if he does, you will never see Jamie Stewart again. You have my word on that."

"You truly believe Kilwylie shot that arrow?"

"With all my heart. And, if you're curious, I'll tell you why."

"Go on," Sir Alexander said, taking the bait, yet all the while conscious of the fact that he was lifting the lid on his own Pandora's box.

"Because for four years there has been a piece of this convoluted puzzle missing—a piece that has now come to Scotland and will shed new light on the misdeeds of my past. Kilwylie will do anything to make sure it never surfaces. Because if it does, he will lose everything."

"Watch what you are saying, Blythe. You're treading on very dangerous ground here. You are attempting to malign the character of one of Scotland's brightest young men."

"He was my friend once, if you'll remember. What I bet you don't know is that he was the one who sprang me from the castle prison, but not to set me free. There was more money to be made off my hide. I was sold for a profit, and a promise that I would receive a fate worse than death. I did. And now I've returned to repay the favor."

There was a long silence. And then Sir Alexander spoke. "Are you saying that you're innocent? You've already pled not guilty once. Now you presume to bang on that same tired old drum again?"

"I presume nothing. I am guilty — of many things — just not the crime I was convicted of."

"So you . . . you claim to have abducted the king . . . because you're not guilty? That's a very dangerous crime to commit for an innocent man."

"I . . . am . . . not . . . an . . . innocent . . . man!" Julius Blythe said pointedly, fervently. "Wrap your head around that first. Jamie Stewart is my insurance policy. I'm simply betting on the fact that because I have the king, you will not let Kilwylie kill me . . . until you can bring me to trial again."

"And he wants to kill you because you have the king?"

"Good," Julius replied, his voice tinged with exhaustion. "Now you're playing. Yes. He forced me to abduct the king by attempting the very same thing himself."

A furious breath exploded from Lord Hume. "You expect me to believe that he abducted the king in the first place?"

"Believe what you like. It's true. And I have a credible witness to verify it, assuming you won't take the word of my men. You know Madame Seraphina L'Ange, Isabeau's governess? She should be at Blythe Hall. You might wish to question her."

"Madame Seraphina wasn't at Blythe Hall."

"Really?" Julius breathed. There was a small pause before he said, "Even better. She's being held captive at Kilwylie Castle then. If you wish to verify my story, send some men there to retrieve her—before Kilwylie kills her."

"This is all very elaborate, Julius. Elaborate and highly entertaining. But you of all people must know that I have no cause to believe a word that rolls off your gilded tongue. You took a very big gamble when you surrendered yourself to me. So why don't you do yourself a favor and tell me where you think the king is."

"Set my men free, and I shall tell you all you wish to know."

"I can draw it out from you in other ways."

"You can certainly try. But I'm committed to take it to the grave if I have to. And you know what an obstinate bastard I can be."

"Then you will die. Because the king, Julius, has never left Edinburgh!" Lord Hume watched as his prisoner searched for something on his person. Then he saw a hand reach out of the shadows and toss a small object through the bars, which landed at his booted feet. Lord Hume bent to retrieve it. His heart stopped beating for the space of a breath or two, because in his hand sat the gold ring of James Stewart IV.

"Set my men free, and I will tell you what you wish to know," said the soft voice again, this time with a hint of irony.

Exasperated, angered, and highly resentful that he had been pulled into this unholy quagmire again, Lord Hume replied coolly, "I think I'd rather wait and see what the turbulent tide brings us tomorrow. Until then, I'm depriving you of your golden horn." He motioned to his jailor and watched as the man slipped behind the bars and pried the instrument from his prisoner's reluctant hand.

"Thank you for humoring me, Sir Alexander," said Julius Blythe once the bars had been locked again. "And because I never had the chance to say so before, know that I'm sorry, and I'm sorry in advance for the hell I'm about to put you through again. Sleep well, my captain." It was a sentiment from long ago, spoken in a voice with the same youthful sincerity. And then the world-weary eyes closed.

"And you stay alive until tomorrow, m'laddie," Sir Alexander advised in a thready whisper. He then turned from the cell, which was now deathly quiet, and left the dungeon, silently cursing his foolish, sentimental old heart.

Chapter 18

WARRIOR
OF GOD

THE SKY WAS THREATENING RAIN, AND SIR GEORGE was threatening to do us harm. We knew this, not only by the baying of the hound hot on our trail, but because we had ridden to the other side of the lake and lay on a hilltop watching from the safety of the low, bushy branches of the juniper we had crawled under. We didn't have long to wait before the first rider appeared at the head of the trail, wading through the tall reeds as he came upon the hidden lake. He paused for a moment, spotted the long-eared hound, and continued to follow it down the very path we had traveled the night before. Then came another rider, and another, and another.

"Holy Mother of God," Gabriel breathed, watching the procession. "There are twenty men down there sent to find a wee lass." He looked at me and remarked with mock wide-eyed innocence, "Dear Isabeau, what did ye do to the man?"

"Stop that," I hissed at the rakish gleam in his eye. He was grinning, and a very knowing sort of grin at that, but I didn't find it very amusing. Twenty of Kilwylie's thugs had just penetrated our sanctuary in the pines, and he was making a joke of it. "This is no joking matter, Gabriel. One doesn't send twenty heavily armed men to retrieve a runaway fiancée. And Kilwylie himself is not among them. That looks suspiciously like a band of assassins to me."

His brightly burning eyes softened in a look of sincere approbation. "Indeed, my heart. And why do you suppose Kilwylie's not among them?" He had already guessed at the correct answer, and it was an answer that lit the fire behind his eyes.

"Too busy?" I offered.

"Doing what?" he probed. "Think about it, Isabeau. You're his fiancée. You are the woman he wants. You also happen to be the only one he believes knows his terrible secret. I've complicated matters for him, however. Those assassins down there are here for me. Not you. He wouldn't be fool enough to hurt you. No, you they'll take back—kicking and screaming if they have to. Now, given all these assumptions, what would be so important about an empty castle that would keep Kilwylie from the pleasure of hunting us down himself?"

I stared back into the crystalline pools of blue as I thought hard about what he was asking. "Because he has something more important to deal with first? Something even more damaging to him than us?"

"Exactly! And what could possibly be more damaging to Kilwylie than you, my love?"

As he spoke, the image sprang behind my eyes, pulling the words from my hopeful lips. "Julius!" I said a bit too loudly. "Julius is alive?!"

"If I were a betting man, I'd bet my life on it." We both grinned like schoolchildren at the possibility, for although we each had our reasons for wanting to throttle my profane brother to within an inch of his scheming life, we could not deny that we desperately wanted him to live. "The wee sly devil," Gabriel remarked placidly, yet even I could see the glowing admiration behind his eyes. "He gave himself up to Hume, and if he's still alive, Hume will keep him that way, at least until he goes to trial—unless, of course, Julius has felt inclined to waggle his raffish tongue. He's the ability, you know, to make Hume regret ever knowing him. Let's just pray, for his sake, that he's alive but blissfully unconscious."

"I shall pray for that very thing," I whispered fervently, and kissed him. It was meant to be a happy little peck on the cheek, but in reality it was something quite different.

"Dear God," Gabriel said at last, trying to catch his breath. On his face was a look of pure and radiant joy. I knew how he felt, and I was slightly relieved to know that only a part of it this time was my fault. The voices coming from across the lake brought us back to our predicament in a hurry, and we looked out in time to see Kilwylie's men leaving the screen of pines. No doubt they had taken a keen interest in the telltale nest of pine needles. "We need to stop these lads before they become a real nuisance. Stay here a moment," Gabriel said, and began backing out from under the squat juniper on elbows and belly. I grabbed his arm to stop him.

"There are twenty men, Gabriel! Twenty armed men hot on our tail says we're going to run, and run fast. I'm coming with you!" I gave him a stern, no-nonsense look. His grin grew broader. It was infuriating and irresistible; it made me want to slap him and kiss him at once.

"Only twenty, Isabeau. I've faced worse than that before."

"Dear God," I uttered, moving from the bush with him. "You can't seriously be considering fighting them?" His softly smiling silence revealed the depths of his guilt. "By the heavens, Gabriel, what kind of man are you?"

"The kind of man who knows he can't outrun twenty men on an overburdened horse."

The rain started as Kilwylie's men followed the hound into the ravine between the two hills that would eventually lead them right to where we were. It was in those moments, watching our attackers grow ever closer, that I began to understand why Gabriel had taken offense back in the Chapel of Angels when I had questioned his ability to fight. I thought he was mad to even suggest facing the overinflated squad of assassins that had been sent for us, and would have argued my point if there was any chance of outrunning the hunting party that was bearing down on us with alarming speed. But there wasn't. Gabriel had waited from our position on the hill, knowing all along what he had in mind to do. I realized this when he placed his helmet on my head and dressed me in his flowing black surcoat. I had insisted he let me help him fight—their presence was largely due to me, after all—and he had been quick to acquiesce. It was refreshing, I thought, to find a man of reason, and I was at once moved by his willingness. He understood that my skill with the bow—which I had demonstrated quite soundly on the battlements of Blythe Hall—was an asset to be used. Yet it was not my deadly accurate aim that he wanted. He wanted my body; he wanted to use me as a decoy. It was an outrage, yet I didn't even bother to argue. Arguing would be useless, for Gabriel the warrior, as I had observed, was a vastly different animal from Gabriel the tormented monk. The tormented monk could be tempted; the warrior, hardened by years of battling under the hot Mediterranean sun, reigned supreme. Besides, he had only the one bow with him and fifteen arrows in his quiver—all tipped with the slim, armor-piercing iron point. And he would need them all. Resigned to my small part in his battle plan, I vowed to put on a convincing performance; our lives depended on it. Dressed, armed, and ready to go, I sat on Bodrum, straight-backed and oozing manufactured bravado, awaiting the signal.

I watched as Gabriel took up position in a patch of greening woodland that lined the opposite bank of the ravine. He crouched behind a boulder, hidden from the oncoming riders in the deep shadows and wet leaves, yet I could still see his refulgent hair now slightly tarnished by rainwater. This line of sight gave me a modicum of comfort, although my nerves still raged within me. Gabriel had been no longer than a few minutes in his hiding place when the hound, far ahead of the riders, came up through the narrow gap and paused at the top of the trail. Here the land opened up to the windswept grasses and tangled brush that rolled over two hills. The dog put its sensitive nose to the ground, sniffed wildly, and took a few tentative steps toward me. I sat dead still, watching from the meager shelter of two spindly saplings. If the dog saw me, I'd have to kill it, and I loathed nothing more than the thought of killing a dog.

But the dog never saw me. It caught the irresistible scent of a man on foot instead. The floppy-eared head jerked up, looked in the direction of the woods, and bounded through the wet grass heading for Gabriel. It disappeared in the thick foliage and never reemerged. That was my signal.

With a click and a gentle nudge of the heel, I urged the noble gray gelding out from the saplings and over to the bald crest of the hill. And there I sat in the drenching rain, wraithlike and unmoving but for the black cloak that bent like a sail to the wind as it billowed and fluttered behind me. Bodrum, catching the scent of the wet and thundering horses, gave a throaty cry.

All heads turned my way. I stared down on the twenty pairs of eyes that held me like a beacon in the night. Bodrum pranced beneath me as I slowly opened my coat to reveal the third weapon Gabriel had carried: a small crossbow, with only three bolts. I held the loaded weapon skyward, making them believe I was waiting for the right moment to begin my attack.

Although the bolt of a properly aimed crossbow could travel a fair distance with accuracy, Gabriel had made me swear that I would not release a single shot until the first rider was a horse length or two away. That way the projectile would penetrate the metal plates of the jack. It was Gabriel's plan to make sure they never got the chance to be that close in the first place.

In response to Bodrum's cry a few of the horses stumbled in the small river that had begun to flow with the rains. Concentrating on getting his horse under control, the last rider, unbeknownst to his troop, was taken down by an arrow. The horse, unprepared for the impact of its lifeless rider, slipped on the wet rocks again and came to a dead stop. Then it bucked and, finding its burden lifted, ran back down through the ravine.

That was the first of a storm of arrows that came silent from the brush flying through the rain-sodden air with deadly precision. I sat breathless, marveling at the speed, accuracy, and fluidity of movement coming from the hidden archer, and appreciated it for the art it was. Kilwylie's men, focused on me and urging their horses to move faster, never knew that their numbers were shrinking with every stride gained.

The attack was swift and deadly. The men toppled like rag dolls the moment the arrows struck, and I saw that they struck deep. My heart was pounding with fear and raw excitement. Every nerve in my body tingled as I aimed the crossbow at the oncoming men. By the time they were nearly level with Gabriel, swiftly closing the gap between us, six riders were left, and every man had his sword out and ready. As the second-to-the-last rider passed Gabriel's hiding place, he sprang from the woods, loosing his last arrow on the run. Aimed for the rider in the lead, it hit its mark, striking the man in the back and throwing him over the neck of his horse. At the same moment the arrow struck, Gabriel dropped his bow and launched himself at the last rider, who had drawn level with him. The man, catching the human, rain-soaked projectile out of the corner of his eye a second too late, spun around, but not before Gabriel knocked him to the ground, taking his horse in the process. It was at that moment, as the rider in the lead fell from his horse with an arrow in his back, that the rest of the attackers began to understand what was happening.

There was a moment of chaos when they saw that their number had been reduced to four—and a moment of sheer terror as Gabriel fell on them with his mighty sword, riding one of their own horses. But the chase was still on, because of the four men left one had broken away and was heading straight for me.

If my brother was a master of the art of leading men to mayhem and mischief with his gilded, rapier-sharp tongue and cheap theatrical antics, then Gabriel was a true warrior-god. His movements, like the words that dripped from Julius's tongue, were lyrical, poetic, and yet so well suited to their task that no one who opposed him was safe from annihilation. I found myself watching him, mesmerized by his skill and agility, when I should have been watching the man who understood who I was. He came at me with sword leveled, his exhausted horse powered by the sheer brutality of the spurs that bloodied the steaming hide. Gabriel, now caught in a three-way brawl, yelled to me, and I understood what he was saying. I waited a heartbeat more and pulled the trigger. The bolt left the crossbow with deadly speed and smashed into the chest of the rider. I watched as his body took the force of the arrow, and then he righted himself and continued to come straight at me. There was no time to reload.

I kicked Bodrum, and the horse jumped out of the way a second before I would have been impaled by the oncoming sword. At the same time Bodrum moved, I swung the empty crossbow and caught the underside of the man's jaw as he careened past. It was enough to throw him back on his horse's flanks. The horse stumbled to a halt. The rider, unmoving, lay with his face pointing toward the streaming heavens, the lethal crossbow bolt lodged in his chest. His booted feet had never left the stirrups.

It was over shortly after that. The heavy rain had petered out to a gentle drizzle by the time Gabriel returned to the hill-top, dragging a battered prisoner along with him. He held the man by the scruff of his shirt and was pulling him along from atop the horse he had taken. Our eyes met, and relief washed through him as he saw that I was unharmed. And then, without uttering a word, his gaze traveled to the dead man still prone on the flanks of his resting charger. A tremor passed under the fine skin of Gabriel's cheeks, and his eyes darkened like the storm clouds overhead. I could tell the thought of what happened frightened him, and I smiled wanly in an attempt to let him know all was well; I was unharmed. But Gabriel, having battled nineteen men himself, chafed visibly to think that this one man had gotten away and that I had been forced to kill him. He pulled his horse before mine and released his prisoner with a shove that brought the man to his knees. Gabriel swiftly dismounted and grabbed him up again, yanking him to his feet and forcing him to look at me. The man's eyes, a maudlin brown, were shifty and reluctant.

"If you wish to live," said Gabriel, his voice low and guttural, "you will fall to your knees before the Lady Blythe, kiss her feet, and beg her forgiveness. Were I in her shoes I would flay you alive, slowly, and watch as the flies lay maggots in your flesh. You are a maggot, a worthless piece of filth. You are not fit to lick the muck off my boots, let alone hers. Beg, lad. Get on your knees and beg the lady for your life, for this is why I spared you." And he released the sole survivor.

Gabriel's prisoner, a young man scared out of his wits, dropped to his knees, crawled through the muddy grass, and, to my horror, began licking the bottom of my shoes. "Stop that!" I said, looking angrily at Gabriel. I saw a grimly satisfied smile cross his lips and wondered at his purpose for further tormenting Kilwylie's young henchman. To say that Gabriel was enjoying himself would be exaggerating, yet clearly he found the spectacle pleasing. I was disquieted by it, and called again for the young man to stop licking the dirt off my shoe.

The young man looked up, wiped the dirt from his tongue with the back of his hand, and turned his long, thin face and pleading brown eyes to me. A fine mist of rain covered his flushed skin, beading on his sparse and patchy growth of brown facial hair. He couldn't have been more than eighteen. "Please, m'lady, please spare m'life. 'Tis worth naught to ye, and 'tis worth even less to me, but to me mum 'tis worth the meat on her plate and the grain in our shed. Should ye kill me, me mum and me brothers would starve for certain sure."

"Humm," I said, playing along. "Are you the oldest?" He nodded. "Well, we can't have that, can we? I'll not be responsible for the starving of your mother and brothers. Sir Gabriel, on the other hand, would think nothing of it, I'm sure." I cast him a wry glance. "Where he comes from they eat children."

"I know," said our prisoner in a tone that was just above a whisper. "And they make whores of their women and slaves of their enemies. I know," he added pointedly, and his pleading eyes hardened into a look of bold accusation. "It was him we were to kill," he said, looking me straight in the eye. "The Hospitaller." He gave a jerk of his head in Gabriel's direction. "The man what took ye from m'lord Kilwylie—*your lord*—and forced ye to his will." There was a particularly unnerving tone in his voice, and an even more unnerving look in his dark eyes. "We all know what he did to ye, m'lady. We all know how he forced himself upon ye. Come away with me now, and I will make it right. I will convince my lord Kilwylie that your good name and virtue has remained intact. Trust me; I will put my life on the line to convince him of it. I know an old crone who specializes in such cases . . ." This speech—this ramble—was delivered in the convincing but desperate manner of a drowning man offering to save the life of his mate who had already gone under the waves: noble but fretfully unwise. And I was rendered speechless by it—and not the least because I knew for a fact that I had been the one to force the Hospitaller to my will. Filling with shame at the thought, I reddened.

Gabriel, standing behind the man cross-armed and swiftly losing patience, gave a deprecating shake of his head while rolling his eyes heavenward. It was, in a morbid way, comical.

I took a deep breath, fought the urge to succumb to the grim amusement, and berated the young man calmly. "You presumptuous, adolescent henchman, you have it all wrong. And how dare you accuse a man of Sir Gabriel's caliber with rape. If you wish to live—if you wish your mother and brothers to continue to be fed—then you will listen and learn the truth. Your lord is the monster here, and not Sir Gabriel! Your lord attacked my castle. Sir Gabriel saved me. And," I said, thinking of the man I shot with a crossbow, "if you weren't supposed to harm me, perhaps you could tell me why one of your men came at me with a sword?"

Of course there was no answer to this. And I realized too late that Gabriel had known that. The revelation left me cold. "You . . . ," I began, my face falling, my heart stopping with the bitter truth of it, "you were sent to kill me too."

The young man kneeling before me, now boldly staring, remained motionless. Heartsick at the thought, I gave a small, derisive laugh. "I'll bet you don't even have a starving mother, do you?" Again I was met with bold silence. "You lie very well, but I suppose that's expected of a maggot. I think," I said, looking at Gabriel, "that we should send this child of the midden heap back from whence he came."

"To the earth? To the maggots?" Gabriel replied, smiling darkly.

"No. To the other maggot. The king maggot."

"Oh? Excellent idea, my heart. I like the way you think!" He gave a broad, effulgent grin. "You're devious! Clever! You think like your brother. Come along, my wee sniveling maggot," Gabriel said cheerfully, grabbing the man by the back of the shirt. He yanked him to his feet with surprising force. "The merciful Lady of Blythe has spoken. She's going to let you live—a courtesy you would not, I'll wager, have shown to her. Gather your horses and your dead and take them back to your lord with this message: *I, sniveling maggot, have failed you. Beat me; brand me; roll me to the gutter. For the Lady Isabeau Blythe lives and is happily ensconced in the protection of Sir Gabriel St. Clair, her lover. The Hospitaller has returned home, and the information he carries will be certain to unleash hell on m'lord's beaten and festering arse.*"

ॐ

I was not a good steward of the property I had been entrusted with. After the trying events of the morning, which had left us both tired, wet, and hungry, I found myself once again sitting behind the saddle with my arms tightly wrapped around Gabriel's waist and wanting him more than ever. I was afraid of my overwhelming feelings for him. I was afraid of losing him altogether. But mostly I was afraid because I knew that I loved him beyond all compare, and no one, not Sir George Douglas, not Julius, not even the King of Scotland, could turn me from him now. Forcing me to believe him an angel had been cruel trickery on Julius's part. Forcing Gabriel to protect me was the low and dirty trick of a vengeful friend, yet there was a remarkable cleverness behind the charade, and I had begun to understand Julius's purpose when Sir George had sent his twenty men. Twenty men sent to kill a man and a woman. The thought still turned the blood in my veins to ice water.

"When did you realize Kilwylie meant to kill me?" I asked softly.

"When I saw the man you killed break from the pack. He had his sword drawn. Until then I gave Kilwylie the benefit of the doubt. I didn't actually believe . . . ," he said, but his voice failed him. He pulled my arms tighter around his trim waist. After a moment of thoughtful silence he began again. "I didn't believe that he'd actually think of taking the life of a woman as beautiful, gracious, and so very, very precious as you." I held him even tighter and rested my head against his broad, rain-soaked back.

"We could have taken another horse, you know," I whispered, closing my eyes and thanking God, and Julius, once more for the gift of him. The rain had stopped, but the sky remained dark and brooding, and we were still in the throes of soaring emotions. We were also trying to find a place to take shelter, and where we could try to make sense of the impending tempest that was building around us.

"We could have," he replied. "But I'm being selfish. I prefer you holding on to me and not to some strange horse."

"That's devious." I let myself indulge in a languid smile, then added, "And also dangerous."

"It is," he admitted. "After the events of this morning, however, I find that I feel like living dangerously."

"Do you mean that?" My voice was soft yet hopeful. "Do you really mean that? You must know that I have no wish to cause you further distress."

The muscles of his stomach quivered as a short burst of deprecating laughter escaped his lips. "'Tis far too late for that, my heart," he replied. "You've been causing me distress longer than you can imagine. I'm a warrior, Isabeau, trained since I was a wee lad to endure the harshest conditions, to battle the fiercest enemy, and never once have I questioned the purpose of my life; never once have I questioned the strength of my faith. This morning I was on my knees questioning both."

"Oh, Gabriel," I uttered, recalling so vividly the image of

him alone in the clearing, on his knees with head bowed before the hilt of his sword—a vision of an archangel. Remorse arose and overtook my selfish joy.

"Don't be sorry," he admonished gently. "God answers us in strange ways. And I received my answer the moment I saw Kilwylie's man draw his sword. In that one instant I felt a clarity I've never before known. I've seen my closest companions fall beside me in battle, Isabeau, and every time a comrade takes a lethal blow, a little piece of you dies with him. You mourn privately, you pray for his soul and his next of kin, you grab hold of his memory, and you carry on—the cause carries you on. But back there, back there it was different. I let a man get past me, a man intent on killing you, and the thought of living in a world without you in it was incomprehensible. Utter devastation. I felt a void so dark and empty it made hell look appealing by comparison. A world without you in it, Isabeau, is a world I won't inhabit. I can't inhabit. Don't you see? Don't you understand? I have been running from you all my life. I became a Hospitaller because I knew you could never love me—and if on the off chance you did, it could never be. I'm a man without land or title. I'm a bastard. Five years ago I removed myself from the temptation to battle a cause more noble than love. I lived with like-minded men and sailed the Mediterranean fighting the enemies of Christendom. I was happy, and Julius mocked me for it. And now the devil has brought me back here—I still don't know how he managed—to face my deepest fear. I have faced it and I have failed miserably. I have lost the battle. I love you and I cannot help that. And now it all makes sense in the senseless sort of way these things do—in the senseless sort of way Julius delights in. He has an uncanny way of finding a man's weakness, and once he does he strips you of all dignity and brings you to your knees begging for mercy. And you beg and you plead and you teeter on the edge of madness until mercy appears. Julius is alive, and I rejoice to hear it. Because I now understand what he was trying to tell me all those years ago. He was telling me that I alone was born to protect you."

"You were born to love me," I corrected softly, my body trembling from that powerful truth. "Just as I was born to love you."

We traveled awhile longer and came upon a farmhouse, where Gabriel bought some bread, cheese, cold chicken, and beer from the goodwife. She was a kindly old woman and pleaded that we stay with her and make free use of her food and a place by the fire, for one look at us likely told her we were in desperate need of both. Yet Gabriel, in his gentle and patient voice, politely declined her invitation. Because we needed solitude. We needed to be alone, and we were desperate to find a place where we could give in to our tempered desires. It was with great restraint that we continued, traveling another five miles under the torture of our warm and eager bodies pressed tightly together—under the torture of my insatiable hands traveling over his taut and trembling skin. We could no longer deny that we were two souls whom God, Julius, or Fate had destined to be together. *And fate?* once said Homer. *No one alive has ever escaped it,/Neither brave man nor coward. . . . /It is born with us the day that we are born.* I was not supposed to have read the *Iliad*. I was not supposed to have done a great many things, including what I was doing now. But I embraced the notion of Fate as I embraced Gabriel, and took comfort in Homer's immortal words.

We finally came to a halt before an old, abandoned croft that was nestled in a wooded glen and overgrown by years of wild vegetation. Gabriel had remembered it from his youth, and at that particular moment there could not have been a more charming dwelling in all of Scotland. Moss and lichen grew thick over the stone. The dirt floor and rafters gave up the essence of a lifetime of previous fires whose remains were still visible in the sooty hearth. There was only the one room, dark and squalid, with a little table and bench in the corner, a pile of logs stacked against the far wall, and a gaping hole in the rotting thatch. Yet on the other hand it was private, and dry, and we couldn't dismount fast enough to get inside the neglected fieldstone walls.

Out of necessity we made a fire, and I watched as Gabriel's strong and steady hands became increasingly clumsy as he rushed through a task he had performed a thousand times before. I knelt beside him, handing him kindling and steadying his trembling hands until at last a glorious blaze sprang from the wood. The fire cast the pale walls in a rosy glow as warmth penetrated the room. Gabriel's eyes, like living sapphires, held mine, bold and unwavering. There was no hesitation now, no second thoughts or regrets. He was completely mine, and he burned with a hunger and urgency that matched my own. Smiling, I took his hand and held it to my face. "Are you, Gabriel St. Clair, Knight Hospitaller and devout brethren of the order, my lover?" I asked, alluding to the message he sent to Sir George.

"God as my witness, I am. Yet you deserve so much more than that."

"I do," I agreed softly, knowing exactly what he meant. For a young, unmarried woman of my status did not run off with a man like Gabriel St. Clair, monk or no, without facing some consequences. He knew that. It was partly the reason he had proudly flaunted his fallen status and mine in the face of Sir George Douglas. There would be public scorn and the wagging tongues of half of Scotland to face unless we were to be married. And marriage was one way to repair such a scandal. "And, thankfully, I happen to be rather good at getting what I want."

"And don't I know that too," he uttered endearingly, helplessly, and then brought his lips over mine.

෨෨

I breathed deeply, indulgently, while lying in the shelter of Gabriel's arm. Beside me, his sun-bronzed body warm and naked, he was completely at ease basking in the afterglow of our urgent and replete lovemaking. I watched his chest rise and fall with the steady rhythm of a body deep in sleep, and marveled at the thought that he could actually be sleeping so soon after such vigorous activity. I was wide awake— deliciously relaxed but wide awake—and I smiled at the thought of him sleeping. I rolled deeper into him, unable to resist nuzzling the tender skin below his earlobe, and then to kiss it. A warm and wonderful sound escaped his lips.

"Are you awake?" I whispered.

"No," he replied to the ceiling. I looked at his noble profile. His eyes were still closed, but his lips were smiling. "I'm dreaming. It's a familiar dream. I know the ending, but it's sweet all the same."

"I know the ending too," I said, and propped myself on an elbow so that I could look upon the face that I had truly believed only lived in my dreams. That he was beside me was beyond comprehension—a miracle that I would never take for granted. There was still a halo around his head, only this one was fashioned not in my imagination but out of a tangle of our bright hair—my fine, pale-apricot strands blending harmoniously with his richer, thicker, sun-bleached umber. His smiling lips were begging to be kissed again. I was not one to resist such a vision. "And it is sweet," I agreed. "I was just thinking how nice it would be to stay here forever."

"I was thinking the very same. I could fix the place up, I suppose," he offered, opening one eye a crack. "Would you have Bodrum living in here too, or do we put him outside with the rest of the beasts?" I looked at the horse—a pale shadow against a backdrop of mottled, earthy hues—now hobbled and resting peacefully. His ear twitched.

"He's docile as a house cat—smarter too—and easier on

the upholstery. He definitely deserves a proper stable, though, for what we've put him through."

Both eyes opened, round, blue, and guileless. "We? You were the one making all the noise, my heart. The poor lad's trying to rest, after struggling for hours under the excess weight of you, and here's you purring away like a cat at the cream. I bet his ears are twitching from the heady ring of it. I know mine are." His lips curled into a purely devilish grin.

Horrified, I covered my mouth and saw Bodrum's ear twitch again. The timing was too perfect, and to Gabriel's delight, I burst into giggles. "You're terrible! That's not at all what I meant!"

"I know. But I couldn't resist. I've never claimed to be a saint, you know, only a monk . . . which is not at all the same thing."

"And you're not a very good monk either," I gently admonished, and leaned down to brush my lips against his yet again, letting him know how thankful I was for that small wonder.

He cradled my face with his hands, weaving his fingers through my drying hair. "That, my heart, was not my fault. I place the blame fully on you," he softly teased. "And when I go to the preceptory at Torphichen, and stand before Sir William Knollis to return my black mantle and renounce my oath, as I know I must, I shall claim the reason for my change of heart regarding the order is that I was corrupted by an angel. One look at you and he'll believe it." Although his mouth twisted in wry amusement, his eyes were serious. I frowned, for Torphichen was the home of the Order of the Knights of Saint John of Jerusalem in Scotland, and the thought that Gabriel had already made the decision to renounce his vows was sobering.

"Are you really going to turn in your mantle and your eight-pointed cross?"

"I'd be living a lie if I didn't. And don't think there are those who aren't living such a lie, because there are. But I won't be among them. I prefer to live honestly."

"Indeed," I said, my voice filling with tenderness. "And I'm glad of it. I only hope this is truly the right decision for you. I couldn't be happy knowing you had second thoughts on the matter or any regrets."

"Oh, I'll have regrets," he said plainly. "And I'm certain you'll give me reason to have second thoughts a time or two as well. And by the end of the year you'll likely be riding to Torphichen yourself pleading with old Knollis to return my mantle and send me back to Rhodes, I'll be that much of a pain to you. But I won't go. Because I love you," he whispered passionately. "And you love me. And that's more than most folk ever get in their lifetime. I have been corrupted by an angel—sweetly, lovingly, joyously corrupted. And I embrace that fact. You, Isabeau my love, have been corrupted by a monk. Let's just say, I wouldn't want to be in your shoes when you try to explain that one to the priest." He flashed a glorious smile, pulled me down beside him, and began sweetly, lovingly, and quite joyously corrupting me again.

⚜

We slept like the dead and awoke in the late afternoon, thoroughly refreshed and ravenous. After pulling an intrepid mouse from Gabriel's pack, we delved into the food bought off the goodwife without ceremony, including the remainder of the tangy little apricots—sharing every morsel—feeding each other until we were sated and fortified with strong beer. Outside, the rain had begun again; inside it was warm and dry, but we knew we would need to leave the safety of our little haven soon, and to understand what was going on and where we were heading. We assumed that Sir George held Blythe Hall and that Julius was being held at Hume Castle. The mention of Julius prompted me to ask Gabriel after the nature of their relationship, and why he believed Julius was the one who had lured him back to Scotland.

"Don't get me wrong, Julius didn't bring me here directly. I haven't seen your brother for over a year now," he said, and took another sip from the flask. "What I meant was that I'm here on-his behalf."

"You haven't seen him in over a year?" I remarked. "But Julius has been gone longer, much longer, than a year."

He looked at me a moment, studying my face with his summer-sky gaze, and then his eyes shifted to the fire. They moved about again, and I could see that the mention of Julius had sent him into eye-roving, disconcerted thought.

"Tell me," I gently commanded, taking hold of his hand and demanding his full attention. "I need to know what's going on, Gabriel. Tell me everything, for there are pieces to this puzzle I cannot figure out on my own. Why does Sir George hate Julius so? Why this shameless play over the king? Where has Julius been these four years, and where is my father? And most important, why have you come here now?"

He dropped his gaze to our entwined hands and, with a long, cathartic sigh, relented. "My relationship with your brother is complicated. We met, as I told you, when we were boys. We had been as close as brothers, but we had a falling-out one day, before the rising of '88, when things were heating up with the nobles. Our falling-out, as I might have alluded to earlier, was mainly over you. But there were other factors too, for instance, the division of the nobles, and whether to support the king or the prince. I had no stomach for any of it, largely because it didn't matter to me. I had no hope of making a name for myself here either way, but like all idealistic men, I did want to make a difference in the world. The one skill I have, Isabeau, is that I can fight, but I didn't want to feed my sword with the blood of my own countrymen. With the help of Sir Oliver, my half-brother, I took my sword and left Scotland, in possession of a letter of recommendation to present to Pierre d'Aubusson, the Grand Master of the Order on Rhodes.

"I was happy there, truly I was," he continued, his eyes soft and distant. "I ate well, slept soundly, prayed daily, and fought the Turks. What more could a man ask? I even made a name for myself in the Hospitaller galleys, where my talent for naval tactics blossomed. I spent most of my time at sea, and was glad of it . . . until one day, nearly three years ago now." He looked at me, and I saw the dark shadow of the memory pass behind his eyes. Reflexively, my hand closed over his, for he was lost in his memory and I wanted him to understand that I was there with him.

"I was in the Aegean," he continued softly, "battling a particularly wicked Turkish pirate, a soulless creature by the name of Curtogoli Reis, the name meaning 'son of the wolf' in Turkish, who was wreaking havoc on Christian shipping in the area. Curtogoli had a sizable fleet, seventeen galleys, and we had slowly reduced their number, but we could never seem to trap his flagship. However, three years ago, after some lucky sailing and bold maneuvering, I finally caught him." He looked up to see if I was following.

"The Turks, Isabeau, make a practice of using Christian captives to row their ships, knowing that a man of God— a Hospitaller—would think twice before taking so many Christian lives. I abhor killing Christians as much as I abhor killing hounds, but sometimes it has to be done. And on this day the price to be paid was inconsequential. I had battled him far too many times to care, and I wanted to see him swinging at the end of a rope at all costs. So, after a hellish battle, we took his ship. But a man like Curtogoli does not give up the ghost so easily. Seeing that all was lost, he set fire to his own ship—purposely trying to kill the Christians he had chained to the oars. It was just another nasty tactic, and I fought to ignore the screams of the dying men as I made ready to take him. It was then that the devil smiled and said he had a friend of mine.

He pointed to where the fire was, and who did I see through the black smoke, chained to the bench? Julius. I wouldn't have recognized him but for the eyes and hair. And of course his sharp tongue. He never lost the use of that cursed gift."

This news, this stunningly horrific news of what had befallen my beloved, wayward brother, caused my eyes to well up with tears, and they coursed down my face unchecked as I asked, "What . . . what happened?"

"What happened? I let the old pirate go and fought like hell to save your brother's life is what happened. Later, long after Julius had recovered, we caught Curtogoli Reis again. Julius had made a friend during his cruise, a quite remarkable young Venetian by the name of Dante Continari."

"I know him!" I cried, wiping at tears. "He was the man who stole my silver! He was the man who returned my sheep!"

"Your silver? Your sheep?" His quizzical look was disarming. "The silver I can imagine, but why, pray tell, did Dante have your sheep?"

"It's a long story—it's been a busy week," I replied weakly, recalling the incident with mild affection. "Julius and his men stole my sheep, kidnapped my shepherds, robbed Blythe Hall, sheared my sheep, and then that dark, rapacious Adonis returned both my naked sheep and my very drunk shepherds. That was all before they kidnapped the king, of course."

Gabriel, with the awestruck grin of a child beholding the sights and sounds of his first fair, nodded as if he understood. It was remarkable, because I didn't even understand it myself. "I didn't know his name. Dante . . . ," I mused, committing the name to memory and thinking of him and my brother chained together in slavery. I couldn't even imagine the horror of it, yet just knowing he hadn't been alone—that Julius had had another beside him—was somehow comforting. It also helped explain the bond between them. "Anyhow, Dante's here. In Scotland."

"Of course he's here," Gabriel said, as much to himself as to me. "Julius saved the young man's life. Dante perfectly worships the ground he walks on." He gave a short, rueful laugh then and added, "Don't we all? I didn't see him though. He wasn't with Julius when they attacked Kilwylie and his army. Julius saw me; I know he did. But I didn't see Dante. I was puzzled by it, but . . ." He thought for a moment, and then, as if arriving at some sort of remarkable conclusion, he swore under his breath. "Forgive me, but this is good news. I mean, it's not exactly good, but it's enough to give one hope." He looked at me then, willing me to understand, and then, like a capricious wind, his brow furrowed as his lips pulled into a pensive and troubled grimace. "The bond between Julius and Dante is very strong, but together they can be dangerous. While it's true that Julius saved Dante's life, Isabeau, both men were badly mistreated during their captivity. Very badly, and old Curtogoli, when they caught up to him—as they eventually did—was instantly sorry that he had ever come across Julius Blythe. I was with them," he uttered. "They were employed on my galley. 'Tis only natural for a man to want revenge, but. . . . I was about to intervene on Curtogoli's behalf—until I learned from the pirate's own lips that he had been paid by a Scotsman to take your brother."

"What?" My voice was thick with astonishment and trembling with outrage. I had to close my eyes then, unable to bear the thought of all this wanton cruelty. Julius, for his crimes in Scotland, was to be hanged. I had always thought he escaped. But what Gabriel was suggesting . . . it was a far more diabolical punishment than hanging. And then, just as a single spark ignites a nascent flame, something Julius had said on that first, unforgettable night at Blythe Hall came into my mind. Upon seeing Sir George, he had smiled mockingly and thanked him for the cruise. I had seen what had become of his beautiful hands; I had seen the ghosts of the once livid scars on his chest. I opened my eyes, already knowing the answer but asking the question all the same: "Who . . . ?"

But Gabriel was not finished. He held up a cautioning finger, begging me to be patient—begging me to let him finish before he lost heart and sickened of his tale. "During their convalescence Julius and Dante stayed with me on Rhodes. We are a healing order, you'll recall—founded on the premise of providing hospitals and medical care for the wounded Crusaders and injured pilgrims in the Holy Land—and we still maintain hospitals throughout Christendom. But I personally saw to their recovery, Isabeau, because it was that important to me. However, I soon learned that there are some things a man never fully recovers from. What had kept Julius alive throughout his captivity was the desire to find your father. Yet as his body recovered, I could see that he had lost the will to continue the search. Julius is a clever and resilient man; no one I know has ever plumbed the vast depths of his ability. But to a sadistic pirate he was the ultimate challenge, and Curtogoli Reis, being the notorious bastard that he was, took great delight in breaking him. And he broke him . . . thoroughly. Julius swiftly reverted to what came easiest to him—his glittering, self-indulgent lifestyle, and on Rhodes he employed his gift of frivolity to its fullest.

"After hearing all that befell him here, in Scotland, and after his refusal to continue his search for your father, I tried to convince him to join the order." He smiled grimly at the thought. "Your brother has many remarkable talents. He could have had a brilliant career serving his fellow man, protecting Christian trade. But the rules, our vows—Julius defies rules; he laughs in the face of devout commitment. Besides, he had discovered that Dante had a gift for numeracy, and together they embarked on a shameful career fleecing the locals of their hard-earned money. They delighted in games of chance—cards, dice, the lot—and enjoyed stunning results.

They began arousing suspicion, and garnering more than a little resentment, so I took them to sea with me, which I instantly regretted.

"The Greeks employed on our ships developed an immediate attachment to Julius and worshipped him like a bloody Apollo. He and his little pet, Dante, not only excelled in protecting Christian trade, they became pirates, and soon started wreaking havoc on the Turks. And, quite wisely, Julius gave half of his profits to the order. The rest he split with the crew. He was loved, and he was making too much money to consider vows of poverty, let alone celibacy. Yet for all his schemes and daring sea raids, there was something desperate about his behavior—something wildly destructive and disturbingly self-loathing. He despised the people he fleeced; he mocked their stupidity. He lost that joyous spark and ease of manner that men clamored to experience. He drank a lot. He dosed himself with powerful drugs from the Orient, and it scared the hell out of me. I could no longer tolerate his behavior. I could no longer sit by and watch him squander what gifts God gave him. I prayed for a miracle. I prayed for his soul. But he grew more unreasonable and quarrelsome with each day, until I could no longer stomach him. I left him; I left Rhodes; and I promised myself that I would never think of him again.

"My resolve lasted less than a fortnight," he said. His blue gaze held mine, and I saw the memory of his pain on his face. "I thought of him constantly, and it was then that I understood what I needed to do if I was ever to be fully rid of him. Julius had been a godsend to me once. And he deserved one last chance from me. That's when I knew I had to find your father."

"My father!? You found my father?" I grabbed him, startling him completely. "He's still . . . alive?"

"Yes," he answered, and a gentle smile appeared on his lips. "Very much so. At least he was when I found him. I shall tell you all about him later, but what you need to know, Isabeau, is that when I found your father, he was ignorant of the plot against your brother, and was positively heartbroken when he learned of it and all that had befallen Julius. He was especially concerned about you, thinking of you here these many years all alone. You must understand that your father's quest is a personal one, and it has consumed him completely. But in his defense, he believed he had everything under control when he left. You were in the convent, and he knew you would spend time at court serving the king. But Julius had been groomed by your father; he was to be Lord Blythe, and he was the man entrusted to be your guardian. In that moment, learning of what Kilwylie had done and knowing he was still in Scotland, Sir William immediately drew up some documents explaining his and Julius's movements in England in the year 1487, signed it, and gave it to me, asking me to make my way immediately to Blythe Hall. Somehow, oddly, he had the feeling that Julius would be returning . . . Isabeau? Isabeau, are you all right?"

"Wh . . . what plot against my brother?" I stammered, a terrible feeling taking hold.

"You know . . . the plot? Dear God, you don't know!?" His eyes narrowed and his face reflected the painful discovery of my ignorance. He buried his head in his hands and breathed, "Isabeau . . . I'm sorry. I thought you knew." He looked up, his face wan and bloodless. "Your brother was framed for kidnapping the Duke of Rothesay—the young prince."

"Framed?" I cried. "He was caught red-handed! He had convinced James to leave Stirling Castle right before the uprising, and James admitted to leaving with him."

"Yes, that's all true. But Julius wasn't selling him to the English. He had uncovered a plot by George Douglas and his uncle Angus, and the knowledge that one of his closest friends, a man who had joined the rebel lords and fought to overthrow the king, was also plotting to sell the young prince. It would have left the throne of Scotland conveniently open for King Henry, and it would have made the Douglases the most powerful family in Scotland. Julius, with his uncanny ways, was able to sniff out the plot before Sir George could abduct James. But the deviousness of Douglas shook him to the core. Julius's one mistake was that he sat on the information, thinking he could stop the rising if James went before his father and the loyal nobles and struck a bargain.

"Douglas, catching wind of Julius's plan, and learning that Julius knew what he and his uncle were up to, acted first and sent men to apprehend your brother and young Jamie on their way to Sir Andrew Wood's ship—where King James was waiting for them. There were also English ships skulking nearby, and it was easy to convince the lords that Julius was aiming for one of those, a job made all the more easy by the incriminating documents Sir George happened to uncover—fabricated documents. The evidence Sir George brought forward was overwhelmingly against your brother, and Julius was taken into custody right before the battle of Sauchieburn. And it was no accident that King James—leaving the field after realizing the battle was lost and heading for the safety of Sir Andrew Wood's ship—was murdered before he could testify on Julius's behalf."

There were tears in my eyes as Gabriel spoke, and my heart, shattered these many years by this event, broke again. Julius was innocent of the crimes he was convicted of, and I had excoriated him along with the rest of the country. My father was still alive. And Julius had finally returned to Scotland to set things right, and now he was wounded and perhaps dying in the bowels of a fetid prison . . . alone.

"Please," I uttered through streaming tears. "We have to save him."

"Of course we do, my heart," whispered Gabriel, and drew me to him, cradling me in his arms. "That's the other reason

I'm here. Your brother inadvertently forced me to find your father, and it was your father who sent me here. Somehow, I don't fully understand it myself, but Julius knew I'd be coming. It still makes no sense at all," he marveled, and then added, purely for my benefit, "and yet I find I don't regret one moment of the hell he put me through." He held me tightly and kissed the top of my head.

I pulled away, holding him at arm's length. "We need to go to Hume!"

"Indeed," he agreed, eyes alight with purpose. "But we can't go alone. We're wanted, remember? I've abducted you, violated you, and slaughtered nineteen of Kilwylie's men—not to mention the broken arm I gave to that sniveling maggot. We won't get within five miles of Hume Castle without help. The king, thank God, is with Dante, and safely hidden somewhere. Of that I'm sure. He's Julius's bargaining chip. As long as the king remains hidden, Lord Hume will not let Kilwylie kill him. Very smart," he mused appreciatively as we swiftly packed our things. "Very thorough. The blessing here is that we don't need to worry about James at the moment. But we do need men, and I know where I can get them. It's time I paid my half-brother a wee visit."

"Sir Oliver, do you mean?" I asked hopefully, for Gabriel's father had sired quite a few legitimate sons. Sir Oliver, by far, was the kindest.

Gabriel nodded with a mischievous gleam in his eye. "Prepare yourself, my heart. We're going to Rosslyn. And we're about to give old Ollie the fright of his life!"

Chapter 19

THE TAKING
OF TWO
KNIGHTS

THE SUN HAD JUST SET ON KILWYLIE CASTLE WHEN three young novices from the local monastery came before the gates with a cartload of beer. To the idle sentries at the gates and the servants left behind after their lord had set out that morning to retrieve his abducted bride-to-be, it was a heart-lifting sight. The lord's powerful uncle had also, thankfully, left with his sizable retinue, but not before doing some heavy damage to the larders and buttery of Kilwylie. The larders could wait, but here was a miracle!

As every man who had traveled the well-trodden roads of Britain knew, monasteries brewed some of the best beer in the world. The reason for this was very simple: men who moved in silence, shunned the pleasures of the world, and clung to the strict oaths of their brotherhood were wont to pour their passions into worshipping higher things—like properly brewed heavy beer. No half-brewed piss water at a monastery! The beer cart, therefore, was a godsend. So too were the novices, for it was common knowledge that young novices—with their heads all aswirl from a hefty dosing of moral philosophy and stuffed to exploding from feasting non-stop on the lofty ideals of their order—were known to strike fretfully awful bargains. Buying beer off a novice was, for all intents and purposes, like pinching pennies from a blind man. And, as every resident at Kilwylie knew, setting a blind man to guard a sack of gold or giving an old widow a prodigious, fat herd of cattle was an open invitation for an easy and indulgently profitable day. Spying the cart lumbering over the causeway, the sentry at the gatehouse gave the order, and the gates couldn't open fast enough for the three spindly lads bedecked in their humble, dirt-smudged robes. They were warmly received.

Less than an hour later the three young novices left a raucous and jubilant Kilwylie Castle, taking their empty beer cart and their short, stout, elderly white-haired priest with them.

☙

It was not the best night's sleep Lord Hume had ever had. To his despair, he found that a good deal of it was spent tossing and turning in his large and damnably empty tester bed. The reason for this was an assault of disturbing half dreams and prophetic visions all strung loosely together in a subconscious tangle of encroaching thought. Even more disquieting was the fact that the fair and insolent face of Julius Blythe had penetrated them all—and with him the haunting, aching emptiness associated with death. Therefore it came as no surprise that he found his nightclothes drenched when he was awakened, shortly after dawn, by an excited servant claiming that Lord Kilwylie was at the gates of Hume. Alexander sat up, wide-eyed and painfully awake, his heart beating away like a demon on a war drum. "Kilwylie's here? What does he want?"

"He wants to come in, sir," the servant promptly replied,

slightly wary of his lord's wild appearance. "The gatehouse wants to know do we let 'im in?"

"Have we any word yet from the party sent to Kilwylie Castle?"

"No, m'lord. No' yet." It was then that the man gently reminded him, "They only left last e'en."

"Right," Sir Alexander acknowledged, and grabbed up his robe. Tying it loosely about him, he crossed to the window, drew back the drapes, and peered out, all the while thinking. Cold sweat still dripped down his spine, and his ears still rang with the wild claim of his prisoner that Kilwylie would come at dawn to kill him. And here was the devil himself—a moment or two late of the mark, but here all the same. It was not, by any means, an admission of guilt on Kilwylie's behalf. Nor did the timely appearance of the realm's most celebrated knight exonerate young Blythe in any way. But it was mightily curious. A tremor of annoyance seized the muscles of his jaw as he peered upon the calm and tranquil expanse of his courtyard, and he silently cursed both men for having the gall to involve him in their sordid affair. For that's what he believed it was—revenge, jealousy, retribution—any or all of the plethora of petty demons that coursed through the veins of young, high-spirited men. Well, like it or not, he was involved, and there was no turning now from the distasteful job thrust upon him. He would tie the noose on either the most promising young man ever to be put under his command or the dark-haired, green-eyed Goliath who four years earlier had exposed young Blythe for what he was.

Lord Hume, settling in for a long and trying day, turned from the window and said flatly, "Go tell the gatehouse to let them in, Robbie. Bring Kilwylie and his men to the hall for refreshments, and have him wait for me there. I'll be down shortly. And Robbie, under no circumstance is Sir George to get near our prisoners. D'ye hear me? He's not to leave the hall until I speak with him."

დო

The gates of Hume Castle opened for Lord Kilwylie and his men as the cocks, scattering before them in the courtyard, continued to crow. Their horses, blowing steam in the heavy morning air, were led to the stables, as the riders, fresh of face and red of cheek, were taken to the hall. There servants had already begun laying out on the board pitchers of weak cider and platters of hard cheeses. Lord Kilwylie, scanning the room, asked after Lord Hume.

"My lord will be down presently," replied Robbie. "Until then he begs that ye relax and take advantage of his hospitality."

"Very good," Sir George said with a smile as he carefully removed his gloves. "Give Sir Alexander my thanks, and tell him to take his time. We're not staying long. I've just come to have a word with his prisoner. In fact, if you'll direct me to the prison now, I can be done with my onerous task before Sir Alexander arrives."

"I'm afraid you'll have to wait here, m'lord. Sir Alexander's orders."

The green eyes, bright and luminous as cut emeralds, held the servant with startling intensity. "Your lord has *ordered* me to stay here?" Kilwylie inquired in a low and pointed voice.

"Yes. But only until he arrives," the servant clarified, and growing slightly nervous under the piercing gaze of the huge knight, he offered feebly: "which should be any moment now."

"I'm curious. Has your lord been able to speak with his prisoner, the Master of Blythe? I only ask because Blythe was near death when I left yesterday. He was unconscious, with one foot already in the grave. Has he, in fact, awakened?"

"Och, awakened! Why, if the wee de'il dinnae arise last e'en with enough sweet racket to wake the dead!" Robbie offered, grinning slightly at the memory.

"Interesting," remarked Sir George, a pleasant smile on his lips. And then, with the speed of a striking viper, he grabbed the servant by the neck and dug his large, thick fingers into his pale flesh. At that same instant his heavily armed guard sprang into action. Within moments all the servants in the hall were powerless to do anything but watch in horror as Lord Kilwylie and his men entered the cellar.

୫୭

If Lord Hume had had a rough night of it, Julius Blythe's had been little better. His body ached from the aftereffects of battle, and his flesh burned with fever. The loose straw he lay on pricked through the fine cambric of his shirt and dug into his sensitive skin like thorn scrub. He kicked it aside, preferring the cold stone of the floor. And most distressingly, the sweet distraction of music was no longer at his fingertips. Without distraction he had no choice but to turn his thoughts loose, where, with ravenous appetite, he would trample, manipulate, and abuse the endless sea of intent and possibility that abounded in the fertile realm of his mind. For this reason he slept little. He relaxed his breathing; his body grew limp and pliant as rising dough, giving over entirely to the gentle pulse of life that flowed through him. And then he let his mind whirl away like a thriving hive of honeybees or a glittering swarm of fireflies on a summer's night. A thousand thoughts fired off at once, each one separate—each one seemingly inconsequential, yet all of them meandering, calculating, until finally converging to point out the path with the most favorable outcome. He closed his eyes and let it come: in words, in visions, in pictures, in sound, in evanescent wisps of thought. And when he finally heard the struggle in the cellar, as he knew he would, and the alarm of the guard swiftly muffled, he couldn't help but smile.

He was desperately in need of a proper bed, and tonight he would get one. Timing was everything; and he waited until the familiar, purposeful footfalls were almost upon him before calling out to the dimly lit corridor with a voice disguised in the innocent tones of gentle delusion: "Mother? Is it Christmas already? I smell roast pig! No, wait. That's just the stink of pig. Why, it must be our intrepid and odiferous guest, gong farmer Kilwylie!" The booted feet stopped.

"My foolish, glittering little harlot," said the knight, his Herculean shadow looming before the iron bars as he peered into the dark cell. The master didn't make a move to be seen. "I am no longer amused, Blythe. Your biggest mistake was coming home. Why, dear God, won't you die?"

"Like the hound that has no desire to hunt, I place the blame on shoddy breeding. Or blame it on dumb luck if you like—or perhaps my stubborn pride that demands retribution for the many wrongs done me. Either way, I'm a glutton for punishment. If it's any comfort to you, Georgie m'lad, you've done an admirably good job of trying to destroy me already. Why trouble yourself further?"

"Oh, I'm no longer going to try, my sweeting. This time I'm going to succeed."

"Excellent. Then all I ask is that if you're bent on killing me, at least let me die with a sword in my hand. For, like the heathen Norseman, I wish to go to that great feasting hall in the sky, Valhalla." His voice, now soft and gently mocking, began, " 'O, *sweet Valkyrie on your steed of ice, devour my soul, I've paid the price, I've fought the de'il and thrumped him thrice, so whisk me away, let me wallow in vice. I've bloody well earned it!'* Besides, an arrow in the back or knife to the gut of an unarmed man is just degrading."

Kilwylie let out a soft chuckle. "But I so enjoy degrading you, my winsome lad."

"Actually, I was speaking of you, Georgie—a knight who basks under a continuous crown of laurels. Did your mother never tell you? Perhaps you were too busy suckling the teat of a swine, but there is no sport in murdering a dying man."

There came a snort of mirthless laughter, and Kilwylie replied, "You expect me to believe you're dying?"

"Well, I'm not exactly thriving in here. Are you going to stand there all day marveling like a slack-jawed dolt at the shit in my bucket, or are you going to unlock the door and come get me?"

"You wish to fight me?" It was, even to Sir George's own opportunistic ears, unbelievable.

"What I wish," said Blythe plainly, "is to be left alone. God, what I wouldn't give for a moment's peace! But if you insist on killing me, then at least do me the honor of fighting me like a man. Unless, of course, you're afraid."

"Oh, I'm not afraid, my angelic one. And I will kill you, and delight in doing so," said Kilwylie, and he turned the key in the lock. The iron bars swung open with a chilling creak. "But first you're going to answer a few questions."

"I take it you saw my golden friend on the battlements?" Julius asked, looking up at the impending form of George Douglas. For the master was in much the same position as he'd been in all night, prone on his back on the stone-cold floor. He smiled wistfully up at his old friend. "A most beautiful sight, is he not? Gabriel St. Clair, unlike us, is a man of pure mind, of clear conscience, and in possession of a heart bursting with the moral integrity of an archangel. He's a living paradigm of virtue, and he fights like a demon in the name of God. Gabriel St. Clair has my sister, thank God. Don't try to tell me otherwise; I won't believe you."

"Gabriel has your sister," Kilwylie concurred. "And I sent twenty men to kill them both. I've also given the order to kill that bitch of a governess, Seraphina. What a vigilant guardian of maidenly virtue she is. How her heart will break when she learns that her angelic charge has not only been abducted and raped but also has been brutally murdered by the rogue and morally corrupt Hospitaller Gabriel St. Clair. It will be the great pity of the nation—such a terrible waste of a pure, innocent, and beautiful young lady. I would have so enjoyed being the one to tame her; I would have been a good lord and master to her. But you ruined everything. You should have thought of that before taking the king." His voice held a tremor of sentiment, but his green eyes were ruthlessly unmoved. "Madame Seraphina, failing to protect her charge, will throw herself out the window. They're all likely dead already, Julius. And you shall see them shortly."

"Doubtful," replied the master with infuriating ennui. "I'm going to Valhalla, remember?"

"You're going to hell," Kilwylie corrected him, smiling with exquisite pleasure as his eyes devoured the pathetic sight before him—the pale hair against even paler skin, the large, pellucid eyes glossy with fever. "I never dreamed it possible, but for once you look less than stunning. In fact, you look very like shit, Blythe. Do you really wish to fight me?" It was said with chiding disbelief. "We can just end it here, quietly, simply, like two old friends duty-bound by the silent code of brotherhood. I shall be humane and put you out of your misery."

"But you are no friend. Therefore, I prefer you be inhumane and fight me."

"Can you even stand?"

"Truthfully, I don't know. I haven't tried. Pull me up." A hand, pale, elegant, and achingly frail, reached up from the floor. Kilwylie, ignoring it, squatted beside the master instead, and began stroking, with sickening gentleness, the sweat-sodden curls.

"I have two questions before I kill you, my debauched, golden harlot," he whispered softly. "My fallen angel. Where is the king, and where is the manuscript?"

"I have two answers, short and succinct. Pull me up and I'll tell you." With a sardonic lift of his dark brows and a vicious twist to his mouth, Kilwylie relented. He grabbed hold of the now limp hand, and with a force meant to pull the arm out of its socket, Sir George shot up, pulling the master with him. Julius, having been prepared for the jolt, staggered to his feet and fell back against the wall. His breathing, for the first time, came in irregular gasps. "All right, here are my answers. Regarding the king: I don't know anymore. Regarding the manuscript: I haven't found it yet. That's the truth." For his efforts, Julius received a vicious punch to the stomach. The force of the blow doubled him over and sent him into a fit of coughing. Kilwylie, not willing to miss a beat, grabbed him by the hair and the neck of his shirt and flung him against the wall, adding a kick to the kidneys for good measure. Julius gasped in pain. The men in the other cells, hearing the beating, began yelling. Kilwylie picked up the master again and tossed him headfirst out of the cell. He landed in a sprawling heap on the floor.

"Give him your sword," Sir George demanded of one of his men. "The bloody wee fool wishes to fight me." The men of Kilwylie laughed at this, for no one in his right mind would willingly ask to go against the blade of Lord Kilwylie. They looked at the man on the floor, fair, frail, and struggling to stand, and recognized it for the suicide it was. The men behind bars, fearful and protective of their young leader, jeered. They were understandably horrified by the thought because they feared the same outcome. Julius Blythe alone seemed oblivious to his surroundings, and he found, to his amazement, a sword in his hand. He gripped it, felt the familiar, comforting weight, and then, turning slowly, he faced his longtime enemy in the narrow corridor of a stronghold prison. He was not under any delusions of winning such a fight, for he lacked the strength to do anything but parry. Yet even a hare could tire a fox, and that's what he intended to do. He just needed to hold out long enough until higher powers intervened. Mustering all his fading strength, and his vast resources of superficial deception, he adjusted his grip on the sword and took his stance.

Bodies pressed against the iron bars that lined the corridor, hooting and cheering him on. On his other side was a wall of solid stone. The lighting was poor and the footing slippery. He noted all this and then nodded. It was then that Sir George Douglas, the most gifted swordsman in all Scotland, sprang his attack.

From the onset it was clear that both men were gifted swordsmen. Kilwylie, tall, dark, thickly muscled, and powerful as an ox, drove his blade with the legendary jarring force and textbook technique that had made him a household name. The Master of Blythe, however, surprised them all, not only because he could, in his weakened state, defend the attack, but because his skill, hidden these many years from public view, blossomed like a thing of wonder before their eyes. The slighter body, the hereditary elegance, the lean muscle in command of the finer bones, moved with an artfulness and precision that demanded respect. These were two different men with vastly different styles, yet both displayed a level of athleticism and prowess that was beyond compare. What started out as a suicide had transformed into a haunting dance to the death, where every flick of the razor-sharp blade, every thrust and parry, rang with the inevitable finality of the outcome.

The men witnessing the duel fell silent, jaws agape, in admiration, until only the sound of clanking steel and the muffled patter of frenetic footwork echoed along the corridor. For this was a modern-day battle of David and Goliath—a mismatched and improbable fight by every definition—and no man present, from callow youth to war-hardened veteran, could pull his eyes from the heart-wrenching spectacle of it.

Kilwylie opened with an attack of malicious intent, driving his powerful body to overwhelm the smaller man. But Julius, with billowing white shirt now bloodstained and sweat-covered, was as quick, as resilient, and as flexible as a sapling. His sword arm, bulging with sinewy muscle, absorbed and deflected each blow with maddening efficiency. His legs, finely shaped and encased in soft leather, moved with the artful fluidity of a dance master. Yet for all his effort, it could be seen that he was not attacking. There was no effort wasted in riposte or counter-thrust, and yet Kilwylie's blade consistently cut into stone and slashed across iron. Those paying close attention saw, with eye-bulging disbelief, how it was done, for the blue eyes of the master, intensely focused, never left the eyes of his opponent; he appeared able to read the living thought as it flashed behind them. In the unimaginably short time it took for the oversized muscles of the knight to obey the direction of his brain, Julius Blythe was already there, anticipating and prepared for the blow he knew would come. It was a display unlike anyone present had ever before seen. It amazed with the same dark and tawdry voyeurism as witchcraft. And more than a few men present wished to see a duel between these two in earnest, and not this shameful abuse of power, where a sword-swinging giant set out to destroy a sick and wounded man.

On some level, Kilwylie knew how Julius worked, and it angered him all the more that he had been fooled into believing once again that his destruction would be easy. The green eyes flashed; the blue eyes understood; and sparks from tempered steel grating against tempered steel ignited the air. The corridor reeked of sweat, and the two men engaged in the vicious swordplay heaved like winded chargers. The spellbinding display that had lasted no more than ten minutes began to lose pace, because both men were tiring. Yet the young Master of Blythe was fading rapidly, and Kilwylie knew it.

"I thought you were dying," Sir George finally said, and drove his blade, with a swing starting at his powerful shoulder, straight at Julius's heart. The smaller man, with shoulders back and square to his opponent, took the hit with the side of his own blade and carried the force of it to the wall, where it bit into stone again, in a continuous campaign to dull the razor-sharp steel. Julius recoiled, disengaged, and, mustering his fading energy, unfurled like a whip, surprising his attacker and landing a blow on the man's shoulder. The cut was not deep but it was enough to draw blood.

"And I thought you'd be smarter than to believe it," Julius replied, his chest heaving, his fair brow dripping with sweat. "'Tis an endearing quality, is gullibility."

Kilwylie, growling viciously, lunged at the mocking face. The master was not quick enough this time and took a grazing blow to the side. Before he could recover, Kilwylie was on him again, driving him with monstrous effort back against the wall. Julius knew that he had nearly exhausted his pitiful re-sources and wouldn't be able to hold on much longer. It had been a risky performance from the onset, and one of his best, yet the thought that he had made it this far only to lose the final and most desperate move rang with an irony too bitter to swallow. He would have laughed if he had the breath for it.

The far wall came up quickly then, because once he lost his footing and let the impetus of Kilwylie's drive push him back-ward, it was nearly impossible to regain the ground he had lost. Not in his condition. He felt it, solid and unforgiving against his fevered skin. He slammed against the hard barrier with surprising force. He was now trapped like a bear in a cage. Pain from his wound radiated through his limbs. And his blade, now limited by the resolute property of stone, was little more than a prop.

And then he saw the flash of the dagger in Sir George's other hand. Their eyes met.

"Let me through!" The cry echoed along the dungeon, ringing loud around them. There had been a commotion, they realized, but it was too late. In the heat of the fight each man had heard nothing but the sound of his own blood rushing past his ears—only the heavy, raucous breath fighting to quench the burning in his lungs. Neither man had heard the guards of Lord Hume arrive. But they heard them now, and they heard Sir Alexander's voice cry out, invoking the regal command of the numerous generations of Humes before him: "In the name of the king, drop your sword!"

Lord Hume had come at last. Julius, looking over the shoulder of his attacker, focused on the man he had always looked up to. On the handsome, stolid face he caught the wide-eyed look of incredulity mixed with the pain of remorse. Reflexively, as if obeying a command in another lifetime, Julius's hand relaxed, and the sword fell from his grasp, landing with quivering finality on the floor beside him. That's when the blade of the dagger came, hard and searing into his body, driving all the way to the hilt. He looked at Kilwylie and saw the victorious grin, chilling in its rapturous joy. "Do you still find a blade in the gut of an unarmed man degrading, my pet? I do hope so," whispered the mouth beside his ear, warm and sweet as a lover's. And then, as swiftly as it cut, the blade came away, leaving in its wake a trail of warm, oozing crimson. Kilwylie held him as his legs gave out altogether. He held him still as his body began to quiver and convulse. And he whispered again into the neat, rounded arch of the finely shaped ear, "I have wiped your race from the face of the earth, Julius Blythe, and nothing will stop me now. Rest assured that I will find the manuscript, and I will learn the secret you have died for." And then Sir George Douglas, hearing the rush of boots descend on him, released his grip on the master.

Julius, without an ounce of strength left in his body, slumped to the floor; his eyes never left Kilwylie. He watched as the knight was grabbed from behind and dragged away. He watched as Sir George cried out, demanding to know on what grounds he was being apprehended—for defending oneself against a traitorous outlaw was justifiable, he argued.

"Sir George Douglas, Lord Kilwylie," declared Lord Hume, "I am placing you under arrest for the abduction and murder of Madame Seraphina L'Ange, governess and loyal servant of the house of Blythe."

"What?" Sir George cried in outrage, his spectacular green

eyes flashing wildly about him. "That's not true! That's not true! 'Tis a lie!"

It was Julius's turn to smile then, and his face held the serene and beatific look of an angel. And he was smiling still as Sir George Douglas, kicking and screaming, was bodily thrown into the very cell the master had occupied a short while before. It was only when he heard the door shut and the finality of the lock sliding into place that his smile began to fade.

George Douglas was still protesting.

⚜

"Dear God," Sir Alexander uttered softly before dropping to his knees beside the master. His gentle gray eyes took in the wreckage, the wanton damage inflicted on the body that had too much promise to end in such a way. And he felt again a pang of remorse, sharp and chastising, that he knew he would never shake, because this was his fault. He discarded his doublet and grabbing the hem of his fine undergarment ripped off a piece of linen. Then, wadding it up, he stuffed it under the abused shirt, pressing it tightly against the gaping wound in the young man's torso. And then, tenderly, he lifted the golden head and cradled it on his lap, like he would if it belonged to his own son. The cornflower-blue eyes, wide and with the melting innocence of a child, held his face. It was not an uncommon look for young Blythe, but this time it was genuine, and it seized Lord Hume's gut and turned his insides to jelly. He would have cursed, but he saw that the young man was smiling.

"What took you so long?" asked Julius.

"I was detained. By God, Julius, what foolish voice in your head made you believe you could possibly fight that man in your condition? I wouldn't have believed it if I hadn't seen it with my own eyes."

Julius peered up at him from beneath lids that had grown

weary. "Normally, I'm quite keen with the idea of trial by battle, but I have to be honest. I wasn't fighting. I was simply defending. I will ask you now again politely, will you please release my men? Douglas has sent a ridiculous number of his buffoons to kill my sister. Call me a mother hen, but I'd be lying if I said I wasn't worried."

"Already done, my lad. And what do you mean, kill your sister? Where is she?" asked Lord Hume, and then his gray eyes narrowed in troubled thought as he took in the scene around him. Anarchy had besieged his slumbering fortress at dawn. His kind and hospitable servants had been roughly handled in his own hall—his prison guards had been subdued, and now he was on his knees in the bowels of his castle, watching as the personal guard of Scotland's most revered knight were being stripped of their arms and tossed into his prison, exchanging places with the rough and broken men of Scotland's most dangerous outlaw. He knew he was going to regret it, but he just had to ask the question: "Would you mind explaining to me what the devil's going on here, Blythe?"

The familiar tone of his voice, the way he said it, elicited an immediate response from the young man, whose face, remarkably placid under the glistening sweat, came alive with wry amusement. It was what Lord Hume feared, and his response was an immediate and deprecating surge of regret. "I would tell you," Julius answered softly, "but I'm afraid the effort might kill me. Might I beg a doctor first? I've a terrible pain in my side, and my head's growing a bit woozy."

"God! Of course! How stupid of me!" And Alexander, wasting no time, turned his head and shouted for his groom to ride and fetch the doctor. "We'll get you to a proper bed, my lad, I promise."

Julius's lips pulled to a smile. "A proper bed sounds like heaven." Then his focus drifted, and he stared at a point just beyond Sir Alexander's head.

"Tell your groom that won't be necessary," came a gentle,

lilting voice beside Sir Alexander. Startled, Alexander turned and came face-to-face with the disheveled and battle-weary figure of one of Blythe's own men. The man's intelligent brown eyes held his curious gray ones, and then he received another shock as the dark-haired man proclaimed softly, "I am a medical doctor. Allow me to introduce myself. Clayton Hayes, former personal physician to the Duke of Bourbon, at your service, sir."

Lord Hume, a man who was not surprised very often but who had received more surprises in the last few minutes than he had in some time, would normally have regretted the words that tumbled out of his mouth: "What the devil is the personal physician of a French duke doing in my prison!?"

"That's a fair question," replied Clayton, mirroring the irreverent smile now on the master's lips. "And it might help to know that I don't serve a French master any longer. I serve a stubborn Scot, a man by the name of Blythe, who was shot in the back while trying to defend his family home. I'm sorry to say I'm no stranger to his particular sort of mischief, and, as testament to that fact, I've patched him up more times in the last two years than I can count. It's what we call in the business job security." His words, as they all knew, were not so much for Sir Alexander's sake as they were for the sake of his Scottish master. "And he is, by all accounts, a resilient and stubborn man. He's a temper on him too when he's out of sorts. If you'll allow me, we need to move him upstairs, and quickly. Cochrane," the doctor called to one of his companions, "come here and give me a hand!" And then, turning back to Lord Hume: "If you'll be so good, I'm going to need boiled water, clean linen, a small cautery iron, needle, thread, and whisky—Dear God, am I going to need whisky!" As the other man arrived to help lift the master, Lord Hume, stunned, shaken, his head perfectly spinning, nodded. He then stood and ran ahead, calling orders like a fishwife at the Market Cross.

"Danny," said the master, grabbing the sleeve of his architect's doublet as he made ready to lift him, "take the men and find Dante. Deliver the message that our friend has finally arrived and he has my sister. He's not to take his package to Edinburgh; he's to go directly to Rosslyn. You know the place; you used to work there. Make sure they get there safely. I have reason to believe my sister will be there as well, and I need her. I need you to bring her to me."

"Aye," said Daniel Cochrane with a grim set to his mouth as he lifted the master. The doctor was at his feet, and he was at the head, carrying the man with a gentleness that belied his gruff and belligerent nature. His eyes, black and shiny as sea pebbles, flicked to the white shirt, now drenched with blood. The sight caused his throat to constrict with awkward emotion, and he uttered, "I'll leave as soon as I see your sorry hide tae bed. An' never ye worry. I'll bring the lass here. An' if I'm going tae make the effort, ye better have more manners in ye than tae die before I return, my canny, muckle-heided laddie." It was a voice that sounded foreign even to his own world-weary ears.

Chapter 20

DANTE'S TASK

DANTE CONTINARI, WHITE-KNUCKLED AND MAD AS hell, watched the attack on Blythe Hall from the crumbling parapet of the old peel tower. He had never sat out a battle. He had always fought beside Julius. But now he had that feeling—that odd, hard-to-pin-down, disjointed, sinking feeling in the pit of his stomach. And he believed that because he was not there to watch the master's back, something terrible was about to happen. He was not, by any means, clairvoyant. He highly doubted his grandmother had been either. What she had excelled at, however, was interpreting gut feeling, and his gut at the moment was feeling positively dreadful. It ached. It yawed. It begged him to be reasonable. It was telling him to commandeer his horse and ride like a banshee head-long into the fray—regardless of the tongue lashing he knew would come. But he couldn't. He really couldn't. Because this time his hands were tied. Julius, damn him, had saddled him with a king.

The master's opening move had been spectacular to watch.

The handpicked band of mercenaries, along with the vengeful tenants of Blythemuir, had sprung an attack on Kilwylie's pillagers and driven them mercilessly back to the site of the main battle. There they had crashed on their own ranks and created exactly what Julius had wanted—chaos. It was hand-to-hand combat from there. Dante followed it as best he could with his eyes, always aware of the master. Watching him fight was much like admiring a work of art, where every precise and delicate brushstroke was integral to the final outcome. And so it was with a sword in the hand of Julius Blythe. The man had an eye for his art. Then, just as he was enjoying the battle, he caught a movement out of the corner of his vision. He turned and saw a sight that the aching in his gut had foretold. It was the fluttering banners and pennants of some local lord barreling across the new-planted fields. The men battling outside the gates of Blythe Hall had no idea they were coming, and he knew it couldn't bode well for Julius. The heavily armed warriors were not reinforcements sent to help an outlaw and his merry band of reivers take back the family home—no matter how much he wanted to believe it. These men had the unbending look of the law about them, and as he was painfully aware, men who upheld the laws of a nation seldom had sympathy for those who delighted in stretching and twisting them to their limits. It didn't help matters any that Douglas of Kilwylie was a man who, like tenacious pond scum, suspiciously rose to the surface on the right side of the law time and again. And Dante, receiving an abrupt but thorough lesson on the nature of the man, knew that Kilwylie would stop at nothing in order to destroy Julius.

All the impetus the master had gained during his feisty attack on Kilwylie slackened when the army arrived. Caught between the burning gates of Blythe and two hostile forces, Julius had no choice but to do what he did. And it broke Dante's heart to see how he sent the men scattering just before turning himself over to the law. The fighting had stopped. He watched his comrades surrender. And then the unthinkable happened. The entire world slowed when he saw that a bolt had been released from the vicinity of Kilwylie. He followed its inevitable trajectory, like that of a comet racing across the night sky, and watched, with his heart in his throat, as it hit the master. Julius had come before the mighty lord. He had surrendered, and the bastard had put a bolt in his back all the same. The lithe and athletic body slumped forward on impact. The gates of the border fortress were broken down, and Blythe Hall, like a gem in an alchemist's crucible, was slowly debauched by the heat, and the violence, and the black-hearted devil who would continue to pillage, rape, and burn until his perverted hungers were sated. Dante, shaking with rage, and with tears spilling from his spectacular black eyes, was gently pulled back inside the tower.

☙

Washed, rested, and dressed from head to toe in luxuriant black, Dante took his guard and headed down the long sub-terranean corridor that led to the secret room hidden twenty feet beneath Blythe Hall. He was very nearly drunk; he had dosed himself with opium, reverting to old habits, and now both sedatives coursed through his veins, relieving some of the anger—some of the anguish—but not all. His mood was still dark, bordering on violent, his temper just barely under control. He had lost it when the men started straggling home after the battle—without their leader. And he had nearly lost it again when accosted by the throng of women and children placed under his care, scared and huddled in the hidden war-ren of tunnels under the tower, wanting to know what had happened. He had told them, bluntly. He had told them they could stay as long as they liked. He had bidden them to eat and drink until all the stores were depleted. And then he had left them to their own devices.

Because he had a job to do.

However, once he had successfully fulfilled his obligation to Julius, like a wolf in the night he would hunt down Kilwylie, and he would cut out his still-beating heart. It was the one thought that made him smile.

As he approached the heavy door of the chamber, he could hear above him the odd, muffled cry of a woman, or a particularly resounding thud indicating that Kilwylie's men were still at it, still violently celebrating their victory. He stood before the locked door, steadied himself, and motioned for the guard to open it.

The sight of the young king, in white shirt and dark hose, sitting at the master's desk bent over a pile of old books, startled him. It was a flash—an ephemeral vision in which his nearly besotted mind had believed he was seeing Julius; for aside from the dark hair, the young king echoed the master's posture whenever Dante had come to this room. And he found it slightly odd that the king should be so enthralled with ancient chicken scrawl and old scraps of parchment when he had a much younger and livelier plaything to entertain him.

That plaything was prone on the bed, dark and sultry, her naked body loosely draped in the fine satin sheets. She was also soundly asleep, and frowsy in the way lively women are after spending themselves in pleasure. He let his dark gaze linger over her body, taking in the roundness of her shapely backside, the way the rosy light of the fire reflected off the alabaster skin. And his eyes remained on her until the young man at the desk could take no more of it. "I will ask you to divert your eyes from the lady. And I will ask it only once," came the soft yet commanding voice.

With a languid smile and eyes boldly proclaiming desire, Dante slowly brought his focus back on the young man. The king was now standing, bristling with outrage and contempt, yet undeniably regal. Dante now had his full and undivided attention. "I see you are an energetic man," he said with deceptive bonhomie while raking his critical dark gaze over the young king. "I admire that. You and the young lady have ten minutes to get ready."

"Why? What's going on?"

Dante, with startling suddenness, turned back on the man, not bothering to temper the inimical look in his piercing eyes. "What is going on, you ask?" His speech was mildly slurred and flavored with a hint of Italian. "Why, Rome, signor, that shining city of seven hills, has been sacked by the barbarian hordes, and I am pledged to see you safely home . . . unless, of course, you'd rather stay here and eat, read, drink, and fuck some more. It is a good life, no?"

"How dare you speak to me like that," James challenged, his tone made all the more dangerous by its softness.

"I dare because you are my prisoner. I dare because I could break your little white neck before you could blink. I dare because you are not *my* king!" And then, with a breath of bitter disdain, he said, "When you are no longer my prisoner, I will give you all the respect you deserve. Until that time, get used to it."

"When I am no longer your prisoner I will see you hanged!"

"Hanged? Really?" Unable to help himself, Dante laughed, showing off the dark gift of his beauty. "Were I a king, I would think of infinitely more creative ways to punish a man than death by a rope! Hanging? What an astounding imagination you have. Tell me, have you ever seen a man impaled? It is a favorite death of the Turks, a nasty, degrading, sometimes even lingering death. Or flaying? There's one that will make a man think twice. Remind me to explain them to you sometime. Hanging," he mocked, and indulged in a bout of unstable laughter.

Neither man saw the woman wake up until her voice rang out: "You! What are *you* doing here? Get out!"

Startled, both men turned in the direction of the voice.

Marion was sitting up in bed, angry, glowering, gorgeous, and holding tightly to the sheet that now covered her.

"You know him?" James cried, incredulity and indignation marring his regal air.

"Intimately," Dante answered, his voice thick with innuendo.

"Barely," Marion shot back with haughty indifference. "His name is Dante. He's Julius's wicked toy. Where's Julius? Go tell your black-hearted master that we're not leaving until he comes and gets us himself! Go! Shoo! Really, you overgrown children are becoming insufferable!"

Dante, thoroughly enjoying himself until the woman mentioned the name of his friend, darkened. Like a breath of fickle wind, his eyes narrowed and the smile was wiped from his lips. "Then you will stay down here and rot, because Julius has been shot in the back by Kilwylie. The balance of good and evil has shifted, my dears. You have ten minutes."

※

An hour later, when Dante deemed it safe, the hoods were removed and the prisoners were surprised to find that they had been traveling in the dark. They were on horseback, riding silently under the glittering expanse of the night sky, with fourteen armed men to guard them. James stared for a moment at the back of the black-haired man in charge, noting the self-possession, the easy and relaxed manner with which he rode. Excusing himself from Marion, he nudged his horse forward and came beside the man called Dante. "Where are you taking us?" the king demanded. "I believe I have a right to know."

Dante looked at him, arched a dark brow, and replied with a stunning lack of concern. "Home."

"Interesting," James replied levelly, his eyes holding the man as if studying a map of a battlefield. "Because I thought you were supposed to sell me to the English."

The Venetian, keeping his eyes on the dark road ahead, answered, "No. I don't like the English. I'm taking you home."

It was incredible. James, unable to help himself, probed further. "You've abducted me so that you can take me back to Edinburgh? That's unique, but I don't believe you."

Dante turned and, without the benefit of a smile, offered, "I like the French. I suppose, if pressed, I could sell you to the French king. But we both know that would be like selling your sister to your best friend. It's too easy; too little money exchanges hands, and it's rather embarrassing for all parties involved. No. I think I'll just take you home. I've better things to do than play nursemaid to a spoiled child."

"What? Do you really expect me to believe you'd go through all this just to return me? I may be young, but I'm no fool."

Dante, smiling to himself, offered a challenge. "Really? Let us put that to the test, shall we? Do you know anything about stars?"

"What kind of question is that?"

"A good one. What star do you think that is over there?" Dante extended a finger to the star-littered sky.

"Which one? The sky is full of stars."

"The star that doesn't move. The North Star. Can you find it?"

"Of course I can!" James, indignant, scanned the night sky, then fixed his sights on the star in question. "There," he said, and pointed triumphantly.

"Excellent! You can find a star. That is the true test of a king. I am satisfied. But suppose we take it one step further. If we agree that is north," he pointed, "then in what direction are we traveling?"

James thought for a moment, then answered, "Northwest."

"Very good. And in what direction lies Edinburgh from Blythemuir?"

"Northwest ... My God! Why?" The young king looked at the disreputable Venetian as if he were mad.

"Do you want the simple answer?" Dante asked, and made a show of peering into the young man's serious face. "It's late. You've lain with a she-devil. I'd best give you the simple answer. Because Julius Blythe loves the King of Scotland. Forgive my brutal honesty, but I cannot imagine why."

James, bitter and boiling over with two days of resentment, replied, "If you are going to lie to me, then at least have the courtesy to pretend to know what you're talking about. I was taken in the dead of night, hooded, roughly handled, and thrown into a ... a ..."

"A paradise," Dante, glittering like the pirate he was, finished for him. "A place for a man who values knowledge, who values the wisdom of antiquity, and who yearns to unlock the mysteries of the universe. I know; it's all there. It is a remarkable collection that few men have ever seen. It belongs to Julius Blythe, the man I have sworn my life to. And he placed you there—into a secure and lavish prison—for your own protection. What is more, you had charming company locked in with you ... and nothing but time to enjoy it. Consider it a gift from a man who deserves so much more than this pitiful little country has ever given him."

"What are you saying?" uttered James, and his eyes, so long blinded by what he thought were the irrefutable facts of the past, were beginning to open with the horrible shock of possibility.

"I'm saying that Julius Blythe has never had any intent to cause you harm."

"If that's true," said James, eyeing his captor with a cautious mix of suspicion and speculation, "then I am not really your prisoner. If all you claim is true, then I can leave you, take the woman, and ride back to Edinburgh on my own."

"You could, but I gave my word you wouldn't. There are armed detachments of men scouring the countryside as we speak, with orders to kill you on sight. I've heard you're pretty fair with a sword, but even a madman wouldn't take that kind of chance, especially one who's responsible for a woman like that. I wouldn't, and I'm a dangerous, disreputable bastard. I think it best you ride with us."

"But who would kill—?"

"Ah," interrupted the smooth, lilting voice. "I see you wish to know the long story. Very well, we've got all night." And Dante Continari—outlaw, slave, mercenary, industrious privateer, and second-in-command of the master's men—settling in for the long journey north, began his tale from the beginning—or what he considered to be the beginning—when he had spent his days chained to the rowing bench of a Turkish galley, and found one day that a yellow-haired Scot had been chained next to him.

ॐ

By the time dawn broke, James Stewart, the young King of Scotland, was speechless and pliant as molten glass. He was also fragile. The tale he had heard in the night, a very hard tale to listen to indeed, had humbled him; it had brought him to weep silent tears. Yet it wasn't until the sky opened up, bringing with it a deluge of rain and a band of Kilwylie's men, that the truth of the Venetian's words was driven home. And only when the men descended on them from the surrounding forest, brandishing swords, did James understand the caliber of men Julius Blythe had selected to guard him. Dante, raven black and deceptively cunning, had spotted the ambush before the attackers broke from their cover. He sent two men around to flank them, and when they were in position he launched two well-placed arrows, each hitting its mark in the woods on either side. He meant to flush them out into the open, and it worked. Kilwylie's men fell on them then, and it didn't take a genius to understand that they were aiming for the king. James was given a sword, dagger, and buckler, for no one would deny him the right to defend himself, but he was closely watched. Since a tender age, as was due his princely title, he had been tutored by the very best sword masters in the realm, and he was quite brilliant. He was more than capable of defending himself. But Julius's men were fiends. They appeared to move twice as fast as ordinary men, and they sprang from their horses, arms whipping about like demonic scythes, their movements as fluid and precise as a beautifully choreographed dance. Although they had been outnumbered two to one, it had never really been a fair fight.

Later that same morning they had seen another curiosity. Far in the distance, from their vantage point atop a bald hill, they spied a single man leading a train of saddled warhorses. The man, wearing Kilwylie colors, also appeared to be cradling his right arm.

Marion Boyd was a trouper. She didn't once complain about the rain, or about anything, but instead kept straight-backed and silent. When they did finally stop to take shelter from the worst of the downpour, and to eat, her stoic silence crumbled, and she filled the air with lavish praise for the bravery and prowess of James, King of Scotland, her lover. Twice Dante caught the proud, snapping brown eyes looking at him, and twice he gave a small nod of approval. It was a silent truce; and Julius, had he been with them, would have marveled to see it.

By midday the rain had stopped and something very curious indeed happened. Daniel Cochrane, a man who was taken prisoner along with the master at the battle of Blythe Hall, came racing toward them, riding with seven of his companions. Dante's exquisite jaw momentarily slackened in amazement, and he pulled to a stop and waited.

"Jesus Christ, ye're a slippery black bastard!" remarked Danny as he paused to catch his breath. A grin, surprisingly white, appeared on the gruff, bearded face. "I've new orders for ye, straight from the master's mouth." The two sets of black eyes locked, and Danny, sobering quickly, answered the unutterable question in the young man's eyes. "Aye, he's alive, but just barely. Kilwylie broke into Hume Castle early this morning. The master put on a grand show of it too, but . . ."

"Dear God," uttered Dante as every raging emotion inside him collided with resounding decision. "We ride to Hume! Now!" His spurs were down and ready to bite into the flanks of his exhausted horse. A meaty hand shot out and grabbed the reins as the spurs hit. The horse, abused at both ends, bucked and capered sideways. Dante's eyes, wild and conflagrating with purpose, bore into the architect.

"Easy, lad," soothed Danny, his insides aching for the young man whose remarkable features were pinched in mortal anguish. Oddly, he knew how the poor bastard felt. "Do not go running off without me telling ye the rest of it. Do ye even know where Hume is?"

"No," he breathed. "Christ! Danny, how do I get to Hume?"

"I know how," said James, coming beside him. "Please, let me lead the way."

"Not so fast," said Danny. The stern look in his eyes was not to be disobeyed. "Those are not your orders, Dante. The master was very specific! He said to tell ye that your friend has arrived. And that ye are tae bring your package"— here he motioned with his head to the king—"to Rosslyn. He believes ye will find his sister there. Find Mistress Isabeau and take her to Hume. For the young master desperately needs to speak with his sister."

"Gabriel." Dante uttered the name in a kind of reverential, lunatic daze. His dark eyes came alive then as he digested this news, which, to the amazement of everyone present, seemed to make sense to him. They watched as he repeated the name, this time shouting it to the heavens. "Gabriel's here! God's glorious warrior has arrived! Holy Mother of Christ! And with Isabeau? How in the world . . . ?" He looked askance at Danny.

In answer to this question all the architect could do was shrug and shake his head.

"I guess . . . we go . . . to Rosslyn," Dante finally declared. And then, as if the thought had just occurred to him, he focused his gaze on Danny Cochrane and cried in despair: "Rosslyn? What the hell is Rosslyn? And how the hell do I get there?"

Dante, a stranger in a strange land, was not having an easy day of it. His nerves, after being hopelessly frayed, were now tied in knots, and the familiar, calming buzz of alcohol had long left his body. Yet he was going to need more than strong drink to get him through the next twenty-four hours. For with a sharp pang of guilt, the name Gabriel had hurled him back to their days together on Rhodes. Dante, with a whimsical and childlike sentimentality, now longed for those days—those warm, sunny, languid days. Julius, Gabriel, and he had lived together on Rhodes, carefree, happy, and close as brothers. On Rhodes, Julius and he had glutted themselves on wine, women, and lucrative vice. On Rhodes, they had lived and squabbled like princes. And it was on Rhodes where they had driven the gentle and dulcet Gabriel, time and again, to fits with their bad behavior. They were unrepentant on Rhodes . . . until the day Gabriel had left them. And now, deep in the rain-soaked, windswept hills of Scotland, the unbelievable had happened. Gabriel had returned, and just as on that day three years ago, he had come in their darkest hour. It was more than a miracle. It was witchcraft.

Dante prayed then, as he seldom did, to accept with gentle grace and humility all the chastisement he deserved; for he was repentant. And nothing mattered more to him than the life of Julius Blythe.

It was then that he saw the young king come beside him,

seemingly untouched by fatigue, the noble carriage unwavering, the warmth and intelligence still bright behind the stormy-blue eyes. "Last night," James began, "a disreputable pirate taught me how to look beyond personal prejudices and preconceived notions in order to fully understand a man's actions and the values that govern him. Today I ask that you let a grateful king lead his new friend to the home of one of Scotland's greatest families. I know Rosslyn well. It is the home of Sir Oliver St. Clair, Baron of Rosslyn. Will you, Dante Continari, follow me?"

"I'd be honored to, Your Highness," Dante replied, and bowed his raven-black head.

NO TWO PEOPLE ON THE FACE OF THE EARTH COULD have ridden with more purpose, or have been filled with a more dire need to reach a destination, than we did, racing to the Midlothian home of Gabriel's childhood. As it happened, we were closer than I had thought. The derelict cottage in the woods had been familiar to Gabriel, and it was less than ten miles from the town of Rosslyn. It was a testament to how far Gabriel had traveled with my unconscious form the day Blythe Hall fell to George Douglas. It was also a testament to the remarkable quality of his horse, Bodrum, who was named, I had learned, after an immense and formidable Hospitaller stronghold on the coast of southwest Turkey. The castle had been dedicated to Saint Peter, but not wishing to name a horse after a saint, he named him Bodrum instead. Gabriel talked fondly of his short stay in the English tower at Saint Peter's castle, when his fleet had been moored in Bodrum harbor. And his memories now lived on in Bodrum, the noble gray gelding. It was a bond they shared that I could never be a part of, and yet, somehow, just knowing of it made man and horse all the more dear to me. Gabriel told me many such things on the road to Rosslyn—in fact, we chatted away like magpies, making up for years of lost time, desperately longing to become a living part of each other's memories. It made the miles fly by. We never once touched on the painful subject of Julius.

Tucked away in a wooded glen and surrounded on three sides by a loop in the river Esk stood the high-walled and formidable fortress of Sir Oliver St. Clair, Baron of Rosslyn. It was dusk by the time we arrived. Torches had already been lit along the precipitous stone bridge and towering gatehouse, while the haunting sound of bagpipes floated on the evening air. It was a scene that evoked in me gentle pangs of nostalgia, and it brought to mind my own home in the days when my father was laird.

"Will they remember you, do you think?" I whispered, feeling Gabriel stiffen as Bodrum's iron-shod hoof hit the first stones of the bridge that spanned the deep ravine.

"Oh," he breathed with pallid cheerfulness, "they could hardly forget me. It's you I'm concerned for. The gates of Rosslyn are notorious for abuse, and Sir Oliver encourages it. Unless I have a foaming army behind me, we're likely in for a bit of ribaldry. It's not going to be the grand entrance I had wished for you, my heart. I beg you to bear with me."

It was a curious statement, and one soundly confirmed the moment we stopped before the great arch of the gates. The sky, awash with a burst of red afterglow, cast its last rays on the rosy stone and the three curious faces peering down at us from on high, steel bonnets glowing as if on fire, lips boldly resisting suppressed joy. The yellow flame burning bright on both turrets underlit the prominent features of each guard, as well as allowing them to see our faces. They had indeed recognized the weary traveler begging entrance. Yet a diligent gatekeeper was not allowed to forgo the formalities of his position. "Who goes there?" the man in the middle called down.

"Gabriel St. Clair."

"If ye are the man ye claim to be, ye will give the password, *Sir Gabriel.*"

Gabriel glanced back at me and whispered with a merry twinkle in his eye, "They want the family motto, and an extra bit." And then, turning to the gatekeepers, he called out: "Commit thy work to God, and to man commit no disgrace."

"And have ye, Gabriel, upheld the family motto?"

"To the best of my knowledge, yes."

"Where do ye hail from?"

"I hail from Rosslyn, Davie Dunbar, and most recently from Rhodes."

"If ye lived here," came the canny voice, "then you'll remember your nickname."

"Sweet merciful Jesus," Gabriel uttered. "They mean to thoroughly shame me before you. If you've ever wondered," he said, casting a glance back at me with a grin of mild disparagement, "why it was I never spoke to you as a young man, you're about to learn. Davie Dunbar's a perfect wee tyrant and a gleeful abuser of the little power he's given. Bear with me, love," he said, and turned to face the gatehouse.

"Don't humor them," I whispered sternly, but Gabriel, plunging ahead, replied: "I've been called many things behind these walls, but the name you'll be looking for is Sir William's Golden Bastard." The men, pitiful fools of the worst kind, could no longer hide their mirth.

"*Sir William's Golden Bastard,*" the man named Davie replied. "The name rings a bell. Tell us, what was your business on Rhodes?"

"Cleansing the earth of ingrates like you. I've come home to continue the work." The men, by now, were laughing outright. The sound brought others pressing to join in the sport. One of them pulled out an apple and, like a giddy schoolboy, handed it to Davie. They balanced it on the bulwark of the overhang and called down, "Can ye put an arrow through this apple, *Sir William's Golden Bastard*?"

"If I take the time to string my bow, gentlemen, I'm going to eat that apple and put the arrow through you, Davie Dunbar. I'm growing weary, gentlemen. Open the gates."

"Not so fast," another man called down with the slow and deliberate speech of one wishing to extend cheap and illicit entertainment. This was, from the looks of it, very likely the most amusement the gatehouse had enjoyed in a long while, and it was obvious they were not in any hurry to see it come to an end. I rolled my eyes in exasperation.

Another man, emboldened by the childish bantering, called down, "Who's the lovely little wench?"

"This is no wench." Now Gabriel's tone had lost all trace of humor. His deep, rich voice was commanding and formidable. "This is a lady, and soon to be my wife. You may abuse me, but you will show her the respect she deserves."

"Wife!" I cringed at the response, knowing what was obviously to come next. "Do they let brother monks marry these days? Or have ye relaxed your vows and loosened your hose strings for the sake of a beautiful face?" It was, to these men of little brains, the absolute height of hilarity. To Gabriel, however, having already chastised himself to the point of madness over the matter, it was the greatest insult they could sling. His body froze, and every muscle trembled with rage. If I had learned anything over the past day and a half, it was that Gabriel St. Clair was a very devout, very proud man. And he was my soul. My body filled with anger and I welcomed it.

"Oh, I've had quite enough of this!" I hissed, and before he could stop me I swung down from Bodrum, stalked forward, and threw out a direct challenge, not even bothering to keep the rage out of my voice.

"Do you see me, David Dunbar—and the rest of you shameless buffoons? You call yourselves gatekeepers? Then open your dim-witted eyes and take a good look at me! I am Lady Isabeau Blythe of Blythemuir. Look at my fine velvet gown of sky blue and cream satin, with beadwork so exquisite it once brought Princess Margaret to tears. It cost more than all of your salaries put together—for an entire year. Now, do you see how filthy I am? How ruined this beautiful gown is? Do you wish to know why? I'm going to tell you why! I am covered in soot because my home of Blythe Hall was taken by force less than two days ago! I'm caked in mud and reek of horse sweat because this brave and noble man—*who is to be my husband!*—saved me from a horrible and degrading death! And you sit there in your cozy little roost and have the audacity to *mock him*? You sicken me!

"I'm tired. I've ridden across half the country on the back of a horse, and if you don't open these bloody gates this instant, I'll string the bow and put an arrow through you myself!" I was heaving after this little tirade, and so busy glowering up at the gawking, slack-jawed men that I failed to see that the gates were already open. Gabriel came beside me, leading Bodrum by the reins. He took my hand and gently pulled me forward.

"Lord Almighty," he said, his magnificent blue eyes sparkling with pride and approbation, "now, *that's* the way to open a gate!"

঩

Sir Oliver St. Clair came barreling toward us from across the courtyard with a harried torchbearer running before him and a servant with an armload of bagpipes bringing up the rear. If anyone were to ever doubt Gabriel's parentage, they only need take a good look at his half-brother. The Baron of Rosslyn was not as tall, or as broad, or even close to Gabriel's prime physical condition, but no one could deny that a voice from a common ancestor echoed in their veins. It was in the way they walked, the noble tilt of the head, the purpose and decisiveness that drove every movement. It was in the vibrant blue gaze bursting with intelligence, the fair coloring, and the sturdy frame that carried heavy muscle with ease. Like my family, the St. Clairs were descended from Norman ancestry. Yet whereas Sir Oliver was thoroughly Scottish, with a florid face molded by generations of hearty, beef-eating, oat-growing whisky drinkers, Gabriel's face was somehow less domesticated. His Scandinavian ancestry was pronounced through higher cheekbones, deeper-set eyes, a gentler nose, and a certain rugged, sun-bleached, windswept air that tended to conjure the image of a ferocious race of men who once spent a good deal of time raiding foreign coasts. Of course, to be equitable, the baron was at least twenty years Gabriel's senior, with a full gray-speckled beard and a sizable paunch.

"Gabriel, m' boy!" he cried, nearly upon us. "My God, is it true? Ye are home from Rhodes? Come, lad, let me take a keek at you!" Without waiting for an invitation, the baron threw his meaty arms around Gabriel, thumping his broad back with astonishing zeal. He stepped back, and Sir Oliver's ginger-gray beard split with blinding joy. "By God, if ye don't look like a mythical Norse god come down to smite my crops with a thunderbolt! We've heard all the stories from Rhodes! Brilliant! I want to hear more—from your own lips this time! Ye made quite a name for yourself, laddie."

Gabriel was beaming, accepting the greeting with all the warmth and mild embarrassment it deserved. Watching them, I thought it interesting that although society didn't recognize these two men as legitimate brothers, at least they themselves had some understanding of the mighty and whimsically branched tree from which they had sprung. Their fondness was as genuine as it was touching. Gabriel, in turn, was full of kind words for the older man, and even complimented the piping, stating that it had improved a great deal since the days he lived at the castle.

"Och! I've had more time tae practice now that the wife's

gone—not dead," he was quick to clarify, "just in Stirling. The piping drove her there!" He laughed knowingly, and added: "God! I've never felt sae free! 'Tis like confession and a mother-naked dip in the sea—rejuvenating mind, body, and spirit at once. Too bad she's only visiting her sister." And then, slowly, as the laughter died away, the two sets of matching blue eyes settled on me: one quizzical, the other apologetic.

I smiled at Sir Oliver, for he had been a friend of my father's. "Perhaps if Lady St. Clair was home, your gatekeepers would be kinder. It's very good to see you, Sir Oliver."

"They're heathens, the lot of them," he said in an off-handed way, adding airily: "Their drink will be stopped for a month. Dear heavens!" he uttered softly. His manner had completely changed from the jubilant host of just moments before to what appeared almost reverent. It made me slightly uneasy. "Isabeau Blythe, my beautiful child. Have ye come here at last? But how . . . ?" He looked at Gabriel, then back at me, his sharp eyes missing little. His wiry cinnamon brows furrowed. Pensive thought took him; and finally, like a young horse given its head, understanding leapt unhindered behind his luminous gaze.

"Oh my dears, is it like that? Oh, indeed! Indeed! Ye are blushing! Well, I cannae say I'm surprised. Wilder things have happened. Come, come inside," he beckoned, and ushered us toward the grand building he had just come from. "We'll get ye cleaned up. They tell me, my dear, ye're in desperate want of a bath. Well, ye shall get one. And a clean gown as well. I'll take good care of ye both, and then ye'll hurry back down for a wee bit of supper and a chat. I've so much ta tell ye."

෨෬

Sir Oliver was as good as his word. After a much needed bath and a change of clothes, I returned to the hall feeling alive, refreshed, and ready to face all that had been laid before me. I was also excited to see Gabriel, looking for once like the well-born lady I was. The gown I was given was one of Lady St. Clair's. It was of excellent quality and cut, and a lovely shade of pale yellow. The fit wasn't perfect, but it was good enough, and I floated down the turnpike stairs like a fairy-tale princess, walking on the light and airy breeze of radiant love. Yet when I arrived at the hall I pulled up, wishing to savor the quiet, familial setting that greeted me.

Gabriel and Sir Oliver were sitting at a small table near the hearth talking softly. The table had been richly set, and the light of twelve candles reflected off Gabriel's golden hair, recently tamed and smartly combed. Gone was the simple, practical dress of the Hospitaller, and in its place was a fine doublet of rich blue velvet over crisp white linen. Gabriel looked positively resplendent, and the feeling that had swept me down the stairs grew to a level near bursting. I was overwhelmed, and could have stood for hours watching them both, for they appeared so much like father and son that it brought a lump to my throat.

I thought of my own father then, and of Julius. I thought of all the disappointment between them—of their final reconciliation; of the disappearance of the one followed so swiftly by the disgrace of the other. I had just learned that my father was possibly still alive. I had also learned that Julius was not guilty of the crimes he was convicted of. And I wondered if they would ever have a meeting like the one before me—two men, from two different generations, with the bond of common blood, slowly, patiently filling the gap of all the missing years. It would be a great pity if they never got the chance, and the reality, I knew, was not hopeful. I felt remorse so acutely then that my eyes began filling with tears. That was when Gabriel turned and saw me.

I was not the only one affected by the transformation in the Great Hall. Gabriel's eyes traveled the length of my body, coming to rest on my eyes. In his I saw a curious mix of awe, tenderness, and an aching question. The question was for the tears that he detected, and I was quick to smile and wipe them away as best I could with my fingertips. He stood then, and, filling with the heady rush of love, I went to join them.

As we sat at the table enjoying our private meal, I saw that Gabriel had done a good job apprising Sir Oliver of our situation. The older man took the news with the characteristic shrewdness of the family, and, thinking quite hard, he answered at last. "I see. You'll be wanting to go to Hume then. William Blythe, were he here, would want his son to stand a fair trial, and we shall see that the lad gets one. Take heart, Isabeau," he said, his gaze softening a measure. "We shall see justice restored, and your lands properly returned. Young Georgie Douglas! I would ha' never guessed that one in a million years. I suppose ye'll be refuting the marriage contract? Oh yes, I heard a rumor about that too. Well, ye cannot marry the man now, especially under the"—he paused to clear his throat—"*circumstances.*" An openly accusatory stare then settled on Gabriel. "And," he continued without altering his gaze, "if it comes to it, I'll give testimony to the condition of the young lady's arrival here, and of the compromised state I found her in."

"Ex . . . excuse me?" I interrupted. The heat of embarrassment filled my cheeks, and I looked at Gabriel. Although thoroughly abashed, he had a twinkle in his eye. I understood then. Sir Oliver, acutely sensitive to the nature of his younger brother's predicament, was simply making assumptions on the young man's behalf, and to his credit, they were quite correct. "Oh?" I said, unable to suppress a grin, "Well, thank you."

"And are you, Isabeau, prepared to receive censure for the ordeal?"

"If you mean, sir, am I prepared to undergo scrutiny in order to marry Gabriel, then the answer is most definitely yes. I take it he has your blessing?"

"Blessing!" He released a peal of warm laughter. "Why, the lad's got my deepest admiration. To marry the lovely Isabeau Blythe! Many a good man has applied for that position. Quite a day's work for a man bound by the oath of a religious order! And," he continued, pointing a sausagelike finger at the younger man, "that reminds me. Ye'll need to reconcile with the order immediately upon your return. Until then, I shall put Lady Isabeau under my diligent protection. Nothing amiss will take place under my roof, laddie."

We were both smiling like moonstruck idiots, so happy were we with Sir Oliver's bold planning, until I remarked, "Return?"

"Aye. From Hume. I'll send word round immediately and have the men ready tonight. Tomorrow, Gabriel, at first light, ye shall ride to Hume Castle to present your information, and ye shall do me the honor of riding under the banner of St. Clair." Gabriel, setting down his wineglass, looked at the other man. It was a moving gesture, and one cleverly meant to elevate him beyond the obstacle of his humble birth. I smiled fondly on Sir Oliver then, filling with admiration and profound gratefulness; Gabriel, like me, was too moved to speak.

"Why, you've led great fleets against the Turks, lad; surely ye can lead a few men on a mission of mercy. Off ye go, Gabriel. You've a big day tomorrow. Find Tommy Hunter and tell him what ye'll be needing, then get ye some rest, as I've my doubts ye've had any since rescuing the lovely Mistress Blythe here. And now my dear young lady," he said, turning his full, glittering attention on me. "I've something very important to discuss with ye. If you're finished with your meal, I'd like ye to come with me."

While Gabriel went off to prepare an army for the ride to Hume, I followed Sir Oliver to a large room on the second floor. It was well known that the St. Clairs, as a family, had a passion for books, and that tradition was strongly upheld and supported by Sir Oliver. The Baron of Rosslyn had an immense library in the castle, and it was to this magnificent room that I was brought. I stood in the middle of the vaulted chamber, dumbfounded by the vast collection of books and manuscripts that surrounded me. The room itself was a long rectangle, with nearly every inch, except for those places already dedicated to tall windows or hearth, filled with the written treasures gathered by generations of St. Clairs. This was a haven for those truly passionate about books, from the thickly upholstered chairs clustered near every favorable light source to the luxuriant Turkish carpet intricately woven in the bold hues so pleasing to men. I thought we were to sit near the fire, the coziest setting for an intimate talk. But I was wrong. Sir Oliver, with a gentle but urgent smile, led me across the room to another door. Without preamble we entered and I found myself, wide-eyed and breathless, nestled in a small scriptorium.

To a man like Sir Oliver, wanting to fill his library, such a room made sense. For such a deeply devout family, and with close access to the remarkable collegiate church on the hill built by Sir William (Gabriel and Oliver's father), known as Rosslyn Chapel, access to talented scribes was not an issue. I had never been inside the chapel, but I had heard it was an almost overwhelming feast for the eyes. This room was little different. Every corner—from the angled writing desks below the tall windows to the chaotic display of ink bottles, quills, and sheaves of parchment—was dedicated to the art of copying manuscripts. There were no scholars furiously copying away by candlelight now, only a quiet, dimly lit room dripping with the promise of a vast and untold knowledge. I knew, standing on the cold floor, that I was about to be enlightened.

With rapt fascination I watched Sir Oliver wander to what appeared to be an antique chest of fine quality. I saw that he held a key, and after a moment of fumbling to unlock it with trembling hands, the lid came free. There was great reverence in his movements as he gently opened the chest. He was a man raised on respect for the written word, and whatever was kept in the box under lock and key seemed to be charged with unusual importance. With both hands he reached in and brought forth his treasure with all the tenderness of a parent presenting a newborn child to a rapt congregation. I was the congregation, and the child was but a sleek, black, velvet sack. This, however, was removed with great care, revealing the true gift inside.

The moment my eyes registered what he held, I understood the care and reverence, for the locked chest had contained a very ancient-looking and quite fragile scroll. Sir Oliver held it under the light for me to see, and answering the question in my eyes, he replied softly, "This, my dear, belongs to your father. He brought it to me five years ago, shortly before his disappearance, asking that I take a look at it. It is a remarkable work, Isabeau," he said softly, his blue eyes grave and tinged with sorrow. "And one that I'm afraid has been responsible for all the heartache and strife that has befallen ye these many years. I am deeply sorry, my dear."

"What?" I uttered helplessly as he placed the scroll in my reluctant hands. And then, as soon as the yellow parchment touched my skin, I felt it, sudden and intense as a bolt of lightning. A blinding light exploded in my head; I saw the white lady; the scent of roses surrounded me, and the anguished voice of my father crying her name echoed through every fiber of my body. It was a vision, a loud, painful vision. A small cry escaped my lips, and I stumbled backward as my legs gave out beneath me. Sir Oliver, horror-struck, broke my fall.

"Come," he breathed, pulling me into his arms. He left the scroll on the floor and led me into the library. The florid face above the beard was now white and pinched with fear. "Sit, my dear. Devil take me, but I'm an old fool! Ye've had a day of it, a weary long day of it, and I've startled ye further. But ye need to sit and listen to me, Isabeau Blythe, because your father instructed me to tell ye all I know."

๕๖

Restored with a glass of wine, and with the scroll returned to its casing and gently placed at my feet, Sir Oliver—sitting across from me with a glass in his hand—began to enlighten me about my father, the scroll, and a man's errant quest to understand what no man was ever meant to understand.

"I'm certain ye dinnae need me, an old fool, telling ye how desperately your father believed that your mother was an angel. Your father was a boon companion of mine since we were chiels, and we were taught in those days, as wee bairns by our mothers no less, that angels guided us, that they watched over us, and that if we devoted enough sweat and toil in the name of God, they will carry us when our last breath has left our bodies, up to heaven. Many lovely people display angelic qualities, Isabeau. Your mother was one of them. No one who knew her would dispute it. But what your father believed was different. Dear William could never be called a devout man. Truth be told, I see a good deal of your father in Julius. A wild, impetuous spirit he was, with a quick smile and an even quicker sword. He was, at best, a God-fearing warrior who worshipped nothing as devoutly as his own freedom. Dinnae get me wrong," he cautioned, watching the amber liquid gently swirl in his glass. "He was a good man, but not the sort tae go bounding off in sandals with a hair shirt under his robes to see the holy sites of Jerusalem." He smiled at the thought. "And he was not the sort to be bound by the strict moral ties of marriage. He was, like many a young man, cavalier about marriage, and the marriage between your mother and father was a contractual one, drawn up when they were both wee bairns. Angelica, your mother, was the daughter of a wealthy French nobleman from Nantes, with strong Scottish ties on her mother's side. That was about all we knew of her.

"The day of the wedding was the first time your father laid eyes on your mother. He was, shall we say, very pleasantly surprised. One seldom knows in the practical bargain of marriage who'll be bearing his children, or what fine qualities she might have. Well, your mother was too fine for him. And William, to be fair, at least had the brains tae know it. From what I recall it was not a peaceful marriage from the start. Your father didn't quite know what to make of a woman of that caliber and spent a good deal of time away from Blythe Hall in the service of his king. But the king soon sent him home to handle matters on the border—and, partly, to make him face his own domestic struggles.

"By that year's end William was a changed man. And if he worshipped anything in his life, it was the very ground Angelica walked on. I had never seen him so happy. He was also humbled. And he was a very good husband to her. It was quite understandable, then, that when she died suddenly and tragically he was devastated. He never fully accepted it, but he got on. And then, during the year of Albany's rebellion, when the Borders were particularly lawless and he had more than his share of ingrates wanting a piece of Blythe Hall, something odd occurred. He never said what, but that was around the time he came to me with a wild tale. He told me then about the miracle he had witnessed at the very moment of Angelica's death. I had never heard it before. He never told me—not until that day. And I was positively stunned to learn that William Blythe believed his wife truly was an angel—a real angel, not a figurative one. It was this one fervent belief that drove his obsession.

"That was the day William found God. He then began creating his glorious shrine to angels. And then, one day, your father arrived on my doorstep bearing this. He asked very politely whether I could take a look at it. It was one of the treasures found on one of his many journeys. Seeing it, and knowing what a glutton I am for old text, I bade him to come inside.

"What little I have been able to make of this has never left me. This is very old, Isabeau. There are writings here that far predate the time of Christ, and contain a name attributed to one of the seven patriarchs of the Old Testament. If that is true, this is, of course, apocryphal—purposely not included in the biblical canon. We also believe this is the only surviving document of its kind. It is a copy. The original was very likely written in Hebrew and was ordered destroyed. This one has passages written in that language, as well as Aramaic and Greek. All of which I know very little about. I can only read the Latin. And there's another writing, a writing so ancient in origin that it simply appears unworldly. It may not even be written by a human hand. We tried as best we could to decipher it using all our resources here, we two sorry old warriors and a handful of monks, but what we really needed was a scholar who understands these things.

"We learned that such a man might have been in London in '87, and I had a small amount of the work translated so that your father and brother could bring it with them when they went to visit the gentleman. The original was to be kept at Blythe Hall. Your father had a magnificent altarpiece made complete with a secret chamber to house it. He wanted it in his chapel, but knew it was too fragile and too important to be on display. I promised I'd take it there myself. I was going to do that very thing when I received a message from him asking that I keep the original here, safely hidden, until his return. If he never returned, I was to give it into the care of his children, presumably Julius when he was to assume the full lands and titles of Blythe Hall. His forfeiture and exile complicated matters. But I never forgot my promise. I was going to give this to ye on the day ye become the Lady of Blythe Hall. And, my dear, I believe that day is upon us.

"I will tell ye the little I know of this. The one name we do know, and who claims authorship of these works is Enoch— Enoch, the seventh-named patriarch in the book of Genesis, Enoch, the father of Methuselah and the great-grandfather of Noah of the Great Flood: Enoch whom the Bible mentions but briefly yet tells us that he was highly favored in the eyes of God, and that he lived only three hundred and sixty-five years, which," he added for my benefit, "sounds like a modern-day feat but is uncommonly short in biblical times, before he was spared death and taken up to God directly, presumably by the angels. We believe this manuscript is a longer, more detailed account of a small and inconsequential incident mentioned briefly in Genesis. There is a good reason why this work, if it is what it claims to be, never made it into the Bible. There is a reason why it should be hidden from the eyes of man. It is likely as heretical as it is unbelievable. And we believe, Isabeau, that this is a firsthand account of the time when a group of angels known as the watchers came to earth and assumed human form. We believe it speaks in great detail of the race of fair-haired, blue-eyed men known as the Nephilim. For the Nephilim, Isabeau, are the blessed and cursed children of a mixed race; the Nephilim are the children these fallen angels sired through the beautiful human women who lured them from heaven—"

"I know the story," I whispered, my heart beating as if it would escape my chest.

He looked at me, his eyes sharpening with keen interest. "How do you know it?"

"Madame Seraphina, my governess, used to tell me of it when I was a child. It was my favorite story," I added as tears began to well up in my eyes.

"Seraphina was your mother's lady, was she not?" I nodded, and his bushy brows lowered in speculation. "That is a very odd story indeed to tell a child. How much of it do you know?"

"It's just a story," I breathed, and felt the hot tears begin to roll down my cheeks.

"But what if it's not, Isabeau?" His voice was gentle; there was no ill intent behind his grave eyes, and yet somehow his words struck deeply and painfully. "What if," he continued, "there is some truth to all of this? Your father never returned from England because he went searching for answers. Could it be that the answers he was searching for were in front of him the whole time? What do you know of the fall of angels, Isabeau? What do you know of the Nephilim?"

"I don't believe in any of them. I don't believe that such things exist."

"But you do," he said softly. "Of course you do. You nearly passed out when you held this scroll in your hands. Why? Tell me, child. What did you see? What on earth did you see?"

There was no point in lying. Sir Oliver had been placed in my father's confidence for a reason, and the least I could do was respect that. I wiped the tears from my eyes and replied, "I smelled her. I saw her. I heard my father calling her name."

"Who? Who is the woman you see?"

I paused; my breathing was unsteady, and then I answered, "My mother." I watched as he silently digested this, looking at me very oddly. It prompted me to ask: "Why did I see her? What does it mean, Sir Oliver?"

"I don't know, child. Heaven help me, I don't know. But I do know one thing, my dear: you never met your mother."

That was when chaos entered, bold and unrepentant, shattering the still air of the library with a cacophony to rival the Last Trump. The shock of Sir Oliver's conversation, still ringing in my ears, running circles in my mind, faded as the clamor from the courtyard below pulled us to the window. I feared the worst. I feared Kilwylie had tracked us to Rosslyn. My heart sank as I saw the dark riders filling the yard below, marveling at how they had gotten through the notorious gates. Gabriel came bounding into the library then, his face flushed and alight with the press of urgent news.

"Mother of God!" he cried, looking at me. "You'll never believe it. The king has arrived!"

❧

No shock could have been greater or met with more excitement. Rosslyn Castle burst to life as the news traveled to the servants' quarters, rousing everyone—from kitchen lad to chambermaid—any and all who had entertained thoughts of retiring for the night. The king had come, and with him, guarding him, was a retinue of twenty-three of the most disreputable scoundrels ever to be seen with a man of noble blood. Gabriel and I followed on the heels of Sir Oliver as he headed to the hall, calling out orders as he went.

We arrived as James entered from the courtyard, coming first into the hall at the head of his rough men, and with Marion on his arm. It was a wonder anyone had recognized him for the king. Both Marion and James were dressed commonly and covered from head to toe with mud. They must have been exhausted, for their arrival, like ours, appeared to be one of great haste, and yet raw excitement, like fine mist, emanated from their every movement. At this first sight of them, relief and joy swept through me, and I left Gabriel's side running to greet them. Marion saw me first; her face was a mirror of my own. She let go of James and met me, arms out and tears streaming.

"I've been so frightened for you," I said, holding her tightly. "I've prayed for your safety. Was Julius very horrible to you?"

"Positively abominable," she whispered softly, and for once I believed she meant it. "You were correct. He's a cold, soulless creature. He's twisted, and perverse, and has no love for anything or anybody."

"I'm so sorry." I held her, comforting her as best I could

because I knew her heart had been broken. Her illusion of Julius had finally been shattered, and from all appearances, my brother hadn't been gentle. Marion had championed him when I had maligned his character, and now, because of Gabriel, our roles had been reversed. Julius was twisted and perverse—life had made him that way. But he did know love, just not the kind of love Marion would ever understand. "I'm so sorry he hurt you. Was he very cruel to James?"

She pulled back, a brave and exquisite haughtiness overtaking her trembling lips. "Oh, I'm not hurt. I'm relieved. And to my knowledge, Julius never talked with James. He communicated through Dante, one of his barmy wee idiots." She turned and pointed to the Venetian who had just crossed the threshold. Like Gabriel, he was a man who stood out in a room, a man who demanded the eye, and I watched as his handsome dark face scanned the hall, looking for his target. His raven head stilled, his gaze sharpened, and then his eyes settled on the refulgent head of Gabriel.

Marion was still talking. "Then they took his signet ring and locked us both in some underground room where no one would ever find us. And they left us there . . ." She paused, noting that my attention had wandered. I was looking at Gabriel, at his reaction at having spied Julius's friend. Dante was the poor man he'd told me about, the one who had shared Julius's horror. He was the man Julius had saved. Unconsciously, my throat had tightened at the sight of him, and I filled with a tenderness I never thought I could feel for such a man. This feeling was carried over to Gabriel, and as my eyes held the man I loved, my heart began pounding away, fearful of the emotions this first meeting must bring.

"Isabeau?" Marion had been watching me intently. She then saw the man who held my full attention. "Oh?" she said, her inflection rising and falling on a wave of curiosity. "Truly, I've no idea what's happening, or how it is you are here, but I do know one thing, my dear friend. I know that look."

I drew my gaze back to Marion, back to the dark eyes shining with uncommon brightness. Her lips curled into a libidinous smile. "My, he is spectacular. And possibly, nearly good enough for you. Wherever have you been hiding him?" I blushed. Her smile grew bolder, and she held me in her all-knowing gaze. Only Marion Boyd could know what I felt.

"He is Gabriel St. Clair," I replied softly, smiling as the name rolled off my lips. "He is the man I'm going to marry. I shall tell you all about it later, I promise. So much has happened since we've been parted. But for now it will suffice to say that the only reason I'm here at all is because of him."

Sir Oliver had engulfed James in a flurry of obsequious welcome and was fawning over the young man like a nursemaid. James, raised with the grace of a king and taught to be charmingly polite, received the attention with aplomb. Yet that didn't stop him from casting toward me a look that silently pleaded for rescue. "Go to your Gabriel," Marion ordered, frowning at my anxiousness. "I hardly think a man like that needs protection; then again, that dark-eyed heathen of your brother's has a way of getting under the skin. Sir Oliver!" she called out, waving. With a sly grin, and a look in her eye that evoked images of a spry cat toying with a sluggish mouse newly emerged from the grain shed, she left me.

Dante, approaching Gabriel from the other side, preceded me by a few paces. Having sighted his target, he did not allow his focus to waver . . . until, out of the corner of his eye, he spied me. His crisp stride faltered, his piercing black eyes looked away, and then he stopped altogether, standing a man's length from Gabriel.

Silence fell as all eyes held the two men in the center of the room. Each took in the measure of the other: prideful black challenging serene blue. There was the space of a dozen heartbeats, and then the stalemate broke with two wide, genuine grins.

"Dante, my dear child of mischief, come here," Gabriel demanded in his deep, rich baritone. In two strides Dante had been gathered in a bearlike embrace. "Lord help me," Gabriel said, stepping back to look at his old friend. "I never thought I'd utter these words, but I've missed you. Peace, I have learned, is as elusive as it is highly overrated. I see you're still a prodigy of nuisance making and thrive on harrying the souls of men."

"It's a hard drink to give up, my friend. And you, Brother Gabriel, you look well, and happy, and . . . I think the word might be . . . glowing?" The smile that illuminated Dante's handsome face was gently mocking, but only gently, because when it fell on me it changed into a radiant twinkle of accusation. The look was hauntingly reminiscent of Julius. "Peace is a noble pursuit, brother," he said, bringing his eyes back to his friend, "but I believe it will escape you yet. My advice: embrace what is placed in the path before you. I would. There is much joy to be found in mischief."

"Indeed. I've been soundly convinced of it," said the Hospitaller, and took my hand, pulling me beside him. "Now, tell me, how are you here with the king? I figured you were protecting him—"

"He was," said James, stepping forward. "How did you know? I only just learned of it myself, today." I saw a curious look pass between James and his captor. "And you, Sir Gabriel, I see you have protected something very dear to me as well." James looked to me then, and beheld me with the tenderness of a friend. "Thank you. And welcome home. Now, gentlemen, would someone mind telling me what is going on?"

It was Dante, surrounded by a throng of Julius's men, who levelly declared: "We are all here, as Fate has planned, to save the soul of Julius Blythe."

That was when all the details came pouring out, and all our various journeys somehow coalesced to shed light on the plight of one very clever man. Julius had come to Scotland to finally clear his name. He had been falsely accused; everyone present was now in agreement on that. He had chosen to resurface on the day I took possession of Blythe Hall. He knew, somehow, that George Douglas would come for me and stake his own claim. And he had gambled everything—his life, his freedom—on the arrival of one man: Gabriel St. Clair. He believed Gabriel had the evidence needed to clear him of all charges. That's why he had surrendered to Lord Hume when he saw Gabriel on the battlements of Blythe Hall. He had ordered the king to be safely brought back to Edinburgh. And then he had been shot in the back by George Douglas.

We then learned how, at the hour of dawn, Lord Kilwylie, let into Hume Castle, had made his way to the dungeons to finish what he had started, unbeknownst to Lord Hume until it was too late. The details of the attack were very hard for me to hear. But I needed to hear them. I needed to understand and feel the urgency of his call. Julius knew Gabriel would take me to Rosslyn, his home. He had made this our rallying point. And now we were all here, his men, the king, and Gabriel. We were all convinced of his innocence, and touched by his forethought; and now he lay in a bed nearly forty miles away, dying.

And he had asked for me.

"We need to leave now!" I said, fear and helplessness tearing me apart from the inside. I cried out in frustration and started for the door.

Marion, learning many of the details about Julius for the first time, was beside me, holding me back, attempting to make me see reason. "We've all just arrived, dear. These men need rest. And you? Look at you! You'll not survive the trip. For heaven's sake, think of Julius!"

"I am thinking of Julius!" I cried. "I've been horrible to him! I tried to kill him! Dear God, if he dies before I can apologize . . . " I gave a little helpless scream and looked to Gabriel for support.

"I was leaving at first light with Sir Oliver's men," he said, holding me in his serene and understanding gaze. "You know you have command of life over me, Isabeau; I would ride now if you ask it—but love, be reasonable. You've been dragged across this country for two days now. Marion's right. Could we not wait a few hours, my heart?"

"I'll go!" said James, much to the chagrin of everyone there.

"God no!" It was Dante, spinning on his former prisoner with respectful violence. "Bloody hell you will! I've risked my hide to get you this far. You're not going back. Scotland, I'm told, needs a king. And if it doesn't have one, Julius Blythe will eat my liver. You and Mistress Boyd are staying here, with Sir Oliver. I'll hear no argument. You're going back to Edinburgh, sire, because if Julius survives his ordeal, he'll be brought to trial. And he'll need you then." The king, naturally, chafed at this, but everyone else, especially Marion, was in full agreement.

"You all need rest!" piped Sir Oliver, acting the parent to all us unruly children. "If the lad's held on this long, he'll hold for another day or two. I forbid anyone to leave until first light! You need fresh horses. You need food, and for God's sake, you'll need clear heads if you're to face Lord Hume and that devil Kilwylie. Go to sleep, all of you, and I'll see to the rest. Now, before you get to your beds, my dears, let us all bend a knee and say a wee prayer for the soul of Julius Blythe."

Chapter 22

DEATH OF
AN ANGEL

UNDER A RICH INDIGO SKY, WHERE THE LAST GLITTER-
ing stars were fading slowly into warmer shades of blue, the
banner of St. Clair fluttered like a sprung sail at the head of
sixty men—and one resolute woman. It was the first of May.
The air, heavy with the smell of verdant life, was cool and
damp, and it came at our faces borne on a steady, cavorting
wind determined to hinder us. But nothing would stop me
from reaching Hume Castle, neither chafing air nor my thoroughly protesting body. A body was simply a body, I kept
telling myself, and my will was stronger. Of course, to say I
was saddle-sore from the onset would have been an under-
statement, yet it was nothing a little ingenious padding
couldn't fix. It also didn't hurt that Gabriel and the men
recently under Julius's command—the very men who had
stormed my home, stolen my silver, and taken my sheep—had
seen to it that I rode on a cloud of kindness and gentle encouragement. Like the thick down pillow beneath my seat,

their words cushioned each jarring step and made the long ride bearable. All along the dusty roads and over the windswept trails of the high moors, I was slowly introduced to these odd men, and they, in turn, were compelled to tell me an anecdote about the brother who had been a total stranger to me these four years. They kept the stories light and entertaining. They spoke of silly things, like high-stakes card games nearly lost and then miraculously won, or times when Julius had gotten them into such bad trouble that the only way out was a midnight dash across the rooftops of some exotic city. They told me of the strange countries they'd visited, and some fabulous tales of the sea. The word *pirate* was never spoken aloud, but I did get the feeling they had made quite a lot of money off the mistakes of other people—and, in turn, had lost nearly as much in foolish ways. They sometimes fought other people's wars for money. They even, at times, engaged in honest trade. Their lives under Julius had been anything but idle, and I understood their need to talk about him, just as I knew I needed to listen, for to these men Julius was more than a brother. He was loved, and revered, and something quite special.

Gabriel had been beside me the whole time listening, amazed, bewildered, smiling in a knowing way at the other men's memories. And then, slowly, cautiously, like a wild horse coming to the fence, Dante came beside us, Dante of the penetrating black eyes and haunting white smile. He had kept to the rear all morning, riding alone, a captive of his own private thoughts. He was a special case, vastly different from the rest of the men, and the very opposite of Gabriel. In fact, one would have been hard-pressed to find two men more at odds in looks, demeanor, and nature than Gabriel and Dante. Aside from the obvious contrast of fair, Scandinavian brawn versus the dark, lithe Mediterranean athleticism, Gabriel was open and honest, and possessed a soul that yearned for the highest ideals of humanity. Dante was guarded and enigmatic, and appeared perfectly content to wallow in libidinous living and vice. Julius belonged to both these men; he was the bridge that connected them. I understood the appeal of Gabriel very well. He had been a childhood friend, and my own heart had been his even before we met. I loved Gabriel; he was a good, dependable, honest man.

But Dante? Dante and Julius had been bound by something terrible and desperate. Gabriel knew what it was; he had hinted of it to me, but he was not comfortable with the details. I didn't need them. I saw beneath the disarming mask; I saw the subtle vulnerability buried deep within the proud black eyes. Gabriel had once loved Julius, but he didn't need him. Dante needed him. Like a drug too long abused, he needed him. And I knew, out of all the men riding to Hume, only two souls felt the pain created by the growing emptiness that burned deep within the heart.

"Dante," said Gabriel in a familiar way. There was a wan smile on his lips that softened the concern in his eyes. "Forgive me for asking, but when was the last time you slept?"

This elicited a small, sardonic curl of the lips. "Do you know? I almost missed your concern. He is like a mother hen this one," he added, looking at me. "He will not rest until all his chicks are safely home, tucked in their downy nests, with warm milk in their bellies."

"I like order," Gabriel was quick to reply. "And you look like you could use a little warm milk just now."

"I could use a lot of things just now, my friend, but warm milk is not one of them." The look he gave Gabriel was full of suggestion. "However, if it eases your mind, I will sleep once I know Julius is safe. You may tuck me in if you like."

"Me too," I added, then clarified, "I mean, I'll sleep once I know my brother is safe." This drew the gaze of both men — Gabriel's gentle blue concern and Dante's dark, twinkling eye. But for the few words flung in the courtyard at Blythe Hall, I hadn't spoken directly to this man. We had kept apart, purposely avoiding each other but for looks and casual innuendoes. It occurred to me that he likely knew as much about me as I knew of him—events, but no specific details. I was, after all, Julius's sister; I shared his childhood. Dante had shared his exile. Julius had come to Scotland to reconcile the two, which left the door wide open to us for speculation and caution. Ignoring his smug delight in Gabriel's fallen status—for that's what his brow was insinuating—I began, "I know we haven't exactly gotten off on the right foot—I mean, what man comes home and robs his own family? But he always was a difficult brother. It doesn't mean I don't love him though."

All childish humor and prideful banter left the handsome, worry-worn face, and he looked at me as I had never before seen him do. "We were very drunk," he offered prosaically.

"Is that an apology?" I asked.

"No." He shook his head without removing his heavy gaze.

"Let me guess. That was not the first time you two were spectacularly drunk."

Dante, still with an achingly serious expression, looked beyond me to Gabriel. "How much have you told her?"

"Just enough. No more . . . but enough." The dark-haired man, absorbing this, gently nodded. I could see how tired he was; I could see how hard he tried to make himself appear invincible. Like Julius, Dante was a fine actor, and my heart broke because of it. There was no need to be cruel or hard on him. I realized then that we were, and had always been, on the same side.

"If it's any comfort to you at all," I said, "I'd like to thank you, Dante—not for stealing my silver or shearing my sheep. Not for being drunk and rude and abusing my shepherds. And certainly not for scaring the king and tormenting Marion—yes, she told me. I am not thanking you for any of the minor abuses we've suffered because of you. But what I am thanking you for is being with Julius—for being his friend.

I've missed him. He may never know how sorry I am for all the mistakes of the past. But God gave him you, and you've been a good friend."

There was a long, silent pause before he spoke. "He talked of you. Often."

The way he spoke, the way he said it, broke my resolve, and my eyes began to sting with the threat of tears. I couldn't speak. My chin started trembling.

"Please," he quietly pleaded. "Don't cry. I don't think I can bear it if you cry."

"I'm sorry," I replied, trying desperately not to cry, but my eyes were being uncooperative.

"I grew up in a house full of women," he said, attempting to make light of it. "One would think I'd be used to tears." Still distraught, he reached under his dark riding coat and pulled out a very fine yet much wrinkled handkerchief. He held it out to me.

I took it and, marveling, asked, "You had a lot of sisters?" The thought was oddly endearing. The handkerchief, I noted, was embroidered with tiny flowers and smelled of exotic perfume. Not quite the gift of a sister, but perhaps things were different in Venice.

"No. I've never had a sister." There was mild relief on his face, and yet his voice was unmistakably wistful. He then added, "I had a lot of aunties though."

I saw the mild look of disgust on Gabriel's face and couldn't help smiling. "I think that must have been very nice." I dried a few more tears and held out the handkerchief.

"No. Please, keep it. I've many of them."

"Thank you. I don't usually cry this much," I offered truthfully. "In fact, I don't usually cry much at all. I've been so tired. It wears the will down. And I know you must be tired as well, Dante. I'd give you the pillow beneath my seat if I wasn't so afraid of collapsing into a ball of pain."

He let out a small burst of genuine laughter. He had a nice, rich laugh. "I understand. I'm more of a mariner myself. Venetians, as a rule, don't take well to land animals. And I'd take that pillow from you if I wasn't so afraid of the man on your other side. He has fists like a joiner's mallet," he added conspiratorially.

"And you would have reason to know. By the way," said Gabriel, his intelligent eyes absorbing everything as his face settled into a look of ease. It was the first time I had seen him relax in Dante's company. "I never asked, but how did Julius know I'd be coming home to Scotland when I hardly even knew it myself?"

It was Dante's turn to look troubled. His dark eyes flicked back and forth between us until finally settling on Gabriel. "Well, that's a fair question. I asked that myself. And the answer I was given was this: he believed he saw his mother, and she told him it was time to come home."

℗

We arrived at Hume Castle at midday, tired, relieved, and thankful that the guards, seeing the baron's banner, had let us through the gates without challenge. Lord Hume met us in the yard. Always an energetic man, he came bounding out with quick strides and a face that was a study in paradoxes. Because of Lord Hume's untimely arrival two days earlier, Blythe Hall had fallen, my brother had been shot, and, while a prisoner in his dungeon, stabbed by his enemy. The man now appeared a stoic wreck. Bolstered by the title of Warden of the East Marches, the air of authority had been tainted by the less heroic emotions of worry, indecision, and utter astonishment. This last blaze of emotion, I realized, was caused by the appearance of Gabriel. Sir Alexander faltered a step or two upon seeing him and then continued as the same odd mix of feelings played havoc with the lines and creases of his face.

We met him halfway. He grabbed hold of me, taking me by the shoulders and looking me straight in the eye. "Isabeau!"

he cried, his voice thick with remorse. "By God, what have I done?"

"What do you mean?" I replied, feeling the fright of his words cold upon my back.

"He's here. Julius is here waiting for you," he said, alleviating my biggest fear. And then, "They've ransacked Blythe Hall. They've destroyed your father's . . ." But he couldn't finish. He saw the look in my eye and couldn't finish. I knew from his expression that he had seen my father's chapel; for no other atrocity than the decimation of a sacred and holy place could make a man like Sir Alexander look so forlorn.

"NO!" I cried, pulling away, tears starting again as I headed for the steps. I dared not look at Dante. "No. Not now. Where's Julius? Please, take us to Julius!"

He looked at Gabriel again. "By God! Gabriel St. Clair!" The words were spoken with reverential awe, and it was little wonder. Gabriel, Julius, and George Douglas had all been under this man's command at one time. And now they were back, pulled from the corners of the earth, and they had brought chaos with them. "What the hell is happening?" Lord Hume demanded softly. It was a question no one could answer.

Holding Gabriel's hand tightly, with Dante grave and silent beside us, we were brought to a large room on the second floor. The door was opened. We crossed the threshold and there we stopped. The sheer curtains on the bed had been swept back, displaying the pale form beneath the covers, head resting on a soft pillow, still and silent as a marble effigy. Light from the tall windows fell across the face, illuminating the golden curls and casting a soft aureole around the head. I stopped breathing and squeezed Gabriel's hand while the other crushed the fine handkerchief given to me by Dante. Julius looked like an angel—perfect, peaceful, luminous, and so very still. We were too late, and the ache of the emptiness that had plagued me became unbearable.

A man, unobtrusively sitting on the other side of the bed, stood when he saw us, his brown gaze settling on Dante. I knew him to be one of Julius's men; he was the doctor Mr. Cochrane had told me about. "Come," he said softly. "You're not too late. He's just resting."

My grip on Gabriel's hand eased slightly. "How . . . how is he?"

"Like Balder," the voice from the bed came softly, "the darling of Frigg. He was slain by a twig of mistletoe . . ."

"And thus brought an end to the era of truth and light, and opened the way for Ragnarok," Gabriel finished, a ghost of a smile on his lips. "I remember that story. You and your pagan tales. Behold a miracle: although the body is wasted, the golden tongue still wags. It's good to see you, Julius. You gave us all a fright."

"I swear," my brother replied, his head having shifted on the pillow. The blue gaze, heavy-lidded and bright with fever, fell softly on Gabriel. "I never saw it coming. But I saw you, brother. Dear Lord, my three children are all here, and they're playing so nicely together. I'm beaming with pride."

"Oh, stop it," I chided softly. I let go of Gabriel and came beside him, slipping into the chair and taking hold of his hand. Julius was not well. He was hot. His breath was a bit gasping, and yet he had remarkable control of his voice. I looked at his neck, letting my eyes rest on the fine, fair skin pulled taut over the elegant muscle. His pulse was weak but rapid. Tears continued to fall down my cheeks. Much to Dante's dismay, I did nothing to stop them. I squeezed his hand, willing his pulse to slow, willing his skin to cool as I posed the obvious question: "Why must you be so difficult? Why couldn't you have just told me what was going on?"

"I believe we've covered this before, Isa dear," he replied, and squeezed back weakly. "You wouldn't have believed me. For four years you've been poisoned against me. There was a lot of poison raging through you. I had to draw it out slowly.

You had to let it go. And now I believe that you have. Besides, didn't we have fun?"

"It wasn't fun," I averred, my chin quivering. "And you wouldn't be here now, Julius, lying at Hume with an arrow in your back and a gash through your stomach, if you had been forthcoming. I hope you realize that Sir Alexander is beside himself with worry."

"I do. 'Tis a pity, an unfortunate casualty in this wicked game we've played. He's a good man. But had I been forthcoming I'd be in the castle prison awaiting the noose—and very likely with an arrow in my back and a knife through my gut as well. And you would be holding hands with dear Georgie Douglas instead of Brother Gabriel. For all his airs and graces, he's a much better catch. I need to speak with you, Isabeau. Privately. But will you allow me to speak with Dante and Gabriel first?"

"Of course." I made to leave, but he was still holding on to me. And then, slowly, he brought his other hand up and brushed it against my cheek, wiping my tears with his fingers.

"Do you cry for me, Isabeau?" he whispered, the question heavy in his bright eyes. "After all I've put you through?" I nodded, tears still spilling from my eyes. "Thank you." He smiled then, a sweet, peaceful smile, and placed his wet fingers on the hollow of his neck, wiping my tears on his own skin. He was so hot that they dried quickly.

"I will make you some tea," I said, trying to hide the fear in my eyes as I looked at him. "I'm going to see that you get better. I think you owe me at least that much."

"You're here, Isabeau. I will get better." I bent and placed a kiss on his forehead. Dr. Hayes came beside me then and gently took my arm. Together we left the room.

⚕

"Is it just me, or does this feel like old times?" There was a mischievous smile on the wan face of Julius Blythe, a misplaced, mischievous smile that a man who had so recently used his body as a pincushion should never wear. It was so pathetic that the other two faces—the one bright and golden as the sun, the other dark and luminous as the moon—likewise grinned. And then they remembered where they were and why. The boyish grins faded. "You two look as if you've never seen me on my back. Prop me up," said Julius. "I'm not fond of receiving male visitors in such a vulnerable pose."

"No," said Gabriel, holding Dante back, because Dante, he knew, had a habit of doing everything Julius wished, like now. "You've put me through hell. You can lie there. Besides, I saw Kilwylie put a bolt in your back, and we've both heard, in great detail, how he carved up your insides. That was no twig of mistletoe, Julius. It was eight inches of cold steel. I know what that does to a man. Stop being so superior all the time and enjoy the humility of the position you've put yourself in. We promise we won't mock." As he said this, he could not, for the life of him, keep from smiling. Neither could Dante. "Now, if you please, will you tell us what's going on?"

For his honesty Gabriel received a cold, basilisk stare. Then, with a sigh of frustration, Julius relented. "Fine. I understand. I'll just lie here on my back and jabber away like a decrepit crone. You're just petulant because my sister has unmonked you. Oh yes, I know." His eyes, a remarkable, guileless blue, stared reflectively into the beet-red, incredulous face of the fallen Hospitaller. "Did I tell you I heard bells? Heaven rings with celestial music whenever a monk succumbs. Bells ring all the time. You just can't hear them because your ear's too close to the ground sniffing out infidels, and listening for the enemies of Christ's most zealous champion on earth, the pope. It must have been glorious," Julius continued, unwavering. "They've been ringing for two days now—sweet, joyful, melodious bells. All those years of burning! All those years of dousing the flames of lust in cold lakes and tepid oceans! All those years of repentant, self-induced torture! All the self-deriding mental flagellation of being habitually chaste! The entire heavenly choir has rejoiced, my friend. Would it be wrong of me to wish I were there too? I suppose so. But only to see your face. Don't be ashamed. Oh, you're blushing! We won't tell. I promise; it doesn't leave this room. Dear God. What are you doing?"

"I'm pulling you up," Gabriel said, seething; his remarkable self-possession had left him entirely. "And God help me if you start bleeding again because I'm going to sit here and watch you bleed out every last drop!"

Sitting serenely, propped on pillows and covered with quilts, Julius Blythe turned his attention to the pressing matter at hand. He was, after all, still a prisoner.

"Lads, from the bottom of my heart, I thank you for coming. I was becoming afraid I might have misjudged the situation."

"I've never known it to happen," Dante said.

"It has. But I've a gift for invention, and I'm good at covering. You of all people know that. I truly wasn't counting on Kilwylie pulling a knife. The rest, more or less, I had guessed. But the hidden knife . . . it was very nearly a fatal mistake." He spoke gravely. Both men understood the seriousness of the matter.

It was Gabriel who asked the question: "And you believe it's not fatal?"

"Your Hospitaller training, of course, makes you a far better judge of these things than I. And I won't lie; I gave poor Clayton a fright. But with you three here, all together, I have soaring hopes. I have a will to live, and that is, after all, the key to a full recovery. Yet I hope you all understand by now that George Douglas will do everything to see that I don't."

"I've heard he's here," said Dante, "locked in a cell."

"Kilwylie's here, but he's being held on trumped-up charges. Hume needed to make an egregious claim in order to hold a lord of Kilwylie's renown in his prisons. He's charged him with the murder of Madame Seraphina L'Ange, which, as Dante and I both know, is not true. However, he meant to kill her. Madame Seraphina was being held captive at Kilwylie Castle, having been brought there with Isabeau. When Isabeau escaped, she, out of necessity, had to be left behind. Poor Seraphina was a bargaining chip—a pawn used to ensure Isabeau's cooperation—but it all went wrong. We have some young friends working to liberate her as we speak. Seraphina is well respected at court and is an invaluable witness who can testify to Kilwylie's planned abduction of both the king and Isabeau. I also have reason to believe she saw Angus there with his men. If Seraphina does not arrive shortly, Lord Hume cannot legally hold Kilwylie and his men much longer."

"But he tried to kill you!" Dante, inflamed, pointed out.

"It could be argued, and quite successfully too, that he was merely trying to save the taxpayers' money and free up the lord justice-general, the Court of Sessions, and Parliament for more pressing matters. I am, if you'll recall, still forfeit in this kingdom, a traitor and an outlaw with a long list of petty injustices to my name. Kilwylie has been exceedingly careful in his movements, and has done nothing boldly against the law. It's more a matter of our word against his."

"Nothing against the law!?" It was the voice of Gabriel, no longer dulcet or controlled. "He sent a group of assassins to kill Isabeau!" he cried, recalling vividly every ounce of horror he had felt when he discovered it. "How is that not against the law?"

"Because, my silly idiot, were you not the most ferociously gifted fighter I know, he would have killed you both and blamed the mess on you. You abducted the man's fiancée." Julius's heavy blue gaze was pointedly accusing. "The king has signed the marriage contract and put his seal on it. It's the document Kilwylie will cling to. Only the king has the power to reverse it. Which reminds me, how is the king, Dante?"

"Excellent," Dante replied, pulling his inscrutable dark gaze from Gabriel. He then looked at Julius and remarked with subtle amusement, "He had an epiphany the other night, riding under the stars, and continues to revere you. He wished to be here now, but we sent him to Edinburgh under the care of Sir Oliver. He went with the young lady. She no longer reveres you." His expressive mouth curled smugly. "That is a pity."

"That is a blessing. And she'd better not have reason to revere you." Sick though he was, he managed to conjure a stern look of warning. "So, James will revoke the marriage contract. Very nice work. Another point, and I don't mean to be indelicate, Gabriel, but I need to know; is my sister still a virgin?"

"What?" Gabriel cried, indignant; he felt his personal life with Isabeau should remain just that: personal. It was not for these two children of debauchery to marvel at, and most disturbing, he saw that Dante had leaned forward, his handsome face a perfect study of probing curiosity. "I thought you heard bells?" Gabriel blurted accusingly. "You said you heard bells!"

"I say a lot of things," Julius admitted with irritating calm. "I'm feverish . . . bordering on delirious. So, do we take that to be a no?" His golden brow rose in question.

"Yes," Gabriel replied, and exhaled forcibly. He was somewhat relieved that it was now over with.

"Wait, *yes*?" Julius repeated, his inquiring eyes enlivened.

"No!" Gabriel cried, losing his temper. "No. She is no longer a virgin! Is that what you wish to hear?"

Julius, feigning shock, smiled. "Thank you. I don't see why that was so difficult to answer. It's a simple yes-or-no question. Not much to think about when you get down to it. You either are, or you're not. All right, now, how about you? Are you, Gabriel St. Clair, still a virgin?" Dante, like the child he was, could not control himself and erupted in a fit of puerile laughter. Julius also laughed but trailed off unheroically in a fit of pain-induced moaning. Gabriel, just as in the old days, was not laughing. "Dear God," wheezed Julius, holding his stomach tightly. "I'm sorry. That was just cruel and juvenile of me. Besides, I already know the answer to that. I heard bells. Remember? Bells, glorious bells. Now that we've sufficiently exhausted that matter, rest assured I will not bother you about it again." This was not said with the most earnest expression, but it was good enough for Gabriel. "And the reason I asked in the first place should be obvious. You now—"

"Oh, it is," Gabriel interjected, cutting him off. "I realized it the moment I stepped foot in Blythe Hall. I realized it the moment I saw Isabeau."

"Did you suffer much?" Julius asked with a convincing amount of concern.

"A little. Yes. As I'm sure you meant me to. You were, after all, teaching me a lesson."

"No." The word shot out like the snap of a whip. Julius, with a face void of all mirth and mockery, looked squarely at him. "No, brother, that I was not. I mocked you all those years ago because I knew that you were running from your own desires. You've always loved Isabeau but lacked the self-confidence to fight for her. It wasn't until you brought us back to Rhodes with you that I saw what you had made of yourself, and I suddenly understood why—even if you didn't understand it yourself. Rhodes made you strong, Gabriel; it made you the man you needed to be in order to fulfill your destiny. And I realized then that your destiny was to be with Isabeau.

"George Douglas was still in Scotland, and I knew that when the time was right he would come for my sister. He told me so himself before he placed me in the hands of the Turk. I knew I needed to return to Scotland, but in order to do that I needed first to be free, and second to find my father. However, by the time you found me I had lost the will to do either of those things. You fought valiantly for our lives, Gabriel, and for that I can never repay you. Yet after all you did for Dante and me, I still could not bear to face my father. I was more than humbled, I was beaten, and I knew that unless I did something, Isabeau would suffer as I had. And then, one day, Providence intervened. You see, I understood that you'd never leave Rhodes—that you'd waste your life and your gifts serving the order. I had to do something, and so I drove you from Rhodes—we drove you," he said, indicating Dante. "Don't look at me like that. It wasn't entirely planned. Yet once you left, I was certain you'd go directly to Scotland, and to Isabeau, but instead you did something even more remarkable. You found my father, didn't you?"

"How . . . how in the world did you know that?"

"I received a message," said Julius Blythe plainly. "And by that time I was ready to face my own destiny. Don't hate me too much for doing what I did," he said, holding up a feeble hand and looking levelly into the incredulous blue stare. "I may have made you face the dragon and slay it, but that dragon was the most precious gift I had to give."

"By dragon, are we referring to Isabeau?" Dante asked, assiduously trying to follow along.

"No," said Julius, not unkindly, "but we can go with that euphemism if you like." He smiled.

"Isabeau is not the dragon," Gabriel said gently. "What Julius means, Dante, is that she is the princess the dragon was guarding—the dragon being the obstacle in the way. Do you see?"

"No." He shook his head. "Not really. Who is this dragon?"

They ignored him. Julius continued. "I take it your feelings for Isabeau are still strong?"

"Overwhelmingly so."

"Good. Because you understand that you will have to fight for marital bliss. I may not have done you the favor you have done me."

"Yes. You have. And," Gabriel said, his open, unguarded gaze beholding the bruised angelic face of his tormentor, "I must thank you, old friend. Oh—before I forget—I have something for you from your father. It may not be the key to hanging Kilwylie, but it will help. He's written a statement describing your business in England and has signed it, clearing you of suspicion concerning all treasonous English connections. I have it safely hidden in my quiver."

"Your quiver? You keep something of this importance in your moldering quiver? How is he—and where is he?"

"Good. And, it's complicated. We'll talk about it later. You need your rest, Julius. You look remarkably better, but not at all healthy enough to go against a frisky kitten, let alone a devil like Kilwylie. I know Isabeau is anxious to talk with you. Dante and I will leave you. We're going to have a wee word with Lord Hume about retaking Blythe Hall. After all, who knows better how to launch a surprise attack from the inside than us?" Gabriel looked at Dante and smiled, indicating with his eyes the labyrinth of secret tunnels and chambers beneath Blythe Hall. "Lord Hume is very distraught at the moment, and we're going to help ease his mind a measure. Dante?" Gabriel said, and stood to go.

"I'll be with you in a minute," Dante replied, looking intently at Julius. With a gentle nod of his glorious head, Gabriel slipped from the room.

"Dante," Julius began softly, "my raven-eyed familiar, we have prayed together at the altar of women, of blood, and of money. Do you think I don't know why you're here?"

"But what if it fails? What if all we've done is for nothing? He attacked you! Kilwylie broke into your cell and stabbed you! Do you think he will stop? What if he succeeds? What if you die? Do you ever think of me?" His dark, fathomless eyes were imploring, and then they fell, and his head dropped, resting helpless against the cool sheets of the bed.

"All the time," Julius replied quietly, and placed his hand

on the night-black curls at the nape of the young man's neck. "But I don't think I'm going to die just yet. And I was wrong. One cannot always revert to the ways of the heathen to solve every problem. Look at me." Dante's eyes came up. "Stay with Gabriel, Dante. Resist temptation, and for God's sake, brother, say a prayer."

"To what deity?"

"Why, to the only deity powerful enough to save our souls."

☙

Dante left Julius and found Isabeau waiting on the other side of the door with a cup of ill-smelling tea cradled reverently between her hands. He smiled at the sight of her. Isabeau, with a shy smile of her own, told him that Gabriel had gone ahead and was sitting with Lord Hume in his chamber. He nodded, thanked her, and gallantly opened the door. He watched her enter, letting his eyes linger over her enticing form a moment too long, and then, with an inward sigh, closed the door behind her. He knew this was an important meeting for them both, and wished them well of it. A part of him longed to be there too—a part of him envied Gabriel, because Gabriel would soon be a part of this extraordinary family. He didn't have a family. Julius was the closest thing to family he'd ever had. And he was not about to let Kilwylie destroy that. He looked down the hall and saw the open door Isabeau had pointed to. He turned and walked the other way, slipping silently down the back stairs.

A commotion on the main floor momentarily drew his attention. He paused and peered around a corner. There was a flurry of activity spurred by the arrival of three spindly monks and a squat little priest. They were in the process of disrobing. He smiled and watched a servant run up the main stairs with the news. It was a good omen indeed, and one that reinforced his decision. He had now fulfilled his obligations to Julius. All would be well. All the pieces of the puzzle had come together. There was just one last thing to do. He had made a promise to himself that he would hunt Kilwylie down and cut out his still-beating heart. There was no need to hunt. Kilwylie was right here, beneath his feet, and no one would notice if he went missing for a minute or two. Dante, with a cold, dark gaze, turned back to the stairs and, like a ghost blending into the darkness, descended into the dungeon of Hume.

ॐ

I stood before the door, clutching a mug of herbal tea, and waited until Dante was finished speaking with my brother. Gabriel, having stepped out alone, came to me and held me tightly, nearly spilling the tea. Whatever had occurred in the room had been straining and emotional, and I was pleased to feel the tension in his body slowly melt away as he kissed me. "Perhaps I should make you some tea as well?" I offered.

"No," he was quick to reply, and then his lips pulled into a soft smile. "I mean, no thank you. Your brother deserves all of that—the whole pot. Tell me, does it taste as bad as it smells?"

"Likely worse. Was he horrible to you?"

"No," he answered softly. I looked into the beautiful blue gaze, deep as the ocean and as full of promise. He then tenderly pushed a strand of hair from my face as he said, "He was remarkable. And he seems to be getting a little better. But don't let him get out of drinking that, aye? I've to go talk with Sir Alexander now. Will you tell Dante to join us?" I nodded and happily took another kiss for good measure.

Dante emerged a moment later looking quietly determined. He was an interesting young man, with a very disarming smile—one that made a woman blush. "Gabriel's in Lord Hume's chamber, just down there," I said.

He thanked me and held the door.

The moment I entered I saw that Julius was looking

markedly better. "You're sitting up," I said, walking to the bed. "Good. You can drink this. I sent your friend Dr. Hayes to bed. You had him worried sick. He hasn't slept in days."

He smiled and patted the bed. "Good. Come, Isabeau, sit beside me. Dear God, what's this?" he said, gingerly taking the mug from my hands.

"I made you some tea. It's one of my groom's famous concoctions."

"Tam's recipe, is it?" He beheld the hot liquid with familiar suspicion.

I looked at him—at his sardonic eyes—and then offered cautiously, "You know Tam? He told me he'd never met you."

"Then he would be a liar," Julius replied. "A good one. He's a remarkable young man, is Tam, and I'm the reason he's your groom."

"What? What are you saying? Tam worked in the royal stables. James sent him to me."

"Yes," he replied. "For a while I made sure he was close to James. I needed him close to you when I went to prison. The switch to serve you was all managed very cleverly between Seraphina and Tam; James would think it was his idea, but the seed was planted by your friends. Do you wonder why?"

"Yes," I uttered, staring at him as if he were a stranger.

"Because, as you've probably already discovered yourself, you and I are different from other people, Isabeau."

I shook my head in fearful denial, while at the same time odd memories came flooding back—the scroll Sir Oliver gave me, the visions of Gabriel, that day long ago in the tower room.

Julius set down the tea, and held my hand. "I didn't want to believe it myself. I realized it that day long ago in the tower room. Do you remember it? Do you remember Rondo, your puppy? He was dead, Isabeau. Your puppy died that day, and you brought him back to life with your tears. Look at me!" he ordered, seeing that I was shaking, seeing that I was unwilling to believe it. "Look at me," he said again, this time in a tone so desperately pleading that I could not deny him. "I was not well, Isabeau. An hour ago, before you walked through that door, I wasn't certain I would live. I was dying. I needed you. I needed your tears to heal me. Give me your hands," he said, and before I could move he took them in his own. I watched as he brought them to his stomach and felt the heat of his flesh through his thin nightshirt. "Close your eyes," he ordered. I did. I could feel him breathe, my hands moving gently with his every breath. "Heal me," he whispered. "Heal me, Isabeau."

"I . . . I don't know how," I said. "Julius, honestly, I don't know how!"

"Yes, you do. Close your eyes. Feel me. Feel my heart beating." I did as he wished, and noted how his heart felt stronger. "Now, concentrate; concentrate on the wasted flesh." He brought my hands over his spectacular wound. The gash was not big, but the blade of the dagger had gone in deep, ripping through his flesh and large intestine, and piercing his liver. There were other wounds as well. I knew this, I realized, because I saw it in my head. My jaw dropped at the revelation. Julius continued. "See my damaged organs and make them whole. Concentrate on the splintered bone and see it mended. See my body as a perfect, thriving, living thing."

As Julius talked I followed him in my mind and felt the gentle hum course through me. It filled me with warm, tingling heat; I felt whole and alive and full of radiant energy. I willed it into him, and in turn I felt it coming back, stronger and stronger. I opened my eyes. Julius was smiling. And he looked . . . he looked like he did the day he came home, the day he wreaked havoc on Blythe Hall. "Dear God," I uttered, and smiled back at him.

"I have it too," he said. "Only not nearly as strong. I can't bring anyone back from the dead. Dear Lord," he breathed, and ran his hands over his torso, marveling and grinning like a fool. "It's amazing—utterly amazing. As I was saying, I'm not a healer. I'm more . . . destructive."

"Really?" I said with pure, juvenile sarcasm. "I hadn't noticed. And you weren't dead, just skewered. But how? How is it possible?"

"Because, dear sister, our mother, although human in nearly every way, had divine blood running through her veins, as do we. Wait," he said, holding up a hand to silence the flood of questions he saw on my lips. "It's not that easy. It's not all good. In fact, I've learned it's very complicated. Let me tell you a little of what I know. Do you know the term *Nephilim*?"

"Yes," I answered slowly, and then looked at him with my mouth agape. "The scroll!" I brought my hand over my mouth. "The manuscript!"

"What?" There was a frightening look in his eyes. "What . . . what manuscript are you talking about, Isabeau?" he asked cautiously, although I believed he already knew the answer.

"The manuscript that drove Father away—the one that speaks of the Nephilim. I have it."

It was his turn to be amazed. "How on earth do you have it?" he asked, keeping his handsome, expressive face under firm control. It was a sign of his remarkable recovery. "I've been looking everywhere for it. Dear God, Isabeau! George Douglas will kill for that. He's destroyed our home looking for it. Where was it?"

"It wasn't at Blythe Hall," I said, looking levelly at him. "It was at Rosslyn Castle. It was supposed to be in the altar in the Chapel of Angels, but Father left it with Sir Oliver on a whim. Now, tell me, Julius," I said, my eyes boring into his with bold challenge, "why would George Douglas kill for it? What could it possibly mean to him? By God, what is going on?"

"Something very, very evil, I'm afraid. Something I've tried to prevent for a long time. Douglas wants the manuscript for the same reason I do, Isabeau. Redemption. We aren't the only ones, you know."

I was staring at him, my body limp, my mind aching and swirling with questions, when the door opened suddenly. We both turned.

"Oh, my children! My poor, dear little angels. I thought I was too late. How my heart has ached for this moment—to see you both together again." Seraphina walked in, her eyes bright with tears. With a spring in her step that belied her age, she crossed to the bed and pulled us both into her arms, just like she had when we were children. "It is time I tell you the Story."

❧

The ring of keys was hanging on a hook in the guardroom. The guard had momentarily stepped out to relieve himself. Dante, black and silent, lifted them and continued down the hall. His heart beat strong and steady; his mind was entirely focused. He stopped and stood, still and eerie as a wraith, before the iron bars. It was dark, but he could see Kilwylie lying on the floor. The man was on his back with his hands cradled beneath his head and his long legs crossed at the ankles. His eyes were closed, but Dante doubted he was sleeping. He watched the huge chest rise and fall with a deep, hypnotic rhythm. He looked at the relaxed face: the smug, insolent set to the lips, the long, dark lashes. And then he visualized his knife taking it all away in one startling moment of pain.

As if Kilwylie had read his mind, his eyes shot open and turned to the door. Dante didn't move. The man's eyes were spectacular, he thought, the piercing light green of a cat's. He saw fear behind them—a fear that gave him pleasure. He was going to enjoy this.

"Who the hell are you?" Kilwylie demanded. "And what do you mean by sneaking up on me, boy?"

Dante only smiled. He took out the key. Kilwylie's eyes fell to the lock. That was when he saw the knife in the young man's other hand. And then he smiled too.

Kilwylie uncoiled and pulled to his full, dark height as the door opened. He was a big man, Dante saw, as tall as Gabriel but thicker, heavier, with muscles hardened under the long use of full tilting armor. He nearly took up the entire cell. "I take it he's dead?" Kilwylie asked, a soft, hopeful smile on his lips. "And does my pretty little assassin have a name, or do I just call you corpse?"

"You can call me death, if you like," said Dante, his voice low and void of emotion. "That is the only name you shall know." And then he moved—with a speed that was nearly inhuman.

Before Kilwylie could lunge at him, Dante was on the floor, rolling behind the knight. He brought the knife up and struck deep into the thick muscle of a hamstring. With a quick jerk of the wrist, he pulled it out again.

Profanity, loud and crude, echoed through the dungeon. Kilwylie spun on his good leg and realized too late that the little creature was no longer behind him. He spun again, and for his mistake received a stab in his thigh. His entire leg was now useless. The little bastard, he thought with grim amusement. He fights dirty, like me. He swung low, protecting his good leg, and finally connected with something other than air. The knife had cut his thigh, but not deeply. Dante flew backward and hit the wall.

Kilwylie, with a mirthless laugh, said, "You mean to cripple me limb by limb. You mean to savor my death. I know the tactic. Very Saracen. How would a nice lad like you know it?" He came at Dante as he spoke, and, anticipating the young man's next move, grabbed left. Dante went right and launched himself under Kilwylie's tree-trunk arm, raking the blade of the knife down the ribs, creating a long, clean slice. He landed on the floor and scrambled to stand. He was almost there.

Kilwylie was quick for a big man, and smart. Turning toward the knife as it raked his side, he fell, letting gravity do what his muscles could not. He hit the young man as he was coming up and pinned the sinewy body under his own, grabbing the kicking legs with his arms, feeling the frantic squirm. Dante still held the knife, and he slammed it down, aiming for Kilwylie's neck.

A loud crash and a yell from a guard erupted from the storeroom beyond the prison. For a split second Dante's relentless focus was removed, and his gaze came up—just as the blade hit. He pierced Kilwylie's flesh, but it wasn't his neck. It was his shoulder. Kilwylie's other arm came whipping across then, knocking the blade from his hand. It flew clattering across the cold stone floor and hit the wall. "Oh," Sir George breathed, scrambling on top of the smaller man, fighting for control over the pummeling fists and twisting body. The lad was strong. There was no doubt. He also knew every fighter's trick in the book; every muscle had been trained to perfection. He was squirming, trying to find purchase with his feet and legs to overthrow the daunting weight that held him to the floor. Against a normal-sized man there would have been no question. The young man was a weapon honed and sharpened to perfection. However, the Lord of Kilwylie was not a normal man. He pinned the arms and legs beneath his heavy body as his other hand, searching, closed over the handle of the knife.

"Oh, I remember you now," Kilwylie said, looking at the tragically beautiful face that had fallen back against the floor; the swollen veins of the neck pulsating with rage; the symmetrical features pinched and fraught with strain; the raven-black hair, fraught with loose curls, pooled on the stone exposing the pale ear. Kilwylie brought his lips close and uttered, "How could one forget such a sweet face? You belonged to Curtogoli Reis, didn't you?" Dante's flashing black eyes stilled and bore, with exquisite hatred, into the light-green ones. "Oh, indeed. You were his boy. Did he buy you as well? He was rather anxious to get his hands on your master. But you already know that. Were all three of you lovers? Or perhaps he shared you with the crew?"

Dante, enflamed with a hatred he hadn't felt in years, jerked with such force that he nearly threw Kilwylie. Another exhaustive bout of wrestling ensued until Kilwylie got him under control again.

The guard had spotted the open door, seen the wrestling bodies, and now he ran toward them.

"My dear boy, you can attempt to drown out the past by living in the bottom of a wine barrel, or by numbing your pain with drugs and a steady stream of cheap women. But you cannot run from what you are, sweetheart. And neither can he. 'Tis a hellish life. I will do you both a favor. I will make it better." Dante felt the point of the knife bite at his skin, high between his ribs. "What will it be, my sweet? A slow and painful death like I gave your master? Or do you want it quick, so you'll be there to greet him when he arrives?"

The guard came bounding into the cell. Dante's eyes, a bitter mix of hatred and sorrow, never left Kilwylie's.

"I'd better make it quick," Kilwylie said, "but I shall send you off with the sweet memory." The knife came as Kilwylie, slowly lowering his head, covered the quivering lips with his own. He savored the twitch of the body beneath him; he reveled in the flood of fear, pain, and heartrending remorse. And he was truly touched by the single tear that fell from the cold black eyes.

The guard, horror-struck at the sight, fell still. His fear made him easy prey for the knife as well.

❦

We stayed on the bed and listened as Seraphina, sitting in the chair beside us, told her riveting story. It was similar to the stories we heard as children, only this one was a little different. I would have thought it unbelievable if I didn't know that it just might be true.

"You, my dears," she began, her eyes calm yet serious, "among all God's children, are quite unique. It is none of your own fault. It happened long ago, when the divine expression of God known as *grigori,* or watchers—the group of angels who kept eternal vigilance over man—had a few members who became so enamored with human women that they wished to experience all the pleasures of humanity. In short, they wished to be human. However, to do this, from the vantage point of the heavens, meant denying God's eternal grace, and knowing, beforehand, that the children of such a mixed race would naturally have sublime power. It has been many, many years since the fall of the angels, and most Nephilim, those with the blood of angels coursing through their veins, or, as the Bible describes them, 'the mighty men that were of old, the men of renown,' have perished. They were wiped out in the Great Flood. But a few survived. Your ancestor was one of them.

"You are not, by any means, immortal. But both of you are capable of great and wondrous things. You, Julius, learned this early. I watched you as a young boy and saw how everything came so easily for you. And I have watched you struggle with the temptation of being able to topple entire nations—to lead men to sin and avarice with a twinkle in your eye, and yes, even to wreak havoc on trade in foreign markets. It is the result of the divine spark that burns within you. It can drive men to greatness, or it can lead to terrible evil. Your curse is always having to walk that fine line, my lad.

"And you, Isabeau, you are specially blessed, yet because of it, you are also vulnerable. Only through you does the divine spark pass. Your children will be as you are. But there are others out there, others of a similar race. It is not easy to tell those of angelic blood from ordinary humans. Many have it.

Many will never know that they do. Your line, however, has been followed closely. Your ancestors are the guardians of nations; through your line are born the guardians of Scotland."

I was dumbfounded by this news, even though I had heard much of it my entire life.

"Is our father . . . ?" I began to ask, looking at Seraphina, for the Blythes had long been a powerful border family and hereditary guardians of Scotland.

"No," she replied. "The Blythes are a noble family indeed, and their sons are brave warriors to a man, but they are very human."

"But the angel above our gates . . . and our motto?"

Her old eyes twinkled. "Your Blythe ancestors were also devout men. Did you know your family motto was established after the Battle of Bannockburn? Your Blythe ancestors fought alongside Robert the Bruce and survived. Battlefields, my children, try men's souls; angels are known to appear on battlefields. And my children," she continued, looking pointedly at us, "it might interest you to know that your mother is descended from William Wallace."

I looked next to me, to Julius, to see what he made of all this. But I saw that he had already figured much of it out, for his cynical eyes mocked my amazement, while his lips twitched with childish smugness. Why was I ever to expect anything less?

"So, our mother really was an angel. Is that why I see things?" Before Seraphina could answer, Julius broke in.

"You see visions like I do," he said, with derision in his voice. "Because every now and then we are allowed a glimpse of heaven—to taunt us, to show us what we'll never have. Do you not think I aspire to that also?" He was looking accusingly at Seraphina. "I want redemption, same as other men, only I know that it will never be, will it? Because that's what our father learned, isn't it? Isabeau is a life-giving vessel of hope and goodness, while I've been condemned to this." And then, as if struck by some invisible force, he froze, his smile fading, his eyes focusing inward.

"What is it?" I uttered.

He looked at me, a horrible expression crossing his fine features, and then, slowly absorbing the shock of it, he shook his head. "I don't know. I felt terribly cold. I'm fine."

I reached out a hand and felt his head. He was warm and looked infinitely better than he had when we arrived. Julius was healing.

"Will you do me a favor though?" he asked, his face still frightfully pale. "Will you check on Dante? He gets a bit emotional when I'm injured. He's supposed to be with your fallen Hospitaller. I just want to be sure." It was a polite request, but I could tell Julius was greatly troubled. I looked at Seraphina and excused myself.

"Wait," she said, her face stricken with panic. "I haven't told you everything. About your family, about the manuscript—"

"I know. I'll be back," I said, and kissed her on the cheek.

❦

Dante was not with Gabriel. Gabriel and Lord Hume were so absorbed in their talk they must have forgotten. At the mention of the name, Gabriel looked at Lord Hume. A living thought passed between them, and Lord Hume uttered, "Dear God, Kilwylie's down there!" Before I could ask the question, both men were at the door. "Get back to your brother and stay there!" Gabriel said, his voice touched with something cold and fearful. He turned and ran down the corridor after Lord Hume.

It was then that I saw Gabriel's gear. It had been brought to Sir Alexander's study and was now resting against the desk. I went to the saddlebag and removed the long velvet sack I had placed there containing the ancient scroll that belonged to my father. The velvet sack was new, yet it smelled musty, old, and now it had a hint of leather. I smiled at that and brought it with me, wanting to show Julius—hoping it might ease his mind until the men returned.

⚬

The moment I walked through the door I knew something was wrong. Julius was in bed, his face still and expressionless, yet his eyes burned with something beyond hatred as they fixed on the space near the door. Seraphina was on her feet, her face frightened, yet her eyes were on me. "Dante . . . ," I began in an attempt to deliver the news; and then I heard the door shut behind me. The back of my neck prickled. I knew who it was by my reaction, and my heart dropped to my stomach as I turned to face him.

"My darling fiancée," said George Douglas, his words and manner belying the ferocity that lay behind the piercing eyes. "In what fictitious world do you live that would make you believe I would not find you? Everything I do, Isabeau, I do for love of you." He came closer, and stopped not more than two feet away. I stood still, frozen to the spot. For the life of me I could not move. "You left me, my sweet," he continued, his eyes filling with gentle concern. It was damnably convincing. "What was I to do? I had no choice but to hunt you down. When you locked your gates against me, what else was I to do but burn them? And when you were abducted by another man, I went mad as a berserker. Forgive me, Isabeau." He moved even closer, until he was a mere few inches away. I could feel his breath on my face and closed my eyes. I wanted to move, but there was something terrible about him that held me still.

"Look at me," he demanded. I opened my eyes.

"Leave her be, Kilwylie." It was Julius who spoke. He was

still in bed, his face hard and suffused with hatred. "Nobody is buying the rubbish you're spewing these days. It's me you want. Let's not be silly and start playing with little girls."

"Julius." Kilwylie's gaze shifted to the bed as a sardonic smile appeared on his lips. "I'm sorry, I nearly forgot you were there. No. It's always been your sister I wanted. And, truthfully, I thought you were dead. I believed this time I had really done it. I must apologize, but when I met that charming friend of yours, that beautiful young man, I sent him along to be with you. You should be proud. He was devoted to the end." He lifted up a hand and displayed a knife. It was still dripping blood.

"No!" I cried, stunned by the biting cruelty of his words and the contrast of the profane smile on his lips. My eyes flashed to the face of my brother then, knowing how much Dante had meant to him—knowing how completely his heart was breaking. But the mask, the implacable mask, revealed nothing. It was beyond torture, and I could take no more of it.

"You soulless beast, how could you!" I cried, and slammed my right hand into Sir George's chest. He barely moved. "By God!" I seethed, "I have never hated anyone so much as I do you!"

"That is a pity, my dear. Because you're going to be with me a very long time. Come," he said, and grabbed me, spinning me to face my brother and Seraphina as he pinned me against his solid, heaving chest. "And if you don't," he whispered softly, yet not so softly that Seraphina and Julius couldn't hear him, "I will take everything from you, everything you hold dear, until you have nothing but emptiness and pain and remorse. You will come to me then, Isabeau; you will come to me then on your knees begging for mercy. Come with me now, or come later; that is your choice."

"No!" cried Seraphina, walking steadily toward us. "Do not listen to him, Isabeau. He has no power over you and never did. Do not listen." And then I saw the flash of a small dagger in her hand. Sir George had seen it too, and lifted his other arm. Realizing too late what he meant to do, I watched as the crimson-stained knife—the knife that had taken Dante's life—spun through the air and struck Seraphina right between the eyes. Aghast, I dropped the velvet sack I had been holding. And then a scream, high and mournful, escaped me.

"Bloody bitch," Sir George seethed, watching as my governess dropped to her knees, still clutching the little dagger in her fist. "I've been charged with your murder, so it's only fair you should die!"

Julius was out of bed and on the floor beside her in an instant, gathering her head and cradling it on his lap. Her blood dripped from the mortal wound, mingling with the dark and crusted blotches already covering his white nightshirt. Seraphina's eyes were heavenward, her mouth was moving as her lifeblood ran in rivulets down her face. It looked as if she was saying a prayer. With a mighty twist I slipped from Sir George's relaxed grasp and fell to the floor, crawling across the polished wood to be with them. I could heal her, I thought, tears pouring from my eyes. Julius had shown me that I could—he made me believe that I had the power to heal. "Let me . . . ," I uttered, but the look in my brother's eye was one of unconcealed fright. And then I saw what he saw. I saw the rays of light emanating from Seraphina's quivering body.

If we had ever doubted my father's story, we now believed it—all three of us. Sir George, soulless devil that he was, stood transfixed, watching the miracle unfold before our eyes. The light that came from Seraphina shot heavenward, momentarily blocked by the ceiling. The plasterwork began to shimmer, until it became translucent, opening to the cloud-speckled blue sky above. And then they came—a host of shimmering celestial beings descending to the earth on radiant light. The beauty of them was so profound that they left us both awestruck and breathless. Mme. Seraphina, my mother's guardian, left her body then, in much the same way a puff of smoke lifts off a flame, quietly evanescent. She was a glittering spirit now, a distinct soul of pure and sublime love. We felt it move through us as she left, carried on the wings of the angels that had come for her. And then Mme. Seraphina, leaving her body behind, was gone. She was, and had always been, a guardian of the Nephilim of our line. I knew this in a way that was unexplainable. "You are blessed," her voice echoed through me. And then all was quiet and still as the light slowly faded away. The ceiling once again became just a ceiling.

Sound came then, loud and distracting, filling the room with the rumble of booted feet. On the other side of the door men were approaching. Sir George, staring at us as we remained huddled on the floor beside our lifeless governess, flinched. It was then that I noticed he was bleeding. Blood oozed from a wound on his left thigh, and a dark, wet stain appeared on the side of his rich green doublet. I wasn't sure if it was his or not. And then my gaze dropped to the floor. His did too, and held the object that had drawn my focus. We were all staring at it as understanding flashed behind Sir George's eyes. Julius made a move but Kilwylie was faster. With a self-satisfied grin he picked up the velvet sack containing the scroll.

"Thank you for this," he said, then added, looking pointedly at me, "I'll be back for you, my sweet." I watched as he limped to the window. The door crashed open at the same moment that Kilwylie jumped. Lord Hume, running in, looked wildly around the room. And then his eyes came to rest on the body of Seraphina. He froze. Still unable to speak, I pointed to the window. He ran across the room and looked out, then started shouting orders to his men. Gabriel walked in then, and in his arms he carried the body of the beautiful young man, Dante.

Julius, having hastily pulled a sheet over Seraphina's body, slowly rose. "Set him on the bed, quickly!" he demanded, his eyes wide and aqueous as they rested on Dante. In four strides he was beside them. Gabriel's eyes, I saw, were wet as well, and I too helped place the limp form on the bed, all of us unwilling to believe what we saw.

"Oh God . . ." The voice, always carefully modulated, always under control, had cracked as Julius looked at the unmoving form on the bed. His hands cradled the still face, urging life to appear with his seeking touch as he yelled his friend's name. It was then that the implacable mask of my brother's face began to melt before our eyes, and the carefully guarded emotions trickled forth, revealing a vast and desperate pain. "Jesus, sweet Jesus, no!" he cried, and then, with soul-hacking urgency, he turned to me. "Isabeau . . . please? I need you to . . . pray for him. I can't do this alone!" His cornflower-blue eyes were wide and pleading.

Unnerved and frightened, I knew what Julius was asking of me. He was asking the impossible. I looked at the young man—at this dark and beautiful stranger who had walked through hell with my brother and had brought him back to me. His stillness was heartbreaking, as was the glistening trail of a single teardrop that had slipped from the dark eyes. With my finger I gently traced the teardrop, feeling the wetness, feeling the warmth of the skin. It was then that I saw Rondo, my little puppy, vivid and alive in my mind. He was happy, wagging his tail. Dante was Julius's Rondo. I closed my eyes, pushing my own tears aside, and nodded.

Gabriel, wrapped in his own silent mourning, had been watching us. There was a question in his eyes as they held me, a question that I longed to answer, but Julius was telling me no.

"Gabriel, you need to go and go quickly, brother!" Julius's tone was demanding, and very reminiscent of our father's. It was a tone no one disobeyed. He wanted Gabriel out of the room. And I knew why. "Help Hume get the bastard who did this! Go, brother! Leave Dante with us! There might be hope for him yet."

With hardly a word, and with tears spilling from his eyes, Gabriel nodded. I took him in my arms, offering what little comfort I could. "Say a prayer for Dante, my love," I uttered as his lips left mine. "And return to me safely."

Then I let him go.

℅

We were alone, we two children cursed with the burden of being semidivine, with two corpses, only one of which still had a chance to be saved. Julius, working quickly, took Dante's knife, now covered with the blood of two souls, and cut the doublet and shirt up the middle, exposing the smooth expanse of unmoving chest. He set the knife down and took my hands, placing them over Dante's heart. "Please, Isabeau," he said, "you need to heal him. Cry for him. If you only knew what he suffered for me, you would cry for him. I cannot let him die like this. I'm responsible for this man just as you were responsible for Rondo. Find him in your mind. See his body and make it whole again. Make it once again a vibrant place for his soul to dwell."

Moved beyond words, I did as Julius wished. We both sat on the bed, Julius across from me with hands placed beside mine on Dante's body. His head was bent in prayer, and his tears fell silent on the lifeless form. It was the first time I had ever seen my brother cry, and the sight of them together—one silent and shaking, the other deathly still—unlocked something within me. My tears fell unchecked then; I was crying for them both. The droplets, fat like spring rain and filled with just as much hope, coursed down my cheeks, mingling with the tears of my brother. I rubbed them into the still-warm skin. And then I relaxed my mind and let it come—the tingling, the rush of warm, radiant energy. I called to Dante; I prayed for his soul. I saw his body healed, but it wasn't enough. The young man was far away; like Seraphina, he had moved beyond the confines of flesh, blood, and bone, and I found only a frangible, tenuous connection with him. Feeling helpless, I spoke my brother's name.

"Keep going," his voice urged. "Keep going, Isa! Do not give up on him."

I didn't.

Following the thread of a connection, and latching on with my stronger energy, I suddenly felt a tug. I was still connected to Dante, but my consciousness pulled free. I was no longer in my own body; I was somewhere else, and I was being urged by the voice of Julius to follow wherever it led me. Like a vaporous wisp, I moved through Dante's body and continued on, traveling down a dark and lonely path.

I was conscious of being in a murky, swirling mist, a place where dark clouds raced overhead and silence pulsed through the ears like haunted whispers. It was an empty place, achingly empty, and I was instantly afraid. I did not like this place. I did not want to be left here, and my fear began pulling me away. I began to retreat until I heard the voice of my brother calling to me, urging me to be brave, urging me to plunge ahead. Like the doting sister I once was, I listened to him.

"Follow him," Julius said. "For love of me, Isabeau, follow him. Release your fear. I am with you. Follow him and bring him back to us." Hearing Julius's voice, and sensing that he was close, I turned around and headed into the darkness. I went deep into the swirling mist until I saw a glimmer of light far along on the path ahead of me. "Dante," I called. "Dante, come back." The light stopped moving. I called to it again. And then, suddenly, I could feel him. I could feel his presence. The light began to grow brighter.

"Come, Dante," I said, reaching out to him. He wanted to, I believed that, but I felt his conflict. I felt his hesitation. I smiled on him then, letting him know how much we loved him, how much we wanted him to come home. I held out my hand and urged him to take it. Still, he hesitated. "Take my hand, Dante," I said again, speaking to the lone and lost spark of pure energy that was him. "It's all right. I want you to come with me."

I felt a fear in him, a dark and terrible fear. But it wasn't of me. It was something else. I was left with no choice. I was losing him; he was fading, and I knew that Julius would not allow that. I would have to be the one to take him. I would have to be the one to pull him back.

I grabbed him; I enveloped his spark in my own light and intended to carry him with me. But the moment we connected I understood why he was hesitant; I understood his fear. Everything he had suffered in his short life—every horror he had lived through—was relived again through me. I felt his pain, endured his suffering; I shared his habitual and complete degradation; I lived in his hell with him, and what I saw was destroying me, shattering me piece by piece. I knew I was not strong enough to fight this vast, soul-devouring evil.

We clung together, two lost specks of light in a swirling darkness. There was an urge to give in to the darkness, to just let it sweep me away; it would be a release; it would end the suffering. It was a tempting option. But Dante's spirit was fighting me, trying to set me free. It was a selfless, terrifying thing, and I would not let him do it. I could not. I could not let him go here alone. I knew then why Julius sent me—to hazard the lonely darkness for one small speck of light. He couldn't come here himself. Because his soul, like Dante's, was possibly already forfeit.

My father was a warrior of Scotland. I may have been born with a spark of the divine in my blood—my mother may have even been an angel—but I was a warrior too. And my father, Lord William of Blythe, taught me that a warrior never gives up a fight he believes in. After living so many years in denial, I finally understood the truth of this; I finally understood the truth of what I was. And I was finally ready to embrace it.

Julius had told me we were a condemned race; I was now ready to believe that we were something quite different. Through our veins ran the seed of hope, and I would not let that vanish with this young man, this lost soul whom Julius had cherished.

And then I thought of what I cherished; I thought of the love that anchored me to the world and made me believe I could do anything; I thought of Gabriel St. Clair.

I saw his beautiful, golden countenance; I heard his heart-felt prayers, and I held on to that. Then we heard the voice of my brother. He was with us, and he had the strength to pull us back.

The tingling, at times very painful, as if a limb had been left too long in ice water, slowly left my body, and I came awake, opening my eyes violently to the world. I was shaking and crying, and I could not help it, because I was utterly terrified of what I had just done. Julius, sitting across from me, was watching me intently. I saw that his eyes were as wide as my own. "Dear God," he uttered. "What just happened?"

"I . . . I don't know," I replied through trembling lips. And then he came beside me and took me in his arms. "I was so scared," I said with a hiccough. "I was so frightened. I thought I would never see this place again."

"Oh, my dear lass," he said, squeezing me tightly. "I'm so sorry . . . so sorry. I should have never made you do it. I should have never asked it of you! Dear God, Isabeau, I couldn't live with myself if I had lost you too. I'm a selfish bastard to the end, and for what?"

"For what?" I replied, and pushed away. Looking into his pained, self-chastising face, I then cried: "For Dante! We did it for Dante. You were right, Julius. We needed to bring him back. We could not let him go without redemption."

I realized then that the chest beneath my hands had been rising and falling. The lungs had been filling with breath. I reached my hand up to Dante's neck and felt the pulse. It was beating again, strong and steady. Still shaking, I turned to Julius and said: "Dear Lord, we . . . we did it."

"Did what? What are you talking about?" At the sound of the familiar voice, we both whipped around, lighting on the still face, on the eyes that were now open and looking at us through glittering tears. "I'm right here," Dante whispered. "There's no need to shout. But would somebody mind telling me what just happened?" A wondrous look of befuddlement crossed his features. Julius was staring at me with the same look in his eyes.

"You . . . you did it?" he uttered. I saw that his hands were trembling too. It had never occurred to me until then that there had been any doubt in his mind. Speechless, terrified anew, I nodded.

Dante spoke again. "Dear God, where was I? I thought I was dying. I swear I saw an angel."

"Angels? Dying? No, you were not dying, my wee fool," said Julius with gruff affection, his eyes bloodshot and overly bright. He looked on Dante with a watery smile and tenderly brushed a lock of hair off the curious face. "Kilwylie, however, did a good job *trying* to kill you. But why did you disobey me? Why, Dante? No," he said abruptly. "Don't answer that. You're going to be in a lot of pain, and it serves you bloody right. You deserve to feel pain for the hell you put both of us through! Look at my sister. And have a care for me, aye?"

"How do you feel?" I asked, as I sat on Dante's other side. I began fussing over his hair as well. Whether he knew it or not, he was now much more to me than just my brother's profligate friend.

"I'll live," he said, and honored me with a smile. "And I saw you," he whispered softly, seriously. "You were there. You were there too, weren't you?"

Thankfully, I never had the chance to reply, because at that moment Gabriel came bounding through the doorway, and in his hand he held the scroll. His face was flushed. "Isabeau, we caught him," he said, his voice strained from the trials of the day. "We caught Kilwylie! He had this—the scroll Oliver gave you." He handed me the velvet sack. "Dear Dante near crippled the bastard, and he couldn't get far. He'll hang now! He'll hang for what he did to the lad."

"What did he do? I can't for the life of me remember."

"DEAR HEAVEN ALMIGHTY!" Gabriel cried, his rich, resonant voice nearly shaking the room. He looked into Dante's eyes. No shock on earth could have been greater to the poor man than seeing a dead man brought to life. Julius, unable to resist, smiled as Gabriel's strong jaw momentarily dangled in utter disbelief. "How . . . ? Holy Christ! I held you in my own arms! I know what I saw! Mother of God and all the saints in heaven! How are you sitting there?"

"Come here, darling," I said, gently taking his trembling hand in my own. "We simply prayed for a miracle, and God answered our prayers. Madame Seraphina was taken from us today, but God did not have the heart to take Dante from us too. He will, of course, now have to mend his ways." I cast the young man in question a pointed look—one that I knew he understood.

"Mend his ways?" And then, overcome, Gabriel began laughing and joined us on the bed. He had a lovely, rich, melodious sort of laugh, and it made us all smile to hear it. He looked at Dante, the young man who had tormented him so, and smiled. "Ha! Mend his ways. That, my lad, is going to take a bit more than a miracle."

Chapter 23

ORDER
FROM CHAOS

Edinburgh,
June 5, 1492

"YOU WISH TO SEE ME, YOUR HIGHNESS?" JAMES, THE young King of Scotland, had been looking placidly out the window of his private chamber, with hands crossed behind his back. At the sound of the voice, he turned. Sunlight streaming through the window like ribbons of soft, shimmering cream fell across the visitor, illuminating the striking blue of the eyes, giving luster and depth to the pale hair, and casting a glow across the handsome, symmetrical features that many an artist's brush would kill to be able to duplicate. But no one, not even the finest Italian master, could ever capture the artful subtlety that moved the features to expression, the graceful control of every muscle, the blazing intellect and lively invention that brought to life the man named Julius Blythe. At the sight of the visitor standing serenely in the opulent room, the smooth, thoughtful face of James Stewart filled with color and ran through a gamut of emotions, finally settling on a warm, candid pleasure. The king walked forward to receive him.

"Alas, heaven and earth have moved, and an overly proud and stubborn boy was finally made to see what the error of four years of spiteful memory and wrongful accusation have done to this country . . . and to me. But mostly to you, dear Julius." He embraced, for the first time in many years, the man he had once idolized to the point of self-destruction. It had been a bitter lesson learned that Julius Blythe was only human, and that he too had been vulnerable to the machinations of greedy men. James, stepping back, added with painful sincerity, "I'm afraid we can never repent enough for the injustices done you."

The easy smile appeared. "You've made a good start of it, James. I never thought I would see this day. I came to thank you for clearing my name and for tearing up that damnable marriage contract between Isabeau and George Douglas. George Douglas? What the devil were you thinking when you signed that?" Julius, gently rebuking, grinned and sat in the proffered chair.

James replied with a self-chastising grimace. "I've been under the influence of powerful men my entire life. I was but a stargazing, brash child when I was encouraged to take the throne from my father, and I've put far too much faith in those men ever since."

"That is the price of having royal blood in your veins," Julius replied, his face turning somber. "And I will defend your actions by reminding you that you took the throne for the same reason many of the nobles sought to remove your father: fear for your own safety. He feared the power of the nobles who opposed him, but he was also afraid of you, James—of your intellect and influence over the men who despised him. And the prophecy of your birth always haunted him. My father, although loyal to his king, saw this, and it terrified him. When he realized that your father's fear of you outweighed reason, he sent me to serve you, and wanting no part of what was to come, he left the country to pursue his own self-interests. Your father's fear and distrust were a powder keg waiting for a spark. I had hoped we'd have been able to avoid it."

"The secret meeting on Sir Andrew's ship," James replied, the shadow of the painful memory touching his strong features. "We never made it, did we?"

"No. We never did. And for that I'm deeply sorry. Things might have been different if we had. But sometimes, for reasons unknown to us, Fate pushes us in directions we fear to go. You led a revolt and became king; I was taken down by a man I thought to be my friend but who was in reality my bitterest enemy. It took me a long time to understand the implications of that day. The truth is, James, I knew of their plot all along. I knew that Douglas and the Earl of Angus had been approached by King Henry. They were playing their own hand in a larger game and sought to ensure a greater fortune, as powerful men often do. But I was young and very vain. I believed I possessed the ability to subvert their plot without bringing it to light and therefore save not only you and the kingdom but my friendship with George Douglas as well—by rendering the very premise for the plot useless. It never crossed my mind that Douglas, pulling me into his confidence and coercing me to sign my name to the implicating documents, had meant all along to get me hanged. Removing me, the heir to Blythe Hall, it left a strategic border stronghold wide open—an easy gateway for an invading army. And I made it even easier for them to implicate me by abducting you.

"The truth is, James, powerful men will always vie for your favor, they will always whisper sweetly in your ear, promising love and loyalty in exchange for the baubles of your kingdom. It is what great men do for the chance to be greater. You have been lucky, however, in those you have chosen as your closest advisors. Lords Drummond, Oliphant, Gray, Hailies, Hepburn, and most especially Lord Hume, in my humble opinion, are good men. You need to put lions before your gates. But will you take some well-meaning advice from an old friend?"

James, hanging on his every word, nodded.

"The Earl of Angus was once like a father to you. I know that trying to placate the nobles and hand out favors to those who have helped you become king is difficult. It's a complicated web of intricacies I would never presume to untangle. But you took the wardenship of the East Marches from Angus and gave it to Hume. His power at court has been slowly and steadily eroded, and yet he protested very little. Do you know why a man like Angus might not speak up?"

"I thought he understood? And then he took his son and left court abruptly."

"Angus left because he is a prideful man and believes his loyalty and his love of you should be rewarded without his having to beg for favors. Hume and Angus, although both wholly committed to the cause of '88, were always at odds. Hume and the Hepburns had your ear, and Angus knew it. His anger was allowed to stew until it became an unholy brew, and all the time he wanted to believe you would call him back to court and give him the power he deserved. When you didn't, and the English knew it, why, it was an easy conversion, like giving a child his first pony in exchange for the key to his father's house—a silly, dangerous bargain made out of a small oversight. The Earl of Angus is a powerful ally to have, James, and the English know it. If I were you, I'd keep him very close. Bring him and his son back to court. Offer him lands. Bequeath to him titles. Endear him to you so that he will never look to the south again for favors. Do not make enemies of those who love you."

"And what about his nephew's influence?"

"Kilwylie was a bad seed in a clever family. He's from the Black Douglas line, and they have a long history with brother England. Angus believed he was entitled to a part of the Black

Douglas lands in Scotland as well, and his nephew Kilwylie was too clever and too powerful for his uncle to resist."

James nodded, ruminating. "Kilwylie was too powerful and charming for me to resist as well. Dear Lord, how we used to gamble! You would have loved it," he said, his eyes wide with elation at the memory. "We once played for three days straight. Angus was with us, as well as Ross of Hawkhead and John St. Clair. I lost forty gold unicorns over it, but damn me if it wasn't worth every Scots penny." He paused, his smile fading. "He charmed us all, and nearly Isabeau as well. But she held out admirably against his many advances, and I often wondered why." He shifted his gaze toward the window, where far below sat the Nor' Loch and farther beyond the wider blue stretch of the Firth of Forth. "He was remarkable to watch in the lists," he said softly. "I admired him greatly, and I believe a good deal of my admiration was because of his connection to you." His dark blue eyes settled once again on his guest. "I fought him once, did I tell you?"

Julius, understanding the younger man's need to reminisce—to mourn another loss—gently shook his head.

"I held my own, but only because he allowed me to. I learned a good deal that day. He was a good fighter, was Georgie Douglas. And now he will never fight again. He's scheduled to hang the morning of Isabeau's wedding. There's irony for you. And I'm somewhat relieved I'll not be there to see him swing. We never were able to substantiate his treasonous intentions, but he could not escape the charge of murder. He's been charged with the forceful takeover and wanton destruction of property at Blythe Hall and the murder of twenty-one men and one woman—Sir Matthew and the men of my Guard, Hume's jailor, and most distressingly, Madame Seraphina L'Ange. We all mourn her loss."

"Thank you. She was an extraordinary woman and will be greatly missed. We've laid her to rest beside the grave of my mother. Old Hendrick's just not the same. He was very fond of her, and Tam has taken her death very hard as well, and chides himself for not being there. Isabeau, however, I believe to be the most affected by her death. Seraphina was, after all, like a mother to her. Thank goodness for Gabriel. He's been very eager to comfort her—too eager in fact. We've the devil of a time keeping those two apart until their nuptials. After all, they did spend a night and a day in the heather . . . alone."

"Alone? Really?" A smile crept onto James's thoughtful lips. "But I thought he was a"—*monk* was not quite the correct word, so he offered, "a devout Hospitaller?"

"Oh, he is . . . or was. I've been told he's taking care of that as we speak. Wouldn't do to have that hanging over a man's head after the wedding they've planned." There were two very unseemly grins. "But my point is, I've strong reason to believe that while left alone in the heather, and having long-standing feelings for each other, they explored some previously unexplored territory."

"No . . . ," James said in the shocking, wide-eyed disbelief of the delightfully scandalized.

Julius, mirroring the look, added: "Indeed. And they're most eager to explore the territory again. However, it's my duty as her brother and guardian to keep her chaste until she's legal. I thought it was going to be a futile task, but I've managed to find a suitable, and rather feisty, governess for her—until Gabriel takes her off our hands."

"Governess? I haven't heard about that."

"No? She didn't tell you? Well, it seems Dante has selflessly volunteered for the position. He's taken it by force actually."

"Dante? That dark-eyed Adonis? Dear God, Julius, do you know what you've done? Putting a man like that to watch Isabeau is the equivalent of putting a wolf to guard a newborn lamb. You forget, but I know the man! He's a charmer. Marion's even told me how he tried to seduce her. I don't blame him, of course. I've done the job fairly well myself, but Isabeau? Dear heavens! If Dante lays a hand on her, Gabriel will accomplish what Kilwylie failed to do, I'm afraid. How does he stand it?"

"Gabriel? Oh, just fine. He's used to Dante, and what's more, he's astonished by our dark little friend's change of heart. But for Isabeau's prayers and quick ministrations, Dante would not be with us, and we're all grateful for that, especially Gabriel. However, in exchange for all the tears Isabeau wept for him, she's made him promise to change his wicked ways. He's still convalescing, you know, but he's making an honest try of it. It's the women of Roxburghshire, I'm told, that aren't making it easy for him. They've been flocking to Blythe Hall since word's gotten out. I'm told Janet Kerr came the other day to visit Isabeau and was greeted instead by a charming, partially clad Venetian. It was very amusing the way Isabeau tells it. However, what the wee fool's managed to do is ignite the ire of all the fathers in the neighborhood who have young daughters, and irk the promising young gentlemen of good standing. I think there might even be a few husbands who would like to skewer him as well. It's nothing he's done but, as I know only too well, old habits die hard—especially when old habits have been ingrained in veins coursing with hot Italian blood." Both men, filling with silent admiration for the Venetian, found amusement in this. "Anyhow, we'll be leaving soon enough, and things will settle back to normal."

James's dark blue eyes stilled. "What? Leaving? But why? Surely now that you've been cleared of all charges, and reinstated as your father's heir, you know that Blythe Hall is yours. I need you here, Julius—with me." The young king, never having begged anyone before, was very close to begging now. "Any position on my Privy Council that you fancy is yours."

It was the first time James Stewart had ever seen Julius Blythe blush and avert his eyes. There was a humbleness about him that was touching, as well as honesty. Above all, James valued honesty. "Thank you, but I've learned that my father's still alive, and I had hopes of trying to find him."

A heavy silence filled the chamber as James digested this news. And then, with admirable graciousness, he nodded gently as his eyes absorbed every detail of the remarkable man before him. "I understand," he said. "Had I the same opportunity I would make the same choice. Once, long ago, there was a young man who tried to offer it. It didn't work out for me. Fate had other plans, but for you, I hope . . ." He paused without finishing his thought, because he understood how the pain of such a desperate hope feels. He offered a wan smile, then changed course, asking instead, "Where is he, by the way? He certainly came through for you in the end. It was his statement, combined with Gabriel's, that removed the shred of doubt from your signature appearing on the document in the plot against me during '88. It proved that your safe-conduct to England, signed by my father, was issued not for the purpose of treason against me but for academic reasons instead. I take it your father didn't find the answers he was looking for?"

Julius, acknowledging his good fortune with a nod of relief and gratitude, eased back in his chair and crossed his silk-encased legs. He was dressed in proper court clothing for the first time since his arrival in Scotland, and the fine tunic of sky blue with cream-and-gold trim complemented, like no other garments could, his golden looks and noble bearing. He had been in Edinburgh for over four weeks, three of which were spent in the castle prison awaiting trial, and one living in the family town house in the High Street wrapping up business before returning to join his household at Blythe Hall. "No," Julius replied, resting his elbows on the arms of his chair and pressing his fingers lightly against his lips in a thoughtful expression. "I believe he's still searching for answers. I'm told he was in Rome for a while, then Alexandria and Cairo, Egypt.

Gabriel eventually found him in the holy city of Jerusalem. He had been waiting for Gabriel at the Church of the Holy Sepulchre."

"Waiting?"

"Aye, waiting. At least that's how Gabriel interpreted it. Call it divine intervention. They are, after all, two men who have blindly cast their fate into the hands of God. Anyhow, Gabriel didn't stay long. My father shooed him away, insisting that he travel to Scotland directly—without delay—and not stop until he reached Blythe Hall. He had even given him specific directions on how to enter the castle unseen—by unearthing an old, hidden escape tunnel. Hendrick and I were the only other souls that knew of it. And an even greater curiosity is that he told St. Clair to go directly to the chapel, for the Chapel of Angels, he had said to Gabriel, is the source of strength and insight for all of Blythe Hall. Gabriel, of course, could hardly resist such temptation; although neither could Isabeau, apparently, because that's where she found him." Both men smiled.

"And thank the Good Lord she did," said James reflectively. "Rome, Alexandria, Jerusalem—God, how I wish I could go with you." It was said not in the wistful tones of a dreamer but with the genuine excitement and desire of an adventurer.

They both knew the impossibility of such a hope, yet all the same Julius replied, "Aye, and maybe someday you will. I'm not leaving, of course, until after the wedding and I see to it that Isabeau and Gabriel are properly settled. Oh, which reminds me, will you sign this?" He took from his purse a document, deftly untied it, and unrolled it on the table before James.

"What's this?"

"A little wedding gift for Isabeau and Gabriel. It's a deed I had drawn up transferring the title of Lord of Blythe and grant of lands of Blythemuir to one Gabriel St. Clair."

"What? Julius, do you really wish to do this? This is—"

"Rash? Permanent? Generous? It is all these things, but it is what I wish. You and I both know that I never was, nor am I fit to be, the Lord of Blythe. You need a warrior before your gates, just as you need lions. Gabriel St. Clair is a warrior of vast renown, and what is more, he's an honest man. I'm too easily tempted by shiny, glittering things. Besides, I have a tower I've been renovating if Isabeau ever kicks me out. I like it there. It's a bit drafty, but the scenery's beautiful." He allowed a languid curl of his lips. James, unable to resist, smiled too.

"Very well, if you insist."

Julius watched as the king took out a quill and signed the document. He lit a candle and meant to put his seal on it, until he remembered that his personal signet ring had been stolen.

"Oh, I nearly forgot." Julius reached into the kid-leather purse hanging from his belt, fished around a moment, and then drew out the ring he had tossed to Lord Hume. "Thank you for letting me borrow this," he said, holding up the band of gold imprinted with the lion and the unicorn holding the coat of arms of Scotland between them. "It very well might have saved my life."

"You're welcome," replied James, taking it back. He dripped red wax onto the parchment and pressed the signet into it. "And you didn't borrow it," he said, holding the ring thoughtfully between his fingers before putting it on. "You stole it from me."

"Dante stole it. Like me, he's attracted to shiny things." There was a smile of pure irony on the king's lips, and he raised a royal brow. "Of course," Julius continued, "he was acting on my orders."

"Of course." James grinned and blew on the wax to cool it. He then rolled up the document, tied the string, and handed it back to Julius. "Here," he said. "Now, let's have a glass of wine and retire to livelier quarters. Marion and I insist you dine with us tonight, and I've been dying to ask you about that room."

"Room?"

"Where you held me prisoner. That room. 'Tis only been a little over a month, but I'd love to be able to arrange another extended stay. The lords are already whispering in my ear that I must find a suitable wife; England's on the verge of negotiating a treaty with France, and there's a bloody and unlawful matter between the Montgomerys and the Cunninghams in Ayrshire that may require royal attention. You wouldn't even need to tell me where it is. I don't wish to know. All I'm asking is if you think we could pull it off a second time?"

Julius laughed aloud. "God no! And even if we could pull it off, I'm done abducting kings." Then, out of the corner of his eye, he caught sight of a snapping brown gaze from the doorway. Like the full moon drawing the gaze of a lone wolf, he turned. Marion Boyd, dressed and bejeweled in a manner befitting a princess, was standing just beyond the threshold watching him. Her eyes narrowed coyly, and she graced him with a smile of pure, delicious irony.

"Maybe you're finished abducting kings, but I say there's not a lass within a hundred miles of either side of the border who's safe from the likes of you! Welcome back, Julius. James has missed you."

ॐ

There was a quiet order that slowly began to settle out of the chaos George Douglas had unleashed on our family. After the trial in Edinburgh where Julius was thankfully acquitted of the long-standing charge of treason against him, and where George Douglas, fighting to the end, was finally charged with murder, I was eventually able to return home. It had been a trying time for us all. On four separate occasions I took the stand on my brother's behalf, and I was the key witness in the brutal murder of Mme. Seraphina. It was with a big sigh of relief that I was back home in Blythemuir, resting, healing, and attempting to come to terms with the fact that Seraphina was no longer with us. There was a haunting emptiness within the walls of Blythe Hall that Hendrick, Tam, and I felt perhaps most acutely. Seraphina was gone, and my childhood home had been ransacked, burned, and badly damaged by Lord Kilwylie and his men. Yet the biggest injustice, aside from the murder of Seraphina, was the violation—the heartbreaking destruction—of my father's chapel, the Chapel of Angels. The room at the top of the tower stairs had taken on new meaning for me, for my eyes had finally been opened to the truth of what I was—the truth my father was still seeking. I now understood that the chapel was sacrosanct; that the works of art, beautiful beyond words, were precious and irreplaceable because they were the highest expression of the human longing to understand the precarious and capricious nature of what it means to be divine. Angels really do exist; and I had been guarded by them all along.

And yet there is a dark side to the light. There were devils who wanted to take it from us. Sir George had been a devil, and he destroyed everything—the artwork; the statues, even the beautiful stained-glass window of Saint Matthew—all in his quest to find the ancient scroll. We still had it, and although the chapel would never be fully restored to its former glory, Mr. Cochrane, Julius's architect, was doing a magnificent job of putting it back together. The scroll would finally rest in the altar my father had made for it.

In fact, Blythe Hall, if I were being totally honest, was teeming with new life and a new purpose. From the ashes was being built something wonderful, and Julius and his men were a big part of it. Most of his men were living with me now until their leader came home. And I had put them to good use. I had just finished working in the kitchen garden with Dr. Hayes, a man who possessed a remarkable knowledge of healing herbs. He had been instructing me on the common uses of some of our new plants, and I was eager to learn, for Gabriel, after all, had taken vows in an order founded on service to the poor and the sick. He had nursed Julius and Dante back to health on Rhodes after their terrible ordeal, and I had resigned myself to the fact that I was also somewhat of a healer. I felt it was· in my best interest to understand and investigate all of what that meant. I stood up, brushing the dirt off my hands, and smiled at the freshly planted black earth next to the budding vegetable garden.

"Very well done, m'lady. I'm sure Sir Gabriel will be pleased to see these when they come up. Angelica, a favorite of the Benedictines and brought from the Archangel Gabriel himself, as legend has it. And lemon balm, marigold, chamomile, basil, sage, rosemary, thyme, sweet marjoram, plenty of cabbage, onion, garlic, leek, houseleek, yarrow—"

"Oh, please don't tell him, Doctor. I want him to ·be surprised . . . if, in fact, anything should happen to sprout at all. I'd best get back to the house," I said, catching the trill of laughter emanating from the direction of my solar. "I left Buccleuch's three ·daughters with Dante, and heaven knows I should not have done that. If Mr. Scott finds out his daughters are here at all, my sheep won't just be shorn, they'll be butchered. Will you excuse me?"

ॐ

It always gave me a start to see Dante, more so now because of what memories lay in my head, and the odd pang that tugged at my heart. It was not a physical attraction; he was not my type. Gabriel St. Clair was my type. No, with Dante it was something different; it was a connection on a level that I could not yet fully comprehend, a connection that had formed when I had pulled him back from that lonely, dark place, the emptiness of which still haunted me. I was thinking on this emptiness when I came upon my sitting room. It was far from empty and was filled with young women, not only the three

Scott sisters who had come earlier, but Janet Kerr, younger sister of Nichole, Lady Hume, and her cousins Sara and Felicity Cranston of Greenlaw had come as well. No one had told me of their arrival. This, no doubt, was due to a combination of two things, the first being that the gates were still under repair and the guards, though diligent, were easily overcome by a pretty face. They were overcome often, for ever since word of Dante—the dashing young Italian gentleman who was so near death at Hume—had gotten out, women had been flocking in. The other reason was because I had recently gained the reputation of being somewhat of a she-wolf guarding her cub and, most disparagingly, I even heard it whispered that I was a convent-bred killjoy, simply because I believed that Signor Continari, as he was now styling himself, needed, above all else, his rest. As it was, young Incubus himself was sitting in a richly upholstered chair, his slippered feet propped on a cushioned stool, while the soft light from the windows fell across his languid form, caressing his dark beauty and domesticating it with the illusion of purity. This illusion was largely bolstered by the simple white robe he'd taken to wearing—a garment that was loosely belted at the waist and revealed with elegant malaise and artful nonchalance a good deal of the smooth and, yes, impressive sculpted chest. The blindfold, however, was a new accessory. With a deprecatory shake of my head, I saw that the game was very familiar.

The six women surrounded the playful invalid, kneeling on the floor and giggling while taking turns feeding him little cakes, ripe berries, and warm honey-milk. His only job appeared to be to eat all that was placed in his mouth, and to entertain his guests with his sharp wit and heavily laid accent as he took disingenuous guesses as to who was feeding him. His hands had been given free license to roam where they wished. It was as transparent as it was shameless. With an extravagant eye roll I entered the room.

"Hush, my dears, someone has entered. I know it. You are

naughty children. It is a signora of gliding steps and swishing silk—it is another Scotch beauty, no? Perhaps another lovely Hume or a spirited Scott?" The girls, seeing me, fell silent.

I walked over and yanked the blindfold from his eyes. "Actually, it's a Blythe."

"Isabeau!" It was accusatory and somewhat abashed. "You . . . you were working in the garden with Clayton," he reminded me.

"Yes, but I'm a very efficient gardener, Mr. Continari." I smiled sweetly. He cast me a spectacularly petulant eye. "Dear me, but you look exhausted. Julius will kill me if I don't have you healthy by the time he arrives. I think you've had plenty of excitement for one day. Will you please say farewell to your guests? And ladies," I said, turning to our disappointed visitors, "I'm so sorry, but I'm afraid Signor Continari is in danger of a relapse if he keeps up like this." After a moment of complaint, I escorted the unhappy young women to the door.

"Really, Dante," I said, walking back to the throne from whence he held his little court, "how long are you going to sit there and let the young women of Roxburghshire fawn over you, feeding you honey-milk and sugared almond cakes?"

"But Isabeau, I am not forcing them," he replied, dropping a good deal of his accent and calling on his overwhelming powers of innocence. "They insist. I swear it. It is quite embarrassing. But I thought you preferred I drink honey-milk rather than other things."

"I do. And they only insist because you encourage it, shamelessly, and reward their forward behavior with kisses. Do not insult me with lies," I warned, seeing that he was about to do just that. "I've seen you! For heaven's sake, you pulled Elspeth Beaton behind the curtain yesterday! You cannot lure young women behind the curtains. And you cannot marry Elspeth Beaton! She's engaged to William Shaw of Kinross."

"Who said anything about marriage? Marriage is on your

mind, not mine. Besides, it was only kisses," he said sweetly. "There is no harm in kissing, my dear Isa."

I stood over him, my hands on my hips. "I beg to differ."

"*Oh?* Oh!" His eyes grew wide as an exquisite smile of conjecture crossed his lips. "So that is how it happened? One little kiss and Brother Gabriel was unstoppable. He is a novice. Kissing to a man like Gabriel is the same as saying, 'Oh, I'll just open the floodgates a little crack,' and then WHAM!" His hands were lavishly explaining along as he spoke. "You are blown on your back with your skirts around your waist and helpless against the raging tide of pent-up lust you've unleashed. A novice," he said, smiling devilishly at my crimson face, "should use caution. But I, dear Isabeau, am no novice."

"No," I replied, recalling every echo of memory he bequeathed to me, and as always, with the memories came a flood of compassion. I stopped ranting and smiled softly. "And I'm sure you know better than I. But all the same, I'll thank you to leave my private life to me." I moved his feet aside and sat on the stool. "So, tell me, how are you feeling? I've been so busy; we haven't had much time to just talk. Are you happy here?" I asked.

He reached down and took my hands, holding them gently in his. They were very warm, and for that I was infinitely grateful. "I am feeling better than I have a right to feel, Isabeau." His eyes, large and expressive as a faithful hound's, held mine. "And don't think that I don't know . . ." He was about to say more, but he couldn't. He paused, searching for words, and just when he was about to speak again, Tam came crashing through the doors.

"M'lady!" he cried, his face flushed with excitement. He brought his gaze to rest on the angelic vision in the upholstered chair, narrowed his eyes, and with mocking vibrato through a snide grin, said, "*Dante*. I just thought as ye'd both like to know that a muckle-gray horse is making its way toward the gates, and the gent he's carrying is a very happy-lookin' man indeed."

"Gabriel!" I cried, and jumped to my feet.

Having the advantage of perfect health and twenty paces, I was out the door and racing my companions to the courtyard. Gabriel had just passed under the archway and saw me coming. So did all the workmen in the yard, but it didn't matter. My betrothed was off Bodrum before the horse came to a full stop, and then I was in his arms, much to Dante's dismay.

"Is it done?" I finally asked, pausing to catch my breath after his kiss.

"Aye. I'm no longer beholden to the vows of the order."

"From what I hear," added Dante, prying us apart with a stern and chiding glare, "you tossed them aside a month ago." We ignored Dante; however, his pretty visitors had spied him and began leaving the sides of their escorts. Gabriel, catching his breath, remembered something. He stopped the boy leading Bodrum away and went to his saddlebag.

"I have a present for you, my heart," he said, carrying the sleeping gift in his arms. "It was a bit impulsive, but I couldn't resist." It was a puppy, a black-and-white collie puppy. My heart stopped as I reached for it.

"A puppy?" Dante said, incredulity dripping off his Venetian tongue. "What kind of gift is a puppy? See, you've made her cry. Did you learn nothing on Rhodes?"

"I love him," I whispered, tears of joy and overwhelming sentimentality welling up in my eyes. "And I love you. Come, come quickly!" Cradling the puppy in my arm, I took Gabriel by the hand and ran back toward the hall. Dante, Tam, and six young ladies followed hot on our heels.

We entered my room panting and slammed the door in Dante's face. "That's my girl," whispered Gabriel as I threw the bolt. We leaned against it, smiling like naughty children and marveling at the curious little face watching us. Angry fists that demanded obedience shook us from the other side;

but we heeded them little, because we were finally alone. "I remembered you had a dog," said Gabriel, his summer-sky gaze quickening the beating of my heart. "A collie. He followed you everywhere. Would it be wrong of me to tell you how I envied him?"

I hugged him, kissing his cheek, and nearly squished the poor little puppy between us. "His name was Rondo," I whispered, feeling my throat tighten from the memory. "And you are a wonderful man to remember such a little thing." I kissed him again. The pounding grew more furious.

"Dear Lord, Dante!" Gabriel boomed, shocking both the puppy and me. "Stop that racket this instant!"

"I stop when you open the door, brother! Get your hands off the master's sister. There is an open-door policy in this house! It is sacrosanct!"

"What self-righteous, ankle-biting little demon has gotten into him? All I want is to be left alone with the woman I have loved all my life. Dear God, Isa, these last few weeks have been torture. Fantasizing doesn't work anymore. I'm scunnered with it. I want you!" He took me up again in his firm and unyielding embrace and, kissing me, moved me away from the door toward the bed. The puppy squirmed and yelped in my arms. "Do you know they ran a brothel out of the old tower?" he said, setting me on the soft pile of comforters. "A quite spectacular one too from what I've heard. And he can stand there—in his white Jesus-on-the-cross robe, looking all pure, innocent, and freshly resurrected, and come pounding on *my* door with this racket!"

"Oh, darling, my heart, don't be hard on him," I soothed, peppering his hot, crimson cheeks with urgent kisses. "He's had a rough time of it. I'm not making excuses . . ."

He pulled back, amused and incredulous. "You have a soft spot for our little Asmodeus?"

"No. Just compassion. He's very dear to Julius, you know."

"You'd better not be on the bed!" the shunned, self-appointed protector of my virtue cried. "If I find you were on that bed, there's going to be hell to pay!"

"Here, excuse me," I said, and taking the fully awake puppy, I crossed to the door. I opened it and placed the perky, nipping fluff ball in Dante's unwilling arms. "Be a dear; he needs to piddle. Oh, and if you think women have a weakness for handsome, partially clad, recently injured men, it's nothing compared with a man holding a puppy, my friend. You'd best get going before you're detained," I warned, looking down the hall where the crimped, frilled, and heavily perfumed gauntlet stood lining the walls, tittering, beckoning, waiting. I smiled and shut the door. Gabriel was beaming with pride.

"Now, my love," I said, crossing over to where he sat on the bed, "tell me, what has it cost you? What sacrifice did the Hospitallers ask of you so that we can be together?"

"Just a pledge of continued support, financial of course, and perhaps the donation of a son or two. I want lots of sons, Isa, my heart," he said, his smooth voice touched with the gravelly tones of rapt emotion. He pulled me into his arms and kept me there.

"I want a daughter," I added, entwining my fingers in his thick, sun-gilded hair and tilting his lips toward mine. A moment later I added, "And sons. I'm not picky. Would you be terribly opposed to starting now? No. Not on the bed. He will have fits. Come," I said, resisting his firm grasp and the powerful temptation to use the bed with divine abandon. "The bed we shall save for our wedding night." I smiled and led him to the solar instead, where the soft rug before the fireplace beckoned to us. But here Gabriel stopped. He looked suspiciously around the room and then, making up his mind, pushed the heavy settle in front of the bookcase.

"There," he breathed, and we both grinned. "You forget, but Dante knows all the secrets of this old castle nearly as well as I do." He then knelt on the carpet and pulled me to him, wrapping his arms around my waist and placing kisses along my torso as he slowly turned me around. We were finally alone, and honestly, we never heard the banging on the door.

৪৩

I knew Gabriel was only to be at Blythe Hall for the night and would be leaving tomorrow for Rosslyn. We were in the final stretch, and he was making last-minute preparations for our nuptials, which would be held in his father's magnificent and breathtaking Rosslyn Chapel. The change in Dante since the incident at Hume was really quite remarkable. He was not pleased with us after we emerged from my room in clean clothes and looking utterly refreshed. Scowling, he returned my puppy and began a scurrilous tirade. Gabriel, unwilling to suffer such biting remarks from Dante, pulled him into a room. They emerged an hour later, both looking a little worse for wear, yet grinning and looking as though they had a much better understanding of each other. Dante never mentioned the incident again, and we, for our part, behaved in exemplary fashion for the remainder of the day.

Gabriel, understandably, was exhausted, yet he insisted on staying up late into the night with the rest of the men. I had left them in the hall, where they lingered together, all of Julius's men, along with our Blythe men, including Hendrick, Tam, and the Mackenzie brothers, who, I had learned, had been encouraged by Julius no less to get themselves thrown into the castle kitchens just so they could keep an eye on things for him. Tam and the Mackenzies had been working for my brother all along. The men had a good night of it, drinking, laughing, and playing cards until the tapers sputtered out. From my bedroom I could hear them in their besotted stupors, clamoring up the turnpike stairs and dispersing on the floors above. Dante had insisted that Gabriel sleep in his room, in the dormitory wing on the third floor. It was a sparsely decorated abode with a small hearth, a small window, and two beds with a night table between them. It would be like old times, Dante had said, cajoling with soft cheerfulness. It was also a way to keep a diligent eye on my betrothed. Dante, I had learned, was a light sleeper.

I was having trouble sleeping as well. This I blamed on my own effervescent excitement—and the whining fur ball in the crate beside my bed. And yet, deep down, I knew it was something else. After hearing the men retire, and feeling reflective, I scooped the puppy out of his box and brought him to Seraphina's room with me.

I had kept her room shut off, not having the strength to face the emptiness yet. But Gabriel had given me the strength I needed, and the puppy, warm and affectionate, was a comfort beyond words. Bearing a light before me, I opened the door.

The silence was absolute, the stillness final and forever unanswerable. I walked in, my heart staggering in my chest, and stood in the center of the lifeless chamber. The curtains fluttered, and I felt a breath of wind, light as a baby's whisper, caress the nape of my neck. I turned to the window, and there, sitting on the sill with its glorious face heavenward, sat a single white rose in full bloom, the soft light of the moon falling on its pale petals. I recognized it as one of the flowers from the rose garden my mother had planted long ago—the garden my father had tended so carefully. My throat had already begun to tighten at the thought when my eyes settled on the feather lying beside it, white as the rose, the soft down of its quill still wavering gently from the breeze. Monochromatic: pure, sacred, white against a vast and swallowing darkness, the image was burned onto my soul, and my heart mourned anew as a tear of sorrow slipped from my eye. I was about to light another taper to chase the vaporous gray from the walls when I saw a form lying on the bed. My heart stopped dead at the sight.

It was the puppy's little yap that awoke him, and Tam, frowzy with drink, wild-haired, eyes puffy from crying, sat up with a start and stared at me. There was a moment of unutterable silence as his eyes, direct and immense, held mine. He looked as if he had seen a ghost, as I suppose to him I was. I had startled him, and for good reason. He wasn't supposed to be in this room. And then I saw the letter clutched tightly in his hand. There was no need for words. I saw the broken seal; I saw the name it had been intended for. I set the candle on the table, shifted the puppy, and gently sat on the bed beside him. It was a moment before I said, "The letter was to me, wasn't it?" He nodded, tears dripping from his eyes anew. It was then that I noted that the lid on Seraphina's chest was still open. Tam, driven by curiosity and, perhaps, a longing to be with Seraphina again, had braved to do what I could not. He had gone through her belongings. I inhaled deeply in order to steady myself before asking, "May I see it?"

He was reluctant to let it go, but in the end we made a trade, the puppy for the letter: a small, warm ball of living fluff in exchange for the cold and final words of the old woman we had loved. When I saw the words, written in the flowing, round hand of Seraphina, I knew why he had been so reluctant.

> My dearest Isabeau,
> If you are reading this then I have left before I was able to fulfill my earthly duty as Guardian of the Angelic Bloodline of Azazyel, fallen angel, son of God, for you, Isabeau Blythe, are the guardian of Scotland for this age, and you will help to usher in an era of light and learning, of prosperity and joy such as this realm has never before seen. But beware, my child, for enemies of peace abound, and the day you were born they struck with a vengeance.
> I blame myself. Your father insisted on a midwife, and I relented. As a carrier of the divine spark, you, just like your

mother before you, will be blessed with two perfect children who will come when God decrees it. Usually one is blessed with a boy and a girl. In this way the divine spark is tempered; for the extraordinary traits of the Nephilim are expressed most strongly in the male offspring yet can only be passed to future generations through female children. However, just as with human women, sometimes twins will be born. With male twins there is little out of the ordinary to fear. With female offspring, however, the divine spark flows strongly through only one twin, while becoming corrupt in the other. And your grandmother, I'm sorry to inform you, arrived with a twin. The bloodline was split, and the fair child, your grandmother, was sent to France for protection. Her twin, dark-haired instead of fair and eyes of green, married into the vast and powerful Douglas clan. Understand that not everyone who bears the name means you harm. And your kin are not entirely evil, just mischievous and gifted with powerful sorcery.

It was your great-aunt Lilith, your grandmother's sister, who disguised herself on the day of your birth. You were delivered safely into the world, and when I left to send word to your father, Lilith drugged Angelica and smothered you, ensuring that her line would rule Scotland. When I came back I found your mother, still weak from the ordeal of childbirth. She was fighting the powerful drugs that threatened her own life, as well as the sorceress, in order to save your soul. A battle of life and death ensued. The result was that Lilith got away unharmed and your mother, left with no other choice, gave her divine spark so that you could live to fulfill your destiny.

You and Julius were born with the ability to heal a mortal body. But you alone possess the unique gift of being able to save an immortal soul. That was your mother's gift to you; long ago she showed you herself how it is done, and you are forever linked to her through that miraculous connection. She

*is your guardian angel, my dear; and she has always, as you
know, been with you and Julius.*

*But abilities are not without their limits, and healing is not
the same as saving. Saving travels beyond death. When God
takes a soul, let it go. When evil forces death upon a body,
choose wisely, for a price is always asked, and a sacrifice will
need to be made. The connection can never be broken.*

*Be kind to Julius. Keep him on course when he starts to
stray. And please take care of Tam for me. He is a dear soul.
Our paths crossed when he was a newborn, helpless against
the fate of a life unwanted. I intervened, and for his own
safety entrusted him to my dear friend Elspeth for safekeep-
ing until he was older. Tam was my angel; I am now his.*

*With love, hope, and cherished memories of
all my little angels,*

Seraphina

I folded the letter and gave it back to Tam. The impact of
the words was as staggering as it was profound, for I had
learned the truth of my birth. Tam, poor soul, had learned,
amongst other things, that old Elspeth was not really his
granny. We hugged and cried in turns, comforted each other,
and when we were finally cried out, I tucked Tam in for the
night, leaving him to hold and be comforted by Rondo. I gave
them both a kiss, blew out the candle, and left Seraphina's
chamber.

A while later I found myself in a sparsely decorated room
on the third floor, kneeling on a little rug between two beds, in
which men lightly snored. I watched as the men slept: relaxed,
limp, indolent, peaceful, angelic—every muscle and thought
given over to the dream world they now inhabited. The air was
heavy with the smell of stale clothing and imported beer. In
sleep, as in life, they were both exquisite. My heart and my future belonged to Gabriel; to Dante, I had given a piece of my
soul. And I felt entirely responsible for both of them. For how

was I to guard Scotland when I could barely manage a castle? These men—the men Julius had handpicked—were to be my sword and shield in a battle I had been unwittingly thrust into the middle of. I wanted no part of it; and I was loath to see these men shed one more drop of blood. Enough had spilled already. I wanted a peaceful life with Gabriel, but I had a strong feeling it was far too late for that.

A little moan of satisfaction escaped my betrothed's lips as he rolled to face the wall. He was deep in the middle of a pleasant dream. Dante, with a start, opened his eyes toward the ceiling before slowly rolling his head toward Gabriel. He was, to say the least, startled to see me looking at him.

"Hush, it's just me," I whispered softly. "Don't worry. I'm not here to make your job difficult."

He smiled. "I don't think that you could, even if you tried. Look at him," he said with ill-concealed affection, and flopped an arm in Gabriel's direction. "He drank nearly a hogshead himself, and I fleeced him for ten unicorns. Is he good for it, do you think?"

"I don't know," I answered honestly. "How about I let you live here, eat my food, and rile my maidservants to foolishness, and we'll call it even. I need to talk with you." At this he rolled onto his side, fluffed the pillow under his head, and beheld me with the soft, inquisitive gaze of an eager spaniel. It was then, looking into the eyes, unguarded and vulnerable with sleep, that I started to falter. How could I ever tell this man that I had trouble sleeping at night because of what I saw through him—the darkness, the emptiness, the profligacy, and every injustice he had suffered? How could I ever tell him that I had died too . . . as a newborn, and that my own mother had given her life in exchange for mine? That because of her sacrifice we both now lived. How could I ever explain how precious was the gift of life, and what his life now meant to me? I couldn't, so instead I said: "Something . . . something miraculous happened at Hume. You know that, don't you?"

His dark eyes, touched with memory, closed as he slowly nodded.

"I just came here to say . . . I just wanted to tell you . . ." I swallowed, took a deep breath, and began again. "Please," I whispered, looking into the fathomless, shimmering orbs now filling with liquid, "do not squander this gift, Dante. Like it or not, you are now a brother to me—to us all. It is a bond you cannot escape. Please, in all you do, try to have a care for me."

His fine lips trembled with a spectacular show of emotion, and then his head gave a solemn nod. "I have always wanted a sister," he said, controlling the tremble with a watery smile. "It was a shabby way for me to get one, though. I heard your prayers, Isabeau. I felt the beating of your heart as you fought and pleaded for me. Only one other person has ever done so. How can I not cherish the gift you gave me? But you must have patience with me. I am not a Blythe. I am an unfettered and malleable spirit who is little better than an animal. I am governed by impulses and physical urges."

"Truthfully," I admitted with a wan but heartfelt smile, "so am I." He raised a brow at this, and then his lips curled indulgently as he let his gaze drift toward the sleeping body in the other bed. "What?" I uttered, my own eyes as moist as his. "Don't look at me like that. We are, after all, human. I'm not asking for miracles here, just . . . discretion."

"You have my word," he whispered. "I shall do my best. Perhaps it would help if you were around to remind me?" With a soft smile he reached into the pillowcase and pulled out another one of his handkerchiefs. "Here, look at us. I am very drunk and you are very tired." He dried my tears, then daubed his own. He then, with surprising litheness, got out of bed and offered it to me. "Come. I know you have a hard time sleeping. Sometimes I cannot sleep either." He lifted the comforter and patted the sheets. "Come," he urged again. "Take my bed. We are family here."

Unable to resist the overpowering thought of sleep, I took

his offer and climbed between the sheets. They were soft, and warm, and had a comforting, familiar male scent about them. It felt right, and I felt as if I could sleep for weeks. I then watched as Dante, with a mischievous grin, pulled the quilt off Gabriel and wrapped it around himself. Gabriel, remarkably, didn't flinch. "He runs warm," Dante explained in a whisper. "He is like a rock that has been under the sun all day. I look upon it as a favor." One more devilish grin, and he curled up on the floor between us, resting his head on the pile of discarded clothing. "There," he uttered, settling down. "We are like a litter of puppies now—all warm and cozy together. Sleep well, my sister, and dream of pleasant things. I always find I sleep much better when I have a friend beside me— when there is someone to watch my back when the shadows come. And tonight, tonight we are lucky, for we each have two."

Chapter 24

THE TAKING
OF VOWS

IT WAS A GLORIOUS JUNE MORNING WITH A WIDE AND vibrant sky of blue overlaid every now and again by the rogue, billowy white cloud. All the birds of Rosslyn were singing, and all the butterflies that should have been hovering near the succulent greenery were now fluttering in my stomach. I was ecstatic, yet more nervous than I had ever remembered being. This was not in any way because of Gabriel, or my feelings for him. In fact, I couldn't wait to see him; it had been an entire week since he'd left Blythe Hall, and just the evening before, my train had finally arrived at Rosslyn. It was Sir Oliver's adherence to foolish traditions that had kept Gabriel from seeing me last night. Truthfully, I just wanted to get on with this day so that it would be over, and Gabriel and I would be married.

However, instead of the small, private wedding we had originally planned, our little ceremony had blown up into the event of the season. This was in no small part due to the man who was scheduled to hang during the hour before our nuptials. Our wedding in Rosslyn Chapel and the hanging of Sir George Douglas, Lord Kilwylie, in New Bigging Street were the two events that had the whole of the Lowlands buzzing, and that they were being held on the same day was added cause for wild speculation. By now everyone knew some of the story, and fewer still knew the real story. Yet the crier had proclaimed at the Market Cross late on the first of June that Sir William, Lord Blythe's son, Julius, Master of Blythe, formerly at the horn, had been cleared of all charges of treason, and that Sir George Douglas, Lord Kilwylie, had been charged with twenty-two counts of murder. They had saved his death as a morbid offering and fitting justice for our wedding; for without Julius's timely intervention, I might very well have been getting ready to become the Lady of Kilwylie. I shivered at the thought.

"Are you cold, dear?" asked Marion. She also had arrived yesterday with the king and his train, and had been busy all morning directing the maids as to how I was to be dressed. Only when I met with her royal approval did she send them away, insisting on doing my hair herself—a cherished indulgence from our days at the priory.

"I'm fine," I assured her, smiling back at her concerned reflection in the looking glass. We had decided on leaving my hair unbound to fall at my waist, adorned with a wreath of spring wildflowers and trailing silk ribbons. As Marion worked the brush, she kept running through the lengthy list of guests who had already arrived. It was an impressive roster; it appeared as if half of Edinburgh and nearly the entire court had come to Rosslyn. And although the thought did nothing to quell the butterflies fluttering away in my stomach, I let her talk. Because Marion had been close to her cousin George Douglas, and she was still coming to terms with what he had done. It would hardly do to let her dwell on the hanging.

I watched in silence as she ran the brush down the length of my hair a few more times before setting it down. And then, falling silent herself, she picked up the wreath and set it on my head, fanning my hair out beneath it. "Oh my dear," she said. "You look lovelier than I have ever seen you, and that's saying quite a lot. I'd hate you, of course, if such a thing were possible." Her arms came around me, and I saw then the tears in her eyes.

It was a moment before either of us could speak, and she chided me for crying as well, saying that it would never do to ruin all her hard work with puffy, tear-streaked eyes. Neither of us wanted that. I was going to miss Marion, for our lives, as we both knew, were moving farther apart in our efforts to seek self-fulfillment. We had finally arrived at our longed-for adulthood, and now we were learning to accept and adjust to the responsibilities that our childish dreams had a tendency to ignore. We were both happy; neither of us had a right to complain, yet still, there was something utterly final about marriage, and being a royal mistress came with its own share of duties and expectations. Marion, still silent, still reflective, picked up a strand of my hair and twirled it between her fingers. A soft smile came to my lips then, for Marion had always loved playing with my hair.

"You've such lovely hair," she whispered. "'Tis just like his, you know—only softer. I do so hope my baby has this lovely hair."

At the word *baby* my heart leapt as my eyes shot across the mirror to hers in a mixture of elation and horror. Marion had wondrous eyes, large and expressive, and they were confirming the question in my own. "You . . . are with child? You . . . are carrying the royal bastard?" I asked, my gaze intent on hers.

"I am with child," she confirmed. "The royal bastard, of course. I'm just saying, would it be so horrible to wish for this hair?"

It was the way she said it, the soft hopefulness filling the eyes that could, with a look, kill. With caution and a good deal of discretion, I asked, "Marion, how many possible hair colors could this child of yours have?"

Her lips twitched slightly. "Really, how could you ask such a thing?" I continued to stare at her until she finally admitted: "Just two. There only ever were two. As much as I flirted, as much as I was kissed and fondled behind curtains, Georgie was very adamant that I remain chaste for the king. Every young man at court knew that. This," she said, running her hands down her still-slender torso, "was his dream. He convinced me that I should be the mother of James's children. Princess Margaret was in agreement as well. And I was certainly not one to argue with that. Please, don't misunderstand me, Isa; I do want this. James is a good man."

"Then for your sake, and the sake of everyone involved, I shall pray your child has auburn hair! Or at the very least a rich, unquestionable brown. If you want a lock of *his* hair so badly, then for heaven's sake, I'll get you one! But, Marion, dear Marion, please do not wish for this." But even as I said it, I knew how foolish Marion could be. And the trouble was, she had no idea what she was asking.

We were startled to silence by a knock at the door. It was a warning knock, and when, without so much as a word from us, the door opened and the man entered, I chose to look at Marion instead. Men, for obvious reason, regarded my friend as simply beautiful. But Marion Boyd was more than that; she was a woman of great courage and deep passion. She was ambitious, and haughty, and yet like me, she had a vulnerable heart. Only one man that I knew of had ever made her blush, and he was standing before us now, looking finer than I had ever seen him. He was dressed for a wedding. The pleated doublet of deep indigo, embellished at the collar and hem with gold stitching, and cinched at the trim waist with a belt of the same gold, was far too fine for a day in the saddle spent wreaking havoc on his fellow man. Under the doublet was a shirt of butter-yellow silk, which could only be viewed through the slashed sleeves. To Marion, judging from the way her eyes lingered on the silk, the prospect of seeing more was obviously tantalizing. But not as tantalizing as the view below the doublet, for there Marion's gaze fell and settled, her bold brown eyes absorbing every nuance of the pristine white, tight-fitting hose. It was, on Julius's part, just cruel to have such a tailor. While my friend's eyes were reluctant to venture above the waist, I was admiring the short black mantle trimmed in sable that matched the bonnet on his head, which was expertly angled to highlight his soft golden curls. It was no surprise that he wore plenty of jewels; Julius only displayed what he wished to convey to his audience. On his bonnet was a beautifully crafted brooch with an alabaster archangel in the center surrounded by the family motto; he also wore our father's ring, and around his neck hung a thick gold chain bearing a truly spectacular sapphire. Gone was my profligate brother, and in his place was a man of surprising and prosperous mien. I couldn't help but smile at the transformation. Marion, lifting her gaze to meet the amused twinkle in the eye of our visitor, and mustering her self-possession, affixed a haughty curl to her lips as she said, "Why, speak of the devil and he shall appear. I see you can dress yourself, but do you have manners? You should know better than to barge into a room where women are dressing. You might get more than you bargained for. Is it time already?"

"Good morning, Marion," Julius said with easy politeness. "Very nearly. I just came to have a talk with my sister. I felt that *someone* ought to explain to her what men expect on their wedding night. My God!" he cried with theatrical flair, bringing his full attention to me. He then pulled me from the chair, scanning my body from head to toe, absorbing the fine gown of pale blue and gold trim, a softer echo of his own ensemble, and the wreath of riotous color atop my hair. Unlike Julius, I wore no jewelry. "You look . . . would it be trite of me to say, like an angel? Truthfully, I can think of no higher compliment than that."

Barely suppressing a smile of extreme admiration, I rolled my eyes; Marion, with cheeks still slightly aflame, rolled hers as well and left the room.

☙

"Tell me," I said as we sat together on the settle, "how is Gabriel holding up under all of this?"

"Well, he's purged himself twice already this morning and has a splitting headache, I'm told, but he cleans up well. By the time he's standing before the altar you'll find him looking magnificent. Clayton may wield a cautery iron like an inquisitor on a heretic, and he's too quick with the bone saw for my taste, but he's a hand with a tonic."

"Dear God, Julius, what are you talking about? What have you done to him?"

"Gabriel?" he said, looking mildly offended. "Nothing. He did it to himself. The poor lad's just recovering from a wee bit of affectionate abuse suffered at the hands of his many admirers last night. We're preparing him for the new set of vows he insists on taking today. After all, one of our ranks has fallen!" he proclaimed with feigned concern. "Another perfectly good man lost to the softness of domesticity. We did what any concerned brethren would do; we took him before the altar of Dionysus, opened his eyes and his mouth, and then, many hours later, he fell to his knees begging to be put to bed—that was after a spectacular thrashing at cards."

"So you got him drunk and took his money; how brotherly of you," I chided with mild disgust. "After today, you leave Gabriel alone. Do you understand me? He's mine now!"

"Oh, don't be mad at me, Isabeau," he said with a smug and suggestive grin. "Gabriel knew what was coming. He's been preparing himself for weeks now. And whatever is ailing him this morning can easily be fixed with a kiss or two from you. You have the unique power to make him feel better, my dear, and I'm not talking about your soothing touch or your healing tears. Gabriel has no idea about any of that, and he never should. He has loved you forever, Isabeau. He loves you for who you are, and what you two have is exceptionally rare. Be good to him, and for God's sake don't do anything strange that will have him tucking tail and running back to that bastion of bonhomie on Rhodes. I'm not fetching him a second time, Isa dear. The first time nearly cost me my life."

"So I've learned," I remarked softly, thinking of all I had learned about my brother and the remarkable way I had learned it. And then I promised, "You shall have nothing to fear from me. I shall endeavor to be an exemplary wife. And I will have no more to fear," I added, holding his gaze in mine, "once I know George Douglas is gone. Our little flock shall flourish indeed."

This made him smile, and then, recalling something, he said, "Oh, speaking of flocks, I've a wee wedding gift for your husband."

"Wedding gift? But you've already bequeathed to him Blythe Hall and your title. It was far too much, Julius. We were happy with the prospect of remodeling the old tower. What more could you possibly give us?"

His face became very still then. Quiet was not normally one of Julius's moods, but today was special; today was a new beginning for us both. With a deep breath and a heart-wrenching look, he said, "Did you ever stop and think that perhaps you mean everything to me? Ours was not an easy childhood, Isabeau. We were never told what we were; we were never made to understand the gifts we possessed. The day our mother died, our father was changed forever. I understand that now, but I didn't then. And then came that day, that day you brought Rondo back to life. Everything came tumbling down around us that day. I knew you weren't lying," he admitted, his eyes distant and burdened with the regret of memory. "You were never a good liar, Isabeau," he whispered through a smile. "I just wanted to make you believe it; I wanted you to feel the pain I felt for being different. I was a wicked, wicked lad. I still am. And I'll ask your forgiveness. All my life I have struggled with the headiness of power, and as much as I restrain myself, I give in to it. But you, you are always an angel."

I shook my head, fearful of the illusion of me he'd created. "No," I uttered, still denying his belief, because the truth of it was that I was just like him. I grabbed up his hand and held it tightly in mine. As I looked into the eyes that were so much like our father's, I thought about the letter from Seraphina; I thought about telling him the truth of what had happened to me that day, and why our mother had really died. That she could have lived if . . . But life was full of ifs. And although one might escape death, one could never turn back the hands of time. And this was not the time to tell him, for some truths are better kept secret.

"I'm sorry . . . ," I whispered instead, fighting tears, "about our mother. I'm so sorry, Julius. But you must know she is with us. She has always been with us. We don't have to see her in order to know she exists. She is in the roses and white feathers; she is in the tendrils of moonlight that spill through our windows. She is the breath that comes on the back of our necks when we are in trouble, and the tickling of a gentle wind that sends a frisson of pleasure tingling down our spines. Her lullaby is the soporific lapping of the waves; her morning kiss comes on the heather-scented air. And the visions? Why must they have to be taunting glimpses of a heaven we'll never see? Why cannot they be a divine gift from her? Do you know I saw Gabriel in my dreams long before you set out to make me believe he was an angel? I fell in love with him even before I ever saw him. And how do you explain your visions for these grand schemes of yours? Are you so vain that you actually believe you have no help in them?

"It was our mother who brought you back to me. She gave us both Gabriel. She was the reason I was able to heal you and bring Dante back from that dark and desolate place. And I know she is with him too . . . our father, wherever he is. Now you tell me, my dear brother, what mother on earth can do all that?"

He was speechless, knowing the truth of it, and I hugged him, offering all the comfort he had ever been denied. And that was when we felt her—the mother I had never met but had always known; the mother who had loved her son but had left him far too soon. She was with us in the room in Rosslyn Castle, a radiant light smiling on us, as she took us in her arms. The moment she did we became filled with a contentment we had never before known. We heard her voice, happy in our ears. And the room filled with the scent of roses.

Neither of us had the power of speech, and we sat silent in each other's company, understanding the gift it was that we had finally been brought together. I then took out the handkerchief Dante had given me. Julius, recognizing the embroidered linen, was mildly amused, and smiling back at him, I dried his tears before drying my own. "See?" I said, holding up the damp cloth. "She is in our tears as well. Now, you were saying something about a gift?"

We both smiled, and the mischievous spark returned once again to his blue eyes.

"Yes," Julius said. "Don't hate me. It's part of the reason I fleeced your sheep. I did it for Gabriel, you see," he explained quickly, calling on his remarkable powers of charm to temper my rising skepticism. And then, comfortably, familiarly, he launched full speed into his tale, opening with the defense, and making it sound utterly scurrilous, as only Julius could: "The man took a vow of poverty, Isabeau. Poverty! Honestly, his slavish devotion to chastity was bad enough. I could almost understand it in his particular case. And his blind obedience to the order? Noble, but impossible to any but the simpleminded and moonstruck to adhere to—which Gabriel, thankfully, is not. All three in my opinion are wholly unnatural. I've done my best to preserve in him all that is noble and virtuous, while showing dear Gabriel the light. I've succeeded brilliantly, and because I've taken great pains to provide for my brother as well, I was forced to fleece your sheep. Don't look at me like that, Isa! It was out of necessity, and a lot of damn hard work it was too. You see, the wool was only a small payment made to a Flemish merchant who is paving the way for the real commodity we trade in . . ."

And that was how I learned of my brother's Cypriot sugar plantation.

"You own a sugar plantation on Cyprus?" I cried, aghast.

"Yes. Weren't you listening? And not I, we do, Dante and I, and we protect it with our lives, or, more correctly, with the lives of pirates. The point I'm trying to make is that sugar is more precious than gold and pepper combined this year. And the courts of Europe cannot live without it. They are all clamoring for it and will pay whatever price we ask. We have taken over the market, and we fight very hard to keep our sugar in demand. As we speak there's a hellishly weighty chest of gold on its way to Blythe Hall, along with the family silver I was also forced to borrow. It was being held in escrow by friends of Captain Wood's to insure the cargo we placed on his ship. Really, all you need to know, Isa dear, is that your husband is not poor any longer. His vow of poverty has been lifted. He doesn't know it yet, but he's now a sugar baron. And don't tell him either," Julius cautioned with a malicious grin. "I want to see his face when he figures it out! He can now buy his wife all the baubles and jewels her little heart desires, and present her glowing and glittering at court. He might also wish to buy himself a nice gold collar now that his mantle has been taken from him. Good riddance to that, I say."

Stunned by his tale and ignoring his condescending remarks about baubles and collars, I asked, "You . . . you grow sugar?"

"Not personally. Again, weren't you listening? We just trade it."

"And ... how did you buy this sugar plantation?"

"I never said that we bought it. All I said was that we *own* it."

"You won it at cards, didn't you!" I exclaimed, knowing perfectly well that's how they did it. I ignored the look of amused approbation. And then, unable to help myself, I laughed. "Dear Julius, what a surprising man you are."

"Indeed, although not nearly as surprising as you. Now, are you ready, my dear? Half of Scotland has turned out to see this wedding of yours, and I can't say that I blame them. For what an oddity is a wedding where the most beautiful maiden in all the land has chosen for her husband a brother-monk? It's got the lads thinking. Why, if I didn't overhear six young knights last evening talking about joining the order themselves ..."

᷄ʘ᷄

On the same glorious day, eight miles away in the town of Edinburgh, a crowd had begun to gather in the streets below the castle and all down the Royal Mile. Many of them had sons or husbands in the service of the king; and many of them were still mourning the loss of the twenty elite men who had been slaughtered in an ambush set by one of their own noblemen. There were still more gathered who wanted to see justice served for the brutally murdered old woman who had been much loved in the town, and was known to many as the very soul of comfort and charity. As the sun grew higher, the crowd thickened, and all eyes, patiently trained on the pillory, watched the long, impending shadow slowly recede in anticipation of the hour George Douglas of Kilwylie would answer for his crimes. The condemned man was in ward at the castle; and a good number of the inhabitants, including His Majesty, King James, and his royal mistress, Lady Marion Boyd, had packed up and left Edinburgh with half their court and a large retinue to witness a much happier, much less morbid event. The wedding of the Lady Isabeau Blythe to Sir Gabriel St. Clair, former Knight of the Order of St. Johns, was truly an event to be celebrated. And it was with a cold and practical eye for irony, as well as good old-fashioned spite, that had caused the justiciar to delay executing the sentence until the hour before the scheduled nuptials in Rosslyn Chapel; for as everyone knew, George Douglas had fought hard and underhandedly for the title of Lord Blythe, and had lost.

The convicted man, patiently waiting in his cell at the castle, stood by the little window and peered down at the Nor' Loch. The morning sun dazzled the rippling blue water. A pair of swans with their gaudy little hatchlings between them crossed below his window heading for the reeds. He smiled languidly. It was a lovely day. It was a day filled with promise, and as he watched the shadows getting shorter, he felt, for the first time, a pang of doubt. He waited a little longer, watching the swans with fascination. Because he knew that timing was everything. And then, finally hearing the telltale sound of a key turning the lock, he let out a sigh of relief. The creak of the small door followed, and yet he waited still, until he was sure that the body of his keeper filled the opening. He closed his eyes, breathed deeply, and turned.

The face that greeted him from within the black robe was cautiously joyful. It was a fair, leonine face, love-struck and determined, and topped with a crown of carroty gold. It was the face of Margaret Stewart, spinster princess and aunt to the king.

"My little fool," she said, walking toward him. "My deliciously naughty, overreaching little fool, what mischief did you get up to? I'm not sorry," she said as her quivering chin lifted to receive his mouth. "Not one bit," she breathed, and felt the heady rush of his passion. "She is far too good for the likes of you. And she could have never made you as happy as

I can. Hurry now, we haven't all day." He dragged the body
of the poisoned guard into the cell and changed into the cleri-
cal robes she had brought for him. "I've a boat waiting to take
you to England. Your men are waiting by the postern," she
informed him as she locked the door behind them. She then
handed him the key. "Keep this, as a reminder of how close
you came to death. Remember my charity. Remember my
love. I cannot offer either again."

ॐ

It was said of Sir William St. Clair that in his later years he
*wished to build a house for God's service, of most curious
work, and that it might be done with greater glory and splendor.* Rosslyn Chapel, in my opinion, had achieved what
Gabriel's father had set out to do. The building itself was part
of a bigger plan, and was to be a collegiate church, dedicated
to Saint Matthew. The construction, when it began forty-six
years earlier, had been so consuming that it gave rise to an entire village of artisans and craftsmen in order to support Sir
William's dream. And yet when Sir William died, some of the
grandeur he had envisioned died with him, but he had left for
his progeny an exquisite little masterpiece sitting high on a
hilltop in Midlothian.

I entered the chapel on the arm of my brother, filled with
excitement, bursting with hope, and overwhelmed with reverence for the place where I was to marry Gabriel St. Clair. It
took a moment for my eyes to adjust, yet once they did I saw
that just as nearly every piece of masonry had been adorned
with spectacular and wide-ranging imagery, the crowd that
filled the nave and overflowed into every vacant space beneath the arches was just as spectacular and diverse. All faces
were turned toward us, all reflecting and magnifying the joy I
felt. And then I saw Gabriel standing before the altar, out-
shining the splendor of the stained-glass windows above him.
Julius was right; he did look magnificent, dressed in the finery

of a knight with his sword belted at his side. Beside him stood Dante holding a wiggling Rondo, and behind them a choir of cherubs began to sing. All my family was here with me, and we were surrounded by our friends and countrymen; not even in my dreams could I have envisioned a more perfect moment—a more perfect beginning to a life I had only dreamed of—including the look of adoration on Gabriel's face. With confidence I walked forward under the soaring arch of the roof, focusing on nothing but the man waiting for me . . .

And then, in the space of one strangled heartbeat, it all changed.

Something terrible had happened. I could feel it. I could see it in the dark clouds that appeared overhead, momentarily blocking out the sun that fell across Gabriel as he stood at the altar. A flash of dread quelled my ebullient joy. And when I saw Will Crichton, a young man in the service of my brother, who was supposed to be in Edinburgh witnessing the execution of George Douglas, standing instead by the magnificent Apprentice Pillar demanding Julius's attention, I knew. I knew that the unthinkable had happened. I faltered in midstep and came to a complete halt, for my ears were ringing with the threat: *I will take everything from you, everything you hold dear, until you have nothing left but emptiness, and pain, and remorse . . .*

I looked at Gabriel. He was everything I held dear; without him I would live the prophecy George Douglas promised. And then I thought of that puppy long ago: Rondo. My father had told me then that I needed to learn how to let go of what I loved . . . because my love had killed him.

The cherubs, noting my hesitation, faltered and stopped singing; the church fell to silent discord as all eyes settled on me. And I watched, trapped in silent fear, as Gabriel's joy melted before my eyes. Dante, standing beside Gabriel, froze as well, but his astute gaze narrowed with unfolding speculation.

It was then that I felt the grip on my arm tighten as a chiding plea hit my ear. "For God's sake and mine, Isabeau, embrace the path before you! Do you not think that I feel it too? I know what you're thinking, and you're wrong, for we are with you now. We will let no harm befall you. God has given you Gabriel; do not throw such a gift away for a petty fear. Look at him!" he whispered in an impassioned voice. "Do not break his heart. You are a warrior too, Isabeau. You are the daughter of Sir William Blythe. It is time to face your destiny. Embrace the path you were born to walk."

I looked at him and saw the respectful fear smoldering behind the bravado. But the smile and the plea were genuine. And he was right; Julius was always right. Bolstered by his touch, I returned his smile. He released his hold on my arm. And then, without another thought, I ran to the altar, where Gabriel St. Clair was waiting for me. I took his hand. I basked in his returning, radiant joy and offered him my own. And then, together, we knelt before the priest, and half of Scotland, and finally allowed our common dream the freedom it had fought so long and so hard for; we finally allowed it the freedom to no longer be just a dream.

DARCI HANNAH lives and plays in Michigan with her husband and three sons. When she's not playing, she's hard at work on her next novel.